The Bells of Brooklyn
a novel

Sequel to *The El*

by Catherine Gigante-Brown

D1246064

Cover design by Vinnie Corbo
Author photo by Carey Kirkella
(as part of her Sisters Project)

Published by Volossal Publishing
www.volossal.com

For my mother,
Teresa DeMuccio Gigante,
a rose among women
who constantly inspired me
with her unconditional love
and quiet grace.

Table of Contents

Chapter One

Something Like Joy

The bells of St. Catherine of Alexandria Church cut through the cold, December air. The sound sliced through the snow which was dirty and gray, and had already melted and hardened more often than anyone could remember. Rose counted the church bells' rings expectantly, relieved to hear each new peal which melded into the one before it. She was relieved because every bell toll brought her husband closer to her, closer to home.

'The bells,' Rose thought. 'The bells are as much a part of our lives as The El is.' Far off in the distance, like the whisper of a promise, she detected the click and clack and screech of the elevated train which snaked through the neighborhood, just a few blocks away. The sound of The El permeated the streets just like bells marked the passage of time. They call us to supper, announce our arrival, herald our departure, ring in the new year. Church bells, school bells, doorbells, the bells on the knife man's cart, the bells on a toddler's shoes, on the counter in a greasy spoon diner, the

7

ring of the telephone. The bells guide us home and usher us away. They are always there, always present, just like the air we breathe is.

It had snowed lightly overnight, leaving a fine crust on the weathered sidewalk, too little to shovel. But Rose could hear Poppa outside already sweeping and it wasn't even fully light. Her father brushed away the snow with the stiff, worn cornhusk broom he favored. Its edge was rubbed to a slant almost to the navy twine which held the bristles in place. Poppa had a brand-new broom in the cellar but refused to use it until the old broom fell apart. "This one's perfectly good," he explained. "Besides, it's wartime."

Even though the Second World War had officially ended in September, to many like Poppa, it didn't feel as though the War were over. Ration coupon booklets and chips—blue for meat, red for everything else—had been long tucked away into dresser drawers, yet some people continued to live with an eggshell-thin frugality, perhaps because they'd done so for almost four years. Some boys were still off in the Pacific Theater or in the dark forests of Europe, finishing their tours of duty when they should have been home with their families. Some families were still waiting, waiting and hoping. Families like the Paradisos and the Sullivans.

Rose knew it was her father sweeping outside without even looking. She could tell by the brisk, no-nonsense strokes. When her mother Bridget wielded a broom, even against a ginkgo's flimsy leaves, the sound was lighter, almost ethereal, as though she didn't want to disturb even the pavement. Poppa would joke that his wife looked as though she were dancing with the broom instead of doing a chore.

These days, Bridget didn't perform many outdoor tasks. Her "bum leg," as she affectionately referred to the right one, wouldn't permit her. Though she could hobble about the kitchen and straighten up the apartment well enough, stairs of any sort were a bother. Her trips to Thirteenth Avenue were few and far between, even with her arm slipped through her eldest daughter's. Bridget called Rose her rock because she now did the shopping for both households. But Rose never complained, and truly, she didn't mind.

Unconvinced that she and Poppa weren't a nuisance, Bridget would shake her head dolefully. "I don't know what we'd do without you," Bridget would admit sadly. "We'd be in the old folks' home or worse." Although Rose would coddle Bridget and "Oh, no, Momma" her up one side of Forty-Seventh Street and down the other, she knew her mother was right. Rose's parents were swiftly aging. Like beautifully-crafted vintage clocks, they were slowing down and losing time.

Poppa's sweeping stopped suddenly and Rose now heard two voices: her father's and her husband's. She could hear the smiles in their speech, and this, in turn, made Rose smile, too.

It was warm upstairs in the Sullivan kitchen but it looked downright frigid outdoors. The frost on the windows told Rose so. The teakettle on the grate forced steam into the air. Rose managed to turn off the burner beneath it before the pot began to scream. She didn't want to wake the boy, not yet. Although it was a school day, he could still sleep a little longer. The boy would be upset that there hadn't been more than a dusting of snow. He'd been counting on a blizzard cancelling out school.

Rose lowered the tea ball into the pretty porcelain pot which had been Sully's mother's. Sully's sister Irene had given it to Rose with the excuse, "Ma always liked you. Even better than she liked me, I think. She would've wanted you to have it." The way Irene's cerulean eyes danced when she spoke, like cut-glass crystals, how could Rose refuse? Although Rose didn't visit with her sister-in-law as often as she would have liked (Irene lived way up in Queens with her husband and sons), the two women talked on the telephone each week, without fail.

Heavy footsteps sounded on the stairs, muffled by the flowered runner which covered them. But instead of Rose's heart brimming with trepidation as it had when her first husband Tony was alive, it oozed with something like joy.

Rose held her breath in blissful anticipation as the door wedged open and a man's frame filled the doorway. She never tired of seeing Sully's pleasantly fleshy, Gaelic face, which was alight in a grin upon seeing her fussing with the teapot in their kitchen. In turn, the beat cop never tired of seeing Rose's sweet, plain countenance. "My Wild Italian Rose," Sully called her in moments of pure love. Sometimes he even whistled the song which inspired her moniker, changing the words of the popular tune to suit her nationality.

And just like that, people began calling her "Rose" instead of "Roe" or "Rosanna," which she'd been called most of her life. It was as though Rose had become a new person. In a sense, she had since marrying Sully.

Patrick Sullivan held his large shoes in one hand and stood in the kitchen in his stocking feet, not wanting to muss the linoleum which had recently been replaced. He arranged his work boots onto the sheets of newspaper laid down in anticipation of his arrival, taken from yesterday's *Brooklyn Daily Eagle*. Sully and Rose smiled. He kissed her softly on the mouth. "How about some eggs?" she suggested.

"Nah," he responded, shrugging out of his heavy regulation police jacket, bulky enough to wrap around his wife twice. Sully draped the coat across the back of an empty kitchen chair. "I wish I could stay and eat. My new partner's quite the stickler," he sighed. "Izzy's nothing like Harry. He's a real by-the-book kind of guy. He's getting a cup of coffee down at Dora's Luncheonette, under the El."

"But I could…" Rose began.

"I told him you'd be glad to put on a pot of Joe," Sully said. "But Izzy thought it was too early to disturb you. He didn't want you to be sore at him." Rose shook her head at Izzy's obstinance, setting an empty teacup in front of Sully. It was also from his mother's Royal Doulton dinnerware set. "I knew you wouldn't be mad and that you'd already be up, but you know Polacks," Sully continued. "They can be so thick-headed."

Rose flashed Sully a challenging look with eyes that were a rich, chocolate brown and sparked with mischief. "Just like the Irish," Rose told Sully as she poured tea first into his cup, then hers.

With Tony, a casual comment like this might have gotten Rose backhanded and sent the china teapot flying. Even now, she had to remind herself that her former husband was long gone, dead and buried in the unyielding earth of Green-Wood Cemetery a few miles away. Sully considered Rose with honest aqua eyes, just like his sister's, as one corner of his mouth curled up in play. "Or the Italians," he offered. "They're stubborn as mules, especially the Neapolitans."

Rose laughed heartily in response. "I'm only part *Napolitano*," she reminded him. "The other half is *Calabrese*. Remember?"

"Even worse," Sully said. "*Capa tosta*."

"Hard-headed? Me?" Without warning, Sully drew Rose into his lap, and instead of protesting, she let him. Rose's spirit felt light as a breeze. She was quite simply happy, something she never thought she'd be when she was married to Tony.

Sully and Rose kissed, first chastely, then deeply. "I hate working through the night," he sighed.

The bedroom door banged open, startling them both, and the boy bounded in. That's the way he usually entered a room: like a small explosion. When he caught a glimpse of Sully and Rose in mid-kiss, the child emitted a distinct, "Eeeeeew."

The couple pulled away slightly until they were nose-to-nose. "Good morning, Stanley," Rose told the boy.

"Morning, Momma. Morning, Pops," Stan said, then peered out the kitchen window. "Did it snow?"

"Not much," Sully admitted. "Barely covered the sidewalk. But it's cold as a witch's…" Rose shot Sully a warning glance. "Cold as a son of a… I mean, it's pretty darned cold out there."

"Damn," the boy declared, then quickly corrected himself with, "Darn. Gosh darn."

"Did you do your homework?" Rose wondered.

"What's for breakfast?" Stan responded.

"Oatmeal," Rose said. "With cinnamon and apples, just the way you like it."

Stan took a seat and dipped his head, indicating that he would permit Rose to fix him a bowl of porridge. She fished a glass container of milk out of the Frigidaire, and poured two cupfuls into a shiny Farberware pot. Gone was her battered, bargain-store cookery. Rose's sisters had chipped in and bought her a brand-new set of Farberware when she and Sully had married seven years earlier, when the boy was almost two.

Rose shook oatmeal into the pan from the red, gold and blue carton, the beneficent Quaker on the label practically part of the family. "None for me," Sully reminded her. "I'm on the clock."

"Did you shoot anybody last night?" Stan wondered in delight.

"No," Sully admitted. "But we did find a Popsicle."

"A Popsicle?" Rose asked, stirring the oatmeal with the roughly-hewn wooden spoon Stan had made in shop class. She still had the spoon her older son Tiger had made a decade earlier.

"A Popsicle is dead body," Stan uttered with glee. "Frozen."

"Probably a hobo," Sully added, for he knew that next, the boy would want to hear all the gory details. "No wallet, no ID. Me and Izzy found him under the El, where the Sea Beach and Culver Line tracks meet."

"How sad," Rose sighed, slipping the apple she'd just diced into the boiling oatmeal. She gave it a final stir.

"It is, but that's life," Sully told her. "And death."

"'Start the day with a DOA,' right?" Stan added.

Rose raised her eyebrows. "You don't actually say that, do you?"

"Sometimes," Sully conceded.

Rose spooned the steaming breakfast cereal into two bowls. Sully refused even a smidgen. His shift would be over soon enough and he would be home. Then perhaps, after breakfast, there would be a few stolen moments with his wife while Stan was in school, in the middle of the morning, no less. Rose relished welcoming her husband home — welcoming him into her bed, into her body, and rocking him there, hastily, desperately, before Bridget or Poppa could summon her to do a minor chore. Her parents seemed to have an uncanny knack of sensing when the Sullivans were pitching woo, and without fail, Rose's folks would suddenly need a task done whenever they were.

During these private moments, the door to Sully and Rose's modest railroad apartment would be uncustomarily locked, but only briefly. Feeling deliciously wicked, Rose would sometimes wait for her husband beneath the covers wearing nothing but a thin chemise, the very same nightie Sully had given her on their wedding night. Most days, Rose usually wore sensible cotton shifts but the chemise was elegant — creamy, ivory-colored silk, which Sully said brought out the warmth of her eyes.

Toying with her oatmeal at the kitchen table, Rose recalled the first time they made love, how tender her new husband had been, how certain his touch was. They had kissed so fervently Rose's lips felt wonderfully bruised afterwards. Sully's hands were as big as bear paws yet they were gentle. Rose remembered how he knew exactly where to fondle her, and how she dampened in response, so much so that it made her blush. The more Rose wet Sully's fingertips, the more persistent his exploration became. With a gasp, Rose felt as though a carpet had been jerked from beneath her, then felt her body deliciously clenching, releasing and levitating. She bit into Sully's shoulder and found herself making sounds she'd never made before. Only then did Sully clasp Rose firmly by the hips and guide himself into her, when he sensed she was ready. Without asking, Sully knew. It had never been this way with Tony, not even in the beginning.

In Rose and Sully's honeymoon cabin, the lingerie box from Henrietta's on Ninth Street in Park Slope lay on the floor, its white tissue paper askew. Henrietta's sold lovely wedding gowns, the unmentionables which went beneath them, and peignoir sets as well. Rose had never owned anything as diaphanous as the chemise from Henrietta's. Maybe it was the silken nightie Sully had given her or maybe it was the fact that they were in the honeymoon cottage at Williams Lake, upstate in Rosendale. (Sully admitted he'd chosen the resort because of the town's name—it reminded him of hers.) Or perhaps it was that Sully had spared no expense, that he thought Rose was worth spending his hard-earned money on. But that night, Rosanna Paradiso Martino Sullivan had finally become a woman.

Sully and Rose's wedding had been on a perfect fall day which had a crisp chill in the air. After the party, they snuck off for a three-day honeymoon. (Rose couldn't bear to be away from Stan longer.) She and Sully drove a few hours north in Poppa's borrowed Buick and arrived at Williams Lake in pitch blackness. They were so exhausted that they fell asleep on top of the covers, still wearing their traveling clothes. The next morning, Rose awoke to a breathtaking view of a shimmering mountain lake. Later in the day, Sully patiently taught Rose how to ride a bicycle. With a similar patience, he made love to her for the first time that evening. And now, several years later, sometimes when Sully came home from the night shift, Rose would slip on the very same silk gown, slide under the sheets and wait for her husband. Sully would always act surprised to find Rose there, although she knew he expected it, looked forward to it, even. It was their ritual a few times each week, like their morning tea. At first, Rose felt decadent, indecent, like a tart as she waited for Sully in bed. But what's a wife to do when her husband works evenings?

A sound stirred Rose from her reverie: the sound of her spoon scraping the bottom of her empty oatmeal bowl. Rose had finished eating the thick, sweet mush without even realizing it. Sully was taking the spoon from her and the bowl from her placemat. He put both into the sink and began washing up. "Where were you?" Sully asked.

"About 100 miles away," Rose said.

"Sleep well?" he wondered.

"I never sleep well when you're walking the beat," Rose admitted.

"I sleep like a log when Paddy's out there," Stan added, unbidden. Then he caught himself. "I mean, Pops. When Pops is out there."

"You'd better get ready for school," Rose told the boy. Although he sighed dramatically and shuffled his feet in protest, Stan did as he was asked. He was a good boy, even though he came from bad people. It was one of those miracles Rose didn't understand but accepted—how a positive could come from a negative. Like the "three persons in one God" phenomenon Father Dunn was so fond of bringing up during his sermons at St. Catherine's Sunday mass, this good-from-evil miracle baffled Rose.

Once, through the screen of the church's darkened confessional booth, Rose had confided in Father Dunn the guilt she felt about the circumstances of Tony's death. It had happened in a scuffle with Rose in the coal cellar. But Father Dunn dismissed Rose's concerns. "You were only defending yourself, child," he informed her gently. "God works in mysterious ways. I truly believe it was the hand of our Lord that saved you in the basement." Rose never mentioned her fears to the priest again and never again felt guilt about her late husband.

Stan reappeared a few minutes after he'd left the kitchen, his wild shock of sandy hair tamped down with water and pomade. "A week and a couple of days and you'll be off for Christmas vacation," Rose said tenderly, to console him. But it made little difference because eight days was a world away when you were almost nine years old.

Stan swung his books on their strap and grabbed his lunch: a brown paper sack containing the heel of last night's Italian bread smeared with butter (his favorite midday snack), a hardboiled egg (still warm) and a crimson apple.

Stan had already slipped on his corduroy coat, scarf and cap. He refused to wear mittens, proclaiming that they were "for sissies." Rose's daughter—who now insisted on being called "Angela" instead of her childhood nickname "Kewpie" since she was now an old married woman, had bought Stan a pair suede gloves from A&S downtown as a Christmas present which were so lush and grown up, Rose was certain Stan would wear them.

Sully buttoned his cape-like coat to his neck and swung his nightstick as he and Stan walked out the door together. Sully would escort his son all the way to PS 131, the same school Tiger and Angela had attended. The boy would even rise up on his tippy-toes to give Sully a good-bye kiss on his stubbled cheek when they parted company.

But before Stan bolted down the steps at home, he ran back into the kitchen and gave Rose a hug. The boy's embrace kept her smiling even after she washed his breakfast dishes, poured herself a second cup of tea, and heard her mother calling from the landing below.

Chapter Two

The Call

"Rose! Rosie!" Bridget's call rang out. Her voice was like a song even when she was shouting from the bottom of the stairs as she was now. But Bridget wasn't angry; you could detect the humor in her words, in everything she said. Poppa often commented that his wife was like the Rodgers and Hart song "Laughing at Life." At this point in Bridget's existence, well into her seventies, she was simply pleased to be alive, and she could find even the tiniest shred of comedy in almost anything. It was one of the qualities that Poppa, and everyone else who knew Bridget, loved about her.

Rose appeared at the top of the narrow staircase in the hallway of the wide-porched two-family house she shared with her parents. Bridget steadied herself by leaning on the polished wooden banister at the bottom landing. Her wonky right leg could scarcely support her these days. Poppa had bought Bridget a regal-looking walking stick festooned with mother of pearl and abalone on the handle. Though the cane was beautiful, Bridget felt like an old biddy when she used it. She preferred sliding her arm through the arm of someone who cared for her and using their body to secure each step. Rose or Poppa, usually, or Tiger, before he'd gone away, and now, Stan, who was skinny but strong.

"Yes, Ma," Rose smiled from the top step. Bridget's hair was not yet pinned up and hung to the base of her spine like spun silk threads of varying shades of silver and sepia.

"First, good morning, dear," Bridget smiled back. Then, after a beat, she added, "It's your father…" Without bothering to hear the rest, Rose took the steps two at a time. "Oh, he's fine," Bridget insisted, "but there's no talking to that man sometimes."

Rose dashed into her parents' apartment. There was Poppa atop the paint-splattered step stool, wrapped in vivid red garland, trying his darndest to fasten it to the wall. "Son of a gun," Poppa cried amid the tangle. Rose busted out laughing.

Bridget was at Rose's heels a moment later, exasperated. "I told him to wait," Bridget chattered. "I told him Sully would be happy to give him a hand when he came in from the night shift. But did your father listen?"

"I never needed help before!" Poppa bellowed. "It's only garland, for Cripe's sake!"

"Pop, you've never been seventy-five before," Rose reminded him.

"…and there he was, dragging the box up from the basement," Bridget finished, then crossed her arms over her chest with a humph.

Poppa accepted Rose's hand and backed down the stepladder's steps one by one to parlor-level, mindful not to trip himself up in the garland he trailed. Rose and Bridget unwound Poppa from his tinsel prison. "Blasted old garland," he muttered. Soon, all three were laughing.

"Blasted old fool," Bridget responded, then gave Poppa a kiss on his rigid mouth.

On the fringed throw rug sat a dusty cardboard crate, packed with Christmas decorations. Rose remembered them from her childhood: lime-green ornaments with "Joy" inscribed on their surface beside a splash of snowy paint, spheres of indigo which shone like the night sky, Betty Boop lights Poppa had bought on a whim and Bridget silently hated. There were peanuts decorated with pipe cleaner arms and legs, googly eyes and hats (made by their neighbor Jilly Mancuso) and knitted ice skates with now-rusted paperclips as the blades.

Poppa tossed the garland back into the box. "I've been climbing the walls since I quit working," he admitted, lowering himself into a Windsor-backed armchair with a huff.

"You and me both," Bridget agreed.

Poppa had retired from the Brooklyn Navy Yard once before, in June of 1941, after putting in almost fifty years there. But once the US declared war on Japan on December 8 the very same year, the day after the attack on Pearl Harbor, Poppa suggested postponing his retirement, an offer his gang boss quickly accepted. Poppa went back to the Navy Yard the very next day. He reluctantly retired again a few months ago, after Hirohito surrendered in August. "I don't feel right leaving the job with Tiger being God knows where," Poppa confided to his son-in-law Harry at the time.

Harry O'Leary understood completely. "How do you think I feel?" Harry had responded as they were celebrating the official end of the war by slipping off to Farrell's Bar and Grill for a drink. No one in the family would look for them in the wilds of South Brooklyn. Harry's limp was more pronounced on stormy days like the one when they'd hidden out in Farrell's. His war wound had shattered his left leg and not his right, so he was still able to drive the Pontiac wherever he liked. But Harry could no longer walk the beat. The police department was munificent enough to give him early retirement, which irked Harry to no end. This was after they offered him a desk job, which he refused; he'd go crazy if he couldn't be out on the street. As it was, Harry missed Sully like crazy, missed seeing his round potato-head five days a week. Though he and Sully lived a few blocks from each other, it wasn't the same as walking the beat day in and day out, eating meals together, shivering together in the January bitterness and sweating together in the dog days of August.

At Farrell's, Houlie set a shot of bourbon in front of both Poppa and Harry without either of them asking for it. Drinks were on the house to toast the armistice, Jim Beam being Harry's adult beverage of choice. He and Poppa clinked glasses and said, "To Tiger," without even thinking. They wanted the boy, the young man, home. Home soon and safe.

Harry surmised that Tiger was somewhere in the Pacific Theatre judging by what his nephew had written in his letters, things which made it past the censors. Codes of sorts, innocently referring to people or places in Borough Park like Wong's or Moskowitz the Chicken Man, when it was really their own secret lingo for Japan or Hitler.

There was a certain comfort in Farrell's, in the dark wood infused with alcohol fumes. There was a reassurance in the familiarity of Houlie and Eddie Farrell, who felt like relatives, almost. Poppa tried to convince Harry to take a booth in the back, for there were no barstools in Farrell's. "If you can't stand, you can't stay," Eddie liked to say, only half-joking. Poppa feigned a bad back but Harry knew his father-in-law's desire to sit was because he suspected Harry's leg ached like a son of a bitch. (It did.) "I can still stand like a man," Harry declared before he downed the bourbon, then tapped the shot glass on the bar, wordlessly requesting a refill. "Even if I can't fight…or work."

"The PD couldn't have sent you back on the street, Harry," Poppa told him as compassionately as he could.

"It's true," Harry admitted. "But I feel like a cad."

"Nonsense," Poppa said. "You gave your all. You did your duty, and with a wife and a little girl at home."

"All gave some," Harry mused, nursing the Jim Beam. "Some gave all." The drink made Harry introspective. "Mike, I know I can't walk the beat," he added. "Hell, some days, I can barely walk at all. And being glued to a desk at the precinct would finish me off."

Houlie stood in front of Harry, already pouring. The bar-back knocked on the mahogany. "This one's on the house, too," Houlie told his friend. Poppa hadn't even finished one drink to Harry's three.

Immersed in thought in the overstuffed parlor chair, Poppa was drawn from his Farrell's flashback by the entrance of another daughter, Harry's wife Jo. She brushed snowflakes from her loam-shaded wool coat and bonnet, then stomped her galoshes in the vestibule. Just like Rose did upstairs, Bridget had laid out a cushion of yesterday's *Brooklyn Daily Eagle* to capture the wet from peeled-off boots. Jo, her green eyes sparkling and a ready smile always on her lips, carried a brown paper shopping sack.

"Can't you ever come here empty-handed?" Bridget wondered, placing a pair of cotton house slippers beside Jo's dripping galoshes.

"Pop said not to bother coming if I couldn't bang on the door with my elbows," Jo winked at her father, ignoring the slippers. Ever since she was a little girl, she padded around in her bare feet "like a wild Indian," Bridget would comment, even in the winter.

Although Jo was now grown woman almost in her forties and a mother herself, Bridget still gently chided her. She rolled her eyes at her daughter's stocking feet, demure seashell-pink polished toenails visible beneath her nylons. "See? They're not bare," Jo told her mother, giving her a quick peck on the forehead. Bridget seemed to be getting smaller, less substantial, each time Jo visited, although she smelled the same as she had when Jo was a child—clean and scrubbed, with a touch of garlic. It was a comforting scent. Bridget smirked, reluctantly suppressing her laughter. "You should be wearing wool leggings in December," she warned her daughter.

Jo kissed the top of her father's head then gave her sister Rose a squeeze. "Normally I would," Jo assured Bridget. "But I have an interview. For a job. I want to look nice."

"A job?" Rose repeated, raising her eyebrows. In her mind, married women took a job only when they were desperate, when their husbands couldn't provide for the family; they didn't work because they wanted to.

Jo unloaded her paper satchel onto the marble-topped coffee table. Inside were several Pyrex containers, a loaf of bread, and in a separate plastic bag, a pair of low-heeled pumps, which she put directly onto the floor. (Jo was well aware of Bridget's superstition about putting shoes on the table—she believed it brought death. "I put a pair of Oxfords onto the kitchen table for a second, and the next thing you knew, President McKinley was shot," Bridget would tell anyone who'd listen.) "Yes, a job," Jo replied, nudging her sister with her hip. "I ran into Anna Pateau on the Avenue and she said they were looking for a girl to answer phones a few hours a week at the insurance office."

Without a word, the women shifted into the kitchen, carrying the contents of Jo's bag. Poppa ceremoniously lifted the *Eagle*, ruffled its pages and began reading. As was his custom, he promptly fell asleep.

"What does Harry think? About the job, I mean." Rose asked, peeking into one container to find a thick, rich chicken soup. Another held a hearty beef and barley variety.

"Harry doesn't say much," Jo conceded. "But I think it would be okay with him. Besides, Anna hasn't offered it to me."

Bridget put the containers into the Frigidaire, piled up like hat boxes. "You've gotten every job you ever went for," she smiled.

"And everything you've ever wanted," Rose added, putting the aluminum coffeepot on to perk. "Anna would be silly not to hire you. You're grand at whatever you do." Jo blushed. "Thanks, Sis," she conceded. Compliments flowed easily from Rose's lips these days. She seemed genuinely happy since she'd begun keeping company with the shy, hulking policeman, and even more cheerful since they'd married. Perhaps Rose's mirth was also due to the fact that an evil ogre no longer haunted her fairytale.

"Josephina, what about Wendy?" Bridget worried.

Jo began placing home-baked oatmeal raisin cookies onto one of the Dish Night plates. She cooked up a storm whenever she was worried or upset. "Wendy's almost nine,"

Jo contended. "She can look after herself for a couple of hours after school. Harry's usually in the apartment when she comes home. And if not, I'll be back soon enough. *If* I get the job."

"Oh, you'll get the job," Rose and Bridget commented in unison.

Jo took out the coffee cups while Bridget lowered herself into a kitchen chair with a sigh. The two sisters exchanged concerned glances. It was not yet ten in the morning and they could see that Bridget's leg was already paining her. "Dr. Lewis says it's nothing," Bridget said firmly, reading her daughters' minds. "Honest. Just old age and old bones."

"You can barely squeeze into your shoe, Ma," Jo prodded.

"Maybe I should go barefoot like you, Nature Girl," Bridget smiled, taking a sweet while Rose lifted the coffeepot from the burner and poured the steaming ebony liquid into four cups. Jo fixed Poppa's, black and sugary, and set it beside him on the end table. When he woke, it would probably still be warm. Jo put a plate with two treats on it beside the cup then softly padded back into the kitchen.

"Where's Harry?" Bridget wondered.

"Home," Jo replied abruptly.

"Under the weather again?" Rose suggested. It was Rose and Jo's code for "sleeping one off," but Rose suspected her mother still knew what they were talking about.

"You could say that," Jo admitted, dunking her cookie into the strong coffee. A piece broke off and disappeared into the cup.

The three women spoke of things great and trivial, laughing and worrying over their morning coffee. Of Mrs. Rosenkrantz next door's sudden demise the month before from a heart attack. ("How will Ti-Tu survive without her?") Of Mrs. Lieberwitz's gout, which was acting up again. ("She's got to stop with the *schmaltz* herring and chopped liver.") And of Tiger, always of Tiger. Was he in Europe or in the Pacific? No one knew for certain. But his two years of service were up, the war was over and he was due home any day now. Only they hadn't heard a word from Tiger for weeks.

The front door burst open, jarring Poppa from his doze. Hurricane Astrid arrived, rattling everything in her wake. Where Rose, Jo and Camille were calm and even-tempered, their sister Astrid was forever in a tizzy. She barreled through a room like a tropical depression. Her wild array of headgear didn't benefit her countenance; it made her look positively batty. A milliner for Macy's and B. Altman, Astrid was distinguished by her whimsical chapeaus. Take what she was wearing now: a detonation of holly berries on a tight-fitting black velvet skullcap, netting pulled over her eyes with a sprig of evergreen thrown in for good measure. Poppa rustled the pages of the *Eagle* and cast Astrid a sidelong glance. "Maggie, it looks like Christmas exploded on your head," he stated.

"It's Astrid," she corrected her father with a tut. When Poppa opened his mouth to protest, Astrid reminded him, "Yes, it's not the name you gave me, but Astrid's the way I see myself, so I prefer it. And I'll have you know that Altman's has already sold two dozen of these ridiculous little things."

"Every mickle mek a muckle," Poppa said, borrowing the Jamaican proverb his welders down at the Navy Yard had taught him. It was perhaps his pet West Indian adage next to "The ghost knows who to scare."

"Yes, I agree, a few pennies can add up," Astrid conceded. "And I'm doing quite nicely for myself, thank you very much. I don't need a husband or a man or a…"

Back in the kitchen, Jo, Rose and Bridget were washing up after themselves but kept the coffeepot on a low boil in case Astrid craved a cup. The dish of cookies stayed on the table, too. Although Astrid was watching her figure, Wendy and Stan would be back from school soon enough, and they would be ravenous as always.

The women each inhaled sharply and went into the parlor to greet she who was Astrid. "Lovely hat, hon, but it doesn't keep your head toasty," said Bridget, "or cover your ears. You'll catch your death of cold."

"It's all the rage," Astrid protested.

"Dying of consumption?" Jo quipped. "It did wonders for that babydoll in *La Traviata*."

"I refuse to wear a *schmata* on my head," Astrid told them.

Rose ignored her sister, which was generally the best way to deal with Astrid. She'd been highly excitable as a girl, when she was known as "Margaret." Astrid had been named for her mother, Margarita, whose pet name was Bridget. As a child, Astrid was also referred to as "Maggie the Baby" by her siblings. Although she wasn't the youngest Paradiso, Maggie was always crying about something. The nickname usually brought on more hysterics. "Here to help with the Christmas decorations?" Rose wondered. Suggesting Astrid actually do something other than complain was a sure-fire way to send her packing.

"Me?" Astrid boomed incredulously. "No thanks, I just got a manicure." Astrid's fingernails were cherry red, no doubt to match the holly berries on her head and the silk of her blouse. "I'll just keep you company."

Astrid's idea of keeping her family company was to follow her sisters about as they hung red garland in the doorways and from the breakfront, which was filled with little knickknacks friends and family had brought the elder Paradisos from across the world: a costumed doll from Greece, a rabbit of Limoges porcelain, a fish of Venetian glass.

Jo and Rose moved onto the golden garland and twisted it beside the red. Determined to be of use, Poppa fed the glittering garland to Rose, who fed it to Jo, who had climbed the stepladder barefoot. Bridget watched contentedly from her armchair—no one expected her to participate because they knew how her sore leg pained her, especially in the gray weather.

Astrid hovered near the tinsel-wielding trio. Having finished criticizing her estranged husband Sam, she was now attacking the government, specifically, what she perceived as President Truman dragging his heels after the War. "I mean, it's officially been over for three months," she spewed, pausing for breath, "and Tiger's *still* not home…"

Nothing got Poppa's goat more than trash-talking good old Harry S. Truman, even if that someone was Poppa's own daughter. "It doesn't matter how long the War's been over," Poppa explained patiently. "The boy had time left to serve."

"The man," Rose commented in a quiet voice.

"Hmmm?" Poppa asked, untying a knot in the gold ribbon.

"He's a man," Rose added. "Tiger's not a boy any longer, Pa. He's been in a war and God knows what he's seen."

Poppa placed the loops of garland into his daughter's hands, as one might pass off a child. His fingers grazed Rose's. Hers were agreeably rough from decades of housework. Poppa's own hands were a mass of healed cuts and scars from his decades at the Navy Yard, but they'd mended, as most things did with time. "He'll always be my special boy," Poppa told Rose.

She turned away and passed Jo the cellophane tape. The box's Tartan design matched her sister's skirt, Rose noticed. Jo tore off a strip of tape and rolled it between her fingertips. "A few months after he went into the service," Rose began, all the while feeding Jo the rope of garland, "he stopped signing his letters 'Tiger,' and started signing them 'Anthony.' I guess we'll have to call him that when he gets home." 'But he never signed them "Tony,"' Rose thought. The name "Tony" was forever ruined for Rose and for the rest of the family thanks to her late husband.

Astrid considered an ornament Bridget was lovingly wiping with a damp rag while sitting in the armchair. It was teardrop-shaped, mercury glass. Poppa and Bridget had many of these unique Christmas treasures since Astrid and her siblings were youngsters. The ornament Astrid held was a deep blue. "Silent Night, Holy Night," was written across it in sugar-snow. There was even a stencil of a church with a steeple, the moon, stars and tall pines on its surface. It had been Rose's favorite ornament as a child. Sometimes she even plucked it from the tree and slept with it cradled in her palm. Rose never let go, even while she slept, and the Christmas ball was still there when she woke the next morning, nestled in her hand, which was often coated with snowy paint.

"Hey, put that down," Rose warned. "There's no tree to trim yet."

But Astrid didn't listen. She weighed the blue ornament in her palm. "When was the last time you heard from Tiger?" Astrid wondered. "The last time he wrote?" It had been almost a month, Astrid knew, but she wanted to make Rose say it. Astrid hated when people lived in safe, little bubbles of denial. Rose refused to answer her sister's question.

"You thought he'd be home for Thanksgiving," Astrid plowed on. "You were sure of it. You even had Momma set an extra place for him at the table. Remember?"

"Yes, I remember," Rose responded in a strained voice. She counted her blessings and was thankful she hadn't received a dreaded Western Union telegram which began: *'THE SECRETARY OF WAR HAS ASKED ME TO EXPRESS HIS DEEP REGRET THAT YOUR SON 2/LT ANTHONY JOSEPH MARTINO, JR WAS KILLED IN ACTION IN…'*

Poppa came to the rescue. "Margaret, you and I can't possibly imagine what's going on over there. Rebuilding. Keeping the peace."

But Astrid wouldn't let up. "Where's over there? We have no idea where he is. The Pacific? Europe? They keep moving him around like a chess piece. My point is…"

Jo tugged for more garland but Rose had it wrapped in her fists like a weapon, like a rope to strangle someone with. When Jo realized that Rose was crying, she slowly came down the ladder's steps. "Enough, Astrid," Jo told her sister. "Enough."

"But I don't understand why…"

All Poppa had to do was flash Astrid a murderous glance and she held her tongue. He didn't even have to threaten to take off his belt like he did when she was a girl. "The look" alone was enough to get Astrid's dander up. She turned on her heels, upsetting the box of glass ornaments on the coffee table beside Bridget. A tiny brass bell tinkled in alarm. Astrid managed to catch the box before it hit the ground but the ornament in her hand rolled free. The snowy "Silent Night" village splintered on the buffed wooden floor, just missing the plush safety of the carpet.

Rose looked at Astrid through tear-stained eyes. "You knew it was my favorite," Rose told Astrid. "You did that on purpose."

"I'll go get the dustpan," said Astrid. As she fussed in her parents' broom closet, Astrid heard Sully's heavy steps in the vestibule, stomping the snow from his work boots. Next came the sound of Sully's merry voice calling out a greeting. He was happy to be home.

As Astrid swept up the mess she'd made, Rose brushed past her. Jo retreated to the kitchen to fix lunch for her parents. She had all the ingredients for Mrs. DePalma's PR Soup, which was heavenly, especially with a loaf of challah bread from Piccolo's, which Jo had bought on the way to her parents' house. Astrid dumped the shards of glass directly into the dustbin without wrapping them in newspaper, without a word of apology. It was clearly time for her to go.

There would be no more decorating until the children finished school in the afternoon. Wendy and Stan's voices rose in delight with each new ornament they took from the box, examining them closely, as thrilled as if each had been a kitten or a puppy. However, the children would have to wait until Christmas Eve to decorate their grandparents' tree, which Sully dutifully carried home on his shoulder each year. It was Sully's ritual to buy the tree from Nino Scapaldi, who sold them in the same spot under the El every December. And every year, Nino would insist, "It's on the house," but Sully would always stuff a couple of bucks into Nino's worn pocket. It was Christmastime, after all.

Chapter Three

The Gift of the Magi

By the time Rose reached the top of the stairs, she could hear Sully splashing about in the claw-footed bathtub. He was warbling "Rose of Washington Square," which he usually sang in the tub. They'd seen the movie a few years earlier at the Loew's 46th and the tune stuck in Sully's head. It was a swell picture, despite the fact that Alice Faye was its star. Even though she was a reasonable actress and singer, Rose couldn't stomach Miss Faye because she reminded her of Tony's cheap, blonde floozy Denise.

In spite of Alice Faye, Rose still managed to enjoy the movie because it also starred Tyrone Power (who Poppa mistakenly called "Tyrone Gable"), who was easy on the eyes. It also co-starred William Frawley, who always appeared to be drunk or at least hung over. (Frawley reminded Rose of a not-so-good-looking Tony, so the actor wasn't her cup of tea either.) But who didn't like Al Jolson, who'd been dubbed "the world's greatest entertainer"? Jolson also being in the picture made it worthwhile.

After his shift was over, Sully usually headed straight for the bath. "To get the stink of the street off me," he explained. Indeed, Sully had to endure all sorts of tawdry characters on his beat: hobos, grifters, hooligans, and the occasional streetwalker. Then there was the "mysterious stench," which, nine times out of ten, turned out to be a body, many days dead, ripening. It was hard enough to swab the infernal odor out of your nostrils, let alone get it out of your pores.

Sully's partner Izzy liked to tell the tale of the floater they found in the Gowanus Canal that past summer, in the height of a June scorcher. By the way he was dressed, they could tell that the fellow was clearly a vagrant, so they didn't expect to find much in the way of personal effects on the body or even a wallet. But Neidrich, their SOB of a sergeant, made them search the poor schmo's corpse regardless. Sully and Izzy found only a penny and a sea slug. Of course, Stan delighted in hearing the story, and often asked Izzy to repeat it. This was the stuff children's nightmares were made of. Even though Stan swore he wasn't scared, whenever the boy heard about floaters, he slept with the nightlight on for several days.

Harry didn't care for the tale, however. When Izzy recounted it at the Paradiso's annual Fourth of July barbecue, Harry smiled politely as Izzy told it to a rapt audience. It made Harry melancholy and pine away for the old days on the beat with Sully. The ex-cop drained his bottle of Ruppert's, immediately grabbed another and reluctantly kept listening to Izzy.

In Rose's scrupulously-clean, checkerboard tiled bathroom, Sully lazed in the cavernous tub, adding hot water by working the faucet with his toes. As he adjusted the towel he'd folded into a pillow for his head, Sully couldn't believe his good fortune. Here he was, wed to the woman he'd carried a torch for since they were kids. He'd suffered in silence as Rose married a no-good bum, bit his tongue and held his temper as that dirty, rotten drunk treated the woman Sully loved worse than dirt.

When Tony finally got his just desserts, Sully found himself in Father Dunn's confessional one Saturday afternoon, still in uniform. There, Sully admitted to feeling thankful about a fellow human being's passing. "Ah, Patrick," the charitable father began, recognizing Sully's voice (it boomed even when he whispered), "The Lord giveth and the Lord taketh away."

Sully had to suppress a laugh behind the confessional's mesh screen barrier. He thought he heard a grin behind Father Dunn's words. It was the only time Sully didn't receive a penance from the priest granting him absolution. No three Hail Mary's and one Our Father. Nothing. "I suspect you've had penance enough," Father Dunn told Sully. "When the time is right, marry the girl." It seemed that everyone knew Sully was head over heels for Rosanna Paradiso Martino, even those who lived secreted away in a rectory. To stress the point, Father Dunn added, "Now, go in peace, my son...and make it right."

If Sully had kept an eye on Rosanna before Tony's death, he did even more so after the parish priest's blessing. Only now, Sully no longer stayed hidden away in the shadows; he was more obvious about his devotion to his Brooklyn Rose. Once at mass, Sully remembered Father Dunn saying in his sermon, "Don't hide your light under a bushel basket." Since then, Sully tried to keep the torch he carried for Rosanna out in the open. Yet, he hung back on the sidelines, anticipating a sign from her. Although her husband had been a monster, Rosanna was still grieving. She was a widow in mourning even though she refused to wear the clothes of bereavement—Rosanna reasoned that she had been in mourning through most of her marriage so she didn't need to wear black after her husband's death. Sully didn't begin keeping company with Rosanna immediately but waited patiently until the time was right.

Christmas Eve 1937 Sully and Harry received a call about an abandoned baby found at an all-too-familiar address. It had been snowing but the burly patrolmen ran to the Paradiso homestead despite the slippery sidewalk. The house was a collage of smells: *fritto misto*, roasted peppers, crab sauce, simmering garlic, and underneath it all, the stench of a soiled diaper. Instead of holding a towering *antipasto*, Rosanna cradled a baby when she met them at the door.

It was a boy. He looked to be several months old, certainly less than a year. Maybe the same age as Harry and Jo's girl Wendy, who was born the day after Valentine's Day. (Sully remembered the date because he was the girl's godfather.) The little tyke was scrawny and pale as dough where Wendy was pudgy and pink. He wore a thin bonnet and was wrapped in a flimsy blanket, both of which looked dirty. The baby's face was blotchy and streaked with tears but he wasn't crying anymore. Rosanna jiggled him and cooed to him as she stood at the open door.

A cardboard box stuffed with rags lay at Rosanna's feet. She passed a note to Harry which she had found amid the foul scraps of cloth. It read:

"This little fucker belongs to you."

That was it. "Pardon my French," Harry added, after he read the piece of paper out loud. "It's what the note says."

There was a dead silence; everyone was speechless. "A real gift of the Magi," Sully offered, filling the uncomfortable void with words. "Like the story. O Henry, I think it was."

Bridget appeared beside Rosanna, wearing an apron and smelling pleasingly of fried oil. She'd probably been preparing the Christmas Eve broccoli, Sully suspected. "It has to be that harlot...Diane," Bridget said. This much was crystal clear, even without the roughly-scrawled note.

"Denise," Rosanna corrected. "This is Tony's boy." The child resembled Tiger so much as a baby, they could have been twins.

"You want us to try and find her?" Harry wondered but he already surmised the answer.

"He's our boy now," Rosanna declared.

"With an abandoned child, protocol is that we turn him over to Protective Services," Sully told Rosanna quietly.

"Then he goes into foster care until we find a family who wants him."

"To hell with protocol," Rosanna blurted out sharply. It was the first time Sully had ever heard her curse, even moderately. Rosanna's arms tightened around the baby, who let out a small squawk. "We want him. It's Christmas, for crying out loud!"

Harry explained, "We'll push through the paperwork so you can keep him for now, without him going to the foundling home. No promises, though. We'll see what we can do."

Rosanna hugged the baby closer and nodded seriously to Harry. "No promises," he repeated, for emphasis. But Sully could tell that Rosanna took it as a pledge, and he loved her all the more for it.

Christmas Eve that year was unlike any other, namely because Rosanna helped Bridget put the finishing touches on the meal with an unfamiliar baby on her hip. The child seemed comfortable there. He was light-haired, light-eyed and serious, taking in every new thing, holding onto it and making it his own.

Rosanna's sisters soon arrived. Jo came with Wendy in her pram, bundled up against the frigid night, a sponge cake in the wire rack beneath the carriage and extra cloth diapers tucked around the cake to protect it. This was handy because that witch Denise hadn't even left her own child with a change of nappies. Jo volunteered to run home to grab some of Wendy's clothes for the boy to wear but the two cops couldn't bear the thought of a male child in a dress.

Sully and Harry made their way to Judy's Nook, the layette shop wedged into a cement triangle near United Israel Zion Hospital under the El. They were pleased to find Judy's still open, even though it was late afternoon on Christmas Eve and the Eve of the Sabbath besides. The proprietress, was extremely obliging to the clueless cops. Even by their sketchy details, she was able to determine the approximate size of the foundling and sold them the items they would need to clothe the boy, at wholesale. Judy was a momma, after all, with four children of her own not two blocks away.

She considered herself lucky that her mother, *kina hora*, could watch her kids while she ran the shop and her husband studied the Talmud—and got Judy pregnant when his head wasn't buried in his holy books. She tried to be a beacon of light and assist others whenever she could with what little she had.

The patrolmen had their evening meal break at the Paradiso place, and by then, dinner was in full swing, with platters being handed around the table and the baby being passed from sister to sister. No one was more surprised than Astrid that the little fellow was most content in her arms, bony and tense as they were. But Rosanna suspected why— the child's mother had blonde hair which came from a bottle, too—so maybe Astrid reminded the tyke of her.

The bathwater had gone cool as Sully fondly remembered the night Stan came to join the Paradiso family. He had added scalding water to the tub twice already and it was time to get out. He did a final scrub with a fresh rectangle of Ivory, the soap's name dimpling the bar's surface. Then he patted down with a thirsty bath sheet stiff from the clothesline. Sully wrapped the towel around his thick waist. Standing at the sink, he added a dash of water to his shaving mug, and stirred the cake of soap to a lather with his badger brush. He thoughtfully painted his chin with the foam.

It wasn't a bad face, Sully admitted, scrutinizing his countenance in the foggy bathroom mirror. He scraped his pearl-handled, straight-edged razor across it. A big, rubbery Irish face, affable enough, with a jaw which sometimes became obstinate. Although with Rose, Sully's thin lips easily curled into a grin. Besides, his wife seemed to like his face well enough, better than well enough. Sully had taken a shine to being married. Even though he'd tied the knot so late in life, when he was almost forty, and to a widow-lady with three kids, he was happy and still stupid in love with Rose.

The little one became part of the Paradiso family as seamlessly as Sully had when Harry brought his new partner to Sunday supper years before. They'd all remembered Sully as Irene Sullivan's taciturn older sibling. Besides being Harry's partner, the fact that Sully was related to Rose's grade school girlfriend was enough for the Paradisos to welcome Sully into the fold. Similarly, the boy, being half-brother to Kewpie and Tiger was enough for the Paradiso clan to absorb the boy into their tender vortex. But Sully suspected they would have been just as loving to any baby who'd been left on their front porch, whether the child was related to them or not. That's the breed of folk they were.

After the boy'd been found, Sully had taken to going to Rosanna's apartment when his shift was over, under the guise of helping out. He gladly washed dirty diapers and sterilized bottles, humming as he did so. Not that Rosanna needed a hand—Kewpie, Tiger and the rest of the family pitched in—but she liked having Sully there. Rosanna liked sharing a nightly cup of tea with him and the way his eyes lit up when he looked at her. Although they'd never gone out on a date, it seemed as though they were indeed keeping company without either of them having said a word about it. If "keeping company" meant folding tiny undershirts, bunting blankets and layette gowns, then Sully and Rosanna were indeed keeping company.

Sully was there when the boy took his first steps. Sully was there through the night when the child barked like a seal with the croup. It was Sully who sat on the edge of the bathtub with the hot shower going so the child could breathe easier, the boy clinging to Sully's chest as the bathroom steamed and the mirror dripped. It was Sully who ran the four blocks to United Israel carrying the toddler when the boy nicked his chin on the edge of the coffee table and required a butterfly stitch. And that very first night, it was Sully who was at Rosanna's side when she found a second note beneath the blankets in the cardboard crate which had been left on the porch. It was Sully who slipped the note from Rosanna's fingers and read it aloud:

"To Whom It May Concern,
I just can't do it no more.
His name's Stanley Anthony Martino. For the only
man who ever did right by me and the man who did me
wrong. My father and his father."

The note wasn't signed but Sully and Rosanna both knew who it was from. The blonde bombshell. The cheap floozy. That witch. (Rosanna was too much of a lady to say the "b" word.) Tony's woman. A wrinkled birth certificate tucked into the bottom of the box named Denise Stephanie Wallaski as the boy's mother and Anthony Joseph Martino as his father.

Rosanna told Sully they had to be careful about the way they referred to "the floozy" around Stan (who now had a name), because she was his mother. They didn't want Stan thinking he was trash because he came from trash. Rosanna was determined to do right by the boy. She didn't want Little Stan to feel he was bad because he was the product of horrible people. That's the way it had been with her late husband—because Tony was part of a despicable family, pretty soon, he started acting despicable himself. Tony believed he was bad ever since he was old enough to realize the type of no-account people he came from, and look what it did to him. No matter how many kindnesses Rosanna and her family poured into Tony, it didn't make a dent. Why? Because Tony had felt unloved as far back as he could remember and was filled with self-loathing, though he would never admit it.

Rosanna needed it to be different with Stan, and it would be. This is why she soon decided never to tell Stanley where he came from. She wanted Stan to truly feel like he was theirs. She made her family swear to keep the secret, even Astrid, who couldn't keep a secret in a vault. But this confidence Astrid kept, for it was a grave one. Stan was only ten months old when he was left on their doorstep, too young to remember his life before 1128 Forty-Seventh Street, so the secret stayed.

After an adequate period of mourning, Sully asked Rosanna to marry him. It was late one evening, after she had put Stan, now a toddler, to bed. Sully and Rosanna were sitting in the kitchen as they often did, silently sipping tea when everyone else was asleep. The silences Rosanna shared with Sully didn't worry her for they were comfortable, peaceful stillnesses. The pair reveled in the pleasure of each other's company without words. It was a rare and magnificent thing Rosanna had never experienced with Tony, although they'd been married for almost twenty years. Sully gently reached for Rosanna's hand as she reached for a butter cookie dusted with granules of sugar. He liked the Kirkman's soap essence of Rosanna. To Sully, it was the scent of honest labor and commitment, a very good smell indeed. Holding her hand and falling to one knee, Sully asked Rosanna to become his wife.

Of course, Rosanna said 'yes.' But she didn't so much as say it as breathed it. Then she started to cry. If the truth be told, Rosanna had been sweet on Sully, though it bothered her to admit this to herself while she was married to Tony. The only other human being who knew of Rosanna's deep fondness for Sully was Father Dunn down at St. Catherine's, and he'd made a vow not to breathe a word of it to a soul, only the Lord, who knew all and saw all anyhow. Rosanna suspected that Sully's sister Irene knew Rosanna shared her brother's ardor, but Little Red (as Sully'd nicknamed her) never said a thing. Through the troubled times with Tony, it thrummed Rosanna's heart that Sully, someone who wasn't related to her, was so considerate. She never forgot Sully's tender mercies, especially after Tony was pushing up azaleas in Green-Wood.

At the battle-scarred kitchen table, Sully and Rosanna shared their first kiss. It tasted of salt and orange pekoe tea and hope. Sully was so overcome with emotion that he almost forgot to take the ring from his pocket. It was a milky, oval opal with two tiny diamond chips at either side, hidden away in a velvet box. He'd bought it from Evvy, the nice Polish girl behind the counter at Milsons Findings in

Manhattan's Diamond District. Evvy was the daughter of
Harriet, the cook at Kreske's who worked with Kewpie.
Harriet swore that her Evvy would do right by Sully, and
Evvy did, selling the engagement ring to him at a fair price.
It looked striking on Rosanna's finger and fit perfectly,
muted violet, aquamarine and orange flickers radiating from
within the stone as though it were alive.

"It's too grand," Rosanna stammered through her tears.
"It's too grand for the likes of me."

"I'm afraid it's not nearly grand enough," Sully told her,
kissing her damp eyes, her hair. Then the baby woke up,
crying, too.

Patrick Sullivan and Rosanna Paradiso Martino were
married on October 8, 1938, in a side chapel at St. Catherine
of Alexandria Church. Rosanna wanted to tie the knot
outside in the church's grotto but it was too cramped a space
for such a large family. Sully suggested hiring a car but
Rosanna wouldn't hear of it. "A waste of money,"
she'd rebuffed him. So, they walked the few blocks to
St. Catherine's, a procession of sisters in handmade dresses
the colors of autumn—red maple, golden ginkgo and the
fiery orange of oak leaves. Sully was already waiting at the
church with Harry, his best man, so he didn't hear the chatter
en route to St. Catherine's like so many starlings, but his
wife—his wife!—recounted the conversation for him later:

*"Astrid, you look like a crazy person with blood spatter-
ing your veil," said Camille, who wore yellow.*

*"Blood!" snapped Astrid, ablaze in a red, kimono-
inspired creation so tight about the ankles she could barely
walk. "Why, if you had a shred of imagination you'd realize
they were cranberries!"*

*"I thought you had a skin condition," admitted Jo, the
matron of honor, a vision in a warm shade of pumpkin. She
turned to her eldest sister for assistance but Rosanna would
have nothing of it.*

"It's my wedding day," Rosanna sighed. "Don't drag me into this."

Rosanna wore an ankle-length dress of ivory Chantilly lace, not white—she didn't want people talking about her wearing white for a second wedding. But they talked anyway. Astrid whispered loudly, "The dress looks dirty," when she knew full well it was off-white. Mrs. Lieberwitz, who'd overheard Astrid, shot her a withering glance. Sadie Lieberwitz figured Astrid's venom was because she'd recently separated from Sam. But who could blame the man? Honestly, they were surprised he could put up with Astrid's shenanigans for almost a decade.

Even Little Stan walked, and he was fairly new to walking. Everyone agreed he looked adorable in his knee-pants and velvet jacket, which had once been Tiger's. Stan toddled between his half-brother and half-sister, holding their hands gingerly. Every once in a while, when he grew restless, they would swing Stan a step forward, his laughter like a melody. Wendy walked beside her mother in a similar shift cut for a child, a miniature version of Jo with the same rusty curls and dancing eyes. There wasn't an iota of Harry in the girl, which was fine with him.

Poppa and Bridget walked slowly behind their daughters and grandchildren, smiling widely. "It's like those Gindaloon weddings in the Old Country," Bridget noted. "With everyone making their way to the church on foot."

Poppa agreed, but added, "Except there are no mules. In Italy, there's always a donkey carrying someone." Bridget laughed heartily, throwing back her head. Poppa thought his bride of forty-seven years looked splendid in her dress of emerald satin, which brought out her eyes. Bridget looked so refined you hardly noticed her right eye, which turned in slightly because of "that damn firecrack" when she was a girl. Poppa himself wore a suit which had long gone out of style but was smartly-cut in its day. The suit had been fashioned by a tailor named Antonio DeMuccio who lived down the block from them on Forty-Seventh Street. Antonio hailed from San Vincenzo, the same village in Calabria Poppa had come from. Gussied up in his dress clothes, Bridget thought her husband handsome and still saw him as a young man. When her grandmother told Poppa this, Kewpie rolled her eyes but inwardly, she thought it was touching, and wondered if anyone would ever love her so fiercely.

Although news of Sully and Rosanna's wedding wasn't published in St. Catherine's bans of marriage, the whole neighborhood got wind of it and were already lining the pews when the profusion of Paradisos arrived. In addition to Sadie Lieberwitz, who took her place next to Mrs. Rosenkrantz, there was Mrs. Rosenkrantz's son Ti-Tu, who'd brought his violin. Of course, Sully's sister Irene, her husband Raymond and all three of their boys were in the first pew on the groom's side. A number of Kewpie's friends from Kreske's attended—Olie Olsen, Harriet Kaminski and Sandra Santiago, who was usually behind Kresge's Notions counter. Kewpie's manager Julia couldn't come and sent her regrets. Julia's eldest, Carol, was in the hospital, gravely ill, and they suspected polio. Even Augie, who had a crush on Kewpie, was there. "You look beautiful, Angela," he whispered as she swished past in a dress the shade of a tea rose. For once, Kewpie didn't roll her eyes. Soon after, she and Augie began keeping company.

Sully and Rosanna were truly moved by the number of people who etched out time from their Saturday afternoon to watch them exchange their wedding vows. Father Dunn kept it "short and sweet," at Sully's request. "After all, it's my second time around," Rosanna explained, apologetically. But Father Dunn believed that any love, even love the second time around, was a point of celebration, especially when it was celebrated within the boundaries of the holy Catholic church.

Rosanna blushed like a schoolgirl when she stood with Sully at the altar. The polished pews were filled with the expectant faces of people she cared for. Rosanna blushed even more deeply when Sully kissed her, lifting her chin with his finger and tilting her mouth up to meet his. Dr.

Lewis couldn't restrain a hearty "*Mazel tov!*" when all was said and done, and Sully finally kissed the bride. Even the good father couldn't hold back a smile. The church broke out into applause.

And thus, Rosanna Paradiso Martino miraculously became Rose Sullivan, who was an entirely altered person.

Out of the corner of his eye, Sully noticed that Jimmy Burns, a street scullion who'd been masquerading as Father Dunn's altar boy, fled as soon as the couple's lips met. Sully thought Burns' disappearance was due to the young boy's distaste for public displays of affection but moments later, the bells in St. Catherine's steeple began ringing frantically. The Burns Boy, who'd once jumped off a garage roof wearing a Superman cape (it was Sully who'd breathed life back into the boy's broken body), was known for his zeal, if nothing else. Father Dunn excused himself to put an end to the frenetic ringing, which soon stopped.

The sun shone through the rosette window and into the chapel, bathing Rose in a peach light. Sully imagined this would be one of the perfect images he recalled on his deathbed—the sun beaming in through St. Catherine's stained-glass windows on his wedding day and the serene expression on his bride's face.

As Sully considered Rose in the chapel, his new brothers-in-law Harry and John clapped him on the back, easing him from his musing. Sully managed to catch the eye of Sam, who had banished himself to the last pew. Sam still considered himself part of the family—they all did, not counting his wife—but officially was not since he and Astrid were legally separated. Sam felt relieved to be away from his estranged wife's relentless nagging but missed his adopted family and spent time with them whenever possible.

Although they were ecstatic for Rose, her brother Julius, Lettie, and their sons Matthew and Carl couldn't attend the wedding. Julius and his brood were back in Mexico, with Jul hired on by Walt Disney for a secret project plus studying with Diego Rivera besides. Rose's brother, Kelly, who'd been ailing in Arizona, had passed away the spring before. Too poor of pocket to travel the great distance with four children, Kelly's widow Sophie Veronica couldn't make the pilgrimage from Tucson in their ancient truck. She was holding on as best she could, running Brooklyn Made, the catering business she'd built with Kelly before his death, and keeping her family afloat. The children also had school and couldn't stand to miss it. Sophie Veronica was there in spirit, though, and sent a winsome double-fluted Navajo wedding vase as a gift. The vessel earned an honored spot on the top shelf of the Sullivans' breakfront.

After handshakes and hugs, the wedding entourage headed to the Rex Manor, where Sully had engaged the upstairs banquet room. Originally, Rose had balked, "It's too dear, too fancy…" but everyone convinced Rose that cooking for her own party wasn't right. Feeling magnanimous, Sully invited everyone who'd come to St. Catherine's to Rex's. It was nearly twice the number of people they'd originally invited. When Rose shot Sully a concerned look, he shrugged, "How often does a guy get married?" Rose couldn't help but agree, and Rex's was more than happy to set up extra tables and chairs, and throw more chops on the grill.

It was at least a mile from St. Catherine's to the Rex Manor, which was perched on the corner of Sixtieth Street and Eleventh Avenue. There was no way the gang could hoof it in their new shoes, especially Bridget, who was already walking on tender feet. The group made their way back to Forty-Seventh Street and piled into all available cars. Augie's dad let him borrow the Studebaker sedan, a solid vehicle, which was ticking like a clock after almost a dozen summers. They squeezed as many as ten into a station wagon, and managed the five-minute drive without incident—although bottoms were pinched, skirts climbed up chunky thighs, garter fastenings dug into legs and erections strained against dress slacks. "Is that a blackjack in your pocket or are you just happy to see me?" vamped Sadie Lieberwitz, masking her Yiddish accent with her best Mae West impersonation. The entire backseat burst into hysterics.

Sully drove to Rex's quite soberly, the vehicle overflowing with a silent joy as Stan sat between his brother and sister. The boy dozed on Kewpie's shoulder as Tiger toyed with Stan's shoelaces. Rose smoothed the ivory finery across her lap. "I'm so happy," she whispered to Sully.

"It's okay to say it out loud," Sully told her.

"Is it?" Rose wondered. "I'm afraid it all might disappear."

Kewpie leaned forward and rubbed her mother's arm. Then the girl tucked a stray wisp of hair into the French braid Rose had let Kewpie make for her earlier that morning. "No one's going to disappear," Kewpie assured her mother.

Sully began to hum "Love Is Here to Stay," which had just come out in *The Goldwyn Follies* months earlier. Tiger had gone to the picture with Poppa and Bridget soon after it debuted in February, on Dish Night. They'd each gotten a soup bowl and a song that stuck in their heads.

Rose smiled in spite of herself. Tiger balked at the hint of gooey romance in the air. "Besides, where would I go?" Sully continued. "Everything I want is right here." Then Stan farted, breaking the magic of the moment.

Upstairs at Rex's, steaming platters of food awaited them. The buffet table was covered with stuffed pork chops, broccoli spears shimmering with butter, crispy steaks, vats of mashed potatoes, and a trough of salad. A metal laundry tub was filled with ice, Rheingold and Schaefer. There was another basin with cans of Hoffman soda for the kids and teetotalers. Mr. Mancuso brought five gallon jugs of his homemade "Guinea Red" and kept them hidden under the table. A three-tiered wedding cake from Piccolo's waited on a side table. People had already grabbled plates and were digging into the feast.

The room looked so splendid that Rose almost cried when she saw it. She knew her three sisters were responsible for the tulle draping the walls and the late summer roses in a rainbow of hues gathered from Bridget and Poppa's garden. Bridget was renowned in Borough Park for both the volume and the fragrance of her roses, a fact which never ceased to make their neighbor Nunzi DeMeo jealous. In addition to the yellow and blush varieties from the Paradiso's front yard, there were also burnt orange and purples from other residents' gardens, even Nunzi's. There were so many flowers, Sully was certain the entire block had contributed to the bounty from their own rosebushes. It was that kind of street, and Sully was elated he would soon be living on it.

When everyone had eaten their fill, Harry and three of his and Sully's cop compatriots pushed aside the tables to make room for a dance floor. Above the din of people carousing came the sound of a lone violin. Ti-Tu stood off to the side with his Knilling tucked beneath his chin. The crowd hushed to listen. The strains of "Love Is Here to Stay" rose to the top of the room like cream to milk, a rendition so heartfelt that lumps rose in throats and tears welled in eyes. Even Mrs. Rosenkrantz was touched. For once, she didn't complain that her son wasn't playing Mozart or Dvorak, and simply enjoyed the music.

Sully put out his hand and although Rose reddened, she took it. She slipped into Sully's arms as easy as a glove. He enfolded her pleasantly-rounded body, encased her, and Rose felt cradled, safe. She moved across the dance floor as one with her husband.

As other couples joined in, Poppa chatted with his cronies at the bar, puffing happily on his pipe. Bridget was content sitting on a chair with Stan on her lap curled up in sleep, his hair matted to the side of his head from all of the sweaty excitement. Sully thought he saw a tear streak down the old darling's face as he led his bride on another turn around the dance floor.

It was during that dance when Sully told Rose they should adopt Stanley, who'd been her foster child since he'd been found on the porch almost a year earlier. The Office of Children and Family Services wouldn't let Rose adopt Stan on her own since she was a single woman. The money she brought in from piecework—making tassels at home for curtains and graduation caps—wasn't enough income for her to support a third child. Even though Tiger and Kewpie pitched in, giving Rose the money they made from their

44

neighborhood jobs, Family Services wouldn't let Rose adopt Stan without a spouse. But marrying Sully changed all of this. On the Rex Manor's dance floor, Rose melted into Sully and softly cried into the shoulder of his suit jacket, knowing that no one could take Stanley from her.

Finished with his bath and his shave, Sully straightened up after himself, wiping his stubble from the sink. Next, he unplugged the bathtub and watched the cold water and the muck of the night shift slip down the drain. Sully was heedful not to burn his ample bottom on the heat pipe which ran from floor to ceiling as he knelt to lightly scrub the sides of the tub with a shake of Bon Ami, noting its perky chick on the label who cheeped, "Hasn't Scratched Yet!" Sully and Stan said this whenever they spotted a pyramid of Bon Ami canisters at Bohack's or one in the cabinet underneath the sink.

"I thought you'd fallen in," Rose joked when Sully finally exited the bathroom, his thick terrycloth robe fastened snugly around his body.

Sully kissed the side of his wife's face. "I do my best thinking in the crapper," he admitted.

"In the restroom, you mean," Rose corrected.

"That, too," Sully said. "Sorry. After a shift, it's hard to slip back into polite society."

Sully noticed that the table was set for tea with the good dishes. 'You don't need an excuse to take out the good stuff,' Bridget liked to say. 'What are you saving them for?' she'd add. Rose usually gave Sully a bite to eat before he turned in after the night shift. It was their custom. "Sorry I was so late," he apologized. "I had a lot of paperwork."

"Rough night?" Rose asked.

"The usual. If you don't mind, I think I'll go straight to bed and try to get some shut-eye before Stan comes back from school."

"I don't mind one bit," Rose told Sully. "Sweet dreams." Maybe, just maybe, Rose would slip into bed beside her husband as he slept, curving her body against his, and reveling in the sensation of his skin touching hers as he dreamed beside her.

Chapter Four

Honey Bunch

Wendy lay on her belly in the middle of Oriental rug which covered most of the living room floor. She was sprawled out like a fallen five-pointed star, Harry noted from the nearby lounger, his war-torn left leg propped up on the ottoman. On bleak, snowy days such as this, Harry's wound throbbed with each beat of his heart, and even the paregoric Dr. Lewis had prescribed didn't take the edge off the pain. But watching his daughter read so intently gave Harry a sense of peace. It was one of the few things which did.

The girl was immersed in one of those "Honey Bunch" books she treasured. They chronicled the adventures of a blonde-haired moppet as she took her first trip to the city, her first auto tour and her first visit to the zoo. It began with *Honey Bunch: Just a Little Girl*, which had been his wife Jo's book when she was a child. They found it stashed in Bridget and Poppa's basement, in a box marked "Jo." (Each of the Paradiso's six children had a similar box in the cellar.) Harry found it delightful, watching Jo and Wendy cuddled together on top of the sunflower-patterned covers in his daughter's first big-girl bed. At the child's request, Jo read it over and over to Wendy's delighted peals of "Again!" It wasn't long before she knew all the words.

At first Harry and Jo thought Wendy had memorized the book but when Jo opened a brand-new volume, *Honey Bunch: Her First Little Garden*, Wendy began reading the words herself. The girl was four. "Is that normal?" Harry whispered to Jo in their bedroom later. He didn't want the girl to hear, in case it wasn't.

"It's normal for her," Jo smiled. Her face was illuminated in the dim glow the streetlamp cast upon their room. Then Jo turned to Harry, hooking her sturdy leg across his. That's all he needed in those days: the brush of his wife's skin on his, and they were off and running. But that was before the War, before Harry came back less than whole with a shattered leg and his dreams of making police sergeant dashed along with it.

A slender, leggy creature Harry sometimes felt he barely knew, Wendy would be nine in a few months. What happened to the chunky baby they'd taken home from Brooklyn Doctors? To the toddler with bells on her white polished shoes and more rolls on her legs than the Michelin Man? To the girl who sobbed, clung to him and begged not to leave Harry's side at nursery school? She was growing up and growing away from him.

Umber waves trailing down her back, jade eyes narrowed in concentration, knees up, wool tights wrinkled around her ankles, feet bobbing—there was such a pure beauty in Wendy that it made Harry want to weep. There was an innocence he was sure would leave her one day, not now, but someday soon, before Harry realized it. Perhaps Wendy felt her father studying her because she peered at him over her shoulder and smiled. He smiled back. A pile of books lay toppled beside her. "Where is Honey Bunch now?" Harry wondered aloud.

"At the beach," Wendy said without looking up. "I'm reading them all in order."

"Again," Harry pointed out.

"Again," she grinned. "Does it hurt a lot?" she added.

"Not too bad," Harry lied.

"It does," Wendy said. "I can tell by the look on your face." She crawled onto her knees and put a velvet pillow beneath Harry's prosthetic foot. This actually made it worse. "Better?" the girl wondered.

"Much better," Harry sighed, patting her cheek. "You get back to Honey Bunch." Wendy did as she was told, delving back into the story.

The O'Leary living room was a cozy space. Harry likened sitting there to being cradled in the comfort of wood, similar to Farrell's, but without the beer smell. There was polished oak paneling, parquet floors inlaid with cherry, pocket doors which Jo kept gleaming. Even Jo's *chachkas* were free of dust, stroked tenderly with a lemon-oil dusted rag once a week. There were Hummels which Mr. Dietrich next door had brought back from Germany way before the War. In addition to the Hummels there was a blown glass rose from Venice, an Indian couple (dot, not feather) sitting on a brass bench, and so on.

Jo had done her best to make the downstairs apartment feel homey but Harry preferred living upstairs on the second floor. Perhaps it was because the light up there was more distinctive, sharper. Perhaps it was because this was where Harry'd first brought Jo as his bride, fresh from St. Catherine's. Perhaps it was because this was where they'd first brought their daughter home, fresh from Brooklyn Doctors. But two sets of tall steps proved to be too difficult for Harry to climb when he came back from the War. In truth, the stone staircase outside was tough enough for him to mount, especially when his leg ached, which was more often than not. The radiologist and his wife who rented the O'Learys' first floor apartment gladly traded places with their landlords. Indeed, both flats were mirror images, except for the light and the irretrievable pieces of himself Harry had left upstairs.

Jo edged open the front door with her shoulder, a paper sack of groceries in her arms. Her cheeks were rosy from the icy air. She was bundled up in her green coat and matching wool bonnet. They also matched Jo's laughing, verdant eyes which shone even brighter when she caught sight of the people she loved best. "Please...don't get up," Jo said when Harry stirred in his chair. "It isn't heavy." But Harry tried to rise anyway. "Honest," Jo told him. "I'm fine." She kissed him on the mouth to show him how truly fine she was.

Wendy was up in a flash, *Honey Bunch: Her First Visit to the Seashore* spine side up on the carpet. She and Jo disappeared together into the kitchen. Harry heard their voices, like music in the next room: Wendy's, the trill of a piano, and Jo's, a deeper, bass, more soulful chords. Harry heard the paper sack crumple, detected the sound of chopping, smelled the savory sizzle of garlic, then onions joining it in a pan. From his lounger by the window, Harry saw that it had started to flurry. A curtain of snow blurred his view of the limestone houses on Twelfth Avenue.

And suddenly, Harry wasn't in Borough Park anymore, but someplace dark. The air was dripping. Harry was soaked to the skin, the coarse material of his uniform impossibly heavy. Once a deep olive, it was now almost black. Harry couldn't decipher where he was going, yet he forged ahead, putting one foot in front of the other on the uneven ground. He imagined there were houses around him but no light shone from them. There was the pleasant scent of dinner on the stove, of meat simmering. It permeated the air and didn't smell especially American. The spices were more exotic. A *bouquet garni*? Was he in France? All Harry knew was that it was cold and it was murky. It could have been anywhere. His hands were frozen to his rifle, his pointer finger tickling the trigger.

Out of nowhere, there was a startling flash and a burning in his left leg, below the knee, not even pain, but more a heat that radiated through his entire body, his chest especially, so intense that he struggled to breathe. Then his left leg gave way beneath him and he was down on the ground, cheek in the cool mud. Harry could no longer feel his leg. Was it still there? He tried to look, but in the lightless night, couldn't see a thing. Instead, he felt it. Yes, his leg was still there. A stickiness covered his probing fingers, too warm to be mud. Then it occurred to Harry that this could be blood. His own blood.

Harry's fingers went inside so easily, inside his own body. He could have sworn he felt bone. His left leg was twisted at an impossible angle but didn't hurt. When he tried to straighten the leg, it wouldn't budge. The mud held it to the ground like a suction cup. Then Harry started to shiver, to shake so violently his teeth rattled. He felt his bowels release, then nothing.

Next, there was the painful brightness of an operating room and glittering viridescent eyes above a surgical mask. "Jo?" He tried to form the word but his lips weren't cooperating. A rubber cup was fitted over his nose and mouth. He detected the scent of decomposing lemons. Jo disappeared in a vapor. Now someone was cutting into his leg. There was a searing hot agony which Harry couldn't stop. He couldn't move. He couldn't scream. He could only take it.

Harry sensed a face looming above his. A set of moist lips grazed his forehead. When he opened his eyes, Harry was in the parlor of his home on Twelfth Avenue. He was back in Brooklyn; he was safe. "You must have dozed off," Jo said.

"Did I cry out?"

"Just once," Jo conceded. "It wasn't too bad this time, though."

"Did she hear it?" Harry worried. Jo shook her head. "I sent Wendy to the basement. To get the Christmas Box." Jo slipped into Harry's lap. "Too heavy?" she wondered.

"Never," Harry told her. Was this really the same lass he'd met under the El on New Utrecht Avenue, fifteen, twenty years ago? Harry had lost track of time. Jo kissed him insistently, moving his lips gently apart with her tongue.

Harry gave into it at first, then pulled back. "In the middle of the afternoon?" he wondered.

Jo shrugged, "It's bedtime somewhere," then went back to kissing him. When they heard Wendy bouncing up the stairs, knocking the Christmas Box into the wooden banister with each step, Jo stood up and straightened the lines of her skirt. "Supper will be ready in about an hour," Jo said. "Wendy and I are making beef stew."

"I peeled the carrots," Wendy added, setting down the box on the floor. "Momma let me slice them, too."

"Smells great," Harry admitted.

"Do we have time to put up decorations?" Wendy pleaded. For emphasis, she folded her hands in prayer. "Please, please, please…"

"I thought you had your fill at Grandma Bridget's," Jo teased her.

"Stan put up the best ones," she pouted. "The glass angel from Italy…the tin butterfly Uncle Jul sent up from Mexico…"

"Well, you can put up our butterfly," Jo suggested. Wendy lifted the items out of the box and lay them onto a worn bath towel which now served as a rag. "Tell me a story," she demanded, with a laugh. The girl craved constant entertainment, Harry noted, just like her mother. "The story of me," Wendy pressed.

"We've told it to you a million times," Harry protested weakly.

"Then let it be a million and one, Pop," Wendy begged. Harry hesitated. "Pretty please with sugar on top. And a cherry," she added.

Jo fished a Manila envelope out of the box. "Once upon a time," Jo began, "A big, brawny policeman…"

"…met a lovely damsel in distress," Harry continued. "It seems that heel of the princess's glass slipper got caught in the trolley tracks as she was crossing the street."

Wendy took the envelope from her mother and slipped out the paper decorations: a round, jolly Santa's face, ginger girls and boys, a Nativity scene, two crossed candy canes and a set of angels with sparkly wings. "Didn't the princess have a magic coach?" Wendy wondered.

Jo laughed. "Not this princess. She was a different kind of gal." Jo slipped an angel from the envelope and held it to the parlor door. She easily found the thumbtack hole from last Christmas and the Christmas before. Into the nearly invisible hollow, Jo pushed a brass thumbtack. Harry picked up where she left off.

"The cop rescued the princess and she was so grateful, she married the lunkhead…" Harry said, half joking.

"The lunkhead was a prince in disguise," Jo added. Her nose had a dusting of glitter across its tip from the angel. "They got married, then the princess's belly grew…"

"And you had me," Wendy finished.

Jo and Harry's gaze flickered to each other, then away. There was no mention of the babies they lost or of the child Hope, who Jo had carried to full term, then delivered stillborn. "Yes," Jo said to Wendy in a voice which trembled almost imperceptibly. "They were going to call the baby 'Hope,' in honor of another little girl, but decided to give her a name all her own."

Wendy cradled a small crate of folded paper figures: snowmen and fir trees. "Was she named 'Wendy' for the girl in *Peter Pan*?" she asked, already knowing the answer.

"No," Harry admitted. "For a different Wendy, a Wendy who made her mom laugh."

Jo lifted the Christmas dishtowels out of the box, refolded them and put them on the arm of Harry's chair. "I was gigantic when I was pregnant with you," Jo told her daughter. "Toward the end, there wasn't much I could do except sit in the movies."

"Your Ma would waddle up to the Loew's 46th and while away the hours while I walked the beat," Harry explained.

"I was crazy for comedies," Jo revealed. "Especially *Lancashire Luck*. It had a new actress in it named Wendy. Wendy Hiller. Boy, did she make me laugh."

"So hard your water broke," Harry added. He could tell his daughter didn't understand what this meant. "It means your mom almost had you at the picture show," he explained. Jo placed one of the snowman figures on the polished cherry end table then moved it a few inches. "I'm thrilled I didn't or else I might have had to name you Loew's...or Augie."

Wendy was busy setting up the Christmas village on the breakfront's ledge. She'd already put down the gauzy cloth and was now carefully arranging the cardboard houses and trees. Jo passed Wendy the oval mirror, which doubled as the ice-skating pond. "Augie?"

"Your cousin Augie was working at the Loew's that night," Harry explained. "And he kept your mom calm until Uncle Sully and I got there." From his chair, Harry managed to pull out the satin drawstring sack which held the tiny wooden figurines who inhabited the Christmas village. Harry'd gotten them at the model train shop at Avenue M under the El.

"This was before Augie was your cousin," Jo added. "Augie and Angela were just friends back then. And now she's an old married lady."

Harry gave his daughter a handful of villagers. He remembered that the blonde girl with the kitten stashed into her ermine muff was Wendy's darling. She put that figurine down first, at the entrance of the church with two steeples. "Augie kept reminding your mom about the movie. Right, hon?" Harry cued Jo.

"'Keep thinking about the little tea shop and that lovely Wendy Hiller,' Augie would say every time I screamed," Jo recalled. "'And remember how it all works out in the end,' Augie said. And it did."

Jo pensively hung an angel in the window. Harry had strung the celestial creature with fishing line so diaphanous you could barely notice it with the naked eye—it looked as though the angel were truly flying. It was the same window where Jo had hung the banner with the blue and silver star during the War. "Your Aunt Rose had gotten to the theater by then, with her coat thrown over her housedress. I swear, old Rosie must have run the whole way," Harry laughed.

"Then what happened?" Wendy wondered, sprinkling Borax onto the mirrored glass to simulate snow.

"Then I had you. Right over there," Jo declared, gesturing toward Brooklyn Doctors a few blocks away.

"Were you scared?" Wendy prodded.

Jo had actually been terrified. She was afraid this child would also be stillborn. Jo didn't want to lie to her daughter, yet she didn't feel it was the right time to share the story about Hope, her older sister who rested soundlessly beneath the ground on a frozen hill in Green-Wood Cemetery. Harry picked up the slack, as he always did. "Scared?" he bellowed, a bit too loudly. "Not your Ma. Nothing frightens her."

'Except perhaps her husband's bleak moods,' Jo thought. She feared the times when Harry sunk so far into the abyss that she didn't know if she could pull him out of it. When he drank too much, mutely stewing, topping off not a shot glass but a juice tumbler of whiskey to sip in the middle of the night when the demons of War wouldn't let him sleep. The times when these monsters invited themselves inside, made themselves comfy and parked themselves on the sofa across from him. Harry told Jo that he didn't want to discuss it, that he didn't want to bring the War home with him, that he'd left it across the pond, in a field in France, in a picturesque town with an unpronounceable name. Not so unlike the little town Wendy was creating on the breakfront ledge in front of him.

Jo excused herself to check on supper. The apartment had filled with the wonderful scent of stew. Three places were already set at the dining room table off the parlor past the pocket doors inlaid with two windows of stained-glass lilies. A hunk of Italian bread sat on a wooden cutting board. "Irish stew and Italian bread don't go together," Harry had remarked once, to which Jo had responded, "Sure they do, like me and you." He had to laugh because it was true.

Jo carried the stew to the table with the potholders Wendy had made herself from a metal loom. Jo set the pot onto a pineapple-shaped trivet Stan had crafted in Mr. Alson's shop class and gave to his aunt (and godmother) the year before as a Christmas gift. Although one of the pineapple's wooden shoots had broken off, Jo still cherished the damaged trivet. "Dinner!" Jo called in a singsong voice. She even tinkled a little crystal bell from her *chachka* collection to get her family to supper quicker.

Harry stood at the head of the table with some effort, ladling out plentiful portions of stew. It was his friend Bobby Ryan's special recipe. Harry had grown up with Bobby, and when they were of age, Harry became a cop and Bobby became a firefighter. Bobby loved the job and was good at it, too. He died in what was known as "The Christmas Eve Fire." But not before Bobby left behind the legacy of his beef stew. (Ketchup was its secret ingredient.) Harry had gotten the recipe from Bobby's widow Della, who'd been pregnant with their second son, Donald, when Bobby passed away. Every time Jo made the stew, Harry thought of his boyhood pal. He was glad his family liked it as much as he did. In this way, it meant that Bobby Ryan lived on. Jo took pleasure in making Bobby's stew because the recipe was not only simple and delicious, but it was her way of paying tribute to an exceptional man who had gone too soon.

With the first spoonful, Harry proclaimed the stew "done to perfection." The gravy was flavorful, the beef was tender and pulled apart with the tip of a spoon, the potatoes were pillowy soft and the carrots were a brilliant orange, firm to the tooth and not mushy. Harry mashed the vegetables into the gravy; his wife and daughter did not. All three ate heartily. Jo switched on the Admiral to serenade their supper.

While Rose complained that Stan didn't utter a word about his day, Wendy regaled her parents with the most minute details–who was caught with a peashooter in their pocket, who got sent to the corner and who had trouble reading *Fun with Dick and Jane* aloud. "Oh, and we saw the Yellow Queen again today," Wendy said matter-of-factly.

"Who's we and who's the Yellow Queen?" Jo asked.

"Me and Stan. And the Yellow Queen's just a lady." Harry and Jo glanced at each other above their steaming bowls of stew. "It's not her real name. We just nicknamed her that. Because she has yellow hair."

Harry chewed his meat reflectively. "How often do you see her?"

"Every once in a while," Wendy admitted. "Sometimes we call her 'The Shadow' because she hides in the shadows."

Jo put down her spoon. "Does she ever say anything to you?"

"Never. But she looks like she wants to. One time Stan went up to her and she ran away. He was just going to say 'hi.'"

Wendy kept eating and swinging her feet under the table. (Her toes were just short of reaching the floor.) But Jo had lost her appetite. "What does this Yellow Queen look like?" Harry ventured.

Wendy shrugged, "Like she was pretty once. But now... she looks tired and a little dirty. Her clothes are old and her teeth are rotten. Maybe one or two are missing. Stan says she's 'The Yellow Queen' because she walks like a queen. And has yellow hair."

Jo washed the dinner dishes at the sink with extra vigor. The rubber gloves almost reached her elbows. Harry sat on a high step stool nearby with a checkered dishtowel. "It's her," Jo whispered. "It's got to be her."

Harry grabbed a soup bowl and dried it. "But we're not sure."

"Who else would it be?"

"It could be anybody." Harry nested the dish within the other two on the Formica countertop.

Jo slipped Harry the utensils. "What does she want?"

"We don't even know it's her, Josephina," Harry said. Jo flashed him *that look*. "So what if it's her, there's no harm in watching. Stan is her kid."

"*Was* her kid, you mean," she stressed. "She gave him up."

"Who?" Wendy asked. She'd gone to rescue Honey Bunch from the parlor carpet, and the book, with its heroine in her pink dress and buttery curls decorating the cover, was wedged under the girl's arm. Wendy was dressed in a flannel nightie which came to her ankles yet somehow made its way up to her neck in sleep.

"No one," her parents responded together.

Born a day apart, Wendy's cousin Stan was the first friend she'd ever had. She was too little to remember how and when he'd come into the family, and Jo and Rose aimed to keep it that way. The first time Stan and Wendy met at ten months old on Christmas Eve, they explored each other's faces, touched each other's hair, and laughed, as though they were looking in a baby mirror. They grew even closer as the years progressed.

In the end, Harry promised Jo he'd bring up "the Denise Situation" with Sully to see if he could make heads or tails of it. This satisfied Jo enough so that by the time they went to bed, she was more placid. Harry noticed Jo was wearing a satin nightgown, á la Jean Harlow in *Dinner at Eight*. He sat on the edge of their double bed in his skivvies, unfastening the strap for his prosthetic leg. Kneeling before him, Jo slipped her fingers over his and undid the leather buckle, easing the padded suction cup-like end from Harry's stump so that it made a soft sucking sound. She propped the false leg beside the nightstand so Harry could reach it himself in the morning. Beside the leg was a wooden crutch Harry used to hop to the john in the middle of the night.

The strap of Jo's nightgown slipped off her shoulder, revealing a pear-shaped breast, full and heavy, an overripe mango dangling from a high branch. The nipple was dusky and ruddy, as though she'd applied lipstick to its puckered surface. Harry felt himself stirring in his shorts in spite of himself. His wife didn't fix her nightgown strap but instead, shamelessly looked into his eyes. Jo reached for the bottle of Jergens lotion she kept on the nightstand. She nimbly unscrewed the cap and tapped a dollop into her palm, then worked it between her hands.

Without a shred of revulsion, Jo massaged the cream into Harry's stump, which was pink and smooth. The scar tissue had faded over the last year. While some might imagine that it was best for a stump to get calloused, this wasn't actually the case. A stump had to stay supple and smooth to fit easily into a prosthetic leg's cup. Usually, Harry lubricated it himself but sometimes his wife took matters into hand. Again, Jo reached for the Jergens and heated it in her palms. But instead of reaching for his stump, Jo reached into her husband's undershorts. Harry inhaled sharply but didn't push her away. He was already half-erect. Jo stroked Harry from root to bud, slowly, watching him grow and stiffen with each slide of her fingers.

A slight smile kissed Jo's lips when she rose to her bare feet. She tipped Harry back onto the mattress, the heavy winter quilt still upon it. Harry fell backwards, helpless as a turtle, his cock as stiff as his stump. Jo lifted the hem of her gown until it was up past her hips. Harry caught a glimpse of her sex, shrouded with the same reddish-brown down which covered her head. Jo impaled herself upon Harry so suddenly, so sharply, that they both gasped. "Did you lock the door?" Harry wondered.

Jo's response was "Shush" as she hunkered down and rode him low like a jockey. "Shush…" For a while Harry forgot—forgot about the War, forgot about his leg, forgot about the pain (both inside and out) and gave himself to the moment. There was only his beautiful wife, mounting him, the scent of *Muguet des Bois* perfume wafting up from between her breasts, the tips of her hair brushing his shoulder blades, the little cry which came from between Jo's lips as he felt her body clutching his and spasming, spasming, spasming. She invited Harry along for the ride, and he finished a few beats behind her.

Afterwards, Harry and Jo lay in bed, just breathing. There was a warm washrag, a kiss and then the heavy bliss of sleep. At least for a little while.

Chapter Five

Corner Plot

Denise stood at the corner of Forty-Fourth Street and Fort Hamilton Parkway with the El at her back, PS 131 before her. She thought perhaps the boy had seen her because he stared straight in her direction, then looked around after she ducked into the fishmonger's doorway. This was right before the shopkeeper shooed her away. "I told you before, lady, quit blocking my entrance," the fishman warned. "For the love of Pete, move your big caboose. You want I should call the cops?"

While Denise had put on weight in the past few years, the nasty, old Hebe had no right to insult her. Why, she had a good mind to knock the stinking skullcap right off his head. That'll learn him. But Denise didn't want more trouble with the police, especially in this neighborhood. Besides, she was getting chilled and the wind was blowing through her wrap as though she were buck naked. She would have to find a proper winter coat. But how? With what dough? Denise pined away for a thick wool jacket, maybe even with a fur collar. She felt certain she could barter for one. Surely a rub and a tug from a good-looking dame was worth a decent winter coat from a horny haberdasher, wasn't it?

The boy had given one final look in Denise's direction before he disappeared through the school's double doors. That annoying little waif was beside him. They were constantly together, like Siamese twins. Too young to be beaus, though. Denise's son would be nine in February if she remembered correctly. But lately, with the drink and her poor health, Denise was forgetting important things like her child's birthdate.

She wondered if they'd kept the boy's name—Stanley, after her old man—as she'd requested. The Martinos had no reason to do anything she asked, given how she'd torn apart their family. But it wasn't all her fault. Part of the blame fell on Tony, though Denise had known darned well that he was married when she started playing footsie with him. Denise swore she would never be with a married guy again, yet she found herself going with wedded fellows time and time again. Her dad had been a straight arrow, tried and true until the end, even after her mother had run off with the Bird Man. That's what everyone called the fellow who kept pigeons on Jackson Place, where she'd grown up, the Bird Man. (His given name was Clarence.) Behind Denise and her dad's back, the neighbors snickered that Enid Wallaski had flown the coop with the Bird Man, like it was some sort of joke. Only it wasn't funny, not to Denise and her father, who never recovered from being abandoned. Neither did Denise.

But it didn't matter now, none of it. 'Sooner or later you'll be gone, with a corner plot in Green-Wood if you're lucky,' Denise told herself. Enid, Big Stanley and Tony were dead and buried. Yet it *did* really matter when all was said and done, didn't it? It mattered to Denise, who was still alive and kicking, but just barely. And then there was her son to consider. *Her son*. Hers and Tony's. Stanley not only looked like his father, but he resembled Tony's other son. They called him something different than his given name, which she couldn't recall either. "Butch," Denise thought it might be. Or maybe "Tiger" because he didn't look like a "Butch." But he didn't look like a "Tiger" either. Denise took a gander at Tony's kid at the Stumble Inn when he was a boy. It had to be eight or nine years ago, before Tony died. 1930 something. For the life of her, Denise couldn't remember. She'd always been sketchy with dates. Especially now.

A man walked toward her. Wide-shouldered, like a four-by-eight, with a boxy build and a pronounced limp. But it was more a rocking rather than a true hobble. Like the way a ship pitches on the sea, rolling from side to side. The fellow favored his left leg then hopped onto the right. He seemed to making a beeline straight to Denise. His hat was pulled down low on his head so she couldn't make out his face. His body was hunched forward, like a bull ready to charge. A dissatisfied john? A surly flatfoot?

Whoever this guy was, Denise didn't like the looks of him. She turned quickly on her heels and made for the El's steel steps. Even in her well-heeled pumps, Denise was quicker than the Neanderthal but panting was by the time she reached the top of the train station's double staircase. She thought she'd heard a frantic, "Miss! Miss!" and then "Denise!" when she fumbled for her token, but she couldn't be positive. Maybe her ears were playing tricks on her.

Lucky for Denise, the West End train arrived a few seconds after she stepped onto the concrete platform. It was even colder and windier up on the El. So chilly, she felt her nipples stiffen under her sheath, and for no good reason. The train was almost empty. She chose a seat far from the door. At least the heat was blasting, but it was so strong it felt like the backs of her calves were roasting. Just as the man lurched his way onto the platform, the doors smashed shut. When their eyes met, a shiver went through Denise's body. She'd have to stop spying on Stanley, at least for a couple of weeks.

The unkind wind made the train sway as it sat briefly in between stations, crawling toward Coney Island. It was too early to set up shop in Ruby's and Denise didn't have the heart to go back to her wretched furnished room on the third floor of the Terminal Hotel. The place wasn't terrible back in the Thirties but now it was undeniably a flophouse in a dreadful state of disrepair. At least once a week, they were carrying out a stiff on a stretcher, an old rummy whose liver finally cried "Uncle!" or a mook who'd said something stupid to someone stupid and got a knife buried in their gut as a reward.

Unlike the Culver Line, the West End went arrow-straight to Coney, with the exception of a noticeable curve before Bay Parkway. In the first car, Denise could see the structures of Luna Park, though many of the buildings had been damaged by fires the year earlier. During wartime, there was no extra money to rebuild a frivolity like an old amusement park, and lately, there was a buzz about putting up public housing for the vets who were coming home in droves. Although it had also been struck by blazes in the late Thirties, "Steeplechase, the Funny Place" had reopened, though. But now, in the dead of winter, everything was shuttered.

The Parachute Jump, which many called "The Eiffel Tower of Brooklyn," soared above Steeplechase. Its cantilevered steel arms reached out into the frigid air, each of which held a parachute attached to a lift rope and a set of guide cables. (They'd all been taken down post-season.) Denise had been on it twice—once as a girl and once as an adult—and both times, she'd been terrified. She immediately had to pee like a racehorse the moment she was belted into the two-person canvas seat which hung below the closed chute. Denise remembered how her heart rose to her throat as the seat was hoisted to the top of the ride, two-hundred and fifty feet above the boardwalk. Her stomach fell into her shoes when the release mechanism dropped her, slowed down by the opening of the parachute. Pole-mounted springs acted like shock absorbers at the bottom "to ensure happy landings." It required a trio of burly cable operators to run each parachute.

On Denise's first ride, the solid girl of ten was seated beside an anonymous fat man whose girth spilled onto her as he was belted into the canvas seat. Once they were airborne, Denise was thrilled they'd put her next to such a fatty because his considerable size acted as a cushion, a human shock absorber. However, it also prevented Denise from being strapped in as tightly as she would have liked. Denise screamed all the way down, the man giving her the stink eye when they were untethered from the ride. Denise gave him the evil eye right back and stuck out her tongue, too. "I'll give you something to scream about," the rotund man threatened, raising his fist before she disappeared into the throng.

Denise's second parachute ride was far more pleasurable. Tony convinced her to try it again a dozen years later. But then Tony could convince Denise to do just about anything. "I'll give you something to scream about," Tony growled sexily when Denise had told him about her first experience on the Parachute Jump. And that he did.

As soon as they were off the ground and out of view, Tony slid one hand under Denise's skirt. The other, he slipped around her back, scooping one of Denise's heaving breasts into it. When Tony found Denise's already-stiff nipple, he squeezed it harder. As the parachute crept skyward, achingly slow, Tony eased aside the band of Denise's bloomers and fished around inside them. He toyed with her thick tuft of pubic hair, damp from the summer heat, caressed her thighs and every now and then, dipped a finger into the depths of her body. The stimulation, coupled with the sheer terror of being suspended above the boardwalk by metal cables, took Denise's breath away. When the parachute began to fall, she pressed her pelvis into Tony's palm, crossed her legs tight and throbbed around his fingertips. She left a garnet lipstick stain on Tony's shirtfront as she thrashed, not caring how he would explain it to his wife when he got home.

Back on *terra firma*, Denise stumbled on her shaky legs. She noticed how the cable operators exchanged knowing glances with Tony and how he winked back confidently, confirming their suspicions. "Better dry off that seat, boys," Tony had joked with them. Even without his blue comment, the crew had probably become adept at discerning whether ladies' weak limbs were from monkey business or from pure, unabashed fear. With a hot tomato like Denise, they tended to assume the former. You'd be surprised how many males got their first grope at the top of the Parachute Jump. Hundreds of feet up in the air on a canvas chair, how could a girl refuse?

The chill seeped in through the open train car doors. How long had they been sitting in the Stillwell Avenue station? A conductor walked by, shouting, "Last stop. All out." Denise grabbed her purse and left. With each weary step, she recalled the many strolls she and Tony had taken from Stillwell to her old place in Sea Gate, how he would head her off at the pass and maneuver their meetings, perfectly timing when she'd be coming home from the office. Once or twice, Tony had guided her into an out-of-service train and had his way with her right there. And Denise had liked it, she had.

But those days were gone, the days of having a steady job in a reputable place. Denise knew that Smith & Associates kept her at the front desk because of her "Ziegfeld Girl" face and entrancing curves. She only had to look snazzy and smile. It had been a peachy nine-to-five job with excellent pay and nothing to do except flip through *Movie Stars*, *Life* or grapple her way through *Dell Pocket Crosswords* until a client came in for an appointment or the phone rang. Since the switchboard fielded the bulk of the calls, people phoning the receptionist desk were generally looking for Denise. Sure, once in a while, she had to fetch some schmo a cup of coffee or stuff envelopes. Denise didn't even mind the occasional manhandling. It had been happening most of her life and she'd gotten skilled at sidestepping fellows with octopus arms.

Then Denise started messing up, as she usually did, calling in sick, coming in late, and looking disheveled when she gave her employers the courtesy of showing up. Even though Denise had a wooden leg when it came to drinking, she couldn't keep up with Tony. Her hourglass figure suffered, everything suffered. Had he been alive, Tony

would have quipped, "Hourglass, my ass. All the sand has
sunk to the bottom."

Denise fussed with her wool beret, tucking her hair up
into it as she picked slowly down the Stillwell Avenue
station's steps. She made her way toward Surf. In dire need
of a dye job, Denise was self-conscious about the brownish
stripe painting her scalp and pulled her hat on tighter. The
last time she'd dyed her hair herself in the sink of the
flophouse's shared bathroom, she fell asleep on the can,
cigarette burning in her hand. Denise's hair had become
a bleached frazzle. Thank heavens she had a few jaunty
chapeaus left from her nine-to-five days to mask her mishap.
You'd be surprised at what you could do with a fancy turban
or an Italian silk scarf wrapped just so.

In the dazzling sunlight, it wasn't too raw on the
Riegelmann Boardwalk, especially after the wind died down.
For a time, Denise sat on a bench, smiling into the brightness
like a tired, old dog. Although she was not yet forty, Denise
felt what she imagined eighty was like. Hers had been a
rough road to hoe, and not just lately. Denise trembled
slightly as she looked at her wristwatch and wound it a few
times. It had been a gift from a gentleman friend and
supposedly had genuine diamond chips around its face. She
would have to pawn it sooner or later. Probably sooner.
A few minutes after ten, it was too early to drink, though
Denise already had the shakes. 'Ah, damn it all to hell,'
she thought, fishing around in the bottom of her purse and
holding her breath until she found the curved neck of a pint
bottle. She unscrewed the cap and took a deep swig, not
caring who saw. The Four Roses went down smooth, like
liquid fire. It tasted of Kentucky: wooden stills, murky
forests, coon dogs and mystery.

Denise felt the weight of a body sitting next to her on the
bench. It was "her" bench, so fellows seeking a quick good
time knew where to find it. "Nice weather we're having,"
uttered a quivering male voice.

"Ah, cut to the chase, why don't ya?" Denise told him,
without even bothering to look at his face. All these johns

were the same, interchangeable. "A rub and a tug or something special?" she yawned.

"The usual," he stammered.

"Well, then," Denise said, standing up and straightening her frayed coat as though it were luxurious. "Meet me underneath in two." Her scuffed pumps made almost no sound on the wide, chipped planks as she worked her way across them and under the Riegelmann.

In less than the prescribed two minutes, the man appeared, slipped Denise a folded bill then undid his zipper. She turned away from him, not looking at his face or his Johnson. The heat of it drew her hand there. This was going to be an easy one because he was already erect. He'd probably been stiff from the time he sat on the bench beside her, maybe even before then. The iciness of Denise's fingers didn't deter him, although to her, it felt like a melting ice cube from the hotness of him. A few strokes and he was a sputtering garden hose, arcing his seed into the sand. He left without a word, fastening his trousers.

As Denise wiped her fingers one by one on a daisy-embroidered hankie too dirty to clean anything, she considered her dilemma: food or drink? Which would she choose? The same one that always won out, which is why her legs were skinny as broomsticks and her belly was bloated. 'Damn it to hell,' she thought, shoving the crumpled dollar into her purse. 'Damn it all to hell.'

Instead of heading straight to Ruby's, Denise tormented herself and walked in the opposite direction, toward Sea Gate. She occasionally did this, tortured herself like a lover might, withholding affection, starting and stopping while doing the nasty instead of giving it up at once. Only with Denise, she withheld booze from herself instead of cuddles. It helped pass the time. Whether it made her drink more or less wasn't clear.

The sky was a vivid blue which hurt the eyes at first, the sort of cobalt that came after a snow. There were a few high, wispy clouds decorating it. One looked like a lion, another like a dragon, but both soon fell apart and blew away. Denise barreled by the Parachute Jump, gated and bolted down for the winter. The parachutes themselves were gone, stored away for the next season. She noticed how the ride's silver paint was flecking off in spots. They would probably have to touch it up next spring. Denise wondered if she'd be around to see it.

A few years before, 1940, she thought it was, a couple had even gotten married up there. "The Parachute Wedding" was the talk of the town in Coney. The photographers, the band and even the wedding party watched from nearby chutes as the couple was legally married, smooched then plunged into a freefall. (To Denise, the act of marriage itself was a freefall.) Denise remembered reading in the *Mirror* how the besotted groom had quipped: "No man on earth is good enough for Ann." Oh, please! They probably did it for the gifts and the publicity. Suckers...

Denise walked past a cluster of bathhouses—Publix, Ocean Tide, and Silver's, which even had a marquee, just like a theater. Behind her was Child's Restaurant, where she and Tony had gone once. It was a yellow terra-cotta fortress three stories high with a rooftop pergola. Crayola-colored mermaids and mermen stared out from above the wide arches and glass picture windows. Inside, there were white tiled walls, creamy marble tables and huge electric fans on the ceilings. The food was pricey, but boy, did they treat a girl royally. Denise would be the first to admit she was treated differently back then. Yeah, she had been a real looker. Nobody would dare suggest she move her big caboose from their storefront. They would have asked her in for tea, more than that, even.

At West Thirty-Seventh Street, the boardwalk came to an end. Denise veered off to the right, to Sea Gate, where she once lived. It was a charming community, "at the ass-end of Brooklyn," as Tony used to say. A guard in a box presided over its entrance, letting a select few come and go. Residents had to leave the names of the guests they were visiting with him or else admittance was denied. Denise could see by the stoop of the guard's shoulders and the baldness of his pate that Herman stood duty. She'd taken a shine to him and vice versa. Denise gave Herman her perkiest, close-mouthed smile, managing to cover her missing tooth.

"Why, Miss Denise," Herman piped, truly happy to run into her. He was so glad that he kissed her fingertips like she was a fairy princess, then engulfed hers in both of his and didn't let go. "Long time no see."

Denise nodded, momentarily taken aback. "I been so busy," she confessed. "You know how it is."

"You look tired," Herman informed her, releasing her from his grasp.

"I been under the weather lately," she admitted, and gave a weak cough for emphasis.

"Well, you take care," he said with concern.

Denise assured Herman that she would. "You mind if I take a look around?" she cooed. "Check out the old digs?"

"Be my guest," Herman responded with a little bow, extending his arm as if to point the way. "A little nostalgic, are we?"

Denise flushed. "You know me, I'm an old softie."

"Where are you living now?"

Denise hesitated but only for a moment. "Oh, me and my beau, we have a marvelous place right on Shore Road, looks out over the Narrows." The truth was that her room at the Terminal Hotel was squalid and overlooked an alley teeming with trash.

"Sounds swell," Herman told her.

"It's positively a palace!" she lied. With a sincere handshake, Denise was on her way. "Thanks, Hermie. You're a peach."

"Don't be a stranger, Miss Denise," he called.

"Oh, I won't." Maybe she would leave through the Neptune Avenue gate to avoid him, Denise thought.

The first place Denise's numb, aching dogs carried her was to the Sea Gate Beach Club. The large, chalk-colored building was boarded up for the season. Its striped awnings were rolled up and secured in place. Denise followed

Atlantic Avenue until it turned into Surf. She headed down toward the lighthouse, the ocean at her left shoulder, Gravesend Bay beyond the tip of her nose. Though some referred to it as the Norton Point Lighthouse, its official name was Coney Island Light. It was situated on the west end of Brooklyn, east of New York Harbor's main channel. If you were docking in Manhattan or Red Hook, which housed a network of piers where the sustenance that fed the city was delivered, you had to come through this channel. And when you were leaving for parts unknown, you had to repeat the same pass through, too. But unlike the ships which came and went through the channel, Denise was sure she wasn't going anywhere any time soon. No place good, at least.

The lighthouse was made of steel, painted a skeletal shade, with a black top. A bloke by the name of Adrien and his family lived there. They were always considerate to Denise, especially Adrien's wife, who could chat up a storm. She was probably just relieved to be away from their seven rat kids. Alice, her name was. Alice and Adrien were from Quebec, and they still had a heavy Canadian lilt to their speech, although their offspring were pure Brooklyn through and through. Alice was quick to dispel the notion that being married to a lighthouse keeper was romantic. Climbing the corkscrew stairs were bothersome to her old man's knees and he had to mount the steps several times a night to wrestle with the 150-pound weight which rotated the lens. Tending the lighthouse made it difficult for the family to go away, and if Adrien was ill, the job fell onto Alice's substantial shoulders. They gave their kids a whopping five cents every time they wound up the lighthouse weight.

Although Alice was pleasant enough, Denise didn't feel like calling on her right now. Tough as a lighthouse keeper's wife's life was, Alice had managed to hang onto all seven of her little darlings, while Denise couldn't even hold onto her one. She'd given away Stan like he was an unwanted pair of shoes before he was a year old. What kind of no-account woman would do a thing like that? A woman like Denise, that's who.

Both the lighthouse's American flag and the Red Cross flag stood rigid in the breeze. Denise continued until Surf Avenue met Poplar. Many of the streets in Sea Gate were named for trees: Maple, Cypress, Laurel. Others bore marine monikers like Oceanic and Nautilus. After some blocks, Highland transected the community, spurring off from Surf. There was no rhyme or reason to the street-naming as far as she could figure.

Denise made a left onto Lyme Avenue, her old place of residence. She'd lived on Lyme for about a decade, longer than she'd lived anyplace. With her former landlady pushing eighty by now and the old broad's money-grabbing nephew living there to "help" her, the Victorian house was falling apart, bit by bit. Denise half-thought that Marilyn Meyer, who everyone affectionately called "Aunt Mimi," at her request, might even leave Denise the joint. But no such luck. When Aunt Mimi grew feeble, the relatives started crawling out of the woodwork like wharf rats, and her nephew parked his skinny tail in Denise's old digs.

It pained her to see paint peeling from the house's once-majestic turrets and from the sloppily-painted steps. A few windows were broken and covered with wood or repaired with plastic sheeting and tape. Tiles were missing from the roof. Denise's wide, sunny rented room had been at the top of the left tower. Aunt Mimi had three additional boarders but Denise had been her pet. The old girl was better to Denise than her own mom had ever been. Aunt Mimi stuck by her when she was pregnant. She even gave Denise her old room back after Tony died and accompanied Denise to his wake. Her landlady did as much as she could when Baby Stanley was born and consoled Denise when she had no choice but to give her son away. However, when she fell behind with the rent, Denise was shut out again. Aunt Mimi howled and carried on, but her nephew insisted on putting Denise out. "It's business, nothing personal," he'd told her. Although she had no ill will toward the old woman, Denise couldn't bring herself to knock on the door to say hello. She couldn't bear for Aunt Mimi to witness the sorry state she was in.

But there had also been delightful times at the house on Lyme Avenue. Denise and Tony spent hours kissing goodnight beneath the gnarled maple tree on the front lawn, now bare and gray-barked. Although Aunt Mimi never let gentleman callers into the *boudoirs* of her female renters— "my girls," she called them—the boughs of the low-slung Japanese maple hid a multitude of sins. If that lawn could talk! And it was the lushest tree in Sea Gate from Denise and Tony's Onanistic grapplings.

Denise lifted a chapped hand to her cheek and found it wet. Mist from the Atlantic? Nothing doing, it was tears. Her tears. Denise was crying and she didn't know why. Hell, she knew why. She was crying for herself, for the past, for the girl she would never be again. And she was crying for the future, as dismal and dark as the boarded-up windows of Lillie Santangelo's World in Wax, with its monkeys playing poker and its exhibit on Lina Medina, the world's youngest mother, a Peruvian youngster who'd supposedly given birth to a child at age five. What happened to Santangelo's wax dummies in December, when Lily's was closed? Where did they go? Were they still and dead and dust-covered while the world went on without them? Or did they take on a life of their own when no one else was looking?

Denise blew her nose into her flower-embossed handkerchief. She wiped her eyes on her coat sleeve and noticed how its red satin lining was coming loose. She would have to darn it when she got back to her room. Denise had a sewing kit stashed in the White Cat cigar box her ma had left behind. It was all she had from the woman except for bad memories and silent rage. Denise suspected folks would be surprised to discover that an old strumpet like herself could indeed sew, and was actually pretty adept at it. 'Yes, I'm good at something besides giving hand jobs,' Denise smirked to herself.

Her legs were ice cubes, and she couldn't feel her feet as she made her way to the Neptune Avenue gate. It was unguarded and only open sporadically. Denise decided to try her luck, and as fortune would have it, the Neptune Gate was unlocked. She walked back down West Thirty-Seventh to Surf outside Sea Gate's black wrought-iron fencing. She hoped Herman wouldn't spot her, huddled against the elements, her ungloved mitts deep in her pockets, her beret yanked over her ears. Maybe Denise should catch the trolley back but she couldn't afford to spend the two bits. The Norton Point Line ran from the Stillwell Avenue station into the depths of Sea Gate and back, but service was spotty at best in the leaden winter. Usually, Denise hoofed it because that's the way she and Tony used to travel the route. After being cooped up in "that damned cage" (the conductor's booth), Tony liked to stretch his legs, especially on a mild summer evening.

Already, the winter of 1945 had been frigid, abnormally snowy and windy. Denise would have been downright cozy with Tony's arm wrapped around her, her body pressed into his. And Tony, the devil rest his soul, was in an even chillier place, instead of beside her. Denise didn't believe in heaven, hell or anywhere else in between. When you were dead and gone, you rotted in the ground, and that was that.

When the trolley clanged its bell at Denise, she quickened her step to show that she indeed wanted to hitch a ride. The trolley operator, a coffee-skinned man with a broad smile, cranked open the door. "Cold enough for you, Ma'am?" he asked.

Her mouth was too frozen to respond. She nodded and shivered. There were two other passengers on the wooden seats, way in the back. When Denise fumbled in her tattered change purse for her fare, the trolley man winked at her, but not in a wolfish way. "Keep it," he said quietly. "Everybody needs a break now and again. Merry Christmas." She almost wept at the stranger's random act of compassion. Denise didn't believe in Christmas either, or in good will toward men (or women). In her book, everyone was out for themselves, Christmastime or anytime. She didn't tell this to the trolley operator, however. Instead, she thanked him in a meek voice, bowled over by his generosity. Denise found herself tearing up and chewed on her lower lip to stop the waterworks in their tracks. It didn't help. Out came the sunflower-spattered hankie. Denise hoped no one noticed that she was blubbering like a madwoman.

Denise chose a seat near the middle of the trolley so the considerate gent who drove it wouldn't strike up a conversation with her. There was only so much niceness she could take in a day. Even in the heated trolley, she couldn't seem to warm up. A juicy cough racked her body as she hugged herself and watched the puce Atlantic as the trolley slowly chugged along. The closed-up rides of Steeplechase Park appeared glum and desolate. Luna Park looked even worse, angrily bearing the scars of its dual fires. Rumor had it that Luna Park wouldn't last the season. Many swore it was the beginning of the end, but for Denise, the grandeur that was Coney Island had already died with her beau.

She was the last one on the trolley, which was nearing its final destination. Denise tugged on the string for the bell to signify that she wanted to get off. The operator nodded his head. He stopped in the middle of the road, almost in front of the Terminal Hotel. "Now, you take care," the driver said, doffing his cap. It was the second time someone had wished this blessing upon her in the same day.

"You, too," Denise told him. "Work safe."

After she stepped off the trolley platform, after the doors closed behind her and after the operator made the left turn toward the Stillwell Avenue station, Denise noticed the oaf with the limp who'd chased her up the steps to the Fort Hamilton Parkway station in Borough Park. Only now, he was dressed for the elements. He wore ear muffs under his watch cap, a thick Tartan scarf, a heavy overcoat and a sour expression on his face. His stocky frame blocked the doorway of the Terminal. Cupping his hands around a match-stick to light a cigarette, his head was down so he didn't see her. Denise scuttled to the boardwalk, toward the Stygian comfort of Ruby's Bar and Grill.

Chapter Six

Bed Rest

Angela didn't want to be with anyone but her husband, and this was mostly out of necessity. Although Augie was a good man, she couldn't stomach the fear and pity in his eyes, mostly the fear. She didn't even want to see her mother. And what girl didn't seek the comfort of her momma in times of trouble? Rose's eyes were even worse than Augie's: like a big, dopey puppy dog's before you tossed it into the Gowanus with a sack of bricks tied around its neck. And since Rose had two natural-born kids of her own plus Stan, she couldn't understand how her daughter felt.

Nothing could coerce Angela out of her funk, not the intricate pattern etched onto her bedroom's icy windows. (When they were little, Rose attributed the wintery decorations on Angela and Tiger's glass panes to the craftiness of "Jack Frost.") Not the "Get Well Soon" card Stan had made for Angela in India ink, complete with a sketch of her standing in front of the house with a baby in her arms. Not the plate of *baklava* Mrs. DePalma had sent over with Anne and Dom, drowning in a sea of honey. (Vincenza had gotten the recipe from her Greek neighbor Theope.) Not the lazy way the snow danced down from the overcast sky. ("Flurries today, it's not supposed to stick," Augie reported to his wife before he left for the theater.)

All Angela could think of was how she had fallen on Thirteenth Avenue last year, and how the pain in her belly gripped her as though she were stabbed. First, Angela had slumped to her knees, then to her side, in front of Moe the Greengrocer's. When she tried to get up, Angela felt a wet thickness slip from between her legs. She knew at once that it wasn't urine but blood. Red stained the front of her shift, where her lap would be, had she been sitting. 'I'm losing the baby,' she thought. 'It's gone.'

Moe, *kina hora*, recognized Angela and knew where she lived. He sent his boy hollering down Forty-Seventh Street for Rose, and meanwhile, summoned an ambulance. Blood tarnished the concrete, flowed down toward the curb. Strangers and neighbors alike tried to console Angela, who closed her legs tight, trying to hold her baby inside, but the tighter she held her legs, the more the liquid flowed. That's when she began crying.

The next thing Angela remembered, there was a bleached-out ceiling and a light suspended from it which hurt her eyes. There was thick padding between her legs and a tenderness in her middle. It hurt to move. There were the concerned eyes of her mother, Augie, and a terrible secret behind their dejected expressions even worse than their forced smiles. Their faces were death masks, sickly jack-o-lanterns. This is when Angela knew for certain…she knew her baby was gone.

But that was a different baby, Angela reminded herself. A different pregnancy. Dr. Schantz assured her that she was fine, that this baby was fine. Her fall down the stairs last month didn't hurt the child, only raised a few welts on Angela's shoulders and hips. Dr. Schantz prescribed one week of bed rest to help Angela recover emotionally. It had been three times that long and she still couldn't seem to leave her bed. She only got up to use the commode and even had her meals sitting up on the mattress. When Angela stood a few minutes, she swore she felt stitches, pulls and stabbing pains in her belly. She imagined she sensed the awful syrupy wetness which had flooded the sidewalk outside Moe's, when in actuality, there was nothing.

Angela was sixteen weeks along, and not even showing yet. Very few people were told about her second pregnancy, not even Grandma Bridget, although Angela gave Rose permission to tell her godmother, Aunt Jo, because Jo had had such trouble carrying a child to term until Wendy came along. Augie was being very understanding, as was his nature, but Angela worried that even her sainted husband would grow weary of her.

Not that Angela was dubious of Augie's love, but every man had his breaking point, even one as virtuous as her husband. Augie was now managing the Loew's 46th Theatre, and making a respectable wage, too. She knew he caught the eye of many a lonely female moviegoer and would be quite a coup if his lumpy, loopy bride were out of the picture. It was the way *film noir* plots began, pictures like *Double Indemnity*, for example. A man could get tired of cleaning up after himself, doing housework, and putting in late hours at the theater. A man could get tired of dropping by his mother-in-law's and picking up a tin of dinner, heating it up in the oven, and serving it to his weepy wife. But even this realization didn't draw Angela out of her sadness and out of her bed.

She knew what Augie did when he took forever in the bathroom. (A man could only wash his face or brush his teeth for so long!) When Augie came out, sheepish and flushed, Angela felt a little pang of guilt, which she mistook for a problem with the baby if she let her thoughts run away from her. The imagined misery served to make her feel less guilty about not being intimate with her husband.

Often Augie drew Angela toward him as they curled up together, preparing for sleep. When she opened her mouth to protest, he told her, "Sometimes I just need to hold you."

How could she argue with that? Angela missed the closeness of Augie's body, too, but then there was the dour, bloody fear, even more potent than missing him. Before Angela drifted off, she felt Augie's body, hard and insistent, wedged into her flannel nightie. It pained her to ignore his arousal but she did. Once, she was even sticky back there when they both woke up the next morning. Augie was mortified. "It must have happened in my sleep," he apologized.

Angela's mother-in-law Conchetta suggested coming by to "help" but Angela wouldn't let her because the well-meaning woman's deeds were laced with judgment. Conchetta refolded Augie's undershirts in the armoire and amended Angela's sock storage method from the balled-up style the young wife favored to tucking in the tops. "It's simpler," Conchetta explained, "and you don't wear out the elastic." She rearranged the food in the icebox and in the Frigidaire, making silent commentary on her daughter-in-law's homemaking skills. This was even before Angela took to bed. In her delicate state of mind, she couldn't bear the idea of someone rifling through her bloomers, even if that someone was Augie's mother.

Angela kept the items she required within reach. She had a tower of books on her nightstand and could tear through one novel in a day's time. (After Kreske's she'd taken a job as a proofreader at *Ladies' Home Journal*, so Angela instinctively read quickly.) Her Aunt Astrid devoured books almost as speedily as her niece did and kept Angela well supplied. She particularly enjoyed *The Green Years*—in ways, it reminded her of the bond shared by Tiger and Poppa, though her grandfather wasn't nearly as roguish as Papa Leckie. But Angela couldn't see what the fuss was about *Earth and High Heaven*, which wasn't her cup of tea. Give her Ernie Hemingway any day of the week. However, Angela couldn't reread *A Farewell to Arms*, which she loved, because of Tiger being in the War and the terribly sad ending with the baby.

Each day, Angela made sure to take a bath, even a quick one in water which wasn't too hot, or the farmer's variety, which was standing up with a basin nearby and a washcloth. She was always relieved that the bathwater wasn't pink with blood when she was done. She would put on a dressing gown or fresh pajamas, comb her hair and pin it back. Even this minor exertion caused a tightening in her belly. Dr. Lewis, who still lived across the street and stopped by regularly, said it was psychological. Whenever she stood, Angela couldn't sit down fast enough. But as soon as her feet were up and her legs were stretched out on the double bed she shared with Augie, the pains soon subsided.

From her parlor window facing Forty-Seventh Street, Angela had a similar view to the one she'd enjoyed as a girl because the house was just next door. Shortly before Angela's fall, their landlady Mrs. Rosenkrantz was found dead on the sofa by her son Ti-Tu. She had been in the midst of a game of Solitaire. Ti-Tu, who was never called by his real name, Abraham, even as a grown-up, lived alone in the downstairs apartment he'd shared with his mother. He often played mournful violin music at odd hours but this didn't disturb Angela. Ti-Tu's peculiar, poignant way of mourning his mother was a strange comfort to Angela. He was a *mensch*, an outstanding human being, if not painfully shy.

Five years earlier, when news had reached Mrs. Rosenkrantz of Angela's impending marriage, the bashful bachelor appeared on the Paradiso doorstep. As Ti-Tu nervously wrung his cap, he offered the Rosenkrantz's upstairs apartment to the soon-to-be Mr. and Mrs. Augusto Corso III at a very reasonable rate. He timidly explained that his mother always had a sweet spot for Angela, and that she liked the thought of having newlyweds in her house. Augie suspected that Mrs. Rosenkrantz also liked the idea of getting into the picture show for free whenever the mood struck, which probably sealed the deal for her. At any rate, Augie and Angela accepted Mrs. Rosenkrantz's gracious offer and gladly took the apartment.

Since his mother's passing, the young couple often had Ti-Tu up for the uncomplicated, satisfying type of suppers

Angela's family made. Every few days, there was Ti-Tu's hesitant knock on the door, even though the response was always, "Come in! It's open!"

After Angela's fall, the tables were turned, and it was Ti-Tu who was consoling the Corsos. Now, it was he who often brought them supper, steaming from his Hotpoint range downstairs: Jewish soul food his mother used to cook. Dishes like brisket (with a whole bottle of Coca Cola poured over it while it simmered), *kasha varnishkes* and stuffed cabbage. Once in a while, Angela would sit at the kitchen table with the men but mostly, she would take her supper on a bedside tray.

After they rinsed the supper dishes, Ti-Tu and Augie played Gin Rummy for a few hours. This was usually on a Tuesday evening, the day before Dish Night, when Augie had to work late. Angela was lulled by the soft shuffling of cards, the whisper of their voices, then either Augie or Ti-Tu's cry of "Gin Rummy." Mostly Ti-Tu's, who was the superior player. He muttered the phrase almost apologetically while Augie's "Gin!" was both triumphant and a surprise. Sometimes Angela suspected Ti-Tu let her husband win, if only to hear his joyful cry of "Gin!" every so often.

Angela read in bed while the men played cards at the cleared-off kitchen table, her feet propped on a pillow, *The Black Rose* propped on her lap. She tried to concentrate on the travails of Walter, the bastard of Gurnie, as he headed east to the court of the Kublai Khan. What a faraway place it was, eons from Brooklyn, even further than where Tiger was. Wherever that happened to be.

Life seemed to make more sense to Angela when Tiger was there. She was sure her brother could talk her out of her fears with a crinkle of his green eyes which tended toward hazel. He could always convince Angela to look at the bright side of things when no one else could, especially when they were younger and their father terrorized their railroad apartment rooms like a troll under a bridge. Where was Tiger now that she needed him most? Where was Tiger when Angela took a bad step and went tumbling down the Rosenkrantz's stairs? Ti-Tu felt horrible it had happened in his house and insisted on contacting the insurance company, at least to cover Angela's medical bills. "I'd feel awful if something even worse happened," Ti-Tu had explained. Where was Tiger when Angela was forced to undress in front of the Prudential adjuster and the insurance company's doctor, and stand there in a full slip, showing them her bumps and bruises, bending this way and that? Where was Tiger when she worried that a twinge meant a miscarriage or that gas pains were the beginning of the end?

Angela would try not to think of these things, or of her brother, as she read of Maryam and of Queen Eleanor of Castile. She barreled through the book, as if getting lost in *The Black Rose* would save her. In a way, it did, but just for the moment. When Angela became aware of her immediate world, the tiny universe of Borough Park, the faint sound of the El constantly in the near distance, she became afraid again.

Angela no longer blamed Rose for letting Tony bully them, for her "sin of omission" that Father Dunn spouted on about from his polished pulpit at St. Catherine's. Angela had forgiven Rose but she could never forgive her father, even though he was dead. She cringed whenever she remembered his drunken fumblings, what had happened that time at Kresge's, for cracking up Poppa's beloved Nash, and all the rest. Although she'd never come right out and told her husband about Tony's abuse, Angela suspected Augie knew by the hints she dropped or from the vehemence which rose in her whenever her father's name was mentioned.

Her profound hatred of Tony was one reason Angela didn't want to be called "Kewpie" anymore. The girl named Kewpie was too weak to stand up to her father but the girl named Angela was strong. Angela never would have suffered through what her father did to her—Angela would have fought back. Angela wouldn't have felt so ashamed. Not only was Angela a different person than Kewpie but Angela was a better person, too.

Mild-mannered by nature, Augie's relations with his young bride had always been sensitive. Both were virgins when they married. Although this had never been spoken, their innocence was apparent by their placid explorations, patient discoveries and new-found delight in each other's bodies. Angela and Augie both enjoyed the pleasures of their marriage bed a great deal, perhaps more than they cared to admit. It amazed Augie how touching the skin of a person you fancied felt electric, thrilling, instead of just like skin. But still, there was the shadow of what had happened with Angela's father, whatever it was, which hung over their bed like a specter.

Because he'd toiled in a movie house since he was a high schooler, Augie was good at picking up on life's subtleties—they were often not as expertly woven as a Frank Capra movie plot, but somehow equally as stirring. Earlier that year, Augie had found Angela sobbing inconsolably in her seat after the credits rolled and the house lights came up when *A Tree Grows in Brooklyn* played at the Loew's 46th. He wasn't certain if it was the picture's alcoholic father or Francie's near rape which drove Angela over the edge, but his wife soon recovered after a cup of tea. In the past, Angela had also grown weepy over films like *Now, Voyager* and *The Grapes of Wrath* (who didn't?) but *A Tree Grows in Brooklyn* had affected her like no other.

When Augie was working, Rose often stopped by, but she didn't stay long. Rose was easily chased away by her daughter's yawns or by her sea-shaded eyes heavy with sleep. Usually, Rose would drop off a parcel of food, linger a few moments and go. There were days when Rose wouldn't even take off her coat. Angela's aunts wouldn't try to come because they respected Angela's wishes—to be left alone with her thoughts. They didn't know the reason Angela had taken to bed after her fall, only that she was ailing. Bridget couldn't visit for she couldn't navigate the stairs but Angela would have let her grandmother in if she'd popped by. Angela could never turn away Bridget. The woman had taken her in when life had become too uncomfortable with

Angela's father, no questions asked, a piercing determination in the old girl's eyes and the Castro Convertible in Bridget's sewing nook open and neatly made, welcoming Angela into the safety of her grandparents' world downstairs. It seemed an entire lifetime ago when it hadn't even been a decade. Now, not even Bridget's indulgences could shield Angela from the fear of miscarrying.

When the front doorbell rang downstairs, Angela ignored it. If there was a package to deliver, Dennis the Mailman knew to leave it on the porch. But when a reticent knock sounded on the apartment door itself, Angela nearly jumped out of her skin. She tried to pay it no mind, but there it was again, insistent, refusing to be disregarded. Angela was propped up in the living room, which was in the front of the apartment, where Angela and Tiger's bedroom had been when they grew up in the almost identical house across the alley. (Angela had told Augie that she wanted to change things up, but in reality, she couldn't imagine laying down her head in a similar bedroom where she'd slept so uneasily as a girl.)

Angela moved her slippered feet from the footstool onto the rag rug which warmed the parquet floor, steeling herself for the sensation of a blood clot slipping from between her legs. (She did this every time she stood.) But there was no blood; there never was, even though Angela half-expected it. She smoothed her hair which she'd recently let down from pin curls, and fixed her dressing gown, a quilted affair Evalena DeMuccio down Forty-Seventh Street had made especially for Angela at the Bay Ridge sweat shop where she worked. (Angela felt cradled by the paisley pattern, she wasn't sure why.) She placed *The Black Rose* onto the chair's seat, which was creased with the shape of her bottom. The book was open to a place near the end where Walter returns to Gurney, a prosperous man, yet still a bastard. Remarkably, the chair cushion wasn't bloodstained either.

"Who is it?" Angela questioned, pausing before she opened the door. It was probably her mother, dropping off a tin of iron-rich pea soup or Ti-Tu with the *Eagle*, which he generally slipped soundlessly beneath the door when he was done reading it.

Instead, there was the lilting "It's me!" of her Aunt Jo. "I'd let myself in but my arms are full," she added through the wood.

Angela opened the door. There was her aunt, scarlet-faced from the four-block walk, smiling. She carried two paper shopping bags with A&S splashed across their sides and set them down onto the parquet. Off came her galoshes, which she put into the rubber boot tray Augie had placed in the hall. There was no stopping Aunt Jo once she was on a mission, and this day, her niece was her mission.

Before Jo had unwrapped the bright red scarf from her neck or had taken off her tam o'shanter, she was chattering. "Grandma Bridget sent me over with some goodies," Jo said with breathless excitement (or maybe from climbing the stairs). "Peas and pasta, sausage and peppers, and Orange Soup." She hung her coat on the hallway rack.

To Bridget Paradiso, Orange Soup was the healer of all maladies, even those of the heart. Especially those. Made with a rich stock of vegetables past their prime, she boiled a cubed butternut squash, a sweet potato, a few carrots, a bit of onion, garlic and ginger (the latter was suggested by Mr. Wong, who owned the Chop Suey Palace down under the El). When it was done, Bridget pressed the softened vegetables through a potato masher, then whipped it with a wire whisk, adding a dash of cream if it was too thick. Then voila, Orange Soup! It went down like butter, and soothed the soul like an edible sunset. Topped with crunchy pumpkin seeds, it was a sensory delight. "Over the moon," as Poppa liked to say.

Without waiting to be invited in, Jo grabbed the paper sacks and was on her way to Angela's sadly-neglected kitchen. "The poor old girl can barely walk, but boy, can she still cook," Jo informed her niece, who hadn't been by her grandmother's for weeks. Angela followed her aunt like an obedient puppy. It never occurred to Angela that since it was *her* kitchen, she should take the lead. This is how upside-down her world had become.

The room was painted a pale orange, less intense than the fruit but reminiscent of its radiance. To reflect the citrusy theme, Angela and Augie had chosen café curtains embossed with tropical fruits—pineapples, limes, lemons and yes, even oranges, in their signature shades—some cut down the middle, dripping with juice. Jo placed the bags on the Formica tabletop and unpacked jars brimming with deliciousness. "So, how are you?" Jo piped.

"I…I really should be lying down," Angela faltered.

"Why?"

"Well…the baby might…" her voice trailed off.

"The baby's doing great," Jo said to the young woman. "It's her mother I'm worried about."

Angela didn't know what to say. Though Augie and Rose had hinted at it, no one had been so direct about Angela's self-imposed convalescence. "We're worried about you," Jo continued. "Your mother told me Dr. Lewis and Dr. Schantz both say you're okay and the baby's doing fine. You can't mope around here all day."

"Why can't I?" Angela pressed.

"Because it's not healthy for you." Jo took the girl's hand in hers. "Because I was there. I lost a baby, too. You were probably too young to remember."

Angela clutched her aunt's fingers which smelled of vanilla and sugar—Jo had been making criss-cross brown sugar cookies at Bridget's table just an hour earlier. "I remember," Angela informed her. "I must have been about fifteen. We didn't see you for at least a month. You didn't come to Easter dinner. I remember missing you."

Jo squeezed Angela's hand. "And we miss you. The old you. The girl with the smile that could light up a room."

"I'm not a girl anymore. I'm a woman now, Aunt Jo. Things happen. Bad things."

Somehow, the woman-child's eyes had lost their sheen, and were a dull, steely gray. Jo looked into Angela's eyes for a spark, for a glimmer of what once shone behind them but found only dimness. She didn't let go of the girl's thin, chilled fingers. "The things that happen...they're called life," Jo admitted simply. "We lose things. We find things. More things get taken away and we get new things in their place. But at least we have each other. Sometimes all we have is each other."

Angela searched for a response but came up blank. How could she argue with what her aunt had said? As Angela gazed at Jo, whose face gleamed with unrepentant optimism, her eyes watered. Before Angela realized it, she was crying and Jo was holding her, cradling her as close as she could with Angela's belly wedged between them. "It will be all right...you'll be all right," Jo cooed.

"How can you tell?"

"I just can. Besides, this family needs you. Especially now, with your brother gone."

Angela's body trembled with sobs. "I miss him," she choked over and over like she was saying the Rosary. Without asking who, Jo knew that "him" was Tiger.

"We all do," Jo assured her. "He'll be home soon."

"It's been weeks since we've heard from him, and Christmas is just days away. At least we haven't gotten a telegram but still..."

Jo could only say, "I know...I know." Her mind counted back to the time when Angela had taken to bed. It was after her fall, true, but to the best of Jo's recollection, it was soon after they received Tiger's last letter. Lost babies, lost brothers...the earth-shattering incidents we have no control over. But what else can we do except muddle through?

When the two women pulled apart, their faces were wet and puffy but their faces shone. Their affection for each other was unspoken but crystal clear. Jo passed Angela the jars and tins of food to stow in the Frigidaire or in the cabinets, which were painted a light ochre. Once they were done, Angela put on the kettle for tea.

Jo told her niece of the job she'd applied for at Anna Pateau's insurance office on the Avenue, which she would probably take. Then, she dipped into her gingham dress's front pocket. "I wanted to give you this," Jo explained. She took out a paper ornament. It was a rustic drawing that depicted a woman cradling a baby in her arms and had sparkles decorating the edges. One of Poppa's pipe cleaners curled at the top, for hanging purposes. "Wendy made it for you," Jo continued. "For your tree."

Jo noticed that there wasn't a Christmas tree in the Corso home, but was certain there would be soon. And sure enough, that very evening, Augie would stumble up the steps, not drunk as Angela's father often was, but he'd tipped back a few. But the real reason for Augie's unsure gait was that he was weighed down by the Christmas tree he balanced on his shoulder. Somehow Augie felt the time was right and his wife was ready to welcome in the season of joy, birth and wonder without fear or trepidation, only with gladness.

And when Augie opened the door to their apartment, pine needles clinging to his hair, his wife was not in her robe, but fully dressed in slacks and a print shirt. She was smiling, and there was a pot of Orange Soup bubbling away on the stove.

"Welcome home," Angela told him. "Welcome home."

Chapter Seven

The Yellow Queen

Stan never felt freer than when he was standing on the precipice of a school vacation. Even though it was Christmas Eve Day, the Board of Education made the poor kids go in for a half-day at PS 131, and throughout the city. "To the bitter end," Stan sighed to his parents just before he left for school that morning.

Sully put a sympathetic hand on the boy's shoulder. "Don't worry, you'll have plenty of time to help me home with the tree," he told Stan. The boy knew that his husky father didn't need his assistance—with the Christmas tree or with anything else—but the very notion of his dad pretending he required his help made Stan feel a little better. They would pick out an immense tree for Poppa and Grandma Bridget's place and a smaller one for their apartment upstairs. Stan and Sully had been doing this happy chore together for as far back as the child could remember.

Wendy breezed down Forty-Seventh Street right on time, as she always did. She was smiling widely, cheeks dappled from the frosty weather, kicking up chunks of ice with her cherry licorice-colored galoshes. Together, she and Stan turned down New Utrecht, following it until it crossed Fort Hamilton. Along the way, they bumped shoulders, pelted each other with snow, paused to pick icicles off a milk wagon and stopped to pet its horse. Their chatter was excited, voices rising with the thrill of the day before them—and no school for a week.

"Eight days to be exact," Stan corrected. "But who's counting?"

"We are!" Wendy exclaimed jubilantly. "Do you think Grandma Bridget will do the *struffoli* this year?"

"She makes it every year, dummy," Stan declared.

"But every year, she says it's too much work, that it's the last year. And don't call me 'dummy,' stupid."

"That's because you believe her, ignoramus?"

Wendy laughed. "Don't call me words you can't spell, you simpleton. S-I-M-P..."

As Wendy spelled the word, she bounced her cousin off her left hip, inching him toward a snowdrift. Although Stan teetered, he didn't fall into the slushy pile. Instead, he crashed into a person, a woman. The lady seemed poised to catch him. Her ungloved hands were tattooed with a snakelike pattern of dry skin. Her coat was old and threadbare, one you might wear on a balmy summer evening, certainly not in the dead of winter. She almost fell from the impact of Stan's wiry body.

Stan looked up into the woman's face to see that it was the Yellow Queen. "Gee whiz, I'm awful sorry, lady," he said. "Did I hurt you?"

The Yellow Queen clutched at her chest, like it pained her to breathe. She pulled her wrap tighter around her distended middle. In addition to not having gloves, the Yellow Queen didn't wear a scarf either. Upon realizing this, Wendy thought, 'It's like no one cares for her or looks out for her.'

After a moment, the Yellow Queen was able to speak but her words were shaky, as though she were chilled to the very bone. "I'm all right, Stanley," she told him.

The boy's eyes widened, as did his cousin's. "You know my name," he gasped.

The El rattled overhead a block behind them at the crossroads of Forty-Fourth Street, Fort Hamilton Parkway and New Utrecht Avenue. The woman opened her mouth but nothing came out, nothing they could decipher anyhow. Before she could say more, a large shadow loomed behind the Yellow Queen and a leather glove clutched her.

"Daddy!" Wendy cried. "What are you doing here?"

"Shouldn't you two be in school?" was Harry's response.

Almost on cue, a loud bell sounded, summoning the children inside. Stan didn't budge at first. "You don't want to get a tardy mark," Wendy warned him, grasping his arm, much like her father was holding onto the Yellow Queen's. In Wendy's mind, little was worse than a red check next to her name. No number of gold or silver stars could erase a red tardy mark, ruining a perfect record like a bloodstain.

Stan looked at the Yellow Queen's face. Once it had probably been very comely; now it was just the opposite. Not ugly but not nice-looking either. It was a sea of used-to-be's, littered with crow's feet, eyes rimmed with pink, runny like a badly-cooked egg, whitish-blonde hair frazzled and unkempt beneath her beret. "I'm all right," the Yellow Queen promised the boy, who turned to go.

When the children were a safe distance, Harry tugged on the woman. "Denise Walters," he snarled. "Fancy meeting you here."

She jerked out of Harry's grip and tried to muster a shred of dignity that was long gone. "It's a free country," she spat. Harry smelled the jagged tang of liquor on Denise's breath, though it was just past eight. "Not where my kids are concerned," he said.

"He's my kid!" she cried out.

"Not any longer," Harry said. "You gave him away. Eight years ago today. Or don't you remember?"

Denise wasn't about to let this nasty old flatfoot see her cry, not him or anyone else. "Of course, I remember," she whimpered. But despite her struggle to keep her emotions in check, her chin quivered as a fat, hot tear slipped down her chilled cheek, branding her skin. She brushed it away before Harry could see, as though it had burned her.

"This one's got trouble written all over her, Harry," Abe the Fishmonger chimed in. "She's here almost every morning, darkening my doorstep. You want I should call the cops?"

Harry considered his options. "No," he told the shopkeeper. "She's not worth it." Then to Denise, "Come on, let's go for a walk." He grabbed hold of her elbow to guide her roughly down the avenue.

Denise struggled but couldn't pull out of Harry's grip. "You mean a limp, don't you?" Harry ignored her. He'd heard worse. Hell, *he'd* said worse. For a split second, Harry felt sorry for Denise. She was shivering like a mouse caught in a trap. He wasn't positive if it was because of the temperature or from the DTs because she certainly had the look of a drinker about her: gin blossom nose, the essence of alcohol leeching from her skin, and a general disarray of appearance. Denise Walters had known better days, that was for sure.

"Let's go someplace. Someplace more hospitable," he suggested.

"It'll cost ya," she shot back. "I ain't cheap."

Instead of arguing, Harry steered Denise under the El, to Dora's Luncheonette. It wasn't the best place in town but it was close by. The bell chimed as they entered. Harry tried to ignore the dirty checkerboard-patterned floor and the dust bunnies, which threatened to become dust alley cats, in the corners. He also ignored the huge, hairy mole on Dora's cheek and the flakes which clung to her shoulders, precariously close to slipping into the mediocre food she served. Her eyeglasses were as thick as pop bottles and speckled with so much muck that Harry wondered how she could even see out of them.

Dora huffed a hello, raising an eyebrow at the fact that Harry was there with a woman who wasn't his wife. "Two coffees, Dora," Harry told her. "And an egg sandwich. Over easy."

Harry showed Denise to a booth with benches of cracked avocado Naugahyde. He hung their coats on the hooks beside the booth. Denise kept her hat, unwilling to expose her bleached rat's nest. The tabletop was slick. Dora rubbed it with a dirty rag to distribute the stickiness then flung the rag onto the counter. She grabbed a battered pot of coffee, a pair of chipped stoneware mugs, and slid the cups noisily across the table in front of the couple. Harry preferred his coffee dark as char, which seemed the safest option, while Denise heaped in spoonfuls of sugar and a river of cream, turning the coffee tan. Dora was meting out the cream and sugar in her head, watching her profits fade the more condiments Denise used.

"How 'bout a little coffee in your sugar?" Dora quipped before barking at Archibald, her long-suffering husband, "Get snappy with that egg sandwich, Archie!" she ordered. He glared at his wife but did as she said, wiping his hands on his apron, which had gone gray with neglect. It was rumored that to spite Dora, Archibald sometimes shifted around the furniture in their apartment above the luncheonette. Dora's eyesight was so poor that even on a good day, she routinely barreled into sofas and ottomans. But with Archie's rearranging, she often sprained a wrist or bumped her noggin.

Denise gulped her coffee before looking Harry in the eye. "Why are you being so nice to me?"

"Maybe I'm just a nice guy," he said.

"Somehow, I doubt that."

Harry wrinkled his brow, pretending his feelings were hurt. "I'm nice to nice people."

"Buddy, you're barking up the wrong tree," Denise sighed. Dora slid the greasy egg, nestled in a split Kaiser roll, across the table to Denise, who tore into it immediately. Denise didn't thank Harry, who was buying it for her, or Dora, who had served her. The yolk dripped onto the plate like sallow blood. Denise mopped it up with her finger, not missing a drop, as though she didn't know where her next meal was coming from. With her mouth stuffed, Denise asked, "So, what do you want?"

"Why do I have to want anything?" Harry wondered.

"Because people don't do something for nothing," Denise informed him when she swallowed. "Not for me. Not for no one."

Harry took a swig of coffee, now gone cold. As he'd suspected, it was acrid. "Sister, who screwed you over?" It was a rhetorical question but Denise answered it anyway.

She looked at him plainly. "Everyone," she said. "Everyone except my Pa." It was too sad for a response, so Harry didn't offer one. "What's your story, bub?" she continued.

"I don't have one."

"Come on," Denise prodded. "Everybody's got a story. You raising him? My Stanley?"

"No," Harry admitted. "But I'm looking out for him. We all are. He's got a family. A good family."

Denise was already done with the sandwich. She'd practically inhaled it, Harry noted. "You sayin' my people ain't good people?" Denise snapped.

"I didn't say they weren't," Harry told her. "I'm saying you're not."

Denise made a move to stand. "Why, I ought to…" but she stayed put. Harry motioned to Dora for a slice of dried-out pumpkin pie. Dora slipped the pie in front of Denise, refreshed her coffee and left.

"You gave him away," Harry said. "How long ago was it?"

"Eight years," Denise choked. "I knew before you said it on the street. Eight years. Only who's counting?"

Harry laid his hand on Denise's which was ready to spear another chunk of her dessert. He saw that her cuticles were mangy, gnawed, and her sanguine nail polish was peeling. "Obviously, you are."

"'Course, I am. He's my kid…" Denise sputtered.

"Not anymore," Harry repeated. "Look, he's being well

taken care of. You can see that. I want you to leave him alone. To scram."

A tear slipped down Denise's cheek, leaving a streak in her face powder. "I can't. He's the one decent thing I ever done."

She was crying hard now, not making any noise, dripping tears onto the Formica table, on her plate, in her coffee cup. Harry gave Denise his handkerchief, which she snatched without looking up—or thanking him. Her boo-hooing led to a coughing fit. She put the cloth to her mouth. Harry studied the crude "H" and "O" his daughter had embroidered onto the cotton square. "But you can't give him a blessed thing, don't you realize that?" Harry said to Denise as cordially as possible. "You can only hurt him."

Denise sat in the booth facing Harry, limp, defeated. "Don't you think I know it?" she sobbed. "I just want to see Stanley every now and again. To make sure he's all right."

"Leave his care to us," Harry snapped. "You best leave him be."

Denise stared Harry down, her eyes swollen and enflamed yet defiant. "Or else what?"

Harry slid a buff-colored envelope across the table. "Williamsburgh Savings Bank" was printed at the top. Harry pushed it closer to her. "Take it," Harry commanded. "Take it and go." She patted the envelope, trying to judge the amount of money inside by its thickness. Then Denise pulled back as though the envelope had given her an electrical shock. She moved away the pie plate, which contained only crumbs. Harry said, "Mull it over and you'll see I'm right."

Denise slid out of the booth with a thump, her face mottled with rage. She grabbed her coat, turned abruptly, then swiveled back to face Harry, taking the envelope but leaving Harry's soiled handkerchief on the table. He noticed a blotch on it. Lipstick, blood, he couldn't be positive which, but he didn't want to touch it. Denise was out the door before he could decide. He stood up to follow her.

Dora watched Denise and Harry's little exchange from behind the counter, her arms folded and tucked into the valley between her breasts and belly. Without waiting for the check, Harry put two brand new dollar bills onto the table. He thanked Dora and Archibald. "Police business," he explained. Archie nodded, not daring to remind Harry that he wasn't a cop any longer.

It seemed colder outside, more raw than it had been earlier. Harry turned up his collar and looked skyward. Jo would dub this "a snowy sky," for it had the uniform ashy shade which foretold of a storm. The El barreled out of the Fort Hamilton Parkway station and toward Coney Island. Harry figured Denise was probably on the train.

Suddenly, Harry was struck from behind, rocking him from his wooden leg. He sprawled face first into a snowdrift, hat flying onto the pavement behind him. Harry caught the flash of a dark coat, chalky hair and a ruddy face. "Go to hell, you fucking gimp," Denise shrieked, then rained the contents of the buff envelope onto his chest. Fives, tens and twenties scattered onto the street. Then she was gone.

Abe, still wearing his fish-stained apron, ran outside to help Harry up. A couple of passersby collected Harry's money from the gutter. "Didn't I tell you that one was bad news?" Abe chided. For emphasis, Abe spat into the slush, as if he needed to rid himself of even the words associated with that hussy. Harry thanked the people who came to his aid then headed toward Forty-Seventh Street with an even more pronounced limp.

And not two blocks away, inside Mrs. McVay's classroom on the second floor of PS 131, Stanley Sullivan was in the process of drawing a picture of a lady, scribbling her hair with a Brilliant Yellow crayon. Very soon after, the noon bell would ring, propelling him and Wendy home to witness the miracle of Christmas.

Chapter Eight

The Day of the Eve

Christmas Eve Day at the Paradiso House was a swirl of
flour, sugar (both brown and white), seafood of countless
varieties, the perfume of crisp, fried vegetables and of the
pure, unadulterated delight of the season. Throughout the
morning, the doorbell rang incessantly from friends and
neighbors wishing them holiday cheer, often dropping off
a special dish. "It's like Grand Central Station in here,"
Bridget would exclaim every time the bell sounded, but she
secretly loved it.

Just past nine, Giovanni had already stopped by with
a tray of his famous rice balls—without the savory meat
stuffing, for Christmas Eve supper didn't include meat. This
recipe abided by the Catholic tradition of not having "flesh"
the night before a major religious holiday. It had to do with
the odd notion that you were feasting on Jesus' body if you
ate meat. This was also the reason they didn't indulge in
meat on Fridays, the day Christ died for their sins. Honestly,
Bridget didn't miss the meat—the creamy mozzarella (made

by Louie, Giovanni's in-law, at Belfiore Meats) and bright green peas made the rice balls mouthwatering enough.

"I don't know how you do it, but they're always as light as a cloud," Bridget insisted. To which Giovanni shrugged and bowed his head, slightly embarrassed but inwardly flattered.

"Mrs. P, I don't do anything special," he said before Bridget enveloped him in a fleshy hug.

"*Grazie tante*," she whispered into his shoulder. "*Buon Natale*."

"*Buon Natale*, Margarita," Giovanni whispered back, his kind brown eyes smiling. Very few called Bridget by her given name and it secretly thrilled her when someone—even someone besides Poppa—did. Her name sounded like poetry on the tip of their Palermo-born neighbor's tongue.

Bridget could usually persuade Gio to indulge in a shot of *limoncello* which she'd made herself and had been fermenting since the summer. Occasionally, she even joined him in a glass. Poppa ambled into the kitchen, when Giovanni and Bridget were in mid-hug. "Sorry to break up the party," Poppa laughed and exchanged a hearty greeting with his friend. In addition to making delectable rice balls, Giovanni was also responsible for New York Telephone doing such a crackerjack job setting up the phone system at the Brooklyn Navy Yard.

That Christmas Eve morning, Giovanni had come and gone, and on his tail Anne Marie arrived, all the way from Twenty-First Street in South Brooklyn. Although she couldn't stay, she dropped off a platter of her husband Anthony's *pignoli* cookies. "Your Anthony makes them even better than Piccolo's," Bridget admitted, unable to resist sampling one. But she couldn't convince Anne Marie to take a sip of Christmas cheer, even a cup of egg nog, no matter how she tried. "Are you sure? It's homemade," Bridget tempted.

"Anthony's in the car with the motor running," Anne Marie apologized. "Plus, I've got to help Katie with the *scungilli*," she added, then was gone with a kiss and a hug and an earnest "Merry Christmas."

Bridget was elbow deep in last-minute Christmas baking when Angela walked into the kitchen nonchalantly, as though the girl hadn't been hibernating in her sorrow for several weeks. It was as if Angela had seen her grandmother the day before, when in truth, it had been almost a month. The old woman's eyes filled with joyful tears as she measured molasses into the tin measuring cup. Bridget swallowed back her emotions and sighed, "Thank God you're here, Ang. Your mother's hopeless with *struffoli*. She always was and always will be. I'm making them after the ginger snaps. Finally, someone who can bake!"

Angela took her place beside Bridget at the table. Her grandmother was all right if she could prep sitting down, for the ache in her leg wasn't as bad when she sat. By instinct, Angela gave Bridget the weathered tin of powdered ginger. She meted out a teaspoonful, then passed it back to Angela. Just a pinch of nutmeg, not the whole half teaspoon the *Settlement Cookbook* recipe called for. Bridget also left out the cloves—"Too overpowering," Poppa had noted once, and everyone else agreed. The only thing cloves were good for in his mind were studding a ham.

Angela sifted together the dry ingredients while Bridget creamed the molasses, sugar and eggs in a separate bowl. Then Angela gradually mixed the powder into the sugary paste. For a moment, Bridget and Angela's fingers brushed. She clutched her granddaughter's smooth hand in her wrinkled one, Bridget's knuckles swollen with arthritis. She raised the girl's unspoiled fingers to her lips and kissed them ever so softly, ever so quickly. It was so fast that even Rose didn't notice, though she was sitting across the table from them, tending to cleaning the *calamari*. Angela kissed Bridget's hand just as surreptitiously. Then she found a saucer and poured a few tablespoons of granulated sugar into it. Angela and Bridget began rolling the ginger dough into walnut-sized circles. Then they rolled the spheres in the sugar, and plopped them onto greased cookie sheets. "These used to be Tiger's favorite, remember?" Rose said sadly.

"Used to be?" Angela bristled. "He's not dead, Ma. Just gone."

Rose caught herself. "No, I didn't mean..." She took a deep breath so she wouldn't tear up. "I was talking about the time he had so many that he ate himself sick. How old was he? Seven? Eight?"

"About as old as Stan is now," Bridget recalled. The back door opened, letting in both a rush of cold air and Sully, who balanced a large wooden box on his shoulder. He laid it on the floor for a brief moment. "What's this?" Rose asked. Sully pulled aside the box's lid to show greenish-brown shells tipped with bands of orange.

"Lobster!" Bridget gulped. "Where'd you get lobster?"

"Did they fall off the truck?" Angela wondered.

"As a police officer, it's illegal for me to accept stolen goods," Sully reminded them. "But a gift is an entirely different matter."

"I've never seen so many lobster before," Bridget said.

"Let's just say that Jumbo had a surplus," Sully hinted. "Where should I put them?"

"There's no room in the Frigidaire," Bridget told him, her voice rising in a mild panic. Rose noticed that her mother became easily exasperated lately. Was it Bridget's age or the weariness which accompanied it?

"How about the back porch?" Rose suggested. "It's like a Frigidaire out there. We'll deal with them after the *struffoli*."

Angela tutted at Rose. "You're not going anywhere near the *struffoli*, Miss Fish Hands."

"Besides, your *struffoli* are like honey-covered pebbles," Bridget added. Sully enjoyed the kitchen patter as he set the box of clamoring lobsters on the porch's wide slats.

Sully's partner Izzy was waiting for him on the sidewalk in front of the modest brick house. They set out on their beat once again, although Izzy would join the Paradiso table later that evening. Most of the Pole's family had migrated from Warsaw to the United States but ended up in St. Paul,

Minnesota. (How Izzy came to settle in Brooklyn is another story.) Bridget prided herself upon having a table which included "Christmas orphans"—this was even before Stan had brightened their doorstep—and Izzy happily became one of them because his wife and kids were at her sister's place in Valley Stream for Christmas Eve supper that year.

Back in the kitchen, Rose busied herself with the endless pile of squid which needed to be cleaned, far removed from the cookie production line at the other end of the table. Rose jumped every time the doorbell rang, her heart leaping expectantly, then drooping when she realized it was another neighbor and not her son. She shook her head at her own silliness. 'If it were Tiger, he'd walk right in,' she reminded herself. 'He knows the door's unlocked.'

The next time the bell rang, it was Consuelo Ortez Vega, with her celebrated flan. Consuelo made at least a dozen for Christmas. She borrowed springboard pans from neighbors who gratefully had them returned filled with her sinful custard dessert, dripping with caramel topping. Consuelo asked after Tiger, lusciously rolling the "r" in his name in her carefully-pronounced English. She and the boy, now a young man, had struck a chord the first time they met at a backyard barbecue years earlier. Consuelo's husband Manny held Tiger dear to his heart from their encounters at the Brooklyn Navy Yard when the child had accompanied Poppa to work there many summers.

The Ortez Vegas had a back seat full of flans, carefully covered with a blanket to preserve them from the deep freeze which had recently descended upon Brooklyn. It didn't stop Manny from popping into the house to share a few words with Poppa about the new foreman who'd taken over at the Navy Yard after Poppa retired for the second time. The fondness and respect these two men held for each other was evident as they looked into each other's eyes, smiles crinkling the corners. They gripped hands longer than was customary, realized it, then awkwardly let go.

Moments later, Jo arrived, shaking snow from her coat and hat. "It smells like home," she said to no one in particular.

"Why, you are home," Bridget told her.

"You're right, Ma, this will always be our home," Rose reminded her, "even though we've made homes of our own."

"You girls keep such nice places," Bridget agreed. "Even Astrid, although I'm scared I'll muss up her white sofa whenever I visit. White! What was she thinking?"

Jo resisted the temptation to complain about her stuffy sister Astrid. "We learned from the best," Jo admitted to her mother. "You taught us how to make a home where everyone feels welcome." Jo kissed Bridget's hair, relishing the wiry satin beneath her lips. Steely, deep ebony and snowy tendrils met at the back of Bridget's neck to form a bun, which was usually slightly unkempt. Poppa fondly called it "her meatball."

Jo glanced at Angela and dipped her head in silent greeting, thrilled to see her but not acknowledging it with words. Then Jo's eyes rested on Bridget, happily dusted with flour, face flushed from the heat of the kitchen, sitting at the table in a straight-backed chair, a spindly throne in her gurgling kingdom of pots, cookie sheets, and love. Jo wondered how many more Christmasses she would be blessed with this image, with her mother's presence, with moments like this. Her eyes blurred with emotion, which she blinked away, deciding to enjoy the moment instead of fretting that it was fleeting. Jo grabbed an apron from the doorknob, fastened it around her waist and set to work on the batter for the *fritto misto*.

Poppa entered Bridget's inner sanctum, which he rarely did when a meal preparation as huge as Christmas Eve's was in progress. It was similar to the way Bridget never entered the garage when Poppa was tuning up Betsy II. This was one of the reasons they'd been so happily married for "forty some odd years," as he so eloquently phrased it—they respected each other's private space. Poppa was in the kitchen long enough to swipe a ginger cookie from the pile on the windowsill and to give his wife a little squeeze. Bridget was content to be surrounded by family, delightfully warmed from the sip of *amaretto* she'd shared with Consuelo

minutes before. 'If I died right this minute, I'd die happy,'
Poppa thought to himself before leaving for the parlor.

The kitchen was getting full but Bridget didn't mind.
Because of her leg, she stayed put in her chair, letting
everyone bring her what she needed—a small mound of
sugar in a chipped Dish Night china cup, six heaps of flour,
already measured out, one glass tumbler of oil, two of
muscatel wine. A jar of honey Angela and Augie had brought
back from a trip to Gardiner, New York that summer, waited
in the wings. Angela recalled the Widmark Honey Farm and
their bears Bo and Objee. Bo immediately turned his back on
the couple the moment they arrived and relished a massive,
enthusiastic dump. The Corsos' visit to the honey farm also
marked the first time Angela had held a baby goat. A tribe of
them had been born the week before and a young boy named
Thomas wondered if Angela wanted to hold one. Not waiting
for her response, Thomas put Dallas, the feistiest of the tribe,
into her arms. Dallas felt light as air and baby soft, too.

Bridget gave Angela a gentle poke, shaking her from her
daydreams. "Baking soda and salt," Bridget recited from
memory.

Angela passed Bridget the red and yellow baking soda
tin and the salt cellar so she could take a pinch of each and
add it to the big bowl. Angela noticed that her grandmother
had a faded, tattered recipe on the table beside her, written in
Bridget's own mother's hand on onionskin paper, in
Italian. It had been mailed to Bridget from Avellino to
America when she was a young bride. Bridget didn't refer
to the recipe for she knew it by heart. She only propped it on
the table to keep her mother and her memories of girlhood
Christmases in the Campania region close by. Above the
recipe, Genoveffa Musto had written: "*Miele per un
matrimonio dolce, e un po 'di vino non fa male.*" Bridget
told Angela that it translated to: "Honey for a sweet
marriage, and a bit of wine doesn't hurt."

Upon hearing this, Angela recalled her own father, for
whom a bit of wine—or a little of anything—was an
impossibility. Tony Martino had turned living by excess into

an art form, and it eventually destroyed him. Angela wasn't going to permit herself to think of anything even remotely sad this Christmas. She'd had enough sadness for one year, for a whole lifetime, in fact.

When Angela looked up, there was her Aunt Astrid, her head a study in juniper berries and smoky felt. Astrid wore a black velvet dress with a stiff collar almost as rigid as she was. "Have the little savages arrived yet?" she wondered.

"If you're referring to the little angels," Jo crooned, "Wendy and Stan aren't due out of school until noon."

Astrid grabbed a shrimp, which was already boiled and cooling in a colander near the sink. She nibbled at it like a ferret. "There's plenty of time for you to escape before then," Rose said to Astrid, moving the shrimp out of her sister's reach.

"Nice of you to come to help," Jo added, because Astrid never helped. Whereas Camille, who had just walked in the front door, stomping snow from her boots, always lent a hand. Slipping off her galoshes, Camille revealed thick cotton stockings. She unbelted and stripped off her red plaid coat and matching hat. Camille hung them on the hook in the hallway and neatly placed her boots on the sheets of folded newspaper. On her way to the kitchen, Camille made a quick stop in the parlor to give her father a peck on the forehead, careful not to wake him. He was taking his morning nap with the *Eagle* on his lap, the sheaves littering the carpet around him.

By the time Camille reached the kitchen, it was a blur of activity. Her sisters niftily side-stepped like ballet dancers in winter wool, passing off utensils, washing bowls without being bidden, wiping down surfaces, chopping, mixing. All except for Astrid, who watched with mild distaste at the manner in which food that would soon enter her body was being concocted. Angela blended into the mix with the smoothness of a child leaping into swirling double-dutch jump ropes.

"Where's John?" Astrid tested her sister, slipping a boiled calamari between her brick-red lips.

"At the Sanders," Camille told her. "Their regular projectionist took sick and he's filling in."

"Oh, I'll bet he's filling in," Astrid said under her breath.

Rose tapped a fingertip into the flour-speckled tabletop and flicked white dust into her sister's direction. The way Astrid carried on, it was as though she had been spattered with acid. "What?" Rose asked naively.

"You know what," Astrid clucked.

"I know you know why I did it," Rose clucked back. "Don't play dumb."

"Maybe she's not playing," Jo posed.

"Girls, play nice," Bridget intervened, as though they were ten, eleven and twelve again.

Astrid disappeared into the bathroom with a washrag, a hunk of Kirkman's and a box of Borax. "Just brush it off with plain water," Camille called after her sister. "You'll only make it worse."

"Like she does with everything," Jo sighed.

"Now, now, it's the holidays," Bridget attempted.

"Maggie never takes a holiday," Jo said. "Pop says she was born in a bad mood."

To this point, Bridget couldn't argue. "Margaret came out bellyaching and she hasn't stopped yet."

Angela was at the stove, bringing the wine and oil to a boil. She couldn't stop laughing. "Let me in on the joke," barked Astrid, her velvet frock dotted with even blacker splotches of wetness.

"Watch your back," Angela cautioned them, guiding the roiling liquid to the table. She poured it into the flour-filled bowl in front of Bridget, mindful not to scorch her grandmother. Using a wooden spoon, Bridget mixed the heated liquid into the flour until it became a thick, tacky dough. She covered the bowl with a dishcloth and set it outside near the windowsill to cool.

Rose was ready to start the *fritto misto*, which Poppa complained made the whole place stink like Dora's Luncheonette. However, the end result of golden-fried, mixed vegetables was scrumptious. "It's but once a year,"

Bridget would remind Poppa, slipping him a tender stalk of batter-coated broccoli to sway his opinion. This usually did the trick. So did going out for a stroll while the fry-fest was in full swing.

The tougher vegetables such as broccoli and cauliflower were already parboiled. Angela sliced the zucchini into quarter-inch pieces. "Not too thick," Bridget said, her breath tickling Angela's neck as she had a closer look. "Ah, just right," she added.

Rose dipped the broccoli into the batter one at a time then dropped the pieces into the bubbling oil. They sizzled away, peacefully coexisting with the cauliflower as they fried side by side. When the bottoms browned, Rose flipped them with a slotted spatula. On the empty back burner was a plate lined with newspaper to drain the oil from the vegetables. Then they were moved to an oven-safe platter for last-minute heating in the oven before they would be served later that night.

It amazed Rose how you could figure out the part of Italy people were from by the types of vegetables they fried on Christmas Eve. The Calabrese, renowned for being *capa tosta* (thick headed), fried broccoli, while the Sicilians (who non-Sicilians argued were not technically Italian since they were from an island and not Italy proper—this understandably angered Sicilians, who were known for their fiery tempers) fried cauliflower. The ritzy Northern Italians liked asparagus, which was out of season in America in the winter, and as expensive as gold, if you could find it. Almost everyone included zucchini in their *fritto misto*—because who didn't like zucchini? (Well, Vinnie Spitone didn't, calling it wishy-washy, neither here nor there.) In her fritto misto, Rose also added fried, sliced onion and even charred cloves of garlic, which mellowed when cooked.

Fritto misto was a labor-intensive dish because it entailed hours of standing at the stove, a task Bridget couldn't handle physically anymore. A bonus was that you ended up smelling like a fry chef. Rose gladly took the baton from her mother and inwardly beamed when Bridget admitted that her daughter's *fritto misto* was far superior to her own. Nuzzling Rose after she fried vegetables for several hours, Sully would always murmur, "What's that perfume you're wearing?"

The front door to 1128 Forty-Seventh Street opened again and closed firmly. Jo recognized the uneven step of her husband, as he favored his left leg, the prosthetic one. The rhythm of Harry's walk, even his new, altered walk, still put a thrill into Jo's heart and her breath caught in her throat. However, there was a tiny ache in her chest when her husband's broad shoulders appeared, framed by the kitchen doorway. She could tell something was wrong. Harry's eyes were downcast and he didn't look at Jo even after her genial, "Hi, honeybunch!"

Jo's affectionate touch found Harry's coat soaking wet. "What did you do?" she asked, laughing. "Go for a swim?"

Harry's eyes finally met Jo's in a sorrowful way. "In a manner of speaking," he told her. Harry shrugged his wife's fingers from his jacket. By his demeanor, Jo surmised that Harry was drunk. But moving closer, she didn't detect the medicinal tang of Scotch on his breath, and felt relieved.

Jo's mind skittered to memories of Rose's husband, the first one. Tony's drinking, his meanness, his violence. Harry wasn't a bad drinker, even when he'd had a few. Sure, once in a while he had one too many, several too many, but the more Harry drank, the more he folded up within himself. With Tony, it had been just the opposite, the more alcohol he consumed, the more blustery and uncontrollable he was.

Jo tried to control the wild roller coaster of her emotions. 'Harry is not Tony,' she reminded herself. 'He's going through a bumpy patch. He'll get through it. We'll get through it. We always do.' Jo put a stiff smile on her face and returned to Rose at the stove. Harry followed. Rose had already filled one plate of fritto misto and needed another newspaper-lined dish. Harry still hadn't answered Jo's question. "Harry?" she prompted.

He glanced at Jo then looked away. "I had a bit of a run-in," he admitted, "with the Blonde."

A cauliflower floret slipped from the fork as Rose tried to lift it from the sizzling oil. It splattered and pinkened her skin. Without a word, Jo ran a dishrag under the tap, squeezed it dry and wrapped it below her sister's wrist as Rose kept cooking. Over the years, Rose had gotten glimpses of Tony's former girlfriend…Diane? Doreen? Denise, she remembered. Who could forget Denise at Tony's funeral, ambling in wearing a skintight black dress, which did nothing to mask the bulge of her pregnant belly. If that hadn't been enough, Denise spat into Tony's coffin. Twice. The funeral-goers were too shocked to confront her, and she was gone in a flash.

That past summer, Denise had been spotted lurking on the corner of Thirteenth Avenue, sneaking a glance at Stan as he sat in Vic the Barber's chair, enduring a crew cut. Another time, when Stan was just a baby and Rose was at Moe's a few feet from the pram, considering the oranges, Denise ventured close to the carriage and peered inside. The peroxide blonde ran off without giving Rose a chance to confront her.

"Are…are the kids okay?" Rose managed to ask.

"Fine," Harry said. "They were already in school."

"And you?" Jo wondered.

"I'm fine, too. A little damp, though." Harry managed an unconvincing smirk, filched a crunchy cauliflower from the platter and popped it into his mouth. It was as hot as a matchstick. His eyes watered.

"Careful," Jo told him.

"You, too," he winked.

Bridget sent Harry into the parlor with a plate of *fritto misto* for him and Poppa to enjoy out of the hustle and bustle of the kitchen. Poppa continued to doze in his favorite chair, a thin, Air Mail envelope on the end table beside him. It was postmarked Tucson, Arizona. A handful of photographs sat beside it. One showed a teenaged Billie in horn-rimmed glasses with her three mop-topped brothers in the background. Another was of Sophie Veronica, petite and chesty as ever, standing primly in front of a Ford truck with "Brooklyn

Made" stenciled on its side. Sophie was making a valiant go of the business she and Kelly had started together. Even though Kelly had died seven winters earlier, she still kept in touch. "You'll always be my family," she often wrote in her letters to them.

Harry placed the plate on the end table. He let Poppa sleep and helped himself to a healthy pour from the amaretto bottle his father-in-law kept on the table so Poppa could offer Christmas visitors "a small glass" to ring in a sweet season. Harry gave himself three fingers worth since his holiday had gotten off to a rough start that morning. He watched Poppa sleep serenely in the Windsor-backed chair. The old man rested deeply, as though he had never known trouble, when in fact, Harry knew he had; heaps of it.

Harry himself was no stranger to trouble. As a beat copy, it had been his bread and butter for almost two decades. Then there was the War, which he'd rather not think about. It was smooth sailing with Jo and Wendy, for they were easygoing girls, both of them. In an odd way, Harry missed the trouble he used to run into on the job. He found himself seeking danger in odd ways: picking a fight with a guy at the end of the bar, drinking more than he should. Things were too good, so Harry had to pick at the scab of life instead of let it be. Likewise, he couldn't leave the Blonde alone to fade into the background, and with any luck, die prematurely of a liver ailment or pneumonia. No, Harry had to pursue her instead of letting her go.

Even though he'd just arrived at the Paradiso home, Harry couldn't stay put. He discreetly dressed in his hat, coat and galoshes, and was back outside in no time. When Jo came out with a plate of ginger cookies for her husband and father to share, she wasn't surprised that Harry was gone, and she had an inkling of where he might be.

Harry's encounter with Denise Walters haunted him. After a few blocks of aimless walking, his stump began to ache and he ducked into the closest watering hole he could find. Like Farrell's in Park Slope, the Stumble Inn closed a couple of hours a day—to swamp out the restrooms and to mop the tiled floors. This was usually about four in the morning but they reopened by six to ensnare the nightshift laborers on their way home. Cops, transit employees, hospital staff and factory stiffs routinely popped in to top off their workday, which ended when the rest of the population was waking up. It was a topsy-turvy way to live but night owls often needed a buffer between their job and fitting back into their home life. Or else, they required help drifting off to sleep when practically everyone else in the neighborhood was greeting the new day.

Harry didn't fit into either category. He was feeling sorry for himself after his second bourbon when Sully caught a glimpse of him through the Stumble Inn's picture window. When the formidable cop entered the bar, the stools surrounding Harry cleared like cockroaches when you flicked on the light. Harry stayed put, looking his old pal up and down, then turning back to the amber liquid in front of him.

Teddy, the barkeep, slipped a tall, slim ginger ale in front of Sully; he knew the neighborhood cop didn't drink when he was walking the beat. Plus, Sully was a teetotaler even when he was off duty. Patrick Sullivan was the rare Irishman without the drinking gene, but he was a decent tipper and a good egg, so it was okay with Teddy. He knocked on the bar with his knuckles, signifying that the soda was on the house. Sully tipped his cap to the barkeep before Teddy disappeared to the other end of the mahogany. "So," Sully said to his brother-in-law.

"So, yourself," Harry said back.

"Funny place for lunch," his friend told him.

"Call it an early supper." Harry took another swig of Gentleman Jim, Sully, of his ginger ale.

The silence between them was comfortable, like slipping into a old pair of loafers. It was undemanding and didn't trouble them. "I saw her again," Harry added, after a beat. "That whore. She should drop dead."

"Come on, they're all somebody's daughter," Sully reminded Harry. "Even whores. Especially whores."

"She's tailing Stan almost every day now." Sully shrugged in response. "And you aren't worried?" Harry urged. "You aren't scared she'll snatch him away." Sully shrugged again, baffling Harry. "What would Rose think?"

"You'll have to ask her," Sully responded. "Look, nothing will happen to him. Stan's a bright boy. Besides, he's always with Wendy. They're like glue. And Wendy's even smarter than he is." At the mention of his daughter, Harry cracked a smile. "I've spotted her, too," Sully admitted. "From the looks of it, the floozy isn't doing well. She's little green around the gills if you ask me."

"Can't you run her in?" Harry offered.

Sully took a fistful of the salted peanuts Teddy had put in front of them. "On what charges? You know better than me she's not breaking the law. Trust me, she won't last in this weather." Sully tossed the nuts into his mouth and chewed thoughtfully. "Don't worry, I'm keeping my eye on her."

"How about the Pole?"

"Izzy is, too," Sully said.

Harry threw back the rest of his bourbon. "Then I've got nothing to worry about." He signaled for Teddy to refill his glass but Sully covered the rim with his palm and waved the barkeep away.

"Izzy's not so bad," Sully added. "I'll never have a partner like you again but that Polish kid holds his own."

"Glad to hear it," Harry told him. "I feel safer already." Harry grabbed his hat and overcoat from a nearby hook. He slipped a few bills toward Teddy on the bar. "Merry Christmas, Theodore." Harry patted Sully on the shoulder, perhaps a bit too hard. "See you tonight."

With a touch of sadness, Sully watched his former partner limp toward the door and shoulder it open to the fading daylight. Sully flipped a single onto the bar. "Happy holidays," he grinned to Teddy. "My regards to the Missus."

Christmas was the only day of the year the Stumble Inn wasn't open. Teddy had seven mouths to feed and some folks had nowhere else to go on the holidays, so he felt he was doing society a service by not closing on the other holidays.

But Christmas Day was an exception; it was for family, so he closed the Stumble Inn then.

"And to yours," Teddy said. "Yours, too."

Chapter Nine

Tiny Miracles

After his visit to the Stumble Inn, Harry wandered around Borough Park. Although it was freezing outside, the air was crisp. He didn't want to be confined indoors, even in the warm, welcoming Paradiso home, not just yet. As he walked, Harry noticed the dragging footprint his left leg made in the snow, which was falling steadily now. So, it would be a white Christmas after all, like Bing Crosby sang about. Wendy and Stan would be happy about it. For a brief moment, Harry longed for those days of innocence, when snow meant no school, sledding and monumental snowball fights. When you grew older, snow meant shoveling, dangerous driving conditions, fear of breaking a limb. Oh, to have a few moments of unbridled joy and to feel the marvel in the declaration, "It's snowing!" as though this were the most astounding thing in the world.

But then Harry remembered the details of his troubled youth, those awful teen years, losing the baby, the War, losing his leg, the whole lot of it, and reasoned that he was exactly where he should be. So many things could go wrong it was a wonder we survived at all. Harry reckoned that a person's existence was simply a series of tiny miracles, nothing monumental on their own but astounding when the events were strung together over a lifetime.

In the dwindling afternoon sun, as night fell, Forty-Seventh Street took on a magical cast, with the lazily dropping snow, the Christmas lights and the streetlights reflecting the cheap tinsel. The snow glowed a pale blue, giving the block the look of a black-and-white film, the movie of Harry's life.

When Poppa and Bridget's house came into view, Harry could see two figures huddled closely together on the top step. Wendy and Stan were shrouded in heavy coats, their necks wrapped twice with knitted scarves, heads topped with caps knitted of the same jade yarn. When he came closer, Harry noticed that the kids' tongues were out and that they were trapping fat snowflakes onto them, swallowing the flakes whole and laughing.

"You'll catch cold," Harry warned.

"Grandma Bridget gave us the old horse blanket to sit on," Stan said.

"Still," Harry continued with a twinkle in his eye, "if you get sick, you'll ruin Christmas for yourself. And the rest of us."

"Oh, Pop, you can take the fun out of anything," Wendy groaned, then realized that her father was joking.

Harry climbed the steps with added difficulty, the chill stiffening his limbs. Was it from the sharp frost in the air or from the drink? Even his false leg seemed uncooperative. Harry steadied himself by holding onto the railing and pulling himself up. (The children knew not to help him—not only weren't they robust enough but it could put him off-balance.) Once he reached the top step, Harry pet first Wendy's head, then Stan's. "Don't eat too much now," he told them. "You'll spoil your appetite."

They grinned up at him. "We won't," they swore. A simple pine wreath decorated Poppa and Bridget's front door. "I don't want to be too showy," she had explained, welling up, then adding, "Especially with Tiger still away." And indeed, there was a blue star adorning her front window, even though the War was over. It would stay up until her eldest grandson was home safe and sound, and eating supper at her table, she pronounced tearfully.

"Come in soon," Harry called behind him. The children promised they would. The radiator hissed in the hallway, the very same one Harry's drunken brother-in-law Tony Martino had cracked his head upon a decade earlier. Harry hung his hat and coat on a hook. Leaning against the wall, he removed his galoshes, then went inside.

As soon as the front door closed behind her father, a shadow fell across Wendy's face. At first, she thought it was the Yellow Queen but its form was slimmer, ghostlike. When the shadow stepped into the lamplight, revealing itself, Wendy's mouth hung open in shock. She elbowed Stan, who was still catching snowflakes on his tongue. Wendy and her cousin said not a word, just grabbed hands as the ethereal figure enveloped them.

In the parlor, Harry was immediately surrounded by warmth. He stepped into the aroma of many dishes intermingling: lobster, lush crab sauce, crackly fried vegetables, sizzling garlic, the sharp sweetness of ginger cookies, lemon-dusted seafood salad, and a host of other scents. The tree was already in its metal stand, undoubtedly brought in earlier by Sully and Stan from Nino Scapaldi's spot under the El. It stood patiently waiting to be trimmed in the corner. They would all decorate the tree together, after supper, and before midnight mass. The Douglas fir looked especially splendid this year, even unadorned.

The table was already set in the dining room with the good dishes, cloth napkins and Bridget's special Christmas tablecloth. As Poppa dozed in his favorite chair, Harry could hear voices crowding the kitchen: Bridget, Rose, Camille and John, Angela and Augie, Astrid and Sam. (Even though they were soon-to-be divorced, Bridget contended that Sam was still part of the family, and insisted on inviting him to holiday dinners, much to Astrid's chagrin.) Although Harry couldn't hear Ti-Tu's voice, he knew the shy violinist, whom they'd inherited after his mother's passing, was there too. Sully and Izzy had popped in on their meal break. Seventeen places were set at the long table, even though only sixteen people were expected. "You never know when a stray will wander in," Bridget explained, for everyone was welcome at the Paradiso table.

The parade from the kitchen began, with everyone except Harry carrying in platters of food for the first course: meatless *antipasto*, seafood salad, garlic bread, cheeses, stuffed mushrooms, stuffed celery, and so on. It appeared too plentiful to fit onto the table but somehow, it did, a jumble of plates, platters, bowls and tureens.

Poppa awakened on his own, perhaps from the easy jab of the food's perfume wafting in from the next room, perhaps from the blend of buzzing voices. He ruffled the pages of the *Eagle* and continued reading the article titled "Meet Our Champs." He thought one of the singing choirboys from St. Augustine's looked vaguely familiar.

"Dinner is served," Bridget echoed as she unfastened the poinsettia-embossed apron from her generous middle. Harry assisted Poppa to his feet as Bridget added, "Call in the kids, would you?"

Since Harry was closest to the door, he moved toward it. But before he could reach it, the door slammed open and bounced off the wall. "Stanley Sullivan!" Rose sighed. "One of these days, you'll break the house down!"

Stan stood there, immobile, out of breath, dripping snow onto the carpet. His chest heaved, as though he'd been running, and he was whimpering softly. Tears streaked Wendy's face as she stepped beside him and again took her cousin's hand but this made Stan cry even more. 'Is it that witch Denise?' Rose wondered, 'Did she try to snatch him?' But in a moment, everyone saw why the children were so disturbed.

There was a flash of khaki and the thump of a duffel bag on the floor. Wendy and Stan stepped aside to reveal Tiger standing there, cap in fist. Bridget put her fingers to her mouth and sunk into the chair John had pushed behind her as her knees buckled. Poppa lifted his spectacles and rubbed a Christmas napkin across his eyes. Rose flew across the floor in one step, it seemed. She would later say that she didn't recall her feet touching the carpet or how she'd gotten into her son's arms. She just remembered being there, swathed in Tiger's bony embrace, thinking how skinny and how wonderful he felt.

No one said a word, which is rare for a large, loud family like the Paradisos. Rose reluctantly let go of her son and held him away so she could get a good look at him. Then she cradled Tiger's face in her hands. His hair felt stiff from being under his cap. She gazed into his eyes, green as a pop bottle, as tears silently flowed. Those familiar freckles still dusted Tiger's nose as they had when he was a boy. Sully was the first to speak. "Welcome home, son," he stammered.

Then the entire family fell around the soldier, asking questions, clapping him on the back, chucking him under the chin, hugging him around the middle. Tiger didn't know who to answer first. Sam sobbed uncontrollably, even though the young man technically wasn't his blood relative. Astrid shook her head in disgust at her soon-to-be ex-husband's raw display of emotion, the juniper berries on her hat rustling. In spite of herself, Astrid gave Sam her lace-trimmed hankie. He thanked her and blew his nose audibly.

Bridget insisted that everyone sit down. Christmas Eve supper was getting cold and besides, Tiger was so thin, he needed to begin eating immediately to make up for lost time and months of eating field rations. "That's not all I ate, Grandma," Tiger told her with a smile. "Actually, the food was pretty good. We had a Colored cook named George who could fry the heck out of chicken."

But Bridget would hear nothing of it. "When was the last time you had a Sunday gravy that wasn't brown?"

They made their way to the massive dinner table, Tiger gently peeling Stan from around his waist so they could take their places. "Probably the last time I sat here," Tiger said. "No offense, Ma," he added.

"None taken," Rose said to him, her eyes radiant.

"Although the *marinara* sauce in Pisa wasn't bad," Tiger admitted.

Bridget pretended to take a swipe at Tiger but instead, hugged him close. As he sat, the small, squat woman's shelf of a chest was eye level and Tiger found himself engulfed in the scent of his childhood: Musterole and garlic and talc and the faintest hint of Evening in Paris perfume. It brought him back to the kitchen table, making *manicotti* and *antipasto* at the elbow of his grandmother as the storm of his father raged upstairs. It felt warm and safe down here.

Suddenly, the old woman released Tiger and was gone quicker than anyone thought possible, limping heavily on her right side. Everyone looked puzzled until Bridget returned a moment later, holding the service banner. When they were finished with supper, she would lay it, and the blue star, to rest, solemnly rolling it into a tube and slipping it into a breakfront drawer where it would never be forgotten.

In Bridget's brief absence, everyone had heaped *antipasto* onto their plates and buttered thick slabs of Italian bread, but no one had taken a bite. "Are we ready?" Poppa wondered. He glanced at his wife, who nodded. "Are you sure?" he urged. Bridget tried to hold back a laugh. "You're not going to go running off like a bat out of hell again?" Poppa asked.

"*Michele Archangelo*, don't say 'hell' at the holiday table...damn it!" Bridget warned. Stan and Wendy snickered, delighted that now their grandma was cursing, too. They all joined hands. This wasn't common for the Paradisos— holding hands at the dinner table. It was a very Presbyterian thing to do, or at the very least, Lutheran, but that day, holding hands to say Grace seemed right.

Poppa could be a man of many words but he was tongue-tied. There was so much to be grateful for. The War was over. Tiger was at their table. Everyone was healthy and moderately happy, even Astrid. Some people, even people a few doors away, couldn't say the same thing. Poppa cleared his throat and said, "I thank God that we're together, and I hope we can all be together again next year."

There were energetic Amens and a few well-disguised tears, even from the men. As the Paradiso clan tucked into the first course, their vigor reminded Tiger of the mess tent, only this was tons nicer. He held back a groan of pleasure as a succulent roasted pepper met his tongue for the first time in over two years. The tang of the charred vegetable, the hint of lemon and capers, the sharpness of the raw garlic was miraculous. He purposely bit down on a spicy wedge, his eyes instantly tearing. It made him feel alive.

Tiger was encased in a chorus of noises. The good silverware tapped against the good china, which was embossed with persimmon flowers and ringed with gold. It was so different than the mess hall's clang of tin utensils hitting tin plates. He reveled in the sound of voices, of women's voices, and the higher register of children's voices which weren't raised in terror. To Tiger, the patter at his grandparents' table was sweet music, better than the Andrews Sisters or even the Ink Spots. Bright conversation swirled around his head and caressed him:

"Please pass the butter…"
"Did you kill anybody over there?"
"Stanley, what a question!
"Camille, how's the insalata di ceci*? Does it need more salt?"*
"Speak English, Grandma!"
"That's the chickpea and spinach salad, Stanley. And it wouldn't kill you to eat a vegetable."
"How'd the girls treat you over there?"
"Look at him, he's a ladykiller!
"Say, mind if I have the last stuffed mushroom?"
"Anyone run into Mrs. Segrell? I hope she's not alone today."

"I think she's going to her son's but I'll make up a plate for her just in case. Calamari, Johnny?"

"Don't mind if I do. Tiger, you sleeping okay. I remember I had a hell of a time getting shut-eye after the Big One. You too, Harry?"

"I always sleep like a baby. Even in the middle of combat. Hey, quit hogging the vino."

"See much of Japan?"

"I got a gold star on my English composition today. It was about you, Cousin Tiger."

"You're such a show-off, Wendy. Can I have more bread?"

"Save room for the macaroni."

"Did you get any medals?"

"I don't want you filling up on bread."

"Aw, nuts. Did you get me anything?"

"Stanley!"

"Momma, should I put the spaghetti in?"

"If the water's boiling. Did everyone have enough?"

A cool hand lay itself on top of Tiger's. "You all right?" Rose asked.

"Yes," he told her.

"You sure?" His mother's eyes were earnest, full of emotion. He'd missed their deep brown sincerity while he was away. Rose smoothed down the cowlick Tiger'd had since he was a boy. It sprung back up, defiant.

As the women cleared the *antipasto* dishes to make way for the pasta, Tiger answered as many of the men's questions as he could. He noticed that Poppa was unseemingly silent and recalled how forlorn the old man had been when he'd learned of the attack on Pearl Harbor. Not only did Poppa grieve for the more than twenty-five hundred souls who died and the one thousand wounded, but he also mourned for the ships that were lost. Many of them had been built or repaired at the Brooklyn Navy Yard. Poppa himself had supervised the task of putting the guns on the *USS Arizona*, which had been hit four times by Japanese bombers before it sunk in the Hawaiian harbor. To Tiger, the old fellow looked slightly misplaced, but perhaps Poppa had merely aged a great deal in the months Tiger had been overseas. His grandfather's eyes caught his, and he smiled. "I still can't get over that you're home," Poppa said.

"Me neither," Tiger conceded.

The questions continued to barrage Tiger like gentle bullets, and he tended to them as best he could while savoring Bridget's meal. Tiger didn't even mind that the dinner was meatless. When they were boys, his friend Jimmy Burns once whispered that you were eating Jesus' raw flesh if you ate meat on holy days of obligation. Sister Patrick Maureen took a sick thrill in elaborating upon this fact, interspersed with references to the fires of Hell lapping at your toes for eternity, possibly longer. There were times when Tiger feared he might never sit at this table again but those days were buried in the past and he tried not to think of them. Not today.

"Why didn't you write?" Aunt Astrid snapped. "You had your mother worried half to death."

"You, too?" Tiger wondered.

"Well, I…" Astrid sputtered then tucked into her plate of spaghetti with crab sauce. To Tiger, it looked as if his hard-hearted aunt might cry.

"I never worry," Bridget piped, saving face for her daughter. "I just pray. A lot."

"Her rosary beads are worn down to nubs," Sully added, and Bridget wacked him playfully.

"Maybe a little," she admitted.

When everyone had finished putting their two-cents in and the table had quieted, Tiger told them, "I didn't have time to write. I had the chance to jump onto a steamer and be home in a few weeks or wait another two months. So, I grabbed my duffel bag and went."

Stan was riveted with the tale of Tiger's voyage: the wonder of going through the Suez Canal, the choice between going to visit the Leaning Tower or a house of ill repute in Pisa (said in a hushed voice to the men as the women fussed in the kitchen with the lobster). Stan was thrilled to be considered a man at age eight, but honestly, they'd forgotten he was there until he inquired, "What's a chippy?"

Sully visibly blushed. Sam stammered. Augie and Poppa laughed; they doubted Ti-Tu had a clue what a chippy was either. Harry was about to answer, as delicately as he could when they were rescued by three heaping platters of lobster and the *fritto misto* being carried into the dining room.

"Why don't we eat meat on Christmas Eve?" Wendy wondered, setting down a bowl of sautéed spinach, glistening with olive oil and browned morsels of garlic. She knew the answer from Religious Instruction but was curious to hear her family's response.

"It has to do with abstinence," Rose offered.

"A penance…giving up something," Angela added.

"Eating more simply," Bridget offered.

"Lobster?" Ti-Tu wondered. "Simple?" The man rarely spoke, but when he did, it was weighty.

"We don't usually have lobster," Bridget explained. "It fell off the truck." Then, realizing how ridiculous this sounded, she sighed, "Oh, I don't know, Wendy, it's what we've done as far back as I can remember. Ask Father Dunn."

With the discarded, scarlet-red crustacean shells piled high atop sheets of the *Eagle* in the center of the table, everyone said they were going to burst. The men cleared the plates, which Bridget called "a true Christmas miracle." She had to admit it was sort of swell to see Poppa with a snowman-patterned apron fastened around his potbelly, scraping plates clean into the trash bin, passing them to Sam (dish towel around his middle) who gave them to Harry. John had washing duties, refusing rubber gloves then lamenting his fate of dishpan hands. Stan and Tiger wiped matching Santa Claus and Mrs. Claus tea towels across the dishes. Ti-Tu stacked the crockery neatly on the counter and Sully put them away in the china closet. Bridget would have to rearrange them later because as she always sighed, "I can't find a blessed thing after people 'help.'"

Meanwhile, the women were setting out the cake plates and carrying in a steady stream of desserts, most of which had been dropped off by their neighbors: Consuelo's flan, icebox cake, not to mention Bridget and Angela's *struffoli* and other sweets. There was also a battered box from a Manhattan baker none of them recognized. "I didn't think Piccolo's would be open by the time I got here," Tiger explained, dish towel still flung across his shoulder. "I hope they're good."

Bridget untied the striped twine and tipped open the box, revealing a mound of *pignoli* cookies dusted with powdered sugar. She stood there and quietly cried, remembering the times she, Poppa and Tiger would sneak the treats into the Loew's 46th for their Dish Night snack or when she and Tiger tried making them, Bridget cursing "that darned almond paste," which was so difficult to handle.

Tiger put his arm around his grandmother's shoulder. "I remembered they're your favorite," he told her. Bridget thanked him and scurried off to put them on a serving plate. (They'd enjoy Anthony Paladino's *pignoli* cookies the following day.) As soon as Bridget put them on the table, Stan slipped one of the "old folks' cookies" to Wendy, who tried to hide it in her lap. They didn't think anyone would notice as they peeled off the pine nuts one by one and tried to split them down the middle. It was challenging to do without having the nuts crumble to dust in your fingers. Wendy's friend Loretta said if you split pine nuts just so, they resembled praying hands. Although Stan and Wendy were having no luck halving the nuts, a pile of pine nut ash was gathering in the lap of Wendy's velvet dress.

When Stan reached for another, Astrid thundered, "It's a sin to waste food. Are you going to eat it or play with it?"

Out of the corner of her eye, Wendy thought she saw a flash of yellow and black at the parlor window which bordered the alley. When she got up to look, there was only the reflection of moonlight on snow and the tinkle of the bell on the reins of Buggy Joe's horse as the rag picker tiredly guided his wagon home. There were rumors that the horse lived in Buggy Joe's house and even had a stall on the second floor of the rickety building on Fourth Avenue. Could a horse climb stairs? Maybe this was just one of Loretta's stories, like the praying hands hidden within *pignoli* nuts.

As the Paradiso clan enjoyed their dessert, Denise Walters trundled toward the El, cursing the snow, the hole in her shoes, and the fact that her son resembled his father so strongly. She swallowed back the ugly truth that she would probably die alone. It was Christmas Eve after all, and not the time to harbor such bleak thoughts.

Chapter Ten

Buon Natale

Christmas morning was almost too much for Tiger to take in: waking to the smell of cinnamon buns fresh out of the oven, seeing his mother's beatific smile, watching Stan's cowlick bobbling as he practically jangled with excitement, taking in Sully's subdued rapture at having Tiger home, the ripping of wrapping paper made from the Funnies and from the *Eagle*, newsprint on Stan's sweaty palms which eventually decorated his nose and cheeks, his brother's protest at having to wash his face again.

It was like a montage from *The Grapes of Wrath*, which Tiger had watched a few months earlier in a makeshift GI theater. Though he'd seen the picture with Poppa and Bridget when it had come out five or six years before, Tiger welcomed watching it again, this time with his friend George at his side. Tiger hoped seeing the movie would make him less homesick, but Jane Darwell bore such an eerie likeness to his grandmother that it made him feel even more wistful and melancholy.

As he sat beside the Christmas tree, Tiger caught Rose looking at him, just watching him, and saying nothing, as though she couldn't believe he were really there. He couldn't believe it either.

At the Paradiso house, Christmas Eve was a bigger deal than Christmas Day. On Christmas Eve, the food was elaborate, the buildup profound. Harry and Jo began holding the Christmas Day festivities at their place to make things easier on Bridget. It was more an afternoon-long buffet than a proper supper but the food was so good nobody minded. Everyone brought their own personal specialty to contribute to the communal table at the potluck of sorts. People came and went all day, beginning at about three in the afternoon. This way, everyone could leisurely open presents at home with their respective families, linger over breakfast, and those who didn't go to midnight mass the day before could go to Christmas services.

Although Bridget said she didn't mind passing the baton to Jo, deep down she truly did. She felt displaced and replaced, even though she couldn't have managed two huge dinners two days in a row, even with help. Now that she was nearing seventy-five, Bridget had stalled almost to an abrupt halt. Poppa would be seventy-six the coming autumn and Bridget noticed how easily he tired, how often he napped, how on bad days, even walking around the house seemed to exhaust him. "We're two old peas in a pod," Poppa had whispered to Bridget in the dark the night before.

She was grateful to rest her weary, heavy body in their feather bed, and too exhausted to argue with Poppa that she wasn't old, for indeed, she felt ancient at that moment, after a day at the stove. "I'm just happy we're around for another Christmas" Bridget told her husband.

"Me, too," he sighed.

"And I'm glad Tiger came home."

"How about that?"

Bridget held Poppa's fingertips, dry as parchment paper, to her cheek. "Sometimes I feel I'm ready," he whispered so softly Bridget had trouble hearing him.

"Ready for what?" she asked, knowing his answer.

Poppa drew his lips closer to Bridget's ear. "Ready to go," he sighed.

Bridget added, "I'm tired, too, you old coot."

"I'll miss you, though."

"I'll miss you, too," Bridget admitted. "We've been married, what, forty-seven years?"

Bridget nestled her head into Poppa's shoulder. A groove was almost eroded into it, as though it were made specifically to fit her pate. "Yes. I was just a girl."

"You were almost an old maid at twenty-eight," he ribbed, stroking the multicolored braid which trailed to the base of her spine, thinner than it used to be but still striking.

"That's because I was waiting for you...waiting for you to come to your senses and propose," Bridget teased.

"And I was little more than a boy when our first baby came along. At least I felt like a lad."

Bridget kissed Poppa's neck, noticing the loose seams and crinkles of skin beneath her lips and liking the way it felt. "You really weren't, though," she said. "You were almost thirty. We've seen a wealth of things, haven't we? Held our grandchildren..."

"And God willing, our great grandchildren," Poppa added. "We lost a child..."

"Oh, how I miss Kelly," Bridget sighed, biting her lip.

"I miss him, too."

"Gone too soon, only forty-one. I hope Sophie Veronica is okay...and the kids. They're so far away."

"They are. They all look well in the pictures she sends, don't they? And they're of strong Brooklyn stock, all of them," Poppa reminded her. "She'll call tomorrow, after she sings the at ten o'clock mass."

"She never misses a holiday, bless her heart," Bridget nodded. "We've had quite a life, Mike."

"That we have. Most of it good."

"We traveled. Remember the trip to Florida back in '41 when you retired."

"The first time. I got to meet the great DiMaggio in spring training."

"We have the picture to prove it," Bridget smiled, then grew clouded. "We survived Tony…"

"That rat bastard…"

"*Michele Archangelo*, mind your tongue."

Poppa took a deep breath. "God forgive me, but I'm glad he's dead."

"Me, too," Bridget told him.

Then Poppa and Bridget did something they hadn't done in a long time. It had been months, perhaps years since they'd been intimate. It wasn't that the spirit was unwilling but the flesh was weak. That night, however, Poppa and Bridget transcended the antique casings of their bodies, floated above the aches and pains, the loss, the sadness and the arthritis, until all that was left was adoration.

The following day, Bridget reddened slightly as she remembered the night before—the conversation and the activities—as if the people sitting around her in Jo and Harry's living room could read her mind. Poppa, beside her on sofa, squeezed Bridget's knee as Wendy lifted the gift her grandparents had given her. The girl shook it and fondled the squared edges of an oblong box set atop a larger box. The girl's face was quizzical; she couldn't figure out what was inside. Stan, who'd torn through his pile of presents like a Tasmanian devil, sat and watched, puzzled himself. He was usually skilled at guessing the contents of a present before it was opened, but not these. Wendy uncovered the smallest box first. "It's a pen," Stan announced, clearly disappointed.

"I love it," Wendy gasped.

"Somebody's got to write down this family's story," Poppa said to her. "I figure it will probably be you."

"A pen," Stan repeated, as Wendy ripped into the other box. He would have been sore if he'd been given a pen for Christmas or even for his birthday, but Wendy was elated. 'She's a strange girl,' Stan decided.

"Not any pen…a Parker '51,'" Poppa explained. "Top of the line, with a 14-karat gold nib." The pen had a sleek fawn body and a gold cap with an arrow pointing down. A silver and gilt ring, reminiscent of a wedding band, circled its body.

In the second box was a book with cream-colored, lined pages and a buff leather cover with the word "Journal" stamped onto the front. It was the sort of book in which you could write great things, important things. Wendy was speechless. "It's beautiful," she said, fingering the soft-as-butter cover.

"No leaving scraps of paper all over the house anymore, huh?" Bridget joked to the girl. Wendy was guilty of writing everywhere: on paper bags, paper napkins, grocery receipts, and they were constantly finding scribble-covered wisps in the oddest places, like lost jigsaw pieces.

Harry studied the journal and the pen for a moment. "They must have cost you a bundle," he decided.

Poppa shrugged it off. "Ah," he told Harry. "It's only lettuce."

Jo put the gifts on the mantle. "Speaking of lettuce, let's eat!" Wendy thanked Poppa and Bridget once again, and hugged them both.

There was a mad dash for the sideboard, which was literally covered with food. Stan tried to cut the buffet line but Sully gave him the hard eyes and the boy slinked to the end, grumbling almost as much as his stomach did. Wendy took her journal and pen from the mantle, settled into one of the corner armchairs, curled up, and started to write. Poppa and Bridget stayed put on the sofa, smiling as they watched their granddaughter.

Tiger leaned lightly against the mahogany breakfront, surveying his surroundings. Even the crowd in his Aunt Jo and Uncle Harry's parlor and dining room seemed trifling to him. Tiger was used to the ship's mess hall as well as the mammoth tents and shacks which served as field dining rooms as he made his way throughout Europe and Asia. The noise in these vast eateries had been overwhelming. You could barely hear yourself think, let alone have a conversation. It was like the buzzing of a million bees. In comparison, this was relatively peaceful. The doorbell rang continually to announce each new guest's arrival.

In the neat, narrow limestone house on Fort Hamilton Parkway, the overlapping and weaving of words was a comfort to Tiger. The laughter, the patter of recipes exchanged, of pleasantries, of Aunt Astrid's customary barbs, which any holiday would be incomplete without. The food, however, was so different than what Tiger had grown accustomed to in the mess tent. No chipped beef on toast, no massive stews doled out in a pot big enough to hold his younger brother, no boiled-to-death vegetables a sickly green. No buddy George doling it out with his cheerful smile no matter how loud or how close the shelling, his skin, shoe-shine dark, glowing in the mess tent's heat. George did the best he could with the abysmal supplies he had, and it was always edible, if not occasionally unusual.

At Aunt Jo's Christmas buffet, there were deviled eggs from Polly Humboldt on New Utrecht, who brought them wherever she went, even to a beach party. (Polly had a special platter to carry them, with divots to hold the halved eggs.) There was a heated tray of lasagna from Rose's kitchen, wrapped in tin foil, towels and secured with string to weather the snowy walk from Forty-Seventh Street. There was the ever-present *antipasto*, this one brimming with olives in two shades of black, shining like patent leather, squares of white and gold cheeses, roasted peppers in Christmasy red and green. There was Erma Rimmer's winter squash soufflé, a festive orange shade, so velvety and sweet it could have been a dessert. There was...

There was a nudge of Tiger's shoulder. He looked up to see his Uncle Harry grinning at him, a tumbler of Johnny Walker in his catcher's mitt-sized hand. "Planning your attack before you swoop in for the kill?" Harry wondered aloud.

"Something like that," Tiger conceded. "There's so much to choose from...and none of it from a tin."

"Beats going hungry."

"I'll say," Tiger agreed.

"Or K-rations." Tiger nodded in agreement. "I had a rough time when I got back," his uncle added. "Now, I'm not talking about the leg. Other stuff. It was tough adjusting to being home."

Harry was a man of few words. It was clear that he fiercely loved his family, but he would never say it out loud. Not in words, anyhow. He took a deep swig of the amber liquid, swallowed then continued. "I wasn't sure where I fit in," Harry told his nephew. "You go off to war and you expect things to be the same when you come back, only they're not. Everything's changed. Hell, *you've* changed."

"Does it get better?" Tiger wondered.

"Eventually," Harry admitted. "Maybe it's that you change again. Not back to the way you were, but almost. A new normal, you know? But I'm not one to judge. I'm still trying to work it out myself, one day at a time."

Jo smiled nervously at her husband from across the room then replenished the Swedish meatballs. Harry returned her smile and raised his glass. Rose checked in with her folks, who were holding court on the sofa, and asked if she could make them up another plate. "I'd start with the *kumpa*," Harry advised his nephew. "Norwegian potato dumplings. They're top notch and they're almost gone."

Finally, Tiger tore into the buffet table, a veritable League of Nations served up on Aunt Jo's Spode luncheon plates. On Tiger's dish, the *kumpa* sat beside the lasagna, which he kept away from the gefilte fish Ti-Tu had made from his mother's recipe. (God rest her soul.) Although Tiger was never a fan of jarred gefilte fish, Ti-Tu's was flavorful and wonderful. There was a dollop of the soufflé left, which Tiger finessed onto the edge of his plate. He forked one piece of *lechón asado*, Cuban-style pork roast, pink, juicy and done to perfection, courtesy of Manny Ortez Vega's wife Consuelo, who'd brought two dishes to the gathering. Consuelo was still lovely, despite the years and the few pounds added to her once-delicate frame. Tiger liked how she said his name. He'd missed hearing it, and missed seeing Consuelo and Manny.

Mr. and Mrs. Wong arrived with gorgeous tea cakes everyone thought looked too pretty to eat. They could stay but a few minutes because the chop suey place was open. Apparently, Christmas was one of their busiest days because those with nowhere else to go—as well as many Jewish folks—frequented Chinese restaurants on Christmas for some unknown reason.

Tiger propped himself into a quiet corner of the parlor, near the window, through which the mid-afternoon sun shone blindingly. A man lingered on the sidewalk outside, gaunt with drink and worn of spirit. When the man looked up to admire the O'Leary windows festooned with decorations, Tiger gasped, almost dropping his plate. At first glance, the man resembled his father so strongly, it took Tiger's breath away. But when he had a closer look, the fellow's nose was too wide and his chin too narrow. When the man walked on, Tiger shook his head at his own stupidity. He began breathing normally again and continued eating his dish of ethnic tidbits with gusto.

"You haven't lost your appetite," noted Manny, suddenly beside him.

"Especially when the grub is this good."

"It's nice to have you back, Anthony," Manny said. "And in one piece," he added, low so Harry couldn't hear.

"It's nice to be back," Tiger said, between bites. "And you can still call me 'Tiger.'"

Consuelo gently pinched Tiger's cheek between her fingertips. "*Ai, mijo* you're so skinny," Consuelo frowned, her eye-catching *café con leche* features furrowing. "You lost weight."

"Maybe a little," Tiger admitted. "I'll put it back on, though. Probably by tomorrow at this rate."

"Come by for *arroz con pollo* any time," Consuelo smiled.

"*Si, muchas gracias.*"

"*Da nada.*" Consuelo left to uncover her container of *moro* on the sideboard. Short for the *Moros y Cristianos* (Moors and Christians), it was a tasty mix of black beans and white rice. "Be sure to get some," she demanded of Tiger. He said that he would.

"I can't call you my Gunga Din anymore, can I?" Manny joked.

"You can call me whatever you'd like," Tiger smiled. Manny nervously traced his pencil-thin mustache. "You've grown into a fine young man," he stated. "I'm proud to know you."

"Thank you."

"If I were younger, I would have…"

Tiger stopped Manny. He was tired of middle-aged men apologizing about not having gone off to war. "Somebody had to stay home to build the ships, right?" he told Manny.

Manny's face relaxed. "Yes, that is true."

Stan approached Manny and Tiger, gnawing on a meatball he speared with a fork and ate like a gravy-coated lollipop. Manny affectionately tousled the boy's hair while Tiger put down his plate momentarily to wipe sauce from his brother's face with a napkin. Stan yakked about *House of Dracula*, currently playing at the Loew's 46th. Tiger promised to take Stan to see it even though Rose had forbidden it. She said it was bound to give Stan nightmares and then he would refuse to go into the basement. (This happened any time Stan saw scary movies.) Happy about the prospect of Lon Chaney and John Carradine (whose dashing Dracula petrified Stan worse than Bela Lugosi's) in one picture, Stan skipped off to grab the last of the *kumpa* Olie and Tomina Olson had ferried on the B-16 bus all the way from Bay Ridge.

Manny smiled as he watched the boy dash, almost knocking over his Aunt Astrid in the process. "Blasted old kid," she muttered, straightening out the excess of holly on her head. Astrid's future ex-husband Sam followed her like a puppy. He hadn't paid that much attention to Astrid when they were married, only now that she was almost in his past, Sam doted on her. One too many hang-up telephone calls in the middle of the night, one too many lovelorn chippies visiting the couple's Kermit Place doorstep had put Astrid over the edge. How could a wife believe her husband's plaintive, palms-raised "I never touched the girl" and "You're the only one for me" claims? What did he take Astrid for, a fool? Astrid Paradiso Fischer was a lot of things but she certainly wasn't a buffoon.

However, the worst Astrid accused her husband of was loving her family more than he did her. This may or may not have been true. Sam had been part of the Paradiso clan for so long, and his family in Tennessee was so far away that Astrid's family still included Sam in on the merriment. But if it were up to Astrid, her association with Sam would end as soon as they were divorced. They'd been separated for going on seven years and she wasn't getting any younger. Plus she had her eye on an agreeable, if not plain-looking fellow who'd come into Bergdorf's when she was at a meeting there. Al Dursi was in real estate with a fellow by the name of Fred Trump, who'd build barracks during the War and was now looking into building housing for returning vets. Al's future was promising, even though he wasn't much in the looks department. It seemed to Astrid that he'd be as faithful as a Saint Bernard, and even vaguely resembled one with his big head and droopy eyes. The first time around, Astrid married for passion (and looks). The second, she decided, it would be for money.

The Christmas guests at Jo and Harry's place happily grazed most of the afternoon. After a few hours, Poppa was dozing in a comfy corner of the sofa. Bridget was presiding over the transition from dinner to dessert on the buffet table like a jovial brigadier general, but in a festive floral shift from Mays instead of a uniform. Without exchanging a word, the women began taking away the platters, plates, tureens and bowls, careful not to stain their holiday finery. Even Wendy and Stan helped. (In their minds, it was an excellent way to get the treats onto the table quicker, plus, when they carried them out, they could sneak tastes when no one was looking.) The men, when they tried to lend a hand, were told to sit down. "They'll just be in the way," Rose said to Camille. The fast pace of the kitchen only confused the fellows who were crackerjack at washing dishes but little else domestic. Camille's husband already had a frilled apron around his waist, and was ready to dig in. "I didn't mean you, John," Rose assured him. "You're a whiz in the kitchen."

John gave Rose a pretend growl—he was really a pussycat beneath his gruff exterior—and followed the ladies through the Dutch doors and into the kitchen, where the table was crammed with desserts. Angela had already started the coffee urn, which was burping its way toward making thirty cups. "Do you think it will be enough?" Jo fretted. But it was, it always was.

Rose had the kettle on the boil. The porcelain teapot her friend Pippa, who'd grown up in London, had given her, waited on the table. It was brown enamel and had a pair of chickens painted on the side. Pip divulged to Rose that the chickens were the two of them, and it would be their special tea pot when they sat around and gossiped, sipping Earl Grey and clucking like hens. Every year, Rose let Jo borrow Pip's special teapot for the Christmas buffet.

Consuelo was measuring out scoops of Café Bustelo for a second coffee pot. The Ortez Vegas, Poppa and even shanty Irish like Sully, preferred Consuelo's potent, Latin American-style espresso. She made the coffee in a special stovetop aluminum pot. Into the basket, she pressed dirt-dark grounds, but not too tightly. Then she set it on the burner to boil.

With a quick shake of the sideboard tablecloth out the kitchen window, Jo replaced the chrysanthemum-patterned cloth and it was ready to receive the procession of desserts. There was Consuelo's flan, untouched from the day before. It was perfect, gleaming on a platter, bathed in a pool of caramel. Hers was slightly different than Gloria Lopez's, with a kick of cinnamon. Flans, similar to the people who made them, Bridget noted, differed from country to country, and she never met a flan she didn't like.

Next was Rose, who held what was left of Bridget and Angela's honey-drenched *struffoli*, also from Christmas Eve. Wendy was entrusted with Carol's cream cheese cake, topped with strawberries their Basque neighbor had canned the past summer. Angela had the ginger snaps, one of which Stan swiped before they even hit the table. Because it was Christmas, she didn't scold her baby brother. Nadia, Jo's new next-door-neighbor, a no-nonsense girl of German and Italian stock, wowed them with her sour milk cake. Finally, there was Eila's dense and delicious chocolate cake, dusted with snowy confectioner's sugar, which was amazingly made without flour.

Stan was tasked with toting in the pile of dessert plates that Uncle John had washed and Tiger had dried, for they'd used the same Spode Christmas-tree dishes for the *hors d'oeuvres* portion of the expansive buffet. Astrid had the forks in one fist, the creamer in the other, while Eila's little one, Max, carefully carried Jo's crystal sugar bowl in his two chubby hands.

An amiable line soon formed at the sweets table while Jo and Camille brought in individual cups of coffee and tea, and set them on one side of the buffet for the guests to prepare to their liking. "Hot stuff coming through," Poppa joked as Consuelo carried in a tray of inky espresso, already liberally sugared to a thick, molassesy consistency. Smiling, Consuelo served Poppa first. Jo took his and Bridget's dessert order— no buffet lines for them—of a little bit of everything. Slipping to the head of the queue, Jo heaped the servings onto two plates, which her parents shared between them. Even the ginger cookie was split down the middle.

Rose flashed Stan a weighty glance, complete with raised eyebrows, when he grabbed two fistfuls of cookies. He wisely put back all but one. "Tomorrow's another day, Stanley," Bridget reminded him, like an elderly, silver-haired Scarlett O'Hara.

There were praises all around, from mouths kissed with rich chocolate, silky caramel and lips coated with honey. No one could get over the fact that desserts made with rotten milk ("You sour it with a squeeze of lemon," Nadia explained.) or without flour, could be so decadent.

By eight, Jo and Harry's parlor was almost empty, except for the immediate family. Everyone had pitched in with the cleanup, washing dishes, packing up leftovers, and it was spic and span in no time. The meal had been going on almost five hours, and they were finally tired of eating nonstop. They sat in the parlor, catching their breath and reminiscing about the day—who'd visited, who hadn't, what they'd eaten, what they should make next year.

This is when Tiger brought out a white paper shopping bag splashed with Asian characters across its front. He'd managed to sneak it in past everyone and hide it under the pile of coats in the bedroom until now. Tiger began to take out the thoughtfully-wrapped gifts. The paper was not only colorful but foreign, exotic, like sheaths of silk. Each gift was tied fast with a rainbow of brightly-hued ribbons.

"But we already exchanged presents," Rose stammered. She still felt badly there hadn't been much for Tiger under the tree that morning, a few generic items she'd bought "just in case" since he hadn't been expected. Rose had apologized profusely but Tiger shrugged it off. "I already have a pretty swell gift and it doesn't fit in a box," he'd told her. "It's being with all of you." Rose bit her lip to keep from crying.

"This is just some stuff I picked up along the way," Tiger shrugged as he lay the gifts out on the coffee table. Tiger's presents were far from insignificant; each was perfect, the best Europe and Asia had to offer. He'd either bought or traded for them, and had done so wisely.

For his mother and stepfather Sully, there was a tin of first-rate English Breakfast tea—they of the early morning and late evening tea powwows. For Wendy, there was a pair of tortoise shell hair combs which would offset her auburn hair perfectly. For Jo and Harry, there was a fragile, milky orchid of English bone china for their *chachka* collection. Packed in a clean, wadded-up sock, it was a miracle the flower made the journey safely. For Camille and John, who both had a sweet tooth, there was a block of superb Swiss chocolate. Astrid and Sam received separate gifts, as they now lived apart. For Sam, there was an ascot of Italian silk, and for Astrid, Tiger had a cloth-covered edition of *India's*

Love Lyrics. As stony-hearted as she could be, Astrid had a fever for poetry and inhaled it before she went to sleep.

Bridget held a pink plastic box in her palm. Its front was stamped with a word too small for her to see without her specs. (It read "Cosenza," the town it was from.) Inside, on a bed of cotton, there was a petite, solid gold cross. "It's from Italy," Tiger informed her. Bridget was speechless. The morning Tiger was to leave for basic training at Fort Dix, Bridget had misplaced the cross her father had given her for her First Holy Communion six decades earlier. 'I know it's here somewhere,' she'd worried aloud. Bridget took losing the cross as a bad omen and even said a rosary for Tiger's safe return. After two years, Bridget still hadn't found her original cross, but by some miracle, her grandson made it home safely, cross or not.

For Angela and Augie's baby there was a tiny flaxen silk kimono, brittle as an oak leaf. (In her initial joy, Angela had written to her brother about her pregnancy.) She pressed the kimono to her belly. The fabric felt soft as rain. Also in the box was a second kimono of fern green. "I couldn't decide on the color, so I got both."

Angela kissed her brother on the forehead, tasting salt and a hint of alcohol. (It's true, he had tipped back a few to celebrate his return.) "Why are you convinced it's going to be a girl?" she teased.

"Aw, the Paradisos always have girls out of the gate," Tiger said.

It was true, for every single one of them.

"Boys can wear kimonos, too," Wendy reminded them. "They're all the rage at Bergdorf's." Everyone, even Astrid, laughed.

Tiger had managed to procure a wooden pipe for his grandfather said to have come from the Black Forest. Its bowl and shank were a burnt sienna and smooth, and a wizened face was carved into it. "I never made it to Germany," Tiger explained.

"Thank goodness," Poppa gasped.

Tiger continued, "I traded for the pipe. I thought you'd like it."

"I do," Poppa declared, trying it on for size.

Tiger saved Stan's gift for last, presenting him with a short, narrow object in a palm-sized drawstring sack. To Stan's delight, it was a knife with many parts. "That's a Swiss Army, a Spartan, with a genuine deer horn handle," Tiger pointed out.

"Wow!" Stan exclaimed. It was such a grown-up present, and far superior to anyone else's, he thought.

"Is it okay?" Tiger wondered.

"It sure is neat," Stan cried, then grabbed his brother in a bear hug.

Rose was ready to tell the boy it was too dangerous a present, that he might take out an eye or worse. Sensing this, Sully cupped his wife's knee under the table. "It's a very grown-up gift, Tiger," he said. "We know Stanley will use it responsibly, with adult supervision, of course."

"Yes, Pop," the boy agreed. Sully felt Rose's body relax under his hand. She nudged him in the side to signify she understood—having a knife was an important rite of passage for a boy. He was a wise man, her husband, Rose decided.

After they got into their coats, Jo gave her family their satchels of leftovers. Stan took two sugar cookies. "He eats like there's no tomorrow," Rose sighed, shaking her head.

"He's a growing boy," Jo told her, giving Rose a paper sack.

"Sometimes I think he remembers going hungry as a baby," Rose whispered when Stan had gone into the hallway to put on his galoshes. "You know, before he came to us."

"He can't possibly remember," Jo said. "He was too little."

Although Harry suggested driving the Sullivans, the Martinos, the Paradisos and the Corsos the few blocks home in a couple of trips, they turned him down. "A *passeggiata* will do us all good," Poppa conceded to Harry. "We'll walk off this great food."

Brooklyn resembled a storybook that Christmas night, painted with gold from the streetlamps reflecting off the snow. Everyone was home within minutes, talking merrily about the rich *smorgasbord* they'd just enjoyed, their neighbor Mickey McGraw who'd shown up "three sheets to the wind," of Olie and Tomina Olsen, who never aged. The joy of the day was in their thoughts and on their tongues as they drifted off to sleep, safely tucked into their beds. All but Tiger.

Chapter Eleven

The Culver Line

Tiger couldn't sleep. It wasn't that he'd had too much to eat or drink. It wasn't even the sound of Stan's breath, heavy with exhaustion, whistling gently through the slight space between his front teeth, the same space Tiger himself had. Tiger couldn't sleep because his mind was restless and hopped from one thought to the next like a bird trying to find the right spot on a branch. For a while, Tiger let his thoughts swirl, following them with interest, curious as to where they might go next. Then he grew weary of this game, put his bare feet onto the throw rug between the twin beds and noiselessly dressed in the same clothes he'd worn earlier that day.

Tiger was heedful not to trip over his own kit bag in the corner or Stan's Erector Set. He could see a half-built bridge in the faint streetlight and various pieces of metal scattered across the floor, even though Rose had asked the boy to clean them up before he went to bed. Stan had been so tired from the excitement of Christmas Day that he'd fallen asleep, clutching the Erector Set's instructions. Tiger wrestled the paper from Stan's hand, put it on the nightstand and covered him with a wool blanket, cautious not to wake the boy as he tiptoed out the bedroom door.

Rose was like an urban panther. She heard every creak, every sound in the nighttime apartment, no matter how trivial. Maybe it came from sleeping alone when Sully was on the beat. Maybe it was because she was so ferociously protective of her family. Although Tiger tried to move as quietly as possible, Rose's bedroom door clicked open and there she was, already in her housedress, prepared to cook at the drop of a hat. "Hungry?" she asked.

"Nah," Tiger whispered.

"You sure?" she prodded. "Because it would be no trouble…"

"Ma, I'm stuffed," he said.

"Do you need Pepto-Bismol? Because I…"

"I just can't sleep," Tiger told her. He reached for his pea coat. "I'm going out for a walk."

He drew his Tartan-patterned scarf (a Christmas gift from Aunt Jo) out from the jacket's sleeve and his watch cap along with it. "Be careful," Rose warned. "It's late."

The second after Rose uttered those words, she realized how silly they were. Tiger had just returned from a war and had managed to come back in one piece without her hovering. Regardless, Rose tucked Tiger's scarf tighter about his neck and straightened his collar. He wondered how his mother had survived his time in the service. Probably the way she weathered everything: with hope and prayer. Both helped Rose sail through.

Tiger kissed Rose on the forehead. It smelled faintly of hairspray, a newfangled thing in a can she had permitted Angela to use on her unruly bangs that morning "It's not so late, Ma," he said. "It's not even ten. Maybe I just need to get reacquainted with the neighborhood." Tiger made his way for the door, which was unlocked, as always. A line of boots stood on dampened sheets of newspaper. "And don't worry, I'll wear my galoshes."

The night air was bracing. The snow-covered sidewalks sparkled as though they were encrusted with diamonds. Tiger made a beeline to New Utrecht, passing Piccolo's Bakery, Dora's Luncheonette, Abe the Fishmonger's and Mario's Pizzeria. Although it had once been his stomping ground, these places looked alien and strange to him now, shuttered against the night. Even the Pink Pussycat was dark on Christmas.

Beyond the El, Tiger saw the hulking monolith of United Israel Zion where Rose had convalesced a decade earlier. He turned toward Green-Wood Cemetery. There his father lay under a blanket of snow, probably uneasily. Tiger's old school, PS 131 was a sandstone giant, taking up the entire block on Fort Hamilton Parkway between Forty-Third and Forty-Fourth Streets. He remembered how Mrs. Curry, his fourth-grade teacher, used to berate the Italian kids, usually the darker-skinned ones. She would snap at Gino Patelli, "What do you wash your hair with? Shoe polish?" Gino would hang his head and blush deep red. To Maria Murro, who would try so hard to correctly answer Mrs. Curry's rapid-fire questions, she once snapped, "If I tied your hands behind your back, would you still be able to talk?" The poor girl had been so mortified that silent tears traced down her cheeks. Tiger wondered where Mrs. Curry was today and hoped perhaps she might already be dead.

He continued down Fort Hamilton Parkway, past St. Catherine of Alexandria Church with its soaring, peaked spire and roof, the same minty patina as the Statue of Liberty. He took in the deep grotto, cloaked in white, the Nativity figures in its crèche half submerged. The shelter, probably made by parishioners, barely protected its inhabitants from the elements. Mary looked placid and unmoved by the Brooklyn winter while Joseph was long-suffering and ignored, maybe because he was almost an afterthought in the Catholic religion. The Three Wise Men were shadows locked within the ivory mantle hugging their shoulders. The donkey seemed to shiver under its blanket of flakes and Baby Jesus's face was obscured. Was it a lowly altar boy's job to swab the Christ Child's visage before the six o'clock mass each morning, Tiger wondered. Probably.

St. Catherine's had been built in 1902, when Tiger's mother was only two. The cross on the church's roof looked as wispy and delicate as a sugar wafer, as though it could snap in half just as easily. The bell in the narrow tower struck once on the half hour. "Don't ask for whom the bell tolls," Tiger said aloud to no one in particular. He'd read a book inspired by the quote when he was overseas, and although it was about the Spanish Civil War, he could relate. That Hemingway fellow could sure write.

Tiger left the church in his wake, moving at a nice clip, barely taking note of the temperature. It was a quality he'd acquired in the service from endless marches in all sorts of weather. Trained not to pay any heed to what was going on outside—rain, snow, sleet, stifling heat—inside, his mind and heart were racing through Borough Park. Only now that Tiger was home, his thoughts were elsewhere; he wasn't sure where he was supposed to be.

Tiger's boots carried him further down Fort Hamilton Parkway. When Green-Wood began at the corner of Thirty-Seventh Street, he crossed the road and began walking beside its high black fence separating the living from the dead. There were signs on the opposite side of the Parkway for streets like Bills Place, Minna Street, Chester Avenue, Clara and Louisa Streets. They were supposedly named for the children of the builder. Tiger's parents had lived on Chester Avenue when they were first married. Had they been happy there, he wondered. Had there ever been a time of tranquility or had his father's drinking always taken control and ruined everything, just as it had when Tiger was a boy? His earliest memories were of his father yelling that blood-chilling screech of his. Tiger seemed to remember hearing it from his crib, before he could even walk. Or was he just imagining it?

It was still Christmas, Tiger reminded himself, the season of peace, joy and goodwill toward men, at least for a little while. Despite what Tiger had done and witnessed in the

War, he thought it was still possible to have a normal life, the different kind of normal his Uncle Harry spoke of. For nothing would ever be the same, not even the streets where he grew up.

At the corner of Fort Hamilton Parkway and McDonald Avenue, Tiger veered left onto McDonald, the snow deeper here because of the drifts at this wide convergence of streets. Vanderbilt, Seeley, Terrace. The names were vaguely familiar. McDonald soon melted into Twentieth Street, then came Prospect Park West, which was called Ninth Avenue by the locals. Tiger made a right turn onto it. He formed the sign of the cross with his gloved fingers as he passed in front of Holy Name of Jesus Church, simply Holy Name to those of the parish. Tiger still believed in some things, maybe not in God exactly, but a bunch of the Catholic rituals still stuck. For example, crossing himself when he passed a house of worship, dipping his head involuntarily when he uttered the word "Jesus." Old habits died hard, especially in Brooklyn.

Catty-cornered from a pharmacy and squashed between Pimm's Delicatessen was Farrell's Bar and Grill. The wide glass front window, draped with silver garland, was unlit. Houlie, arguably the best bartender in the County of Kings, had probably gone back home to his family in the wilds of Long Island. Yes, even Kevin Houlihan had a family, had people who loved him. So did Tiger. Then why was he out in the December chill, the sole soul on Ninth Avenue? Because Tiger felt he was in a sort of limbo, neither here nor there.

Was Dan Fiorino home? He and his brothers lived down Prospect in a narrow limestone house with their folks and Grandma Bridie, who hailed from County Cork. Tiger gave a little chuckle when he remembered how the lace-curtain Irish lady had come home in a tizzy from midnight mass one Christmas Eve because, as she complained in her bitter brogue, "those hooligans from Farrell's were hooting at Father Shine." Grandma Bridie vowed never to go to midnight mass again. And she never did. From that moment on in the Fiorino household, "hooting at Father Shine" became a euphemism for being rip-roaring drunk.

Although Dan was probably home, the Fiorinos were undoubtedly asleep and Tiger decided not to bang on their doorbell, even though Dan's mother insisted Tiger was welcome there any time, day or night.

The Culver Line was across the street from Farrell's and went all the way to Coney Island. Frigid as it might be at the lip of the Atlantic, Tiger felt the relentless tides of Coney pulling him there, so he went. He descended into the station across the street from Farrell's.

The night was so murky that Tiger could scarcely see when the train ruptured out of the tunnel after Church Avenue. He could decipher a crooked hodgepodge of rooftops, the outline of pigeon coops, unfettered clotheslines and water towers, but little else. Every so often, there was a light burning in one of the apartment windows but most panes were unlit. It was rare to decipher the shape of a person in a window, shifting in front of the glass like a ghost or else seated at a lonely table, staring off into space or into the depths of a cup. It reminded Tiger of the paintings of a man named Edward Hopper: lugubrious, blank, interchangeable faces as seen through the window of a diner, an automat or in a deserted hotel lobby.

The wide curve the elevated train made when it hooked toward Coney Island didn't thrill Tiger the same way as it had when he was a boy. The carcasses of the Cyclone, the Wonder Wheel, of Steeplechase and Luna Park were etched into the night sky, unmoving, as though dead. Come spring, Tiger knew that like the trees, they would also come to life. The Culver train screeched into the Stillwell Avenue station, braking brutally. Tiger's father had been a conductor, not a motorman; he didn't have a job as important as drive the train but opened and closed the doors. Tony also made announcements, usually slurred from drink or from general carelessness, naming the next stop or telling riders to watch the closing doors. Occasionally, Tony would cap it off with "You rotten bastards" after he turned off the microphone. A few times, Tony had burst forth with a litany of obscenities when he'd over served himself from his medicine-bottle flask and was suspended with a day or two on the street without pay. But that was a long time ago.

By the second-to-last stop, Tiger was in the train car alone. When the doors crashed open at Stillwell, he and a few passengers from other cars scattered onto the platform, pulling their coats closer to their bodies, fighting the unforgiving ocean breeze. Tiger was the only one without a satchel. Everyone else had shopping sacks filled with gifts, opened or unopened. Watch cap pulled low over his eyebrows, Tiger bumped into a grizzled man in Transit Authority blue and apologized. The fellow's bloodshot eyes were first perturbed then flickered in recognition. "Tiger?" the man said. "Tiger! It's been a dog's age!"

It was Sean McBride, his father's old stationmaster when Tony was working out of Stillwell. "Old donkey rummy prick," Tony used to call the gin-blossom-nosed Irishman. Instead of using his father's epithet, Tiger put out his hand and grimaced, "Mr. McBride."

"How the hell are you?" McBride wondered. "Why, I remember you when you were knee-high to a tadpole." McBride repeated this every time he ran into Tiger, from age five on up.

"I'm good," Tiger told him without thinking, even though he wasn't quite certain what he was.

"Your pop's been gone, how many years?"

"Going on ten, Mr. McBride."

"Time flies," the seasoned drinker nodded. "And quit calling me 'Mr. McBride.' That's my Pa's name, the rat bastard. I hear you were away."

"You heard right. In the European Theatre mostly, then a few months in Japan."

"Those Eye-talian gals treat you okay?"

Tiger was mainly in Holland but he didn't want to encourage the ancient lush into a deeper conversation. McBride's breath reeked of gin and Tiger couldn't quit staring at the man's unruly ear hairs. "They treated me fine," Tiger conceded.

"What brings you down this way?" McBride wondered. Tiger shrugged. "Monkey business, no doubt," the old boozer winked knowingly.

"Just taking a look-see around," Tiger told him.

The bells of Our Lady of Solace sounded a few blocks away on West Seventeenth Street, slicing through the numb air. Tiger lost count of the tolls. "If you want an honest, steady job, keep in mind the TWU," McBride said. "There's plenty of overtime. So what if it's on Christmas. The benefits are top-notch. If the TWU was good enough for your old man, it's good enough for you."

Tiger couldn't imagine anything he wanted less: to follow in his father's footsteps. He didn't say this to McBride, however. Instead, Tiger shook the man's hand again and wished Mr. McBride a Merry Christmas. The TA worker wished him and his family the same, then considered the crooked rooftops of Coney Island for a moment. "There's not much open this time of night," McBride said. "Whorehouses, a few opium dens, but Ruby's never closes."

Chapter Twelve

Ruby's Bar and Grill

Tiger stood at the end of Steeplechase Pier, listening to the ocean. He couldn't distinguish the line between sea and sky, yet he could sense it, the dormant midway and rides lurking behind him like sentinels. How many times had he and his sister whiled away an entire day at Coney Island, sharing five dollars between them, and coming home with their pockets jangling with change? How many times had Kewpie given him a piggy-back ride home from the trolley when he was too tired to walk? Countless.

In Europe, Tiger had touched the Atlantic, the Mediterranean, even the Adriatic and North Seas. (Although, in Asia, he was there too briefly and didn't have the luxury to sample even one body of water.) Tiger needed to touch his home ocean, even if it wasn't technically the Atlantic but Coney Island Channel. Maybe it would help him feel like he was truly home. The sand was firm beneath his boots and it shone in spots from the drifts of snow. He stood stock-still with his boot tips aimed at Breezy Point and watched the

foam engulf them. Bending his knees, he trailed his fingers
into the surf then recoiled. The water was so cold it hurt,
but it made him feel alive. He turned and headed back to
the Riegelmann Boardwalk, struggling to read the signs for
Stauch's Baths and Hygrade Franks along the way.

There were three people in Ruby's when Tiger pushed
through its sea-worn wooden door, including the barkeep.
Ruby's was vast and gloomy, a somber barn, and with about
as much personality. Tiger hadn't been there for at least a
dozen years. His father occasionally took him to Ruby's
from the time he was about eight. Tony would sit him up on
the bar, feed Tiger cream soda and pickled hardboiled eggs
while he himself guzzled boilermakers. Although Tiger liked
going to work with his dad, he hated going to Ruby's because
they would be there for hours instead of on the rides or on
the beach. As a boy, Tiger often fell asleep in one of Ruby's
booths, only to be roughly roused and forced to practically
sleepwalk the lengthy block to the Stillwell station.

Ruby's hadn't changed since then. There were the same
dirty mirrors behind the bar, the same soiled, striped
paper decorating the walls, the same jumble of photographs
behind grimy, nicotine-stained glass, the same sticky wooden
planked floor. Ruby's probably hadn't been cleaned since
the day it opened in 1922. In one way, it familiarity was a
comfort, but in another, it was unsettling. Bars, even bars
overseas, always reminded Tiger of one thing: his father.

"What'll it be?" the barkeep asked, sullen and crotchety
he had to sling beers on Christmas night and serve low-life
losers. The bourbon, served straight up in a squat, filmy
glass, would take the edge off Tiger's uneasiness. It
always did.

Two men sat a barstool away from Tiger, speaking in
low voices, hunched toward each other. One was short and
wiry, so thin he looked ill, his robin's egg blue eyes set into
hollowed-out scoops in his skull. The second was bigger,
pulpy, with the jolly countenance of one who had never seen
war. "Welcome home, soldier," offered the shorter fellow.

Tiger tried not to look startled that the man could tell he'd been in the service. "Merry Christmas," Tiger responded. "How did you know?"

"You have the same look I did when I first came home," he admitted.

"Oh? And what's that?"

"Lost," the smaller man told Tiger. "Like you're not sure where you belong." He put out his hand. Tiger took it. "Roy," the man nodded. "And this here's Joe."

"Anthony," Tiger said.

"Pleased to meet you, Tony," Roy smiled.

"It's Anthony," Tiger corrected him. "My father was Tony. I'm not."

"Oh, I get you," Roy nodded. "I had one of them, too. Rotten bastard. Ran out on us when I was twelve. If it wasn't for my sister Evelyn, we would have starved."

"Where's your old man now?"

"Calvary? Yours?"

"Green-Wood," Tiger answered.

"I'm glad. You?"

"Yeah, I'm glad, too," Tiger admitted with a sigh and a sip of bourbon. "Good riddance to bad rubbish."

"Where were you stationed?" Joe wondered.

"European Theater. Holland. A little in Italy. Then Japan. You?"

Joe reddened so Roy piped up. "Joey here was 4-F. Flat feet, the lucky duck."

"I held down the home front," Joe said.

"He was beating them off with sticks, Joe was," Roy quipped. Again, Joe flushed.

"What branch?" Roy pushed.

"Army."

"I was Air Force, a paratrooper."

"I'm impressed," Tiger admitted.

"Don't be," Roy grimaced. "Son, three things fall out of the sky: precipitation, bird shit and assholes."

Tiger was speechless and even more impressed. Roy took a deep gulp of his beer, draining the dripping mug in one long slug. Tiger signaled for the bartender to give Roy another, which he did.

"Roy was captured by the Krauts in Holland," Joe said. "He was in a POW camp until the Brits liberated them."

"I heard about that place," Tiger admitted. "I was in Italy at the time, on the way to Antwerp. Kamp Erika, was it?"

Roy stared off into a corner of Ruby's, as though he were studying something that wasn't there. "It was brutal. I thought I was hungry growing up only it was nothing compared to the camp. Your body starts eating away at itself. I was there almost a year and I was only 85 pounds when they set us free. April 11, 1945."

"Wasn't that where the Butcher of Ommen was?" Tiger probed.

"Herbertus Bikker," Roy spat. "Nastiest God-damn prison guard you ever want to meet. Fat Nazi bastard. Killed Jan Houtman, a Dutch kid in the Resistance. Bikker...what a sick, sadistic fuck."

Tiger was afraid to ask but had to. "What ever happened to Bikker?"

"Dunno," Roy admitted. He'd emptied his glass, which the bartender refilled, rapping on the damp wood to signify the drink was on him. Roy looked around the almost-empty bar and confirmed they were alone. "Can you keep a secret?"

Tiger leaned in closer. "Sure."

Roy told him, "Me and a few of the boys, we're pooling our resources. We're going to send a couple of the fellas back there...and not for no pleasure trip, if you get my drift."

Tiger licked his lips. "Do you think they'll find the Butcher?"

"Him *and* his friends. Holland's a small country. About twice the size of New Jersey. They'll find him, alright."

Tiger studied Roy's face in the dim bar light. It was emaciated and lined, but his body was thickening out some. Roy wasn't a large man yet he had an imposing fierceness about him, like a scrappy alley cat. One look at Roy and you got the silent message not to cross him, ever. "How will you decide who gets to go?" Tiger wondered.

Roy shrugged. "Draw straws, maybe. I wish I could be the one but I don't see how. The wife's expecting our first in a few months. Betty would die if I went away again, and I couldn't tell her about it. Besides, I got a job down at the Navy Yard."

"My grandfather used to work there. Retired a few months ago," Tiger stated. But it was almost as though Roy didn't hear. He might have been somewhere in Holland, perhaps dangling helplessly from a tree near Ommen, his parachute tangled in the branches.

Roy finished his beer and stood abruptly. "Well, I've got to hit the trail. Betty'll be worried." Roy put on his heavy wool coat, lifted a Fedora from a nearby chair and plopped it onto his head at a jaunty angle. "Nothing against the little woman," Roy added. "It's great being home. But sometimes...sometimes I've just got to get out. I can't stay cooped up indoors, as nice as Betty keeps the apartment."

"I know what you mean," Tiger admitted. "That's why I'm here instead of in my warm bed. I get antsy." Tiger dug into his slacks pocket and pulled out a ten spot. He crumpled it into Roy's palm.

"What's this?" Roy asked.

"A contribution for your collection," Tiger told Roy.

"You're a real *mensch*, Anthony," Roy said, visibly moved.

"You are, too. I hope you find what you're looking for."

"Same to you."

Roy and Joe left Ruby's, letting in a frosted rush of air. Tiger noticed that he had barely touched his drink as he listened to Roy talk. He finished the bourbon and signaled for another, although he didn't start on it right away. "Some story, huh?" Tiger commented to the bartender.

The barkeep gestured to the statuette of three monkeys on the shelf behind him: Speak No Evil, Hear No Evil and See No Evil. "I'm the middle guy," the barkeep said and knocked on the bar. "This one's on me. Welcome home, soldier," he said. "Merry Christmas and all that."

"And to you," Tiger wished him back.

A woman came out of the shadows. Her hair was as colorless as straw, except for the roots which were brown and laced with hoary strands. Her body was stocky and solid with bird-thin legs but she still had a reasonable figure, a poor man's Mae West. Tiger was unclear on how old she might be, perhaps between his sister and his mother's age, but she was unlike either of them. This woman was hard of face and mouth, accentuated by the red lipstick she wore. It reminded Tiger of the color of a drop of fresh blood. There were lines beside her mouth like sets of parentheses, from smiling or frowning, Tiger couldn't discern which. It was probably the latter, judging by the furrow between her penciled-in eyebrows. Something about her was vaguely recognizable but Tiger shrugged it off—women like that were a dime a dozen.

"And to you, too," Tiger told the woman. "Merry Christmas to you."

"Merry? Ha!" she choked. "But thanks just the same."

The barkeep wiped the down the mahogany with a dingy rag. Tiger caught his eye and nodded, then gestured toward the dishwater blonde. The barkeep slipped a semi-clean glass in front of the woman and gave her a healthy pour because he was feeling generous. "But I ain't got the dough..." she began to complain.

"Relax," Tiger said. "It's on me." He slid a bill toward the barkeep. "Keep the change," he said.

"Ain't you the high roller," the woman remarked. She downed her whiskey in one great gulp, slapped the glass onto the bar then wiped the corners of her mouth with the tip of one pinkie. "Thanks," she muttered.

"Anything for a lady," Tiger said.

The barkeep stifled a wry cackle then turned away. The woman flashed him a tempestuous look, then attempted to fix her mussed hair. "It's been ages since someone's called me a lady," she admitted. "And it don't feel too bad." She held out her hand. "I'm Denise."

When he took Denise's hand in his, Tiger noticed that her fingernails were chewed down to nubs. Flecks of polish clung to what was left of them. "Anthony," he told her.

"It's a pleasure," she bubbled.

"The pleasure's all mine," Tiger said. Denise smiled, revealing two rotten teeth and a missing front molar. She covered her mouth with a flea-bitten paw when she caught Tiger staring.

"Where you from?" she wondered.

"Down the road," he said. "You?"

"Almost around the corner."

"The Terminal?"

"Ya know it?" Denise asked, leaning in.

"Heard of it." She pulled a half-smoked cigarette out of her coat pocket. As Tiger lit it for her with a matchstick, he wondered if she'd found the cigarette butt on the ground. He studied Denise as she smoked: the wrinkled print dress, grubby around the collar, the worn-down heels of her scuffed shoes resting on the unpolished brass footrest, her stockings, baggy at the ankles. Tiger immediately felt sorry for her. He wanted to slip her a fiver but was afraid she'd take it the wrong way.

Denise blew a steady stream of smoke beyond Tiger's face. "Why ain't you with somebody?"

Tiger took a sip of his Four Roses. World's best-selling American bourbon, his dad used to remind him every time he filled his cough-medicine bottle flask before his shift on the El. "I'm with you guys," Tiger replied, gesturing to Denise and the bartender. The smoky, perfume taste of the bourbon caught in his throat, his nostrils. "You're somebody. You and..." Tiger looked to the barkeep.

"Dermott," he offered.

"You and Dermott," Tiger nodded.

Although Dermott would have rather been back in Park Slope with Lucy and their kids, he tipped his glass to the young man and imbibed liquid holiday cheer. God save

Lucy, alone with the three boys, ruffians each one. But as loud as it could be in their flat, it beat the hell out of the dead quiet of Ruby's on Christmas night. "Cheers," Dermott said.

Denise started up with Tiger again. "How come you ain't got a sweetheart?"

"Who says I don't?" Tiger prodded.

"'Cause if you did, you wouldn't be here with our sorry asses." Denise flashed Dermott a quick, alarmed look. She'd been thrown out of Ruby's more frequently than she cared to remember for gutter talk and innumerable indiscretions. "No offense," she added.

"None taken," Dermott told her.

Tiger felt himself blush when he explained to Denise, "I just got back, from the War yesterday. I haven't met anyone yet."

"You mean, you didn't have a gal waiting for you at home? A handsome devil such as yourself?" Denise pressed. Tiger shook his head. He could tell she didn't believe him.

Denise flashed her greenish teeth. "The War's been over for months now. How come you're just getting back?"

Tiger shrugged. "Somebody's got to clean up the mess."

"I suppose so," Denise conceded.

Tiger gave another signal to Dermott, who filled Denise's glass to the brim. "Last call," the bartender announced.

"Damn it to hell, I thought Ruby's never closed," Denise whined.

"Have a heart, Denise. It's Christmas," Dermott said. "It's time I go home to the Bride."

"Aw, you been married for ages, Dermie," Denise drawled. "The Mrs. ain't a bride no more."

Dermott shrugged. "She'll always be 'the Bride' to me."

Denise rolled her eyes. "Why, ain't love grand."

Dermott turned his back on Tiger and Denise. He began rinsing the soiled glasses in a tub of soapy water. "I thought I was in love once," Denise piped in a small voice to no one in particular. "Then he went and died on me, the creep."

"I'm sorry to hear it," Tiger told her. He hoped Denise wouldn't start crying. He hated when women bawled because he never knew what to do when they did.

Suddenly, Denise's face brightened. She looked younger, almost pretty, but only for a moment. Her eyes took on a dreamy cast as she traveled back in time. "I remember when the War ended," Denise said. "Everyone was so happy, hugging and kissing in the street." She traced the edge of her shot glass with one finger, smearing the lipstick print on the rim. "I was at my friend Fannie's place in Borough Park. She has an apartment right next to the El. When news came the War in Japan was over, people opened their windows and started banging pots and pans, just like New Year's. We were all so relieved the War had ended. A train filled with servicemen pulled into the station. They stretched out their hands to us and we stretched out ours to them. We almost touched but couldn't quite reach. Then the train pulled away. I'll never forget it."

"I live in Borough Park," Tiger said.

Dermott flicked the lights like they do at the theatre when intermission is about to end. "Hate to break up the party," he pressed. Dermott was already wearing his hat and winding his scarf around his neck. It looked brand new, like he'd just gotten it that morning. He slipped on his coat, tucked in his scarf and did up the buttons from top to bottom. Dermott left the glasses on the bar. As with most messes, they'd be there waiting for him in the morning.

Tiger shrugged into his jacket. He held up Denise's wrap for her and noted how lightweight it was. He wondered how it could possibly keep out the cold, especially with the steady wind coming in off the Lower Bay. She slid into the sleeves one by one, avoiding the frayed, torn lining. When Denise saw Tiger looking, she crooned proudly, "Lord & Taylor's finest. Oh, gentlemen used to buy me presents all the time. This coat was really snazzy back in its day...I was, too."

Denise accepted Tiger's arm when he presented it to her on the boardwalk. The sky was a deep indigo. It had clouded over so even the stars were hidden. She pulled her slouch hat onto her head and dug her fists into her pockets. "Here, take these," Tiger posed. The gloves would be swimming on her but they were leather and lined with rabbit fur, so they'd keep her warm.

"You sure?" she asked, shivering. Denise took them without waiting for Tiger's response.

"Sure, I'm sure." Tiger said. "I have two pair just like them at home. I showed up unexpected. Last minute presents, you know."

Denise slipped the gloves greedily onto her raw hands, reveling in the silkiness of the fur. "I didn't get no Christmas presents," she frowned, "'Cept for these…thanks a bunch, Anthony. You're a real peach." She kissed Tiger on the cheek, hastily, shyly, like a young girl might have done. "They're nice and toasty."

"I'm glad," he told her.

Denise steered Tiger toward Stillwell Avenue. It was wide, empty and windblown. Lonely. Still. The snowdrifts were high in the corners of some buildings, and the sidewalk blown clear in others. Across from the train station was a slumping row of buildings. A neon sign in front of one flashed "T-e-r-i-a-l H-o-t-l" in alternating red and blue. "The Terminal Hotel's seen better days, too, huh?" Denise sighed. It was the first time she seemed ashamed about her sorry situation. Moments later, when Denise's stomach grumbled like a creaky door, was the second.

"You hungry?" Tiger wondered. "I could go for a nosh myself." The reality was that Tiger's belly was still full from the mountain of food he'd had at Aunt Jo's. He couldn't take another bite.

"I could eat," Denise shrugged.

"Good," he said. "I'm buying."

"If you're buying, then I'm eating," she agreed.

There was a little hole in the wall all-night diner around the block on Mermaid Avenue. The Mermaid Grill's windows were so grimy with grease that it looked closed. The broken neon sign which didn't light announced, "Open all nite!" The interior looked gray—walls, floors, tiles—and was probably once white, a poor choice of color for a greasy spoon. The Mermaid Grill's lighting was garish and unkind, especially to Denise, whose countenance diminished in its harsh glow. It made her complexion appear even sallower and unhealthier. Every surface in the Mermaid Grill was sticky, from the menus to the shabby wooden chairs to the plastic tablecloths to the dented silverware.

Tiger ordered a cup of tea with lemon while Denise requested the Lumberjack Special—two eggs any style, two pieces of toast, two strips of bacon, two sausage links, two pancakes and hash browns. "I can eat brefast day or night," Denise admitted, licking her lips to keep her salivation at bay. And that's the way she said the word, "brefast." It made Tiger feel embarrassed for her, feel sorry for her more than he already did.

If his mother were there—and Rose most certainly wouldn't approve of a woman like this—she would have reluctantly admitted that Tiger was always taking in strays. As a boy, he once snuck out little saucers of milk for a litter of abandoned kittens in the backyard. Neither Rose nor Poppa nor Bridget would call him on it. Especially after their neighbor Mr. Greco took the whole lot and drowned them in a burlap sack in his garden trough because he claimed they were peeing on his beloved tea roses. Tiger looked high and low for those kittens, under the grape arbor, in the garage near Poppa's heavy bag, even under the back steps. "Maybe they've just gone someplace else," Rose told him. Tiger reluctantly agreed with his mother, but deep down, he knew the kittens' fate.

Tiger's hot tea was tepid, and the lemon was dried out. He pushed it to the side of his saucer and drank the tea without even sugar—the contents of the sugar bowl were speckled with the carcasses of deceased ants. Tiger sipped his cool tea and watched Denise tear into her "brefast" with fervor, wondering how long it had been since her last meal. Denise violently broke the egg yolks with the corner of her toast and smeared them over the pancakes. She picked up a bacon strip and chomped on it like a stray dog might if it had fingers.

When Denise got to the sausage, she stabbed one with her fork and nibbled on it, pointing out her pinkie in a refined gesture. The potatoes went down practically in one gulp. Then she mopped up the remains of her meal with the toast, smacking her lips when she was through.

"You positive we haven't met before?" Denise wondered after her eating deluge. "You look so familiar."

"People say that to me all the time," Tiger conceded.

"You remind me of someone," she pressed.

"I get it a lot, too. Still hungry?"

Denise covered her mouth, grinning, and nodded. "A tad."

"How about a slice of pie?"

"Pie would be delightful," she admitted, then yelled out, "Hey, Millie, ya got banana cream?"

Behind the counter, the waitress, was adding up a bill on a tattered pad. "If I were you, I'd go for the chocolate," she responded.

To Tiger, Denise said, "You don't have to tell me twice." To Millie, she shouted, "Chocolate cream it is."

Denise and Tiger looked at each other in the awkward silence that had grown between them. "I swear I've met you before. It's something in your eyes. When were you born?"

"1926," he said.

"A baby. You're not even twenty."

"I've seen a lot, though," Tiger admitted.

"I bet you have," Denise giggled coquettishly.

"In the War, I mean. Things I would rather forget."

"Then do," she told him. "Half of my life I wish I could forget so I pretend it never happened. Then poof!"

Tiger laughed. "It's gone? Just like that?"

"Poof!" said Denise, throwing up her hands into the air like a haggard magician's assistant.

Millie arrived with the pie. "Made it yesterday morning," she said. "The banana cream's past its prime, if you ask me."

"Thanks, Mill, you're a doll." Then lower, so Tiger couldn't hear, Denise whispered, "And I haven't forgotten about the two bits I owe you." Tiger heard, though, but then again, Tiger heard everything.

"Sure," Millie snapped, half believing her. "I haven't forgot neither."

The ting of a bell called the waitress away. "Order up!" shouted the man in a yellowed undershirt from the window separating the kitchen from the counter. The eggs, over easy, slightly slimy, toast and oily hash browns looked strangely forlorn as Millie scurried past with the plate.

Denise stabbed at the pie with her fork, first with trepidation, then with great zeal. "Wanna taste?" she asked, her mouth full of brown mush.

"No, thanks," he responded. "You enjoy it."

As Denise ate, Tiger thought there was a familiarity about her, too. Perhaps it was just that every worn-out floozie and washed-up bar girl had the same used, wrung-out-by-life look. Only there was an aspect of Denise, like the flicker of a forgotten dream or the glimmer of a childhood memory long gone, but stashed deep inside, that was buried on the periphery of Tiger's mind, on the tip of his tongue. He couldn't retrieve it, so he let it go.

Denise had demolished the pie. She was now picking up the remaining crumbs of graham cracker crust in her plate with the back of her fork, which she then licked. It was both such an intimate and desperate act that Tiger had to turn away. He watched a pair of flies wrestling in the corner of the window. "Borough Park," he heard. "You said you was from Borough Park," Denise repeated.

"Yes," he nodded. "Born and raised there."

"Had a beau once who was from Borough Park," Denise informed Tiger, absentmindedly toying with the tines of her fork. He half expected her to lick the plate.

"Where are you from? Originally, I mean," Tiger wondered.

"Here, there and everywhere," Denise shrugged, momentarily treating Tiger to a glimpse of her ruined teeth. "Mostly in Coney. I was born here and I'll probably die here."

"Not soon, I hope."

Tiger didn't know about the blood-dotted handkerchief stashed in Denise's purse. She fished another bent, half-smoked cigarette out of her pocket and slipped it into her mouth. Now, her lips were practically invisible since their paint had worn off from the food she'd consumed. This time, Tiger lit her cigarette butt from the book of matches on the table. Denise drew in the smoke deeply. She thought it was a minor miracle that she hadn't had a coughing fit in the time she'd been with him. Maybe the liquor had coated her throat. Maybe she was getting better. But she knew the truth; she was getting worse.

"Ya never know when your time's gonna come," she told Tiger philosophically, taking another drag. Denise realized that smoking probably wasn't the best thing for her. It made her throat burn more than it already did. It relaxed her, and besides, she reasoned, who did she have to hang around for? What was the point? Every day was a struggle and she owed money to virtually everyone on Mermaid. The rub-and-tug trade dwindled in the winter months. And this kid Anthony wouldn't go for a hand job, she could just tell. He wasn't the type. An upstanding guy, a prince among men. Denise was grateful her belly wasn't empty and happy that at least someone was treating her like a somebody instead of like a common piece of dirt.

"*Never send to know for whom the bell tolls; it tolls for thee*," Denise spoke, coming out of nowhere.

"Hemingway," Tiger said.

"But first, John…John Whosit," she grappled.

"John Donne. We read him in PS 131, eighth grade, Mrs. Coughlin's English class. "*No man is an island…*""

Denise picked up, "*Every man is a piece of the continent, a part of the main. If a clod be washed away by the sea, Europe is the less…yadda, yadda, yadda…Any man's death diminishes me…*" Tiger looked at Denise, stunned she had memorized Donne's poem. She ducked out the cigarette stub and cackled out a laugh. "You believe that horseshit?"

Tiger swallowed the last dregs of his tea, ice cold. "Well, yeah. We're all part of the same crazy swirl. My Grandma Bridget says, 'We all come from the same place.'"

"And you buy that crap?"

"Don't you?"

"*Isn't it pretty to think so*," Denise quoted.

"More Hemingway?"

"Surprised I can read?"

"Nothing surprises me these days," Tiger told her.

"I used to read like some people breathe," Denise cooed. "Loved me those Agatha Christie mysteries and that dime-store trash, too."

"You don't read anymore?"

Denise shook her head. "Don't have the mind for it. Can't seem to concentrate. Plus, my eyes are going bum."

"Why don't you get glasses?"

"Ha!" Denise sputtered, indicating that she hadn't the money or the inclination. "Can you picture me in specs?"

"Why, sure," Tiger said, but he actually couldn't.

Tiger and Denise sat silent for a few moments, their unacquaintedness weighing heavy between them. She stared off onto Mermaid Avenue through the smeared windows. "What would you say if I told you I had a kid once? A little boy."

"Once? What happened to him?"

"I gave him away. It was the best I could do for him. I ain't cut out to be nobody's mother." Tiger wanted to disagree but he surmised she was right.

"What was his name?" Tiger wondered.

A weak smile curved Denise's lips. "I named him for my Da, the one man who ever treated me like a queen. Stanley. I named him Stanley."

Tiger felt a sharp claw dig into the pit of his stomach. He saw a blonde woman at his father's casket, a doughy face in the shadows of the Stumble Inn almost ten years earlier, a suitcase by her feet, the brief swell of her belly, and then, like smoke, the image was gone.

Chapter Thirteen

Afternoon Tea

Tiger woke in the snug, soft sheets of his childhood bedroom. Beside him, his brother's cot was empty. Judging by the sounds filtering in from the kitchen, it was past breakfast time. When Tiger listened closer, he heard the heavy, dense timbre of supper being made—chopping, as opposed to stirring, and pots being navigated. He had the vague recollection of coming home late, the iciness of the El, and before that, a chaste kiss on the cheek from a broken-down lady. What was her name? Diane? Dolores? Denise? It was Denise.

Was there also an affectionate, enveloping hug from Denise? From what Tiger remembered, it was as though she draped her body over and around his. Or was he just dreaming it? Was there the quick slip of a tongue in his mouth, lips which tasted faintly of chocolate, leaving him aroused and horrified all at once? Or did he dream this, too?

Tiger felt the weight of a late night upon his brow and a sweet ache in his bladder. He didn't remember how much he drank but seemed to recall a short, angry man named Roy in Ruby's, a barkeep named Dermott, and Doreen. Or was it Denise? Yes, Denise. During the two days Tiger had been home, Stan had chattered about someone he called the Yellow Queen who often followed him and Wendy to school. Tiger noticed how Rose visibly stiffened when Stan mentioned the woman. Now Tiger knew for certain why— because the Yellow Queen was Denise, Stan's birth mother. Tiger was sure of it, even though he didn't dare say anything about it to her.

Leaning against the cool bathroom tiles, Tiger emptied his bladder, noticing the clean smell of Kirkman's soap and bleach, permeated by the pungent, alcoholic stench of his own piss. How many mornings had he heard his father "drain the dragon" after a night of being overserved? Tiger was unclear about what he wanted to do with his life but there was one certainty—he didn't want to be his father.

Now in corduroy slacks, a wash-softened flannel shirt and slippers (the latter a Christmas gift from the day before), Tiger made his way into the kitchen. Rose's face brightened when she saw him. She kept trimming the *prosciutto*, then chopped it. The onion had already been coaxed from its papery jacket and minced. "Cup of tea?" Rose asked expectantly.

Tiger nodded. "I think I can keep down a cup of tea."

"Piece of toast, too?"

"Just the tea," Tiger said.

Rose busied herself with the complexities of tea-making. She fished a few bags out from the tin where she stashed the tea. Its top was embossed with the company's name, Lipton's, and "THE MOST DELICIOUS THE WORLD PRODUCES" in bold, slightly tarnished letters. Tea balls... Rose called them "tea balls," Tiger remembered. She selected "his" mug from the cupboard. It was brown inside and out. The water in the kettle began to hiss soon after Rose lit the burner with a match. "When did I come in this morning?" Tiger asked her.

"About three," she said, without judgment. "I heard the bells at St. Catherine's."

"I'm not going to do that again," Tiger stated with a finality.

"You're a man now," Rose told him. "You've been to war. You can do whatever you please."

Tiger stepped close to his mother, who was reaching for the sugar bowl. It was tawny and hive-shaped with a honeybee on its lid. Rose put it on the table. When Tiger kissed the side of her head, he felt her smile. "I'm not going to drink. Not like that," he clarified. Rose caught the kettle before it started to howl and turned off the flame beneath it. "I don't like the way it makes me feel," Tiger added.

"Ah, the hair of the dog," Rose offered, pouring water over the flo-thru tea bags she'd stuffed into Pip's pot.

"More than that," he said. "It makes me feel bad. Like I'm following in his footsteps."

"You're nothing like him," Rose admitted, bringing her son the cup.

Tiger stirred in a heaping teaspoon of sugar from the bowl. Then he added a splash of milk from the glass bottle which came from the dairy where his father had worked when Tiger's parents started keeping company. Borden Dairy. Tony had delivered milk with a horse and cart. His father used to regale Tiger and Kewpie with stories of how Tony's horse Gertie knew the way to Rose's doorstep. That's how often he would visit his beau. They would all laugh no matter how often Tony recounted the story—until something set him off. Tony was a mean drunk. Usually, it was a harmless comment which got his goat, and then supper, if not the entire day, would be ruined. Tiger remembered a time when...

"Honest, you're not," Rose told her son.

"Not what?" Tiger asked.

"Like him. Like your Pa." Rose placed a Christmas sugar cookie on a paper napkin in front of him.

"I hope not," Tiger said. He took a bite. It was crumbly and sweet. "You do these the same way?"

Rose nodded. "The dough rolled flat with a wooden rolling pin then cut out with a jelly glass. Just how we used to when you were little."

Tiger smiled. "Some things never change."

Finished with her chore of trimming the *prosciutto*, Rose was now searing it in oil in the heavy pot. She stirred it with a wooden spoon so it would brown evenly. It sizzled so loudly Rose had to raise her voice to speak above it. Next, she added the onion, still stirring. "You've changed, though," his mother said.

"How so?"

Rose fished around into an already-opened can of whole plum tomatoes, fit one into her fist, and squeezed it into the pot. "You look thinner, older, more serious. You must have seen some bad business over there, Anthony." She did the same with another tomato, stirring the sauce with her free hand.

"Yes," he admitted. "But also some incredible things… the sunset over Pisa. Snow on the Alps. Buddhist temples in Tokyo. The grateful sobs of a woman I gave a loaf of bread. The smile of a boy I gave a chocolate bar. It all evens out, I suppose. The good and the bad."

"I like to think so," Rose stated, squashing another tomato. When she had squeezed them all into the pot, she rinsed the inside of the can with a splash of water then added it into the sauce as well. She mixed it thoughtfully with a wooden spoon.

"Is that the same spoon I made in Mr. Alson's shop class?" Tiger wondered.

"It broke right after you went overseas," she told him. "This one, Stan made."

"Mr. Alson still around?" Tiger asked. She told him he was.

Rose was like an alchemist now, adding a few twists of ground black pepper, one pinch then another of dried basil. With a teaspoon, Rose tasted the gravy, smacked her lips, was pleased with the result. She filled a second spoon, blew on it and held it out for Tiger to sample. It was deep and complex, sure and solid, the color of the "Terry" bricks which comprised the building they were standing in. (Tiger knew the bricks' origin because his Uncle John had a job briefly at the Terry Brick Factory upstate in Kingston, and had told him so.) "It's good," he told her.

They sat at the kitchen table, sipping their Lipton. After a time, Rose stood to check on the sauce. "I met her," Tiger said.

"Her who?"

"Stan's mother." The spoon dropped from Rose's hand and into the pot, splashing the Wellbilt's top, but she uttered not a word. "I saw her once when I was a boy," Tiger continued. "At the Stumble Inn. She looks different now but I'm sure it's her. I ran into her at Coney Island. In a bar. She's in a bad way."

Rose spoke harshly through her teeth in a voice which wasn't hers. "She should rot in hell, that one."

"We're all God's children," Tiger said plainly. It was something Rose used to tell him as a boy the rare occasions he'd been mean-spirited.

"Not all," Rose admitted. "Not her." She gave the sauce one final mix with the wooden spoon then covered the pot. She poured herself another cup of tea, but didn't drink. Instead, she stirred it silently.

"She doesn't want Stan back," he promised her. "I mean, how can she take care of him? She can barely take care of herself."

Rose looked at her son. Tiger didn't think he'd ever encountered eyes as mournful as his mother's could be. Eyes which could sparkle with an equal joy, depending on the occasion. "She just wants to see that he's okay," Tiger pushed. "I'm sure of it."

"Why wouldn't he be okay?" Rose took a deep sip of the hot liquid, wincing. "He calls her 'The Yellow Queen,' you know. He watches her watching him. Wendy, too. That witch shows up at school. Harry tried talking to her but there's no talking to that one."

"Does Stan realize who she is?"

"No," Rose said emphatically. "I'm certain he doesn't."

She warmed Tiger's tea with a splash from Pip's teapot. "Does he know he's not…"

"But he *is* ours," Rose added quickly.

"I know he is. I wasn't going to ask that."

"He doesn't suspect he's adopted, if that's what you're getting at. He's my son, Anthony, he's my son like you are."

Tiger nodded. "He is, Ma. Stanley's my brother. Not my half-brother. My brother. Just like he's your son."

Rose trembled as she raised the cup of tea to her pursed lips. It was then Tiger noticed the two neat rows of tears streaming down her face, yet she was smiling. Tiger reached across the table for his mother's hand and held it. He rubbed her fingers, raw from all the holiday cooking, and the scrubbing of pots, pans, and dishes. She didn't pull away.

The apartment door burst open and knocked against the wall. Without looking, both Tiger and Rose deduced it was the boy—this was Stanley's way of making an entrance: an eruption, a circus child shot from a cannon. Stan cringed at the noise he created. "Sorry, Ma," he shrugged, red-faced from the cold.

"Slow down, cowboy," Tiger told him, grinning.

Although some might accuse Stan of bounding wildly through the world, as many almost-nine-year-olds do, nothing got past the boy. He noticed every trick, took the whole of it in, took it all to heart, every ragman and street beggar, every abandoned kitten. Perhaps this was because Stan had once been abandoned himself, even though he didn't know it yet. This built-in empathy was part of who the boy was. "Why are you so blue?" Stan asked his mother.

"I'm not blue," she said.

"Then why are you crying?" he wondered.

"Didn't you ever cry for happy?" Tiger demanded. Rose wiped her eyes on her evergreen-embossed apron.

"No," Stanley declared. "But I'm not even nine so there's still time." He took the bottle from the table and poured some milk into a glass covered with a spray of starbursts which reminded Stan of silent fireworks. Then he grabbed three treats from the tray: oatmeal, chocolate chip and sugar.

"One at a time," Rose said. Stan put back two, keeping the oatmeal after brief consideration. "Gloves off. Coat off. Hat off." Stanley did the three in reverse order then sat like a gentleman, feet flat on the linoleum. (He knew "Sit down" would have been Rose's next command.)

Stan dove into a detailed litany of what he'd been doing up until that very moment: built a snowman in the front yard with Wendy, constructed half of an igloo in the backyard with Poppa supervising, had hot chocolate with Grandma Bridget, had a snowball fight with Darius, the mean boy from Forty-Fifth Street who put rocks in his snowballs and thought no one knew, had another cup of cocoa with his sister Angela across the way, and then came home.

While the boy talked excitedly, scarcely taking a breath, Tiger and Rose smiled at each other. Rose couldn't remember what her life had been without Little Stan in it, except perhaps quiet. Yes, it had definitely been more quiet, but it had also been more empty. Sully was as fond of the boy as Rose was; they all were, and no one could imagine Stanley not permeating their days with a sense of awe and wonder at even the simplest thing. And suddenly that bleached blonde crone turned up after almost a decade, without warning, like a sudden snow squall.

"What does she really want?" Rose asked Tiger after Stan bounded back down the stairs and outside, refueled, refreshed and thawed. Tiger and his mother stood beside each other, her washing the tea dishes, him drying.

"You'll have to ask her," Tiger told Rose.

"Oh, I couldn't!" Rose cried. "I couldn't even be in the same room with that awful woman." The saucer slipped from Rose's soapy grip and cracked against the porcelain sink. It broke straight down the center and wedged itself neatly in half. A trickle of Rose's blood went down the drain in a crimson ribbon. Tiger carefully scooped up the sharp dish and put the pieces to the side.

"He's legally ours," Tiger reminded her. "You and Sully adopted him after you got married."

"But she's his ma," Rose declared mournfully. "She's his blood."

"We are, too. Me and Kewpie. It counts for something, doesn't it?" Tiger fished a scrap of discarded wrapping paper from the trash, bound the broken plate in a golden snowflake pattern, and pushed it deep into the pail. "I think now's the time," Tiger told her. "I think you've got to tell Stan."

"No!" Rose said emphatically. She stood at the sink, gripping the sides, breathing deeply. "I'll have to think about it, mull it over with Sully," Rose said, wiping her hands on a chrysanthemum tea towel. The bleeding had stopped. Rose couldn't detect the place where she'd been cut. Soon, she would forget all about it. But other scars didn't heal as well.

"Rose! Rose!" Bridget's voice rang out from the landing below.

"Coming!" Rose answered, untying her apron. "I'll be right back. Keep an eye on the sauce," Rose said to Tiger, then went downstairs to find out what her mother needed. When the door opened moments later, Tiger thought it was Rose returning. Instead, his sister came in. Angela lowered herself into the kitchen chair beside Tiger and sighed. "I'm big as a house," she told him.

"You look beautiful, Kewpie. Like a beautiful house."

"Thank you," she conceded. "It's 'Angela' now, though. Remember?"

"Pardon me, Astrid," Tiger ribbed his sister.

"Hey, Angela is my real name, not like her. Besides, 'Kewpie' was another person."

Tiger tried the name on for size. "Angela...I don't think I ever called you that before."

"Well, you can call me 'Angie,' if you prefer."

"Gee, thanks."

Angela heaved herself up from the chair and peeked into the pot. "Boy, oh boy, *prosciutto* sauce. I usually get plain old *marinara*."

"I *am* her favorite," Tiger said. They both laughed. When they were growing up, Rose swore she had no favorites; that she loved each one best. Meanwhile, Poppa would tell them he also had no favorites; that he disliked each of them equally. Of course, they realized he was joking.

"How about you?" Angela wondered. "You're a man. Aren't you sick of being called 'Tiger'?"

Tiger bit into a ginger snap and shook his head. "Poppa gave me that name."

Angela took her seat beside him again. She admitted, "He gave me the name 'Kewpie,' too, but…"

Tiger finished for her. "…but you hear him calling you that." *Him* being their father.

"Yelling it," Angela corrected. "In that terrifying voice. It sounded like a bark or a growl. And I'm not the same girl anymore, Anthony."

Tiger smiled. "Anthony was his name."

"No one ever called him that."

"Still…"

"I'll keep calling you 'Tiger' then."

"I'd like it if you did." After a beat, he added. "I saw her yesterday, his old beau. His *goumada*."
Angela noticeably stiffened. "I heard she'd been around, skulking about like a rat."

"Do you remember when we saw her with him at Coney?"

"You were on the carousel and dropped the brass ring," Angela said. "Seeing them ruined a perfectly nice day."

"But we got through it, Kewpie," Tiger told his sister. "We survived."

"It's Angela," she reminded him, and served herself some tea.

Chapter Fourteen

Music Box Mine

Christmas vacation moved far too fast for Stanley's liking. The days slid one into the next, as if slipping by on ice. He couldn't understand how the time in school dragged snail-slow but the holidays sped by as if on a conveyer belt. Stan's winter break was peppered with countless possibilities. One day he, Wendy and Tiger went sledding in Owl's Head Park. It was a long trek but well worth it because of the killer hills, the steepest outside of Green-Wood. Only who in their right mind would want to go sleigh-riding in a cemetery, even without the danger of the guards catching you. That's why they opted for Owl's Head. The trio also went ice-skating in Prospect Park but none of them could get the hang of it.

Angela and Tiger finally took Wendy and Stan to the Saturday matinee of *House of Dracula* at the Loew's 46th. They hit the jackpot because Augie was working that day. He not only got them in for free but even let the kids choose one movie-sized box of candy of their own. (Stan picked Black

Cows and Wendy, nonpareils.) Augie was able to watch part of the picture with them. Out of the corner of his eye, Stan noticed his brother-in-law rubbing Angela's belly as he sat beside her. The movie scared Wendy so much she dug her nails into Stan's wrist and actually drew blood. Some people didn't appreciate a good fright, Angela explained to him later. Stan himself had to sleep with the nightlight on for three days because the film was a triple threat—it included the Wolf Man, Dracula and the Frankenstein Monster. They all agreed that John Carradine outshone Bela Lugosi as Count Dracula but missed the humanity of Boris Karloff's Monster. "Glenn Strange just doesn't cut the mustard," Stan conceded.

Once during Christmas week, Tiger even brought Stan all the way to Manhattan. "It'll be boys' night out," he told Stan. "Just you and me on the prowl." Tiger managed to nab tickets to Radio City Music Hall's Christmas Spectacular. It would mark Stan's first time at the opulent theatre. As Rose helped him get dressed for the outing, she recalled her first visit there and how she'd marveled at the finery—all of the gold, the red velvet and the graceful folds of the curtains. It made the Loew's 46th, and even the Fortway, pale in comparison.

Rose combed Stan's hair so straight it hurt and even rubbed in Kreml Hair Tonic to keep his cowlick in place. But it didn't last for long. Stan could feel his unruly shock of hair creeping up in the middle of the show as a striking, brunette ballerina named Helen Wood simultaneously played violin and danced in a number called "Music Box Mine."

Cowlick and all, Stan felt very grown up as he headed to the City with Tiger. Maybe this had to do with the fact that when Stan walked to the El with his big brother, Tiger didn't clutch his hand like Rose did, as though she were afraid someone might snatch Stan away if she didn't. Since Tiger had been overseas in the War, he knew that nothing, not even holding onto someone as tightly as you could, made any difference. They could still suddenly slip away without warning.

Side by side, Stan and Tiger crunched through the light layer of shoveled snow on the sidewalks, Stan in his galoshes (so as not to ruin his dress shoes) and Tiger in his military-issue boots. It was shivery on the train platform which loomed high above the streets but Stan steeled himself against the cold. He tried not to hunker down and shudder, and did his best to emulate his brother's dignified, armed-services posture. It looked almost as though Tiger had an oaken rod running up his spine, even when he sat. Tiger smiled at Stan and wound the boy's scarf tighter around his neck, a scarf Bridget had knitted with deft fingers as gnarled as tree trunks.

The brothers spied the West End train coming down the tracks several stations away, its lights bobbing and nodding in the dimming daylight. "My father used to work on the trains," Tiger said to the boy when the doors opened in front of them. He neglected to mention the fact that Tiger's father was also Stanley's father.

"You told me once," Stan recalled. "A long time ago." The doors slammed behind them. It was entirely possible that the conductor had tipped back a few as their father had been known to, especially when the weather was wintery. "What did he do?" Stan wondered. "Drive the train?"

"Nothing so important," Tiger said. "My Pa liked the drink. He couldn't be trusted as a motorman."

"Did you ever go in with him?"

"A few times," Tiger admitted.

"Was it fun?"

"Not really. It was pretty boring."

"Did he ever let you work the doors?" Stan asked.

"It wasn't allowed."

"Aw, nuts. I bet that would have been a kick."

When the train's doors opened at Ninth Avenue, the last stop outside, there was a gush of frigid air. A man and woman, bundled up against late December, barreled in. The daylight faded as the train burrowed into the tunnel. The sound of its wheels upon the steel tracks became louder indoors, so loud it became difficult to have a conversation.

"Was he nice, your father?" Stan wondered. The man and woman sitting across from them lifted their heads to hear Tiger's response.

"When he wanted to be," Tiger conceded. "But he drank a lot and it made him mean sometimes."

"I'm glad mine doesn't drink," Stan told him. The boy assumed Sully was his father and no one had ever said any different. Sully was the only dad Stan had ever known, and Rose, the only mother he remembered. It was easy to let Stan go on believing this fantasy, at least for a little while longer.

"You're lucky," Tiger smiled.

Miss Subways, "Lovely Rita Cuddy," shed her light upon Tiger and Stan from her poster, which hung on the train's wall across from them. Rita had a friendly smile and her description said she had blue eyes but they looked gray in the picture. "I am," Stan admitted.

Beneath the dapper topcoat his Uncle Harry had grown out of, Tiger wore his Army dress uniform. He'd wanted to store it in mothballs but Stan begged Tiger to wear it on their trip to the City, just this once. He was proud of his brother and besides, Aunt Astrid and the others agreed that Tiger looked smart in it, and that the olive khaki brought out the green in Tiger's eyes. He felt self-conscious wearing his uniform because everyone made such a fuss. Worn down from Stan's pleas, Tiger agreed to wear his uniform for their Manhattan adventure. Rose even pressed it beforehand. As much as she tried not to cry, a few tears slipped out and onto the stiff material. They dried in a moment under the heat of the steam iron. Many sons didn't come home from the War; hers did. Rose was crying for them, for the lost boys. It was an honor to press Tiger's uniform and a joy to have him home.

The ride to midtown Manhattan was long and slow. Soon, Stan tired of talking and his head grew heavy, lulled by the motion of the train. Tiger felt his brother's head lolling, then finally resting on his shoulder. He liked the sweet weight of it. How many times did Tiger do this on his sister's shoulder when he was Stan's age? History repeats itself again and again. Not solely in bad ways, but in good ways, too.

To avoid being roasted by the train's heater, Tiger moved his heavy boots around in a silent tap dance, a Brooklyn version of Gene Kelly, the hoofer/actor who had recently replaced Fred Astaire in Poppa's heart. The old fellow usually called him "Kelly Gene" by mistake but Tiger always knew who he meant. "That Kelly Gene can really cut a rug," Poppa had exclaimed, wondering if Tiger had seen *Anchors Aweigh* overseas. (He hadn't.) "And that Frank Sinatra fella sure can sing…he's not from the dancers, though." For some reason, Poppa never mangled Italian names, just Irish ones.

In the overheated train car, Tiger opened the front of his coat, exposing the top of his uniform, just a few bars and stripes. The couple sitting across from Tiger and Stan, now thawed and rosy-cheeked, smiled at the young soldier and the young boy. "You're a good father," the woman told him. Tiger nodded his thanks and didn't bother admitting to her that Stan was his brother, not his son.

As the couple exited the train at Fourteenth Street, the man saluted Tiger. "Thank you for your service, soldier," he said. "Welcome back."

Again, Tiger nodded. "I'm lucky to be home."

At Thirty-Fourth Street, Tiger thought of waking Stan so they could look at the decorations in Macy's windows and walk the mile to Radio City, but the weather was too cold. With the sun going down soon, it would grow even more frozen. Tiger also wanted to guarantee there was time enough to eat. He had promised Stan they could have supper wherever he chose, and the boy puzzled over it for days.

Tiger began to gently rouse Stan so by the time the train rolled into Forty-Second Street, the next stop, the boy would be fully awake. First, Tiger nudged Stan's shoulder. His head bobbed. Then he flicked at Stan's nose. The boy woke with a start. "Are we there yet?" he wondered.

"Almost," Tiger said. "You still want to go to the Automat?"

"Do I?" Stan grinned. "Wendy told me all about it. I can't wait!"

"The one in Times Square is the grandest I've ever seen."

Christmastime, the streets surrounding the Great White Way were more crowded than usual. People politely zipped every which way, the men doffing their hats, the women clinging to their escorts' arms, the children wide-eyed at the lights, traffic, and activity. Stan instinctively held Tiger's hand as they waited to cross Sixth Avenue. Rose instructed him to do this once they got to the City. Tiger liked the roughness of his brother's woolen mitten in his palm. The mittens had also been made by Bridget and matched the scarf around Stan's neck. Curiously, these were the only mittens the boy would wear because they'd been knitted by her.

Horn & Hardart's Times Square location was nothing short of magnificent, especially to a young boy. Both of its brass doors shone and the silvery filigree above them was spotless. Red neon block letters announcing its name in a field of black beckoned you inside. The words were flanked by bright red signage which declared "Automat." Inside, the ceilings were high and the whole place glowed. Beyond the revolving doors, an elegantly-coiffed woman sat in a glass booth with a bucket of nickels and rubber tips on her fingers.

Tiger let the boy choose the shiny, lacquered table where they would eventually sit. It was close to the silver wall where the food lay behind little glass windows. Tiger himself would have picked a more private table in the back, but Stan was clearly in awe and didn't want to miss a heartbeat. When he took off his coat, Tiger became even more conscious of his uniform; the other men were in civilian clothes. But Stan was only aware of one thing: the marvel of the automat.

"How do they get the food in there?" Stan puzzled.

"The kitchen's behind the wall," Tiger told him. "The workers put the plates of food onto the shelves and replace each plate once it's taken."

"Wow…"

"Come on, let's eat. I'm starving." The boy stayed put, amazed at the profusion of food on passing people's trays: pot pies, macaroni and cheese, creamed spinach, baked beans, Salisbury steak, mashed turnips, prune and apricot pie, and even coffee, which was dispensed from a spigot. It was the kind of food you didn't find in Bridget or Rose's kitchen.

"I don't know where to start," Stan said.

"Let's take a quick look see," Tiger suggested. "They're famous for their chicken pot pie and spinach." Stan wrinkled his nose at the mention of "spinach." But Tiger assured him, "Trust me, you'll like it. It reminds me of Grandma's *minestra*."

Stan was perplexed at how almost a dozen vegetables, including potatoes, carrots, celery spinach, onions, and garlic and spices, plus hunks of stale Italian bread, boiled to a smooth pulp then savagely beaten with a wooden spoon could taste so delicious. Or clean out a body so effectively and abruptly as *minestra* did. In light of this, Stan resigned himself to try Horn & Hardart's creamed spinach, but only on the stipulation that he could have a slice of pie afterwards. Only which one? The banana was piled six inches high, toppling over with the weight of the fresh whipped cream, while the coconut...

Tiger eased his brother out of his pie trance. "First dinner. Then pie. If you have room."

They made their way back to the woman in the glass booth. Tiger tried to buy a stack of nickels but she waved his cash away and pushed him a roll of coins. "Your money's no good here, soldier," she said to him with a wide, snaggletooth smile. "It's on the house." "Audrey," as her nametag silently proclaimed, gestured to the manager, who kept an eye on the proceedings at the Times Square Automat, possibly H&H's busiest. Tiger began to protest but Audrey cupped her hand over his, closing the roll of nickels inside. "Take it," she whispered to him. "These old Hungarians are tight with a dollar, so when they offer to pay for your meal..." Tiger nodded; he understood. "He lost his son and nephew at Anzio," the girl went on. "It's important you let him do this for you."

Tiger felt tears rising in his throat. He nodded twice, perhaps one nod for each lost boy, then and walked away, leading Stan to the wall of chrome and glass. When Tiger looked up to find the manager to thank him, the man was gone. Yes, this would definitely mark the last time Tiger wore his uniform in public.

Little placards beneath each food window announced what awaited inside. They made their selections. Tiger opted for the coconut custard pie—the chocolate and banana cream reminded him of the time he'd spent with Denise in Coney Island—and tapioca pudding, too. The boy delighted in putting nickels into the slots, turning the knob, hearing the door click open, lifting the door and helping himself to the food almost as much as he enjoyed the food itself. Although Tiger had warned Stanley to take it slow, the table was covered with plates. 'Your eyes are bigger than your stomach,' Rose often warned Stan, as she had with Tiger when he'd been the boy's age. And it was true, as it is with most children.

"I'm going to ask Poppa if he could build a wall of those windows between the kitchen and the dining room," he told Tiger, bacon-flecked baked beans filling his mouth. "Poppa can build anything."

"Grandma Bridget wouldn't go for it," Tiger said. "She likes watching people enjoy her food. It wouldn't be the same having them grab it through little glass doors."

There was a tumbler of chocolate milk for Stan and a cup of coffee for Tiger, who let Stan pump it from the dispenser. It was special coffee, Tiger had explained, tempered with chicory, the way they serve it in New Orleans, a city down south Tiger had read about and always hoped to visit. His Army buddy George was from The Big Easy, Tiger continued. He let Stan take a sip from his cup. Unimpressed, the boy announced that it "wasn't as bad" as normal coffee but needed some sugar.

"I can't wait to tell Grandma Bridget about this," Stan gulped between bites. "Poppa, too."

"Oh, they've been here," Tiger said. "But not for a long while."

"They're pretty old," Stan concluded. "Aren't they?"

"I guess they are," Tiger admitted, then sampled the macaroni and cheese. The *ziti rigati* was crispy on the outside and bathed with a creamy cheese on the inside. "But then, I thought they were ancient when I was your age, and here they are, still alive and ticking," Tiger added.

The boy dug his fork into a fish cake. It made a little crunching sound as it broke through the golden-brown breading. He made a grunt of pleasure at first bite. Tiger tried it next. Stan was right; it was good. Lulled into a contented place from their supper, Tiger decided this was the perfect opportunity to plunge into talk of Stan's past. "What do you remember about your childhood?" he ventured. "When you were very small."

Stan thought for a moment. "Lots of people, lots of noise, but happy noise. The sounds of people yapping, eating, laughing, cooking together. I remember playing under the kitchen table while Grandma Bridget and Momma made supper together."

"With my lead soldiers. I used to do the same."

"Boy, how Grandma would curse when she stepped on one of them, or on the dog."

"Butchie. That Pomeranian was always underfoot," Tiger admitted.

"'You dirty stink! I'll break your nut!'" Stan cursed, just like Bridget.

Tiger smiled. "Remember anything before then? For instance, when you were a baby?"

Stan pierced the crust of the chicken pot pie and let the steam escape before taking a forkful of the succulent meat and vegetables in a sea of creamy gravy. "Not much. Being carried everywhere or looking up at the street, the trees, the houses, from the carriage. And a party. A huge party."

"It was probably Angie and Augie's wedding," Tiger told him.

"No, I remember that one. I was real little. My christening?"

"Nah," Tiger said. "You couldn't possibly remember your baptism. You were a babe in arms then." Tiger took a chunk of pot pie. It was piping hot and burned the roof of his mouth, so scorching his eyes watered. "I have no clue what that shindig might have been," Tiger lied.

The party Stan described had been Rose and Sully's wedding; Stanley's baptism transpired days after he'd been left on the Paradiso doorstep. The party was a quick, serene celebration in Poppa and Grandma Bridget's dining room, seamlessly incorporated into the next Sunday dinner.

The two brothers managed to make a dent in the food covering the table, almost cleaning their plates. A Colored man in a white jacket came by with a pot of coffee—they hadn't noticed anyone getting their mugs refilled. Tiger gratefully accepted the coffee. "My cousin Tremaine was KIA in Normandy," the man explained, a touch of chicory in his speech, like the coffee. "God bless you," he choked.

To which Tiger replied, "I'm sorry" and "Thank you" and "God bless you, too."

"What's KIA mean?" Stan wondered after the man had left.

"Killed in action," Tiger said plainly. Yes, he would definitely pack his uniform in moth balls and store it in a box in the back of the basement bin, perhaps as soon as he got home. It was starting to itch uncomfortably.

It seemed to Stan that the entire world was right there in Times Square. There were people from all walks of life, fancy ladies in furs as thick as a wolf's hide with diamonds on their fingers—or were they rhinestones?—as dazzling as the stars in the brittle winter sky above them. There were beggar ladies selling apples along Broadway. (And really, who wanted a rotten, old apple with the H&H Automat so nearby?) There were men with skin as shoe-polish dark as Gunga Din's, the star of Tiger's top movie, escorting women with painted red dots in the center of their foreheads who wore iridescent robes. There were inky-skinned Colored folks and beer-bottle brown people, too, bemused, smiling, and in their Sunday best. There were blondes with hair so blonde it was white and ginger-headed girls with seas of freckles so thick it made their skin look rusty. There was everybody from everywhere and it was all good. There were fat, mustard-colored taxicabs like swollen, metal bugs, buzzing through, and cars of every type: Fords, Packards, delivery trucks, Buicks, Studebakers and Chevys, vehicles as varied as the people who drove them.

Tiger had to tug his brother lightly along as Stan oohed and aahed over everything he saw. When they spotted a blind, one-legged bloke selling pencils, Stan wanted to buy one until Tiger pointed out the man's leg tucked inside his great, long coat. They saw an organ grinder with a dress-wearing monkey and a scribbled sign that read: "No pennies please!" There was a bum who sang opera as superb as Caruso. When they saw these poor unfortunates, Stan felt guilty. Although his family wasn't rich, there was "just enough," as Poppa always pointed out, while the Times Square beggars barely had the wherewithal to keep from starving.

So, when Tiger rushed Stan past a skeleton-framed girl in a dirty, ragged shift without a coat, the boy dug deep into his pocket and gave her the quarter he'd been saving to buy his Ma a trinket from Radio City. He also gave the girl the unwrapped sucker he was saving for the middle of the show. Although it had grown fuzzy in his pocket, he didn't think she'd mind. The girl, with her hollow, hunted eyes, was too stunned to thank him. Stan and Tiger walked on as she popped the hard candy into her mouth and sucked so intensely, her cheeks caved in.

It was only about eight blocks from Times Square to Radio City Music Hall but Stan felt as though they'd moved through an assortment of hemispheres along the way. He was suddenly very tired...until he saw the theatre. Stan's spirit leapt in joy as he spotted the red, white and yellow letters soaring up toward the night sky. Electric blue lights surrounded it, making the whole façade glow like gems.

In the near distance, a church bell rang out on the half-hour, deeper and throatier than the bells of St. Catherine's. "What's that?" Stanley asked.

"The bells of St. Patrick's Cathedral. It's one block to the east," Tiger said. "A cathedral is bigger and fancier than a regular church. Why, four of St. Cat's back home could fit inside St. Pat's."

"Can we go see it?" Stan wondered.

"Let's save it for another time," his brother suggested. "You've had enough excitement for one day. And it's far from over."

Tiger had the show tickets in his breast pocket. He gave them to Stan so he could have the grown-up job of giving them to the ticket taker. This was something Poppa had done every Wednesday with Tiger when they went to his childhood Dish Nights at the Loew's 46th. It was an awesome responsibility, and Tiger often feared he'd lose them on the few steps from ticket booth to ticket taker but he never did.

Although Stan did almost drop the tickets when he caught a glimpse of Radio City Music Hall's Grand Foyer beyond the lobby, paneled in warm, golden wood, with a sweeping, twisting staircase which led to a mural. Even though their seats were in the orchestra section, Tiger suggested they go upstairs to the mezzanine level so Stan could take a closer look. The mural depicted a scene of mountains, hills, clouds and trees, perhaps in China. There was an old man in it with a staff who gazed out upon the landscape. Stan thought he looked vaguely like Mr. Wong. "It's called 'The Fountain of Youth,'" Tiger told him.

"How do you know so much stuff?" Stan gasped.

"I read," Tiger said. "You learn a lot when you read."

"Ah, fudge," Stan groaned but he supposed it was so. He vowed to read more but probably wouldn't.

In the center of the Grand Foyer was the *piece de resistance*—a giant chandelier with hundreds of cut-glass pieces, teardrops strung with gold. It was flanked by countless lights, long tubes lit from within, probably as tall as Tiger if not taller.

His brother asked if Stanley needed to use the restroom. Of course, he did. The men's room seemed the size of a dancehall with shiny black floor tiles intersected by silver diamond-shaped ones. The sinks were turquoise pedestals. There had to be at least twenty urinals, whose porcelain went all the way down to the floor, and a long row of stalls. It was so sparkly, you could probably eat off the floor or drink from the urinals but Stan decided not to. He did his business in a stall, too self-conscious to pee in front of grown men. He didn't talk to anyone just as his brother had instructed. "Boy, you should see the john!" Stan bubbled to Tiger when he returned. The people within earshot chuckled at Stan's wonderment over the lavatory.

Radio City Music Hall was so impressive that Stan almost forgot to give the man the tickets. After they were torn, Stan handed the stubs back to Tiger, who returned one to Stan in case he had to revisit the bathroom. He was so excited he might just have to. Stan decided he would keep the program forever and that he might even read it. Well, at least part of it.

The theatre itself was a study in gold. There were no columns to spoil the view and it was so huge, it looked as vast as a football field. Sweeping arches curved at the ceiling. Staircases rose up the side toward the back walls. The curtain across the stage was a shimmering gold.

"It's the largest indoor theatre in the world," Tiger said.

"Man, oh, man," exclaimed Stanley.

"Look at the curtain," Tiger gestured. Stan nodded. "Also the biggest in the world."

And if that weren't enough, Tiger continued, "There are twenty-five thousand plus lights in this place."

The sound of a pipe organ startled Stan and made him jump. "Relax, it's only 'The Mighty Wurlitzer,'" Tiger explained. "The pipes range in size from a few inches to thirty-two feet. They're kept in eleven different rooms, if you can believe it."

"Oh, I can believe it," Stan told Tiger, even though he had a tough time taking it all in. The boy didn't want to forget a thing, and he never wanted to leave.

"The fellow who designed Radio City Music Hall called it 'An American People's Palace.' Donald Deskey went for grandeur over glitz, elegance over excess. I think he did a bang-up job. How about you?"

"I wish I could live here," Stan sighed. A couple behind them chuckled when they heard his response.

The theatre went dark, so dark Stanley couldn't see his hand in front of his face. His eyes soon adjusted. The acts were extraordinary, each better than the one before it. The Christmas pageant itself, with the Living Nativity onstage, including camels and sheep, was stunning—not to mention a special appearance by Santa himself in a sled drawn by the Rockettes. Stan couldn't believe how they could persuade a camel onstage, let alone how those leggy Rockettes managed that precision. Their high kicks left Stan breathless and with a strange tingling in the front of his slacks.

Stan's favorite part of the show, however, was a number called "Music Box Mine." He didn't know why. It wasn't the dancer's skimpy ballerina costume or her muscular legs. Maybe it was her joy in dancing and playing the violin at the same time, the stark simplicity of it. Or perhaps it was the fact that she looked right at Stan, in the center of row FF, seats which must have cost his brother a bundle but were worth every penny.

But Helen Wood, the Music Box Dancer, wasn't looking at Stan, he decided. She peered right through him, out into Radio City Music Hall's Grand Foyer and beyond. She gazed past the lights and the shadows and the fancy murals, wall coverings, lush carpets, precious metals and gold foil, then back into the very depths of the boy himself, as if to say, 'Isn't this wonderful? All of this?' It was a secret the two of them shared. The Music Box Dancer smiled benignly before the luminescent curtain came down between her and Stan, and went black again. But just for a moment.

Chapter Fifteen

Slip of the Tongue

Before anyone knew it, New Year's Eve was upon them. Bridget spent most of it where she was happiest—in her kitchen. True, it wasn't modern and the linoleum was curling up in a few places where it met the cabinets Poppa had built years earlier (with a little help from Camille's John), but the kitchen was her domain. Bridget kept it scrupulously clean. She preferred scrubbing the floor on her hands and knees with a rag and a bucket of Spic and Span to using a newfangled squeeze mop. But this was getting harder to do as time went on. Some days Bridget felt she needed one of the Navy Yard's cranes to lift her from her knees. She managed to rise on her own if she did it slowly, holding onto a chair to steady herself. Her daughters chided her for doing too much around the house, and even said they'd do the housework, but she always turned them down.

Bridget was in decent shape for an "old battle ax," as Poppa endearingly called her. She liked it even better was when he referred to her as "my old gal," because it had been decades since anyone thought of her as a gal or even a girl. Bridget would be seventy-five the next year, God willing, trailing Poppa's landmark birthday by six months. And they had celebrated their forty-seventh wedding anniversary in October. Who would have thought? Would they make it to fifty? Now, that would be something.

Bridget scattered a fistful of flour across the top of the butcherblock table, which was usually covered by an oilcloth, except when she was baking. It was before six in the morning and the sun hadn't come up yet. This last morning of 1945, everyone else in the house was asleep. It hadn't been the best year because for the bulk of it, the country had been at war. Then those awful bombs were dropped on Hiroshima and Nagasaki in August, ending the battling abruptly.

But good also happened in 1945. Tiger came home, Angela was pregnant again—and it looked like the baby would come to be, God willing. The girl wasn't nearly as frightened of losing the child as she'd been at the beginning of her pregnancy. In fact, Angela had recently grown round, radiant and pink-cheeked.

Bridget caressed the wooden tabletop as though it were the skin of a person she loved. Perhaps she did love this table, which held the silent voices of laughter from the wonderful meals which had been created upon it. The wood captured the feel of the vegetables chopped on its surface, the texture of the thick, marbled slabs of meat tenderized atop it, the tackiness of the cookie batter kneaded, risen and shaped upon it. The table retained the essence of the quick lunches and long, lingering cups of coffee with old friends, many gone, which had been enjoyed upon its surface. Then Bridget realized that she didn't love the table so much as she loved what it symbolized.

The dough was just right, having risen overnight in the deep Pyrex bowl Bridget had covered with a dishtowel. She left the bowl on top of the stove so the heat of the pilot lights would coax it to grow. Bridget was making lard bread, a dish which sounded terrible but tasted incredible. Oh, the way the dime-sized drops of pork fat melted on your tongue, a salty, smoky blessing. Bridget rolled out the dough with the ancient pin which had mellowed into a walnut shade from decades of being buffed by butter and olive oil. It felt good in her hands. After rolling out the dough, Bridget cut it into long strips with her sharp paring knife, precisely, in one fluid motion, like Dr. Lewis might use in the operating theatre.

Bridget had already browned the pork bellies in the cast iron skillet and was surprised the aroma hadn't roused Poppa. She noticed that her husband slept a lot more heavily lately, and a lot longer, his naps as he read the *Brooklyn Daily Eagle* growing lengthier and more frequent.

The crumbly bits of fat-laced meat waited patiently in the pan until Bridget was ready for them. She shifted the now-cool skillet to the table beside the strips of dough. With a pastry brush, Bridget painted the dough's skin with the rendered fat, humming happily. She began singing softly under her breath:

> *"Don't sit under the apple tree with anyone else but me,*
> *Anyone else but me, anyone else but me, no, no, no,*
> *Don't sit under the apple tree with anyone else but me*
> *Till I come marching home."*

On the next verse, a "no, no, no" and then a giggle joined Bridget. It was Stan, still in his pajamas, barefoot, without his winter slippers. "You'll catch your death of cold," Bridget told her grandson. It was her brusque but loving way of saying "hello."

"It's warm in here," Stan announced.

"That's because the oven's on," she said. Stan swooped in behind Bridget, hugging her, reveling in the flour and pork scent of his grandmother's skin. "I couldn't sleep," Stan yawned. Then before she could ask why, he added, "I was too excited."

"It's just another year, no big deal," Bridget smiled.

"I like New Year's Eve almost as much as Christmas," he admitted.

"Wash your hands," Bridget ordered, knowing he would want to help just as his brother did before him, and Rose did before that.

"They're clean," Stan protested, holding them up.

"Wash them anyway," she suggested. Stan did, at the kitchen sink. "Use soap," she added, without looking. Stan briefly slid his fingers across the cake of Kirkman's in the porcelain dish, dunked them in water then dried them on the dishtowel. He held them up for his grandmother's inspection. She nodded, "Good boy, Stanley."

"Can I do the painting? It's the best part," he admitted. Bridget passed Stan the pastry brush so he could coat the dough's surface with olive oil. In Stan's wake, Bridget drizzled bits of pork onto the glistening dough. When he was done with the brushing, Stan added the pork cracklings. Although he was more heavy-handed than she, Bridget didn't mention it. 'We each have our own ways of doing things,' she thought to herself. 'They're not right or wrong, only different.'

Next, Bridget doused the dough with pepper. There was enough salt in it from the cured pork, so she didn't have to add any, she explained to Stan. Bridget showed him how to roll up the dough into small, pinwheel-shaped mounds. Stan modeled her, all thumbs at first, but soon got the knack. When Stan and Bridget were through, there were a dozen little lard breads, sitting in a row like miniature, meaty beehives. Most, they would eat that night but a few Bridget would give to friends who had a fondness for the deliciously greasy treats. It was an acquired taste, to be sure, but one savored by those who appreciated the labor-intensive dish. One was for Dr. Lewis across the street and another was for Rose's friend, Sadie Lieberwitz. Although both were Jewish and kept Kosher, they suspended the rules once or twice a year for these delicacies.

"So, why do you like New Year's Eve so much?" Bridget finally asked her grandson when the lard bread was safely in the oven. She suspected it had to do with the noise of the holiday: the neighbors on their front porches banging pots and pans, people setting off "those damned firecracks" they'd judiciously saved from the Fourth of July. Even local churches got into the act, giving altar boys free rein to ring the bells madly at the stroke of twelve. This was why so many people in Brooklyn called midnight on New Year's Eve "The Bells"—because that's when all the church bells would ring.

Mothers would tell their sons, "It's okay for you to go out for a few drinks, just be home by The Bells."

Or fathers would tell their daughters, "Stay at home until The Bells. Then you can go out with your sweetheart."

And, "Come over before The Bells and have a nosh with us."

Unless you had experienced it yourself, it was impossible to know how stirring The Bells actually was. The whole of Brooklyn rose together in a disjointed song of church chimes which called out wildly every few blocks. In those days, Brooklyn had almost as many churches as it did bars; there seemed to be one on every street corner. The Bells enveloped you, surrounded you, resonated from deep inside your chest as you stood on your front stoop or leaned out your tenement's window and beat a wooden spoon against a pot to join the racket which welcomed in another year.

Stan considered his grandmother's question for a moment. He thought for so long that Grandma Bridget had already eased herself into a kitchen chair and was peeling an onion. She had a damp rag on the table beside her to absorb the onion's juices so it wouldn't make her cry when she chopped it. "I like New Year's so much because we're together," Stan began.

"We're together most holidays," Bridget told him. She put down the paring knife and placed a head of garlic in front of Stan. It was his job to separate the cloves and slip them from their paper coats. She didn't even have to instruct him to do it; he knew.

"Yes," Stan admitted. "But nothing else gets in the way. No turkey, no presents, no Easter eggs. There's just us."

Bridget slipped the onions into a waiting Pyrex bowl. Astrid had gotten her a set for Christmas, all the colors of the rainbow. "I saw them in *Gourmet* and...," she'd enlightened her mother.

"What are you doing reading *Gor-met*," John had asked, purposely mispronouncing the magazine's name to irk Astrid. "You don't even cook."

"Irregardless," Astrid had boomed. "You can be a gourmet and not cook. Pyrex is all the rage. You can mix, serve and store in the same bowl."

Whether Pyrex was rage-inducing or not, Bridget favored them because they were sturdy and dependable, like Poppa, who was still sound asleep two rooms away. "I can understand that," Bridget admitted to her youngest grandson. "Just us is more than enough sometimes."

Stan took a garlic clove, lay it on the cutting board, pressed the blade of a dull knife to it and slammed down on the blade with the meat of his palm. His violent act popped the garlic out of its thin cloak. Then he slid the naked garlic clove to Bridget. "Easy does it," she warned him. "You'll wake Poppa and you know how he needs his beauty sleep."

The boy tried to smash the next clove more calmly. Bridget chopped as the boy slammed, until the whole head of garlic was denuded, then finely minced. Next, Bridget chopped the fresh parsley. "What's the garlic for?" Stan wondered.

"Veal *spiedini*. They're your brother's favorite."

"Ma says veal is too dear."

"It is," Bridget conceded. "But then, so is your brother. I'm happy to have him home safe."

Bridget poured herself a second cup of coffee from the stainless-steel percolator pot. She put another mug on the table and slid it in front of Stan. "Only half a cup," she warned. "Any more will stunt your growth."

Again, Stan hugged Bridget around the waist, this time after she'd put the pot back on the range top. "Thanks, Grandma." He topped off the coffee with a heaping teaspoon of sugar and a swirl of cream.

Next, Bridget took what was left of yesterday's Italian bread from where it lay on the top of the stove. The pilot lights had warmed the enamel top and in turn, warmed the bread. She cut two thick hunks of bread, split them down the middle and coated them generously with butter. Bridget let Stan finish them off with a light sprinkle of sugar from between his fingertips. "*Basta*," she said. "You don't want to rot your teeth. Then you'll look like poor Mr. Smith around the corner."

For a brief second, Stanley pictured the friendly, goblin-toothed old man who lived in a tenement apartment on New Utrecht, under the El. Stan stopped his blizzard of sugar and folded the bread closed. He passed Bridget the slightly-larger piece. Wendy had told Stan that giving someone the bigger share was a sign of caring, and he believed her. Stan hoped his grandmother knew this, too. But then, Grandma Bridget seemed to know everything, so he was confident she knew that he loved her. She ruffled Stan's hair. Then she dipped the corner of her bread into her coffee, and he did the same.

Before long, the lard bread was ready to come out of the oven. Bridget sensed the perfect moment by its aroma, which was divine. The tops were golden and the tiny, charred dots of pork popped through, freckling the surface. Bridget was lulled into a soothing happiness from the heat of her kitchen, the scent of food enveloping her, and the company of her grandson. "Your father used to love these," Bridget said.

"Used to?" Stan questioned. "He still loves them."

A shiver prickled Bridget's skin. She cleared her throat and stared down at the floured tabletop; she couldn't bear to look the boy in the eye when she lied to him. "I mean, sure, he loves them, but they give him *agida*, so he..." Her voice trailed off, then she came back on track with, "You're right, he still loves them. Yes." Stan was staring at Bridget when she glanced at him. He was struggling to understand what had gotten his grandmother so flustered. But she wouldn't quit talking, "Like Poppa and my red peppers, huh? He loves them, only they don't love him. But a little Pepto-Bismol

197

sets him right, doesn't it? Like the time you ate a whole jar of *lupini* beans sitting under the kitchen table so no one could see."

"The Pepto made me upchuck," Stan reminded her.

"Sometimes that's the best thing," Bridget said, laughing nervously. "Why once, your brother Tiger ate an entire tin can of olives, hiding in the same spot. And I remember..."

But Stan wasn't listening anymore. What did Grandma Bridget mean? Wasn't Sully his father? Stan felt he belonged in that house, to those people, only when he thought about it, he'd never seen any pictures of himself as a young baby. He'd never seen snapshots of Rose pregnant with him—there were photos of her "expecting" with Tiger and Angela. Augie took so many snapshots of his sister bursting with child that she often asked him to stop. And Stan looked nothing like Sully or Rose, but he was the spitting image of Tiger, right down to the cowlick. So perhaps Stan did belong to them, he just wasn't sure where.

Maybe Grandma Bridget had a slip of the tongue, but then why was she so jittery and jumpy. Maybe Stan should ask her straight out, as he had the Christmas before, when he'd suspected this whole Santa Claus business was a ruse. Bridget had told Stan the truth then, and she would tell him the truth now. But maybe Stan didn't want to learn the truth. Because if he didn't belong to these people, then where did he belong?

Poppa disturbed Stan's thoughts and Bridget's soliloquy about various foods which had induced nausea throughout Paradiso Family history. "Who's making all this racket?" Poppa wondered. "Can't a guy get a little shut-eye?"

The old man was wearing his burgundy robe, the one with the pattern of feathers wafting down its silky material. Astrid called it a smoking jacket and got miffed whenever he called it a robe. "Sleeping in?" Bridget joked. "It's nearly seven. Why, if young Stanley wasn't here, I'd be lost."

Poppa's thin silvery hair was mussed from sleep. His eyes looked pin-sized, startled, mouse-like, because he wasn't wearing his spectacles. "What does a fella have to do for a cup of mud around here?" Poppa wondered. He chose a seat across the table from Bridget. She wiped the space in front of him clear of flour with a dishrag.

Stan hopped up, grabbed a mug from the cupboard and gingerly lifted the percolator. He poured his grandfather a cup of the steaming liquid and put it on the table. Poppa nodded his thanks to the boy before taking a deep sip. "Strong and black," Poppa proclaimed. "Like Lucifer himself." Bridget sighed and shook her head. "What's for breakfast?" Poppa wondered next.

"I just this minute pulled the lard bread out of the oven," Bridget said. Stan took out three plates, the everyday ones with the blue cornflower pattern. Bridget selected one of the bread pinwheels and cut it into three pieces. Stan could see moist spots where the juice of the crunchy pork had seeped through. Bridget placed a flowered plate in front of each of them, then broke off a piece of hers to taste it. "It's good," she declared.

"Of course, it's good," Poppa told her. "It's always good."

Bridget looked up at him and smiled, reaching for the hardboiled eggs, which had been cooling in a pan on the stove. Stan helped Bridget peel them, remembering the trick she'd taught him: breaking a nick in one of the rounded ends, peeling away a bit of shell then putting his lips to it and blowing to separate the invisible membrane from the egg itself. It worked like a charm, allowing the shell to be peeled away neatly from the egg. Bridget put the peeled ovals in another bowl until she was ready to chop them.

Poppa observed the scene contentedly, young boy and old woman toiling quietly together. Every so often, he had a sip of his coffee and a mouthful of lard bread. "What?" Bridget asked, catching her husband looking at them, grinning.

"Life is good," Poppa admitted.

"Life is always good," Bridget said. "Even when it isn't." At first Stan didn't understand. He screwed up his forehead as he pondered.

"Consider the alternative," Poppa reminded him. "Anything's better than the alternative."

As usual, Poppa was right.

Bridget worried herself sick about what she'd said to Stan earlier that morning. Should she tell Rose? Was Bridget all worked up about nothing? Did the boy suspect something? He seemed all right when he went upstairs after he finished his breakfast, chattering about finishing the igloo he and Wendy had started days before, but Bridget couldn't be sure.

Just as she'd promised, Rose came downstairs at eight to start the *spiedini*. Bridget hemmed and hawed about admitting her transgression to her daughter. Would Rose be cross at her? And if so, could Rose ever forgive her? Who knew how much time Bridget had left on God's green earth and she couldn't abide by Rose giving her the cold shoulder. After all, they lived in the same house. She heard her daughter's footsteps above her every day as Rose moved through her life and through the second-floor railroad apartment. Bridget heard when Rose got up to check on Stan in the middle of the night and when she got up to put the kettle on in the morning. If Rose were cross with her, she truly didn't know…

"Momma," Rose said, jolting Bridget out of her litany of worry. "You've chopped those eggs more than enough."

Bridget looked down at the hard-cooked eggs, which were ground into a powder. "I suppose so," she admitted. Next came a mound of freshly-grated Pecorino Romano cheese, looking like a pile of newly-fallen snow. This was followed by a cupful of breadcrumbs made from the stale heels of leftover Italian bread. Without consulting her mother, Rose dropped in the minced garlic, so wispy and thin, it looked as though it had been shaved with a razor.

Rose had learned her excellent knife skills at the elbow of Bridget when she was a child. She'd been easily roused awake by the aroma of a Sunday sauce bubbling on the burner, and would ask if she could mix the meatballs, roll and tie the *braciole*, fry the sausage. And Bridget's response was always, "Of course, you could," even if she were afraid the girl would chop off a fingertip or get splattered with hot grease. "How else will she learn?" Poppa would remind Bridget. And learn, Rose did. Bridget even thought her daughter was a better cook than she, that Rose had perfected the dishes her mother taught her how to make. Bridget would even bet that Angela would grow to be a far superior cook than Rose.

Whenever Bridget complimented Rose, the woman blushed and denied it up and down. "No one's better than you, Momma," Rose insisted. "No one." Bridget accepted the flattering words silently this time.

When Rose slipped the chopped parsley into the bowl with the garlic and egg, Bridget mixed it with her wrinkled, paper-dry fingertips; she never used a spoon. "It's not the same," she explained. "You've got get messy to be a good cook." Rose nodded in agreement, her fingers slick with an egg, oil and garlic sheen. It was something many people didn't understand—the necessity of getting dirty prepping food—but Rose did. She'd learned it from her mother.

It was after the veal had been pounded with the wooden meat tenderizer, after it had been christened with a healthy measure of the chopped egg mixture, after it had been rolled up and fastened shut with toothpicks, placed onto greased cookie sheets and put into the oven that Bridget finally told Rose about her little slip of the tongue. They were sitting at the kitchen table, taking a breather, mugs of tea at their elbows. Although first, they spoke of veal.

Rose worried, "It must have cost a small fortune."

"Ah, Sal gives it to me wholesale," Bridget reminded her.

"Me, too!" Rose laughed.

"After all these years." When they were teenagers, Bridget's daughter Jo and Sal had briefly kept company. Jo would come home with an assortment of culinary gifts: a few slices of mouthwatering, paper-thin *prosciutto*, a couple dozen Kalamata olives in a waxed paper bag. Even decades later, Sal gave Bridget special dispensation at his Liberty Meats. Bridget had been kind to him and had taken him into the family, albeit for a short time. Although it was long ago, soon after Sal's mother had died, he never forgot the Paradisos' kindnesses to him as he grieved.

"Josephina must have been a real pip," Rose quipped.

"Still is," Bridget responded, nudging Rose.

Between the preparing the veal and rolling the *prosciutto* around breadsticks, Bridget had the courage to confess about her faux pas with Stan earlier. Although her daughter's face dropped and her mouth hung open in shock, Rose told her mother not to worry. "He's so caught up thinking about firecrackers and eating those *spiedini*," Rose pointed out to Bridget, gesturing at the Hotpoint where the delectable morsels were sizzling away. "I doubt he realized what you said."

Bridget's brow was still furrowed in worry. Rose patted Bridget's hand for comfort, yet her own stomach was suddenly in knots. Rose shivered briefly, feeling a chill even in her mother's overheated kitchen. 'Stanley is a smart boy,' she thought to herself. 'He doesn't miss a trick. He knows. Of course, he knows. He knows, and then he won't want to be with us. He'll want to be with her, and I'll lose him.'

Rose noticed a tear slip down Bridget's cheek. She squeezed her mother's fingers to reassure her. "Don't worry your pretty little head about it," she said to Bridget. "It was a slip of the tongue, nothing more."

Chapter Sixteen

Ring out the Old, Ring in the New

But Rose couldn't help worry, and it showed. Her voice trembled when she asked Sully to fasten the dainty golden locket around her neck which he had given to her that Christmas. Rose shook too much to do it herself. "You're a bundle of nerves," Sully commented, slipping his work slacks on over his union suit. He easily clipped the heart-shaped charm around his wife's throat. Sully kissed the back of Rose's neck, reveling in the softness of the tiny, translucent hairs hidden there, invisible to the eye but detectable to the lips.

She lifted the locket on its chain and opened it, examining the photographs inside: one of Angela and Tiger together as children, and the other of Stan at twenty months of age—it had been taken at Rose and Sully's wedding. She was careful to hide wedding snapshots of Rose in her gown and Sully in his suit which also had Stan in them. Rose didn't want him to connect the dots and find out the truth, that she and Sully weren't his birth parents. The boy was Sully's and Rose's in terms of emotions, in terms of heart, and that's what mattered. Did Stan already know that he had been born to the Yellow Queen, and she'd left him on their doorstep eight Christmas Eves ago? Rose shuddered to think.

"Why am I'm so shaky?" Rose fibbed to Sully, as she leaned toward the bedroom mirror and applied rouge to her cheeks from a little brass compact. "Maybe it's the New Year. You never can tell what next year will bring. Good, bad. Usually it's something you don't expect."

"It's the same every year," Sully told her. "We don't know what's going to happen until it does. But I'm here, right beside you, come hell or high water." His gentle kiss was full of courage and promise.

Halfway across Brooklyn, in a flophouse called the Terminal Hotel, Denise Walters was doing her best to make herself presentable. She didn't have the energy to haul herself out of bed, let alone put a stick of rouge to her cheeks, which she could see were a pallid, deathly tone, even in the dim glow of the bare light bulb that hung from the ceiling. The bed sheets, though ringed with soil and smelling slightly sour, felt cool against her feverish skin. The pine floorboards were strewn with discarded takeout cartons: the bright yellow and green of Nathan's wrappers, cardboard boxes from "the Chinks," as she called the Chinese take-away place, and paper sacks with scraps of long-forgotten meals in them. A number of items were so rotted, she couldn't even venture to imagine what they had once been. Sort of like Denise herself, she laughed without making a sound, only it was more tragic than comical.

Seeing what she was now—worn, broken and tubercular—it was difficult to believe that Denise had once been beautiful, a shapely would-be chorine, the envy of every woman, the lust of every man. Her hair had been dyed a Peroxide shade of blonde not found in nature, and coiffed into short ringlets. She had a curvaceous physique, smart clothes and stylish shoes. And then there were her hats! Denise's hats had been purchased in the best shops, many made to order, on a whim whenever the mood struck her. They were the sort of hats Astrid Paradiso Fischer designed.

But now, now Denise's hair was showing through a mousy gray at the roots. It was the consistency of dry grass and just as brittle. She found hanks of it on her pillow when she woke each morning. There were clumps of it in her ivory comb when she cared enough to pull it through her locks. Denise couldn't remember the last time she'd hobbled to the shared restroom down the hall at the rooming house to bathe or to even do her business. Lazy, exhausted, Denise kept a chamber pot by her bed which was starting to stink. She'd have to empty it soon.

It was New Year's Eve, and in a matter of hours, 1946 would replace 1945. "Different year, same shit," Denise muttered out loud. She often talked to herself and realized this was a sign of insanity, but was it still twisted if you *knew* you were doing it and just didn't give a hoot? Denise would have to ask Tony. Oh, that's right…Tony was gone, dead. It would be ten years this coming September, ten crummy years.

Lighting a cigarette butt she found on her bureau, Denise thought of the mess she'd made of her life. She had not one thing to be proud of, not one thing she'd accomplished. Not a one. Nothing except her son Stanley, who she'd given away when he was a baby. He'd soon be ten, or was it nine? No, it was definitely nine because Tony would be dead ten. The dirty rotten fink.

Even though she'd ditched him, Denise found herself drawn to her son, but only recently. She rarely gave Stanley a thought after she'd left him on the Martino Family's large front porch. She'd waited behind a burgundy Dodge across Forty-Seventh Street to make sure Stanley had been taken inside. Sure enough, a young tyke who'd been peering out the window, probably looking for Santa and his sleigh, came bounding onto the porch to discover the evaporated milk carton which held Denise's son. This boy was probably Tony's son, his other son. "Ma!" the kid wailed, and two women immediately appeared at the door, wiping their hands on their aprons.

"Heavens to Murgatroyd!" blurted out the oldest one, her gray hair pulled into a messy bun, her cobbler-style apron straining against her generous breasts, hips and belly. The second woman bent down. She had lackluster hair and was homey-looking with moon eyes. This was Tony's wife, Denise guessed. Instead of lifting the cardboard box, the woman scooped the child into her arms and held him close to her heart. At that moment, Denise knew her little Stanley would be well taken care of, much better than she could care for him herself.

Crouched behind the Dodge, Denise stood and turned to go, choking on her tears. As she walked away without looking back, she heard the excited bustle of voices coming from the house's open door. She'd even caught a glimpse of the Christmas tree inside, strung with popcorn and sparkling ornaments. The windows were decorated with construction-paper candy canes and tinfoil stars. It would be a fine place to grow up, Denise decided, and her son would be loved. Maybe they even loved him already.

She was still bawling like an imbecile by the time she reached the Fort Hamilton Parkway train station at the corner. Denise almost plowed into two beat cops who were hurrying down the street. "Watch it, flatfoot!" she barked at the tallest one, who'd practically run into her.

"Merry Christmas to you, too, Ma'am," he told her.

Every so often, Denise returned to the unassuming brick house on Forty-Seventh Street between New Utrecht and Twelfth Avenues. She just needed to see the boy, to see he was all right, and of course, he was. One time he would be toddling about, holding his grandmother's skirt and the next, he'd be on a red tricycle, the next, on roller skates, clattering down the pavement. Not counting the time on the Avenue, when she peered into his pram outside the fruit store, it was just lately, when she'd begun feeling poorly, that Denise had grown brazen enough to draw closer to the boy. Often, she watched him go to and from school. Then once, he crashed into her and apologized—such a polite boy—and she'd made the mistake of calling him by name. Right after that came Denise's encounter with the gimp who bought her brefast and warned her to stay away. He'd even tried to bribe her to scram, the schnook. What sort of girl did he take her for?

Denise ducked out the cigarette on the bureau. Its top was scarred with similar burn marks. She knew she shouldn't smoke with her condition but smoking was one of the few acts which calmed her nerves, even though it usually set off a coughing fit, as it did now. Denise grabbed a hankie and hacked into it, expecting a red, flowerlike splotch of blood. Sometimes it looked like a hydrangea. Others it resembled a rose or a geranium, but it was always a bad portent no matter what it looked like, and it was happening more often.

It was too disagreeable to go outside and seek gentleman callers, but Denise couldn't bear the thought of greeting the New Year in her dank, dreary rooming house. Not long ago, she'd danced in the decade at the Ritz, even the Plaza once, and she'd turned heads. Now people turned away when they saw her stumbling down the street. They pulled their kids away from the broken-down woman she'd become. Holed up at the Terminal, Denise convinced herself that she would feel less gutted if she saw him. Stanley. Her son. She forced herself to dress.

For her New Year's Eve outing, Denise selected a pair of shoes which had the fewest gaps in the bottom, first padding the soles with newspaper before slipping in her feet. She shrugged into a sweater with holes at the elbows but was otherwise passable. Then she fastened her tatty coat over the sweater, and smashed a wool beret down onto her head. Didn't she have long johns somewhere? Denise recalled a fellow dressing in haste and forgetting them. Damned if she couldn't find the long johns when she needed them most. But at least she had gloves, thanks to that nice young man she'd met at Ruby's. Anthony. That was his name. Anthony.

Wendy and her parents made their way down Twelfth Avenue with the girl leading the way, skipping in her red galoshes, even though she carried a satchel filled with goodies. "Careful," Jo warned, slipping her arm through Harry's and holding him close. They smiled at each other, their teeth feeling the sting of the cold. Jo managed to balance the tray of baked ziti, covered with tinfoil, as they walked.

"Don't slip," Harry added. He realized that his wife cleaved to him not purely out of affection but also to steady him. Harry's prosthetic leg felt unsure on the ice-slickened slate sidewalk. It was snowing lightly. The air was frosty and clear. The stars seemed sharper in the sky, despite the snow, shimmering like chipped ice in black velvet.

"I won't slip," Wendy chirped, still skipping.

It was a few short blocks to the Paradiso House but the wind was sharp, prompting them to walk even faster. Harry's bad leg left a crooked trail in the dusting of snow, Jo noticed as she looked over her shoulder. "What?" he asked.

"I thought I saw something," Jo told him. "A person."

"I wouldn't take a knight out on a dog like this," Harry quipped, repeating the punch line of an old joke. He always said this on bitter evenings, and it always made Jo laugh. Then she saw it again out of the corner of her eye: a wool beret, a flash of white, a dark coat, but it was soon gone. "What?" Harry repeated.

Jo shrugged. "The Ghost of New Years Past, maybe." They walked on, turning down Forty-Seventh Street.

Denise was trembling like a stray. Twelfth Avenue was such a wide street, it caught the wind like a canyon. She cursed the breeze, cursed the snow, cursed everything under the winter sun. Denise thought the woman and maybe even the young girl might have spotted her, so she cursed the child, too. That brat was constantly pointing out Denise to Stanley when she lurked near school or by the candy shop. The child was indeed cute, too cute for her own good, with auburn curls peeking out from beneath her smart felt cap and eyes the color of a smoky emerald. 'But she'll see,' Denise thought to herself, 'I was once a darling little girl myself. And look what happened to me. *Life* happened to me.'

It was so frigid outside that Denise's lungs felt as though they were on fire each time she took a breath. She tried to breathe shallowly, softly sluffing the air in through her nose instead of through her mouth, but that hurt as well. No matter how she breathed, Denise didn't seem to be pulling in enough air. She would have to quit smoking once and for all. And drinking, which didn't help either. Only not tonight. Definitely not tonight.

Denise unclasped her purse, extracted a silver flask and gulped from it deeply. The initials "AM" flashed in the streetlight's glow. She had gotten it for Anthony Martino, her Tony, their first Christmas together, and it had cost a pretty penny. At the time, Denise thought he was worth the money she spent since she was newly smitten and freshly in lust. Had she ever loved him, truly, madly, deeply, in the George Gershwin "The Man I Love" sense? No, it was in the powerless, Oscar Hammerstein "Can't Help Lovin' Dat Man" sort of way. Denise would do anything for Tony, and often did. And look where it had gotten her.

She tailed the happy family down Forty-Seventh Street from a safe distance. The stable woman at the man's side, her arm slid through his while balancing a tray, conversed amicably, glancing up at her husband, smiling. It was clear to Denise that the woman loved him by the way her body listed toward his. She thought she recognized the fellow. An old john? A former beau? No, not this palooka. He seemed above associating with her type. Denise vaguely recalled a meal or at least sitting at a table with him. But when and where? Her stomach sunk when she remembered pushing him into a snow drift not too long ago. What was going on with her? What was wrong with her? Why was she so addled? Why did she feel so weak? Another slug of gin made Denise forget her worries. And they really didn't matter anyhow, did they?

Wendy reached the front door of 1128 Forty-Seventh Street first, bounded up the steps and waited for her parents.

The very idea of still being awake and outside so late excited her. The bells of St. Catherine's had already rung nine times when they were almost ready to leave the house. It was probably close to ten now. Beyond the closed door, Wendy could hear voices and laughter. Through the window, she caught a glimpse of her Uncle John steering her Aunt Camille around the parlor in a dance. Her aunt protested, at first trying to push him away, but then she let him lead her around the carpet. The chords of "I've Got a Crush on You" came through the iced-up windows in a whisper.

Wendy saw her cousin Angela lower her large body onto the sofa and briefly rub one swollen ankle and then the other. Her Aunt Rose held a wine glass, which was mildly shocking—Aunt Rose never drank, even pooh-poohed it. From kitchen and neighborhood gossip, Wendy gathered that her aunt's late husband was a drunkard. "A stone-cold lush," Wendy's mother declared, while her father's "degenerate drunk" was even less charitable. So, Aunt Rose never went near the stuff, until that evening.

A light touch on Wendy's shoulder made her gasp and jump. "I ought to book you for being a Peeping Tom," her father laughed.

Wendy laughed, too, and without thinking, squealed, "Pop, you're not a cop anymore." Her father's face dropped and she knew she'd hurt his feelings without meaning to.

"I'm not anything anymore," Harry mumbled under his breath. But Wendy heard him and so did Jo as he held the door open for them.

"Pop, you're everything to me," Wendy told him as she slipped past him, hugging him briefly.

Jo kissed her husband hard on the mouth. "You're my everything, too," she said. But it made little difference to Harry.

Stan lay on his stomach on a corner of the parlor rug. Wendy joined him there after she hung up her hat and coat, and slipped off her galoshes. Stan was putting together a jigsaw puzzle of World War II warships, which included the *Arizona*. Poppa peered over their shoulders from his armchair. "My men mounted the guns on most of those beauties," he began, "right here in the Brooklyn Navy Yard." Although Stan and Wendy were already aware of this because their grandfather had shared this story before— numerous times—they didn't remind him. Instead, they listened politely as though it were the first they'd heard of Poppa's work as a journeyman.

"All the puzzle pieces look the same," Wendy sighed. "They're all gunmetal gray."

"That's why it's so challenging," Stan said. "And fun."

"Too bad they don't make a Honey Bunch puzzle," Wendy told him, halfheartedly toying with a piece.

Astrid and Sam bounded into the parlor on the boreal breeze. She was wearing a thick, curly fur of mouton lamb and had a matching hat clamped onto her head. "I declare," Astrid complained. "What's become of this neighborhood? The bums, vagrants and unsavories flock here like sheep."

"They're poor unfortunates, sweetums," her ex-husband corrected. "Imagine having to live outdoors on an evening cold as this."

"Pish posh," Astrid snorted, waving Sam away like a bug. "People have no one to blame but themselves for the predicaments they get into."

Harry shook Sam's hand and kissed his sister-in-law's cool cheek in greeting. "Sometimes it's just tough luck," he told her.

Jo grilled her sister, rolling her eyes. "What is it now?"

"Some washed-up rummy dilly-dallying inside the gate," Astrid sneered, shaking the snow off her coat. Sam took her jacket and hung it in the hall closet. He already knew it was too refined an item to suspend from a coat hook—he'd been scolded for doing this once and would never forget it. Astrid demanded a padded satin hanger for her fur jacket, which Sam grudgingly fished out of the closet.

Rose dashed to the front window, fogged over from the heat indoors meeting the cold outside. She searched for the mystery woman with a heaviness in her heart but found only blackness. "Oh, she's gone now," Astrid added. "I chased her away like a stray cat."

"Why, she even hit her with a rolled-up newspaper," Sam added for emphasis.

"Did not," Astrid huffed. "But I would've if I'd had one."

Bridget appeared in the doorway between the parlor and kitchen, fastening an apron which had champagne glasses and popped corks ironed onto its front. She dug it out of the breakfront drawer every December 31. "Chased who away?" Bridget wondered.

"The hobo lady," Stan said, studying the puzzle. He fingered the outline of a piece he hoped might complete the *USS Nebraska* but it didn't fit, no matter how he tried.

"Don't force it in. You'll ruin it," Wendy told him.

"It's mine to ruin," Stan responded.

Poppa's youngest grandkids weren't accustomed to being up past eight, and here it was approaching ten. "Somebody sounds cranky," Poppa commented. "Like they might need a nap."

"Not me," Stan swore to his grandfather, puffing out his chest.

"Me neither," Wendy added.

"Good," Poppa said. "Because I could use a hand or two."

"Good," Stan grinned at his grandfather. "Because we've got four."

"But mine are clean," Wendy pointed out, holding them up to prove it. They were indeed spotless and even scrubbed under the fingernails, which Wendy was permitted to paint a pale pink for the occasion.

Stan wedged his fingers underneath his body. "So?"

While the women reheated the food—"Just a few snacks," Bridget had told them—and the men set up the extra chairs, Poppa sent his grandchildren into the depths of the basement, which each of them secretly dreaded but neither would ever admit for fear of being called a fraidy cat.

Stan made Wendy go down the rickety steps ahead of him. "Ladies first," he offered, with a sweeping gesture. How could Wendy refuse? Her knees trembled through her woolen tights as she took the stairs one by one, holding onto the roughly-hewn wooden banister. Stan followed close behind. They kept the hall door open. "What if she's down there?" Stan wondered.

"Who?" Wendy pushed.

"The bum lady."

The very thought terrified her. Wendy almost peed her bloomers out of sheer terror. Without meaning to, she let out a tiny scream, and quickly swallowed it like a hiccough. "How could she be?"

"Maybe Poppa forgot to lock the cellar door," Stan suggested. "He's always forgetting stuff lately. He's getting old."

"But he never forgets things like that," Wendy said, to soothe herself as much as to defy her cousin.

They were at the bottom of the cellar steps by now. Stan didn't protest when Wendy grabbed his hand instinctively. He reached overhead, grasping for the flimsy strand of the light's pull chain. The bulb flickered on, illuminating the boxes, discarded toys and dusty tools with a sinister glow. The two children crept through the basement, inching their way toward the coal furnace in the front of the cellar, its ochre flame licking at the damp air. They were looking for a milk crate covered with a dishtowel, marked with the words "New Year's Decorations." It held tin noisemakers and cardboard horns which tasted vaguely of dust and other people's spit.

Although Stan preferred to bang a kitchen pot with a wooden spoon at the stroke of midnight, he liked the horns, too, and those noisemakers with the red handles which spun around and made a creaking sound. Stan couldn't resist blowing a horn when given the opportunity. A pudgy mouse waddled across the cement and into the dirt of the coal cellar. Both children gasped. "I peed a little," Stan confessed.

"Me, too," Wendy admitted. She squeezed his fingers tighter.

Stan and Wendy braced themselves for the life-sized cardboard cutout of Father Carmine, Poppa's brother, who'd been a Jesuit priest for decades before he died. Although Father Carmine had been a kind man who they vaguely remembered (he'd died when they were toddlers), the cutout of this munificent relative scared them almost as the Frankenstein monster did. It had been the same for Tiger and Angela when they were kids, Tiger had confided to both of them separately.

Wendy spotted the milk crate they were seeking before Stan did. It was exactly where they'd left it last January, on a shelf about chest-high. But it was Stan who snatched the box first. "This is where it happened," he told his cousin, pointing to an indistinct place on the ground. "The dirt in the coal cellar is darker there."

Wendy couldn't see a thing. The light was too dim. "Where what happened?"

"Where he died."

"Who?"

"I'm not sure. It might have been the coal delivery boy," Stan ventured. "I overheard Mrs. Lieberwitz and Mrs. DePalma once. When I asked them about it, they wouldn't answer." Stan wedged the crate against the wall to get a better grip. He continued, "Some guy slipped and fell. He was a drunk, everyone said."

"Everyone who?"

"People who know, silly," Stan teased. "Mrs. Lieberwitz for one."

"Calling me names won't make me see it," Wendy warned. She studied the red dirt on the floor of the coal cellar. "Boy, they saw you coming! They know you'll believe anything and everything."

"They didn't even know I was listening," Stan insisted.

"Did, too!" Now Wendy was talking just to hear herself talk because the thought of someone, even a drinker, dying in the basement, petrified her. "Race you to the top," Wendy piped, then ran.

"Hey, no fair!" Stan struggled to pull the chain to shut the light while holding the crate.

By the time Stan had puffed to the top of the basement steps, Wendy was already munching on a cheese puff pastry. Everyone else was there by then. Tiger nibbled on a pig in the blanket while Angela reported how she had waddled over from next door, with Ti-Tu and Augie supporting her on each elbow so she wouldn't slip on the ice. Camille and John recounted their treacherous drive from Sunnyside, way out in Queens. (They'd packed a satchel and were spending the night on Bridget and Poppa's Castro convertible so they didn't have to make the pilgrimage home in the wee hours.) The only one missing was Sully because he and Izzy had nabbed a few hours of overtime. But he promised to pop by before The Bells.

Maybe that's why Rose was drinking—because she missed Sully. She hated when he had to walk the beat on such cold nights. Despite the layers of *muthandies* she made him wear underneath his thick uniform and city-issue topcoat, Sully became chilled to the bone. The one thing that would thaw him out was a long, hot bath in the claw-footed tub.

Every time the doorbell sounded, there was a chorus from inside which sang, "It's open." Friends and neighbors traipsed into Poppa and Bridget's parlor, eager to wish them a heartfelt "Happy New Year!" with a handshake, a hug and a bottle of cheer. Already, the sideboard resembled the shelf behind the bar at Farrell's, decorated with an array of liquors from the lands from which the bearers hailed. There was Cuban rum from Sandra Santiago, (*añejo*, the best, she said). There was *krupnik*, a honey-infused liqueur from Poland, where Sadie Lieberwitz was originally from, and Jack Daniels from Tennessee, where Sam had grown up, plus wine from their friend Celeste's father's basement operation in Bensonhurst.

Tiger surveyed the sideboard and noted to himself that his father would have probably disappeared with a bottle. Oh, Tony would have been a giddy, loving drunk at first, then would transform into a *Jekyll and Hyde* understudy even more unhinged than Fredric March and Spencer Tracy combined. It wouldn't take much to thrust Tony over the edge—a guest looking at him faintly askance or making a playful compliment which Tony's drunken brain would misconstrue. It wouldn't take much for him to give Tiger a swat that would send the boy's head spinning or, in private, to shove Rose against the wall, grab her by the throat and snarl into her face before storming off. His father never raised a finger to Angela, but Tony made her suffer in a multitude of other ways.

Out of the corner of his eye, Tiger saw Rose examine a bottle of Guatemalan *cuxa*. It had been brought by Juan Marcos, who used to work with Poppa at the Brooklyn Navy Yard. "You'd better not," Tiger warned her. "It's Mayan moonshine. Firewater."

Undeterred, Rose poured herself a shot. "A small glass," she shrugged. "Can't do any harm."

"Sure, it can," Tiger told her.

"Your father used to say you wouldn't get a hangover so long as you didn't mix your colors."

Tiger couldn't follow. His mother was tipsy already. "Colors?"

"You know," Rose slurred. "You don't mix the brown ones with the clear ones. I'm on the clear ones."

"So, I see," Tiger noted. "But that's hogwash. Like most of the things Tony said. Pure hogwash."

Sam chimed in, ever the Southern squire, nursing a tumbler of Gentleman Jack with exactly one cube of ice in it. "It's the sweet stuff you have to watch out for," he warned. "Those girly drinks with umbrellas and fruit juice. They'll do you in."

Rose lifted the glass of *cuxa*, took a sip and winced. "It tastes like lighter fluid," she stated before downing the rest. "I'm just celebrating," she added for Tiger's benefit.

"Celebrating what?" Astrid snapped, her refurbished nose permanently out of joint.

Rose thought for a moment. "The end of the War. Tiger being home. Life in general. And so on."

Rose's brother-in-law John slipped the cut-glass jigger

out of her grip. "How about celebrating with a bite to eat?"
John steered Rose over to the buffet table, where Jo had
placed the bubbling pan of baked ziti. There was a platter of
pigs in the blanket alongside a pile of potato *latkes* which
Ti-Tu had made from his mother's recipe. Mrs. Rosenkrantz,
God rest her soul, claimed *latkes* went with anything, even
Italian-American barbecues. (She was right.) Dr. Lewis's
wife Eva carried over a heaping bowl of *kasha varnishkes*
from their house across the street, the buckwheat and bowtie
pasta an inviting combination. Not to mention the mushroom
pan gravy which accompanied it. No New Year's Eve
celebration would be complete without a dish of lentils and
pig's trotters, which Italians believed brought good luck and
prosperity in the coming year.

And then there were the desserts. Rainbow cookies from
Anthony Paladino, which Stan loved as much as Tiger had at
the same age. There was Sadie Lieberwitz's chocolate *babka*,
as puffy and fluffy as a genie's hat. George, Tiger's Army
buddy, even came by earlier with his wife Elaine, all the
way from Jersey City, to bring one of Elaine's world-famous
banana puddings, made with real vanilla wafers. Despite the
late hour, their children were well-behaved and darling, with
starched gingham dresses and tight plaits on the two girls,
neat bow ties and close-cropped military issue crew-cuts on
both George and his sons. The banana pudding was lovely
to behold, made in a transparent Pyrex serving dish to show
off its layers of hand-beaten, whipped cream set against
fresh bananas, the top nicely toasted. ("You'll have to come
visit us in Jersey City to return the bowl," Elaine suggested,
to which Bridget agreed.) This perfectly complimented the
trifle made by Vanessa Ucco down the block.

Rose surveyed the table. "I guess I could eat," she conceded.

Poppa convinced her to "*cop a squat,*" mangling the
French phrase with a touch of Brooklynese. Rose obediently
sat while Angela made her a plate. "A little of everything,"
she said unevenly, and Angie complied, adding tiny mounds
of food so Rose could sample it all. One *latka*, a spoonful
of sour cream, hold the onions. A teaspoon of marinated

mushrooms. Mrs. DePalma's roasted red peppers (seasoned with a bright dash of lemon juice, not vinegar). A healthy ladleful of baked ziti, with no extra sauce. A slice of lard bread. A few olives—black, not green. A modest square of zucchini pie.

Feeding Rose seemed beneficial at first, but as Angela set the plate in front of her mother, Rose's stomach began doing calisthenics which grew more vigorous the harder she looked at her plate. The oil from the peppers bled onto the ziti which leaked ricotta onto the olives. Mr. Mistretta had gone into the restroom off the kitchen, so Rose eyed the front door, which was closer. She made a dash to the porch, as limber as she had run on the relay race team when she was a girl. Rose leaned over the porch railing and let out a fetid stream of vomit. It burned, leaving an acid in her nose and throat. It was mostly liquid, she noticed, clear liquid which had turned a sick orange when mixed with her bile. It splattered in the snow.

Out of the corner of her eye, Rose spied Sully coming up the walk with his partner Izzy. Close by, crumpled on the porch steps, was the shape of a body, lightly covered in snow. The spindly legs of a woman stuck out from beneath a thin coat. Hair the color of straw peered out from beneath a light hat. Sully and Izzy ran when they spotted the woman, unconscious, while Rose let out another spray of sick, and moaned.

Chapter Seventeen

The Bells of St. Catherine's

Sully heard the bells of St. Catherine's from the hallway of United Israel Zion Hospital. The sound mingled with the bells of other churches in the area, Immaculate Heart of Mary, possibly even Holy Name of Jesus in Park Slope. The midnight air was alive with church bells, which all rang riotously to welcome in 1946.

As with most new years, the fine people of Borough Park were hopeful that this one would be full of positive change and prosperity. The War was over, both in Europe and in the Pacific. Young men and women were still coming home from overseas and no new men and women would die, at least not in this War. There would be more jobs, more food and more elation. There would be more promise. For the Paradiso Family, 1946 would be a period of great flux and adjustment, but also great joy, signified by the church bells ushering in the new year.

Still on duty, Sully stood outside Denice Walters' hospital room. She was lucky to have been found by him and his partner, unconscious and in the early stages of hypothermia, on the Paradisos' porch steps less than an hour before the bells began pealing throughout Brooklyn, and the rest of the city. She was lucky because she was still alive, but just barely.

Sully was sorry he'd missed spending the moment of The Bells with his family, as he had done every year since he and Rose had been a couple. Whenever Sully was working, as he was that night, he would plan it so he would be at his in-laws' apartment when the church bells sounded. There would be a chaste kiss with his wife, hugs and the anticipation of good things to come.

But this New Year's Eve was unique. Sully had the unpleasant task of accompanying the ambulance carrying Denise Walters to United Israel. He told his partner Izzy to make a quick stop home to kiss his own wife, Belkis, and their kids, who lived in a tenement apartment on Forty-Fifth Street under the El, a few blocks from the hospital. Izzy said he'd meet Sully at United Israel on foot, and he did.

Sully guarded the ward-type hospital room which housed nine unfortunates besides Miss Walters, vagrants mostly, women with no one who loved them, or at least women who'd alienated themselves from the people who cared about them. And it had come to this, a narrow hospital cot in a county ward on the dawn of a new year.

It pained Sully to leave Rose, who was visibly shaken by the discovery of Miss Walters unconscious on the front steps. Rose's worst fear had come to be and now they would be forced to tell Stanley the true story of his birth and who his blood mother was. There was no way it could be avoided. Sully noticed that Rose was unsteady on her feet, reeling like a drunk, but she rarely drank. His wife was a teetotaler at best. Perhaps Rose's condition was due to the shock of seeing the lifeless body of her son's mother sprawled out on the stairs. Rose retched and vomited over the porch railing as soon as she spotted the woman there.

Stan and Wendy were upset witnessing the lady they called "The Yellow Queen" laid out on the porch's icy brick stairs, as though dead. Harry had told Sully he'd given the lush a firm "talking to" not a week earlier. Being on the job, Sully had to be careful to keep his distance from the woman, though he longed to caution her to stay away. It might be taken as a police officer threatening a civilian or misusing the power of his badge. Harry was another story, though. Since Harry was retired from the force, he could take the liberty of reading Denise Walters the riot act. So, Sully was helpless to do anything except stand stock straight outside of Miss Walters' hospital room, waiting.

Back at the house on Forty-Seventh Street, Stan and Wendy were placidly putting the pots, pans and wooden spoons back into their proper places in Grandma Bridget's kitchen. In their eyes, the highlight of the New Year festivities was banging on kitchen items, screaming and yelling at the top of your lungs, and watching grown-ups cry and kiss, but it just wasn't the same tonight. Not with the ghost of the memory of finding the Yellow Queen on the porch, the dribble of blood oozing out from the corner of her mouth and frozen to her bluish face.

Izzy and Sully sprang into action. They moved the woman's body from being sprawled across the steps to lying flat on her back. The young Pole about to give the unconscious victim mouth-to-mouth resuscitation until Sully noticed the blood and stopped him. "Could be TB," he warned. Instead, they roused her into consciousness with blankets and warmth, and by smacking her hands. Beneath her men's fur-lined leather gloves, the woman's skin was chapped and flaking.

Rose still clutched the porch railing, white-knuckled, without a coat, not feeling the cold. It wasn't until Angela ushered her inside and upstairs that Rose began shaking uncontrollably. Her trembling wasn't from being outdoors without a jacket, however; it was from something more, something deeper. It was from fear.

Tiger checked on Rose after the ambulance left with Denise and Sully inside it. Rose was shaking, even with a blanket draped over her shoulders as she bowed in front of the toilet. Angela had a difficult time getting onto her knees with her big middle, so she stood behind her mother and rubbed her shoulders, holding back her hair as Rose vomited. "How is she?" Tiger asked his sister from the doorway.

Angela shrugged. "I've never seen her like this."

"Me neither," Tiger admitted. "She almost never drinks. A sip for a toast and that's it."

"One drunk in the family is enough," Angela said. "Was enough. More than enough."

Rose murmured into the porcelain, so low they couldn't figure out what she was saying at first. "It's over," she whispered. "It's over." Tiger knew what Rose meant but didn't let on. Now wasn't the time to explain who Denise was to his sister.

"What's over?" Angela wondered.

"Everything. He'll know now. She'll take him away," Rose moaned.

"Who?"

"Her," gasped Rose.

Then there was another stream of sick into the bowl. Tiger looked away, slightly pallid. "Can I help?" he wondered.

"No," Angela told him. "You look like you're going to hurl yourself. I don't need two sick people to take care of."

The discovery of the mystery woman on the front steps had cut short the family's New Year's Eve festivities.

Although they stayed together for The Bells, they disbanded soon after. Camille and Jo were covering and putting away the food. Harry, Sam, Augie, Ti-Tu and John were stowing the chairs. As she tossed the linens into the laundry basket, Astrid scolded Sam, who looked like a reprimanded puppy. "Our divorce was just finalized," Astrid reminded him. "Why would I marry you again?"

"But I..."

"You don't have to ask me to marry you every time you have a couple of cocktails," Astrid chided. "Or every time you get sentimental. Everyone's sentimental on New Year's."

"Astrid…" Poppa warned her.

"But I'm only trying to talk some sense into the man," she began.

"Don't be mean," Poppa cautioned.

"I wasn't being mean, I…" Just as it had been when she was a child, all it required was a glance from her father and Astrid knew it was time to button her lip. The damage had already been done, however. Sam hung his head and after that night, never came back to the comfort of the Paradiso home, not even on holidays or holy days of obligation.

Through with her kitchen chores, Bridget was making up the sofa for Stan, who didn't question why he was sleeping downstairs. His sister Angela was tending to his mother upstairs and was going to spend the night at Rose's side. His father would be home in the morning, after the night shift, and then things would be back to normal, Stan told himself. Camille and John were putting sheets on the Castro convertible in Bridget's sewing room. Augie and Ti-Tu went back to their respective apartments next door. The house grew silent as everyone left by ones or twos.

Tiger kissed Bridget on the forehead. "I'm going out for a walk," he told her. "I shouldn't be long." Tiger soon found himself under the glaring lights of United Israel Zion and in a stiff-backed wooden chair by Denise Walters' hospital bed. Sully and Izzy nodded him past, and didn't even ask why he was there.

In the women's ward, Tiger watched Denise's alabaster chest rise and fall as she slept fitfully, furrowing her brow, and biting her dry lips. There was dried blood in her nostrils and a rust-colored crust in one corner of her mouth. Her wrinkled, powder blue hospital gown was tied loosely about the neck. Sitting beside Denise's bed reminded Tiger of the time his mother had been in the same hospital, but Rose had a semi-private room thanks to the TWU's health benefits. She hadn't been subjected to the indignities of a public ward. There had been three, maybe four beds in Rose's room, tops, whereas Denise's room had almost a dozen. In the pastel-colored hospital frocks, each a faded floral shade, the women looked like broken blossoms. They were sorrowful, shabby and beaten down by life. They took turns moaning, shouting out, and cursing. They tried to climb out of the high, steel hospital beds. One lady made it as far as the doorway, a slice of her sagging bottom peeking out from the johnny gown, before an exasperated nurse caught her and guided her back to bed.

"You rotten bastid…"

"Son-a-mon-bitch…"

"Do it again and I'll have to tie you to the rail…"

"You wouldn't dare…"

"Ugly witch, what did you do with my clothes?"

"Happy New Year to you, too, dearie…"

"Hey, cutie, looking for a little fun?"

Tiger tried to ignore the toothless woman with the bloodied patch where her eye had been. "Yeah, you, cutie," she persisted. "I know how to show a fella a good time." She began to lift her hospital gown above her scabbed knees.

The young man felt a rugged meat hook on his shoulder. "I'm sure you do," Sully's voice boomed behind Tiger. "Which is probably what landed you here, sister."

The woman spat out, "You dirty coppers always spoil a girl's fun."

Denise slept through it all. The nurse had given her a sedative so she would rest easier. Although Denise tossed and turned, she didn't wake, not even with all the noise in the ward. Sully pulled up a chair beside Tiger. "How did you meet her?" Sully wondered.

"By chance Christmas night, down at Ruby's," Tiger told him.

"When did you know?"

Tiger shrugged. "I put two and two together." He cleared his throat. "Saw her once when I was little, Kewpie did, too, only I don't think my sister recognized her on the porch. I might not have either if I hadn't run into Denise last week. I tried to tell Ma about it…"

"But she didn't want to hear it, did she?" Sully finished.

"How did you know?"

224

"I know your Ma. I know how scared she is. She doesn't want to lose the boy. She doesn't even want to tell him the truth. But I don't see how we can avoid it now."

Tiger toyed with Denise's bed sheet. "That's not right, is it? Not telling Stan, I mean. It's not fair to her or him." Sully didn't say a word. "Why are you here?" Tiger asked his stepfather.

"I have a few questions when she comes to," Sully said. "How's your mother?"

"She was still throwing up when I left."

"She's really shaken up," Sully admitted.

"Oh, she's more than shaken up," Tiger told him. "She was cross-eyed drunk."

"Drunk?" Sully repeated in shock. "Your ma?" Tiger nodded. Sully barked a short laugh. "Well, there's a first time for everything. Rosie will definitely feel it in the morning."

"Will this one pull through?" Tiger asked, gesturing to the bed.

"It's touch and go," Sully admitted. "The doc says she's dehydrated, malnourished and her liver is shot. Along with pneumonia, she's got TB. It's pretty far along."

Tiger sighed, "It doesn't look good, does it?"

"No," Sully admitted. "It doesn't."

Denise's eyes fluttered open. They landed first on the uniform, then the hat and badge. "Am I in trouble?" she rasped.

"Not yet," Sully said. "I just have some questions."

She licked her lips with a parched tongue. "So tired," she sighed. "Later." Then, "Water."

Sully left as Tiger held a ceramic cup to Denise's mouth, only she couldn't lift her head to drink. On the metal bedside table, there were crackers, a washrag and a paper straw, the kind they put into soft drinks at the soda fountain, but this one was much longer. Tiger put it into the cup. Denise drank. "Thanks, Tony," she croaked. "Hey, where've you been? It's been forever." Tiger wasn't sure if he should explain to Denise that he wasn't his father or just go along with it. It would only confuse her, so he was silent. "I've been looking after our boy as best I could, only somebody snatched him," she continued.

"You rest," Tiger told Denise. "Try to rest."

"How can I rest without my boy?" Denise began to fuss with the tubes taped to her arms. She tugged on the bag of clear fluid which went into a vein through a tube but she was too weak to remove it and soon gave up. "I must look a fright," Denise said, trying to fix her hair. It stood up around her head like a clown's, except it was a mousy blonde instead of electric red.

"You look beautiful," Tiger lied.

Denise broke into a grin. "Aw, gee, Tony, you always knew how to make a girl feel special." She grabbed hold of Tiger's wrist, then immediately drifted off to sleep. After about an hour, Tiger felt Denise's grip loosen. Her hand fell away like a leaf to the slate sidewalk. When Tiger saw Denise was in a deep slumber, he got up to go.

Sully was still parked outside on a walnut chair with rollers, the sort you might find behind a teacher's desk. His eyes were closed and his head lolled to the side. "Sleeping on the job?" Tiger wondered.

"I'm officially off the clock," Sully admitted. "I already sent Izzy off." He rubbed his face, his eyes. "You know, this is the first time I've dreaded going home to your mother since we've been together."

At first, Tiger didn't know what to say. "Ma needs you," Tiger offered. "Especially now."

"I know."

"She's scared."

"I'm scared, too," Sully stated plainly. "Only I can't tell her that. One of us has to be strong, and I guess it's me. I don't feel strong, though."

"Regardless," Tiger pushed. "You have to go home. Eventually."

Sully cracked a smile. "What do I do? She'll just cry. Sob like her world is coming to an end."

Tiger shrugged. "Just hold her. Sometimes all you can do is hold someone and let them cry."

Unraveling himself from his wooden perch, Sully stood. He towered over his stepson. "How'd you get to be so smart?"

Tiger shrugged once more. "I just call 'em how I see 'em."

The beat cop and the young soldier left the overheated hallways of United Israel Zion and were greeted by the teeth-rattling January clime. Stooped against the raw weather, they walked close together, as one, as they slowly made their way down Fort Hamilton Parkway. When they reached Forty-Seventh Street, they stopped. "This is where I leave you," Tiger said, and Sully nodded. He understood. "There are things a fella has to do alone, and this is one of them."

"Where will you go?" Sully asked.

"The Pink Pussycat's still open," Tiger replied. "They had a party."

"Your father's favorite place."

"After Houlie banned him from Farrell's," Tiger conceded.

"And rightly so," Sully said. He watched for a moment as Tiger backtracked down Fort Hamilton Parkway. Sully's eyes watered from the arctic air and his vision blurred. He imagined that his son would take the ten or so blocks briskly and would be there in no time, drinking in the shadow of Green-Wood Cemetery, where Tony was laid to rest in a particularly unpicturesque section near Tenth Avenue, not far from the Thirty-Eighth Street train yard. His son. Yes, Sully thought of Angela as his daughter and Tiger as his son, as much as he did Stanley, while in truth, all three were the children of one of the few truly evil individuals Sully had ever met.

It was a night of new beginnings, Sully reminded himself as he scaled the five brick steps which led to the porch. Sully unlocked the front door as inaudibly as he could, and did the same with the inner door. There was a faded stain on the carpet, blood from where Tony had fallen years earlier, cracking his skull open on the radiator. Sully's eyes drifted to the spot unconsciously whenever he came in, although he always tried not to look at it. His eyes were drawn there like a moth to a flame.

As Sully mounted the stairs, he heard it, an unearthly sound. A keening, like an animal in agony, perhaps a sheep on the way to the slaughterhouse. Except this wasn't an animal, this sound was human. The next time he heard it, Sully recognized the voice. It was his wife.

Chapter Eighteen

The Overlook

Rose was convinced Denise had given her the evil eye as the woman lay prone on the front porch while Sully and Izzy tried to revive her. Both old school Italian-Americans like Rose, as well as those born on "the other side" like Bridget, were confident the *malocchio* could be combated on a daily basis by wearing amulets dubbed *i corno* (the horn), pinned to their undergarments or on a chain around their necks. Resembling a sheep's curved horn or a chili pepper, *i corno* was said to protect the wearer from an unhealthy dose of the evil eye, which many called "The Overlook."

Midday on New Year's Day, Rose had recovered enough from her brain-crushing hangover to discuss with Sully the matter concerning Denise. Rose vowed never to take another drink for as long as she lived—and she held fast to her word. She recalled that Sully had come home in the wee hours, and had sensed his presence in their bed which bowed from the weight of the large man. Rose had a vague recollection of Sully being there as she scurried for the bathroom to embrace the bowl. She didn't think it fitting to use the slop bucket Angela had left on Rose's side of the bed. She was grateful she managed to convince the girl to go home to Augie and leave Rose alone with her self-inflicted misery.

Sully rubbed Rose's back as she moaned, curled away from him on the mattress. He stroked her hair until she told him, and not cruelly, that she felt so poorly even her hair hurt. Then Rose bolted for the toilet again.

Stan was concerned. The boy had never seen his mother so ill, not even when she'd had the influenza. Stan, a notorious early riser, had slept in because he'd gone to bed so late the night before. Tiger, who'd come in shortly after the bells of St. Catherine's had tolled the hour of three, was burrowed beneath the covers in the room he shared with his brother when Stan finally woke. "I'm worried Ma is going to croak," he whispered to Tiger. "I never heard a person puke so much."

"It's nothing," he convinced Stan. "She probably has a stomach bug. Once I barfed for days," Tiger exaggerated, and commenced to tell the boy about the time he and Jimmy Burns had eaten their way through Borough Park one temperate summer day—pizza from Mario's, a chocolate egg cream and salted pretzel rod from Dora's Luncheonette, a Charlotte Russe from Piccolo's, and to top it off, an onion bagel, which sent him over the edge. "I ate myself sick then threw up a river of puke in the street. It flowed down the gutter like lava. Then Uncle Harry found me and took me home."

Stan was fascinated and immediately forgot about Rose's tender stomach. His mouth hung open in awe. "Did you get a spanking?"

"Nah," Tiger told him. "I guess they figured throwing up that much was punishment enough."

Downstairs, Bridget worked well with Angela in the kitchen, almost as seamlessly as she did with Rose. It was something particular to the Paradiso women, excluding Astrid, who had no culinary sense whatsoever. Bridget and Angela moved effortlessly about the kitchen together, handing over a spoon when it was thought of but not yet requested, deftly dancing out of the way when the other had to pass behind with a steaming tray of stuffed artichokes. Although Angela had envied this kitchen dance as a girl, it was a skill she acquired by osmosis when she grew to be a woman. Angela was an intuitive *sous chef* as she and Bridget went from one dish to the next easily, even without Rose's help.

New Year's Day brunch was simple: a "kitchen sink" *frittata* (meaning everything but the kitchen sink was folded into it—a few leftover roasted red peppers, lowly cubes of cheese, almost-forgotten olives), a mountain of pancakes, a heap of French toast with real maple syrup from the Sullivan Family's Vermont expedition that summer, fresh-squeezed orange juice made with the crate Julius had sent up from Mexico, bacon, sausages and breads, sweet and salty (date nut, *panettone*, pepperoni and lard, mostly odd pieces remaining from the festive days prior). Of course, there was intensely-flavored coffee, the best Lavazza had to offer.

"It's nonsense, Ang," Bridget told her granddaughter when Angela mentioned Rose's evil-eye fears. "The *malocchio*? From the likes of *her*?" Bridget's fingers were coated with egg wash as she dipped thick slices of yesterday's Italian bread into the yellow mixture. Angela sprinkled more cinnamon, also sent up from the Paradisos in Mexico, onto the French toast. "That *puttana* couldn't give the evil eye to a flea."

"Still," Angela said. "We should do it."

"The Overlook Prayer?" Angela nodded and drizzled extra Mexican vanilla into the egg wash bowl. She gave it a quick toss with a bent fork Bridget kept solely for the purpose of beating eggs just so. "The Overlook is not to be taken lightly. It's very powerful."

"It is," Angela admitted. "But Momma's been so moody lately, even with Tiger home."

"She's afraid we'll lose Stan," Bridget said thoughtfully. "Our own Christmas miracle." The cast iron frying pan had begun to smoke under its light brush of butter. It sizzled gratefully beneath the ovals of egg-soaked chunks of Italian bread. Bridget insisted on naming the dish "Italian toast," since it was made with Italian bread.

"Who could blame her?" Angela pointed out. "That woman has been skulking around like a graveyard ghost, coming up to Stan outside school, peering into our windows."

"Even Harry couldn't talk sense into her," Bridget sighed. She flipped the fried bread with the spatula Angela had wordlessly given her grandmother the moment the bread was ready to be turned.

"Teach me how to do it," Angela told Bridget.

"French toast? Why, anyone could do it. Anyone except Astrid."

"You know what I mean, Gram." Angela nudged Bridget with her belly. "The Overlook Prayer. I'm old enough."

"Your mother doesn't even want to learn it. It scares her."

"True, it's powerful," Angela agreed. "But I'm not afraid."

One by one, Bridget removed the slices of Italian toast to a flower-patterned platter. When she was done, Angela slipped the plate into the oven which was set to less than a proofing temperature of two-hundred degrees. "You used to do it when Tiger and me were little, when we had a headache that wouldn't go away or a fever that wouldn't break," Angela mused.

Bridget smiled in reminiscence. "Making the sign of the cross with salt or oil on your forehead…"

"…then throwing the basin of water out the window when the prayer was done," Angela finished.

"I also did it when someone was jealous or 'overlooked' you. Afterwards, you give praise to God."

"Always. That's where its strength comes from, right?" Bridget nodded. Angela closed the door on the enamel Hotpoint, then asked, "Would you teach me the Prayer?"

Bridget thought deeply about her granddaughter's request. It was an awesome responsibility. The Overlook Prayer protected your family and friends from the evil eye.

It was so potent that it could reverse bad luck even after the evil eye had been cast. As Italian superstition dictated, the Overlook Prayer could only be passed down from woman to woman, in the same family. In addition, it could only be taught on two sacred days each year: Christmas Eve and the Feast of the Epiphany. Bridget believed in the Overlook Prayer the way she believed Poppa loved her: with all her heart and all her being. To Bridget, the Overlook Prayer was the embodiment of the power of faith.

Fruitful with repetition, the Prayer consisted of nine straightforward lines, combined with an invocation from the Apostles. Bridget only knew the Overlook Prayer in Italian, a language Angela didn't understand. The Prayer could be written down, but if so, the slip of paper it was written on had to be destroyed by midnight that very same day. If its steps were not strictly adhered to, the Overlook Prayer would lose its power for both the teacher and the taught.

With another round of egg-infused bread frying in the blackened pan, Angela said to her grandmother. "Otherwise, if you don't teach me, the Overlook Prayer would die with you."

None of Bridget's daughters believed enough in the strength of the Prayer to learn it, although Bridget had used it often to aid them in times of trouble without their knowledge: when Tony was terrorizing the entire family, when Jo was unable to carry a child, when Tiger was in the European Theatre and then in the Pacific, and also for Harry. (Bridget was convinced that without the Overlook Prayer, Harry would not have survived his injuries.) She also used the incantation to rid Patrick Sullivan of his crippling shyness so he would finally ask her daughter to marry him—plus she employed the Prayer so Rose would have the wisdom to say 'yes.' And here was Angela, begging to be taught the mystical lines which would end with Bridget if she didn't. There was only one answer.

"Christmas Eve has come and gone," Bridget said. "And who could learn something so important with all of the cooking going on?"

The girl's face brightened. Angela hugged her grandmother. "I know you used it when I got pregnant again," she whispered into the silken, multicolored bun at the nape of Bridget's neck. "I know because suddenly, I felt better and I believed everything would be all right."

"That leaves January 6th," Bridget announced officiously, turning off the jet beneath the burner. "It gives us only a few days to prepare."

As Bridget and Angela stepped to the table, they each grabbed a knife and a cutting board, and set to turning the succulent Mexican oranges into juice. They moved quickly, halving, squeezing, straining, then starting over. As they did, Bridget explained the finer points of the Overlook Prayer to Angela, what she could and couldn't do. Angela listened as voraciously as she did when the skinny, blue-eyed singer Frank Sinatra came on the radio. (Most of the neighborhood girls thought Tiger resembled the crooner from Hoboken, and the Paradisos did also.) Angela nodded, cut, juiced and absorbed. It was decided that early on Sunday morning, before Bridget started the gravy, she would take pen to paper and translate the Overlook Prayer into English for Angela to learn by midnight.

Angela carried the pitcher of orange juice into the dining room with Bridget close behind her, toting a platter of sliced *panettone*. Poppa was asleep on his favorite chair in the adjoining parlor, unaware of the bustle around him. Astrid, Stan and Wendy had already set the table. Jo was slicing the pepperoni bread she'd brought, hot from the oven at her place. Camille was folding the linen napkins into festive fans. The men—Harry, Sully, Tiger and John—were gathered around the radio, listening to Oklahoma A&M and St. Mary's battle it out in the Sugar Bowl. Stan flipped through the Dick Tracy comic books he'd gotten for Christmas, half listening to the game.

"It's men against boys," Harry taunted.

Sully challenged him. "The 'boys,' as you call them, are no slouches. You'll see."

"The Okies have seven war vets," Harry added. "Including Jim Reynolds."

Tiger had seen Reynolds in passing, both a football and wartime legend, but had never spoken to him. All the GIs were in awe of Reynolds. "Flew fifty-two missions over Germany," Tiger added.

"Don't forget Bert Cole," John pointed out. "Shot down over Yugoslavia, spent months among the blasted Chetniks and made his way back to allied lines. No small feat."

"Is it true, Pop?" Stan wondered.

"Tis," Sully said, taking a sip of the blackberry brandy Poppa had given him when he came downstairs. He'd never had a taste for the sugary liqueur and just took it to be polite. Then the old man proceeded to "rest his eyes" even as the football game blared on the radio.

"St. Mary's doesn't have a chance, though," Sully pushed. "What with the flu bug that bit them a few days ago."

"Don't be too sure," John challenged.

How a person could sleep in that racket was beyond Bridget, but there was her husband of "forty-some-odd years," out for the count. If it hadn't been for his soft snoring, Bridget might have moved closer to him and anxiously listened for the sound of his breathing. Her *Michele Archangelo* had slowed down a great deal lately. He didn't take long walks like he used to and when he did, they became shorter since he grew winded easily. At times, especially when he first woke up, Poppa seemed dazed. He didn't follow conversations as deeply as he once did, but he soon returned to Bridget, his eyes sparkling with recognition. When she taught Angela the Overlook Prayer in a few days, their first entreaty would be for Poppa, for life in general had given him the Overlook as he aged.

"Who else is coming?" Astrid pushed, trying to sneak in a bite before they said Grace. (This time, it was a fallen crust of pepperoni bread she didn't think anyone would miss.)

Gently smacking Astrid's hand from the bread, Jo replied, "Just us," as if more than a dozen was a wee number. People were always coming to the Paradiso home unexpectedly, and they were always welcome, for there was always enough. And of course, there was the ever-present Ti-Tu, Augie's phantom brother, a tacit part of the family now.

"Where's Rosie?" Astrid wondered, when she knew full well where her sister was.

"She's, uh, under the weather," Sully said.

Astrid gave a quick bark somewhere between a laugh and a sound of scorn. "Paying the piper, you mean," Astrid added. Stan didn't understand the reference. He couldn't imagine a flute player in the john with his mother, and he hadn't heard anything remotely resembling flute music, just lots of retching and moaning to accompany the smell of sick. Sully flashed Astrid an annoyed look, to which she responded, "What?" However, she ceased and desisted.

Bridget's familiar touch on Poppa's shoulder woke him. He ruffled the pages of the *Eagle*, as though he'd been reading it all along. "Brunch," she told him, brushing her lips along his forehead. Poppa rose and took his seat at the head of the dinner table with the seltzer bottle at his feet, ready to dispense a spritz at a moment's notice. Everyone occupied their unofficial places at the table, Rose's seat between Sully and Stan noticeably empty. Platters were circulated in an orderly fashion, with no one serving themselves too much or too little. Bridget always coaxed when she thought an adequate amount hadn't been taken.

When the plates were filled, there was a pause, and heads were bowed, although Sully had to poke Stan to put down his fork. Poppa cleared his throat and said what he did at the start of every family meal: "I thank God that we're together, and I hope we can all be together again next year." Then he added, "And to those who are here in spirit, on their knees, praying to the God of Porcelain, we think of them, too."

Everyone, even Stan, knew that Poppa was referring to his eldest daughter, Rose, though the boy would have to ask Tiger later what the reference to the deity of ceramics meant. The meal, though delicious, wasn't as buoyant as most were at the Paradiso table. Perhaps this was due to the events of the previous evening, the unconscious vagrant woman found on their doorstep, providing a curious ending to 1945. Perhaps it was the fact that Rose was absent or that Tiger was so newly present that he didn't feel part of the family just yet. Still, there was quiet laughter, good-natured ribbing and the sound of food being savored.

Rose lay curled up on the sofa in her parlor, directly upstairs from her parents' dining room. She was covered with an afghan crocheted in a wavelike pattern in varied shades of azure. Each of Bridget's children and their families had at least one but in different colors. Astrid's was in hues of green, Jo's was variations of peach and Camille's was a rainbow of reds. (Even Julius and Kelly's families had them, in yellows and browns, respectively. They carried them across the country and around the world, wherever they went.) Lying beneath the blanket her mother had so lovingly created made Rose feel better, made everyone feel better when they were ailing. Rose listened to the muffled voices of her family downstairs, which was also a comfort to her.

When the telephone rang in Poppa and Bridget's place downstairs, Rose figured it was Sophie Veronica, her brother Kelly's widow in Tucson, for she phoned on every holiday, major or minor, albeit briefly. It would be just before the ten o'clock mass at St. Cyril's Roman Catholic Church, where Sophie Veronica sang each Sunday and holiday. (In addition to this being the first day of the New Year, a good Catholic girl like Rosanna Maria knew January 1st also celebrated the Solemnity of Mary, the Holy Mother of God.) In spite of her queasiness, Rose smiled at the sound of Bridget's raised voice when she spoke on a long-distance call. (They often joked that she didn't need a telephone to be heard.) Sophie Veronica held it all together after Kelly passed away from leukemia not a year after they'd relocated to Arizona. It had been almost eight years now, and during that time, Sophie Veronica had not only kept their catering company, "Brooklyn Made," afloat, but also had a weekly column in the *Tucson Daily Citizen*. None of this would have been possible without their daughter Billie, who not only looked after her three siblings but made catering deliveries, too.

Rose drifted off to sleep to memories of her deceased brother and the echo of her mother's voice sifting up through the hallway, the barf bucket an arm's length away, just in case.

It took Sully several days to summon the courage to talk to Rose about Denise Walters, and even then, he knew he had to tread lightly. Subtlety was never the lumbering man's strong suit. Sully kept searching for the right moment to discuss "the Denise Matter" with Rose, only it hadn't come, not for five days at least.

On the Feast of the Three Kings, Stan was abuzz about the lesser but thoughtful gifts the Three Wise Men had left for him in exchange for the boy putting out hay, a carrot and a dish of water for the Magi's camels. He didn't believe in Santa Claus anymore, but the "Three Wise Guys" were another matter entirely. (This is what Consuelo mistakenly called them in English, as though the Three Kings were a comedy team like the Marx Brothers.) Though not an Italian tradition, leaving out food and drink for the Three Kings' beasts of burden was such an agreeable tradition that Poppa had borrowed it from his Panamanian workers at the Brooklyn Navy Yard when he'd first heard about it. After several decades, the tradition was still upheld. It was so close to his own children's hearts that they carried it on with their own families as well.

Stan was thrilled with his little treasures: a bar of Hershey's chocolate, a brightly-painted wooden top and a shining pink Spaldeen ball. True, it was not the gold, frankincense and myrrh the Magi had left for Baby Jesus, but these items better suited Stan's needs. Besides, who had a clue what myrrh was? Or even frankincense. Stan sat on the parlor rug, spinning the top on the bare wood and trying to knock it down by rolling the Spaldeen (whose real name, he had noticed was "Spalding," except everyone in Brooklyn said "Spaldeen.") Stan had permitted himself two sacred rectangles of the chocolate and was saving the rest for later.

Sully watched the boy alternately spin, roll and nibble, and figured it might be the right time to approach Rose, who was "resting her eyes" in their bedroom in the middle of the afternoon, which she had never done prior.

Downstairs, Bridget was trying to teach Angela the Overlook Prayer. It wasn't going very well. Though it had less than a dozen lines, the girl found the repetition confusing, and rightly so. Bridget remained patient, although the hours of the day were dwindling away. Her granddaughter would have to memorize it by heart by midnight or else the Prayer's power would be lost, and it would never be carried on to future generations of Paradisos. This was a great deal of pressure but Bridget tried not to fret. She reminded herself how hard it had been to teach the child how to make the shells for *manicotti* or how to chop the garlic fine enough for *spiedini*. But once Angela got the hang of something, she got it forever. They pressed on.

By Rose's breathing, Sully could tell she was awake. She lay in bed with one arm splayed across her eyes even though the room was dim. When Sully sat on the edge of the mattress, Rose looked at him. After all these years, he thought Rose's eyes beautiful, deep and dark as Hershey's kisses, even when clouded with fear or worry. "Still feeling poorly?" he asked.

"I'm in such a funk. I don't know what it is," Rose told him. But she knew; they both knew. "Maybe it's just the New Year's Blues."

Sully cradled Rose's hand and stroked the skin which was slightly rough yet alive with washing, chopping, baking and kneading, chores which turned a house into a home, their home. "It's going to be a good year," he pronounced. "I can tell."

"You can?" Rose wondered. "There's so much loss, so much sadness. Eichmann's escaped and…"

"But *Show Boat's* back on Broadway. I promise to take you soon."

"Can we afford it?" Rose wondered.

"I bet Johnny's buddy still moonlights at the Ziegfeld. I'll see what I can do."

Rose's face brightened for a moment. "That would be nice."

Meanwhile, at Bridget's kitchen table, she decided that the best way to teach Angela the Overlook Prayer was to show her. They'd had an early Sunday supper. Instead of making a spaghetti sauce, Bridget decided to heat up the Frigidaire full of leftovers (or "planned overs," as she called them). The family enjoyed another plentiful *smorgasbord*, a no fuss meal. For once, Bridget felt relieved at not having to cook a Sunday gravy. She was bone tired from all the kitchen activity these past few weeks, and welcomed the break. Now she had the rest of the afternoon to teach Angela the forceful incantation, which began with the sign of the cross.

Upstairs, Sully took a deep breath and a leap. "I know why you've felt so bad," he ventured, then paused, waiting for Rose to protest. "It's because of her. You're afraid." Tears oozed out from the corner of Rose's eyes, but Sully didn't stop. Instead, he plowed forward. "We're all afraid. We don't want to lose Stan either."

Rose bit her lip to staunch her crying. "You don't understand. She could…she could…"

"She can't do a thing," Sully told her. "Stan's ours. We adopted him fair and square. It's legal, on the up and up. She signed the papers."

"She was probably drunk when she did," Rose sneered.

"It was still legal. You realize that, right?"

"I do," she admitted. "But…"

Sully smoothed the hickory-shaded hair from Rose's face. It was beginning to become threaded with silver, just like her mother's. Somehow, this made her even lovelier in Sully's eyes. "We have to do it," he said. "We have to tell him. And soon."

Rose shook her head from side to side like a stubborn toddler. "I don't even know how."

"Neither do I but we have to. Stan deserves the truth."

"That we've been lying to him? That he isn't really ours?"

"He is ours," Sully said forcefully, then added more softly, "What scares you the most?"

Rose thought for a moment. "That he won't feel like he's part of us."

Sully grasped Rose's chin. It looked insignificant and childlike in his fingers. "He's ours as much as Tiger and Angie are ours. We just have to make sure he feels it." Rose was silent. The tears flowed steadily now. "She's dying," Sully told his wife. "She asked to see him before she passes." Rose sat up with a start. Her pleasant, pretty face became rock, immovable. "No!" she barked. "No!"

From behind the closed bedroom door, Stan called, "Ma? You okay?"

"I'm fine," Rose tried to convince Stan, though she clearly was not.

Sully held her firmly by the shoulders. "The real question is, can you live with it? Can you live with denying a dying woman her last wish?" They both knew Rose couldn't.

In the well-used kitchen downstairs, Bridget and Angela, hands joined, were just finishing the Overlook Prayer. The girl recited it in tandem with her grandmother, a few beats behind her. Toward the last few lines, they both began to yawn, and Bridget laughed. "When you start to yawn, it's working," she told Angela.

Poppa came into the kitchen, looking for a snack. "But you ate two hours ago."

"Just a piece of bread and *provolone*," he said. "Maybe a slice of salami, and a little glass of wine to wash it down."

Upstairs, Rose climbed out of bed. She began to change from robe to housedress. "How about we have a little supper? Something light, maybe *pastina* and eggs." She added, "It's strange, but suddenly, I feel better."

Downstairs, in Bridget's kitchen, just after sunset (when the might of the Overlook Prayer is strongest), she and Angela were in the process of burning the copy Bridget had carefully written out for her granddaughter in English. Angela turned on the gas jet while Bridget scraped a matchstick against the box's strike strip, then touched it to the burner. The jet lit in a halo-like blue flame. Next, Bridget held the sheaf of notepaper to the fire. The paper disappeared in a curl of ash. All that remained was the echo of the words the paper had once held. Moments earlier, the Prayer had reverberated on the kitchen walls, young voice mingling with old, mixing with the scent of countless good meals (and a few bad), memories and love. Now, it was just dust.

Angela had no need for the cheat sheet anymore for she remembered every word of the Overlook Prayer flawlessly, and she would do so until the day she died, decades later. So would the daughter she carried.

Suddenly, Angela was very tired and couldn't stop yawning. Neither could Bridget. They both retreated to the comfort of their respective bedrooms and slept peacefully through the night.

Chapter Nineteen

The Visitation

It went better than they had expected. Sully called Stan away from another game of pink ball versus wooden top in the parlor. (It had become his favorite game of late.) Rose was already waiting in the kitchen with a steaming mug of hot chocolate, sprinkled with cinnamon, the way Stan liked it. At first, the boy thought he was in trouble. He followed Sully onto the kitchen's checkerboard floor with a drag in his step. But when he saw the cocoa waiting at the table and a ginger snap on a plate beside it, Stan figured he was in the clear.

Sully sat the child down and without sugar-coating the story, explaining to him how he'd come into their lives and how they'd loved him from the very start, from the moment they'd laid eyes on him. "And we still do," Rose told Stan, putting another cookie on his plate.

"Who's my real mom?" Stan asked, taking a bite of the molasses-sweetened circle.

"I think of myself as your real mom," Rose confessed to him, her voice wavering. "But technically, it's that woman. You and Wendy call her 'The Yellow Queen.'"

"So, that's why she's been following me," Stan said, chewing thoughtfully.

Sully cleared his throat. "When you were a baby, the Yellow Queen couldn't look after you, so she gave you to us."

"Why you? Why here?" Stan wondered.

Rose looked at Sully, giving him silent permission to tell but he cowered. "Because she knew we would take care of you," Sully said.

"And because…" Rose began. "Because Tony is your father."

"The same dad Tiger and Angie have?"

"Yes," Sully and Rose responded together.

"Then I *do* belong here," Stan stated with a certainty. "Can I have another cookie?"

Rose ruffled up his hair. "No. Supper's soon. Italian wedding soup, for starters."

"With those tiny meatballs?" Stan gasped.

"Of course," Rose told him.

"My favorite!" When Stan hugged Rose, she thought she'd burst with happiness. "Thanks, Ma," he said into her apron. Sully turned away, rubbing his eyes with a handkerchief white as the snow starting to come down outside the fogged-up window.

Ready to prepare supper, Rose grabbed an egg from the carton on the sill. "There's just one more thing," she began.

It had already been arranged. After school the following day, Stanley Sullivan would finally meet the woman who had given birth to him. They were careful not to call Denise Walters Stan's mother because in its truest sense of the word, she wasn't. A mother brings up a child, nurtures a child, and teaches a child. Denise did none of these things for her son. She had merely brought him into the world. Rose reminded herself of this fact as she walked to Stan's school on Fort Hamilton Parkway to meet him.

She was a Nervous Nellie about the visitation all day while Sully walked the beat and Stan did his lessons at PS 131. Only it wasn't the same paralyzing fear she'd known the past few weeks. Instead, this was a normal, rational apprehension. Poppa did his best to quell Rose's worries when she stopped into her parents' apartment before she left. "I forget he isn't ours," Poppa told her honestly. "Because he *is* ours. Truly, the boy is. You must realize that, Rosanna Maria."

"I do, Pop," she admitted. "At least my mind does, but my heart is scared." Her voice cracked on the last word. "Scared we'll lose him."

Bridget kissed Rose on the cheek. "The heart is foolish sometimes," she said to her daughter. And in Bridget's mind, she recalled the second line of the Overlook Prayer, the one which began, "*The heart against the mind…*" Bridget knew at once the Prayer had worked.

Rose had dressed in her best winter coat, the slate-colored wool wrap from A&S downtown which was as toasty as a blanket. It had a built-in scarf and a smart matching hat, complete with a stylish red feather. Rose rarely wore it because it was too fancy for every day. She'd made sure to dress Stan in his Sunday best, and scrubbed behind his ears with a damp washcloth that morning. "Nobody's going to look back there, Ma," he protested, wincing.

"They might," she conceded, scouring his skin diligently. "And you're wearing clean undershorts?" she continued.

"Yeah," he sighed—he wasn't. Although he'd worn them the day before, he thought they still smelled moderately fresh.

Rose smiled at her memory of the boy's face before he left for school that morning. She pictured the same dusting of tan freckles across his nose that Tiger had, the bottle-green eyes which always sparked with the potential of laughter, even when he was serious. Rose's boots crunched in the light cover of snow. She hoped Stan

remembered to put on his own Totes over his shoes after
school, though he complained about having to wear them.
She walked through the sea of children, recently released
from being educated. It was as though a floodgate had been
opened. They giggled and jostled each other, flush-faced
with the weather. There was an occasional, "Hello, Missus
Sullivan," to which greeted each child by name.

Stan was waiting for Rose on PS 131's front steps as he'd
been instructed. He wore not just his galoshes but his hat and
gloves as well. Wendy was beside him, chattering happily. Jo
must have told her to stand there with him, Rose decided. Jo
also must have also told Wendy about Stan's true parentage.
She could see by the girl's eyes. Wendy hugged her favorite
aunt as warmly as ever. To her cousin, she whispered, "Good
luck," and kissed his hat. "Remember, this doesn't change
anything," Wendy added. "You're still my stupid cousin."
Stan gave her a little shove and Wendy shoved him back.

When the boy took Rose's hand without her bidding, she
smiled on the inside. It was five blocks to United Israel Zion,
and they moved quickly through the chilled, windless air.
Sully was to meet them in the lobby before they went up to
the women's charity ward. He was already standing there
when they arrived. Together, they boarded the crowded lift
to the third floor, the elevator operator slamming the gate
shut and closing the grate noisily behind it. Sully greeted the
man, whose nametag read "Liam." 'My pop seems to know
everyone in Borough Park,' Stan thought with pride.

The crammed elevator was a microcosm of society, with
simple pea coats brushing lush furs, the scent of curries
mingling with last night's corned beef and cabbage and
heavily-garliced tomato sauce. The elevator inhabitants had
the look of Brooklyn itself, a comfortable mix of people
from a myriad of places, yet they were, all of them, home,
even if they weren't born there. Stan felt lulled by the by the
closeness, by the aroma of life cradling him.

The elevator's bell dinged before the cage, and then the
door, slid open. "Third floor women's ward!" piped Liam.

Amid "Pardon me's," the three made their way out of the elevator, but not before Sully told Liam, "The best to your Mam and Pap."

Liam responded, "Same to your in-laws. Tell Uncle Mike that Liam said 'Hey.'"

"Will do," Sully agreed. He led the way to Denise's ward slowly, walking abreast with Stan and Rose. "There's no danger you'll catch it," Sully assured his wife. "TB's contagious, but she's been on meds for a week or so. It's harder to catch than you might imagine. Even the docs and nurses don't wear masks." Rose nodded. Her biggest fear wasn't catching the disease; it was something larger than that.

"It smells funny in here," Stan announced.

"It's the medicines, the cleaning fluids," Sully explained.

The boy shook his head. "It's different. It smells like sick people. Sick people and something else."

They stopped at the ward's wide doorway. Inside, there was bed after bed of anonymous women in washed-out hospital gowns lying on white sheets. "This is it," Sully told them. "She's in Bed Number Five. It's by the window." He took their jackets, Stan's hat and gloves, then nudged the boy forward but the child didn't move.

"I can't go in alone," Stan said. "I want Ma to come with me."

Rose was surprised by her son's request but did as he asked. Again, he grabbed her hand. Stan's fingers felt clammy and unusually small in Rose's. "Sorry, it's sweaty," he apologized. Rose felt Stan's fingernails sharply pressing into the meat of her palm and made a mental note to cut them when they got home.

"It will be okay," Rose convinced the boy.

The two entered the ward. Rose barely recognized Denise. She vaguely resembled the curvy chorine who'd walked up to Tony's casket and spat on him. Denise was even greatly changed from the person who'd collapsed on the porch steps days earlier. Diminished, languished, a lily pressed into a forgotten memory book. Her skin appeared colorless, almost translucent. Rose could see the veins, painted a wan blue, beneath her flesh. The woman's pulse beat rhythmically in her neck. She was connected to tubing that led to glass bottles which were hung upside down from a stainless-steel tree.

It didn't seem possible but Stan grasped Rose's hand even tighter. Sensing their presence at the foot of her bed, the woman opened her eyes. "Stanley," she breathed. "Sit."

A wooden chair waited beside the bed. Rose pointed the boy toward it, slipping her fingers from his. "Go," she told him. "I'll be right here." To give them privacy, Rose took a few steps back. Stan glanced at her with a worried expression on his face, then sunk in the chair.

"My Stanley," the woman in the bed said. With the words came a stench: like what wafted up out of a sewer in the summer, what dogs leave behind on the pavement. Stan decided it was the scent of death coming to get you. He didn't know what to say to the woman, so he figured he would wait until he thought of something good. Instead of talking, he searched the lady's pasty face for a fragment of remembrance, for a piece of her that resembled a piece of him, but came up empty. Tears rolled down the woman's gaunt cheeks. Her fingers scrabbled to the sheets, as though seeking something. His hand? Stan wouldn't take hers—he was afraid to touch her, afraid she might break. Instead, he grasped the railing on the side of the bed with his fists.

Denise licked her lips but they were still cracked and dry. "You look just like your brother."

"How do you know Tiger?" Stan asked, in awe.

"Our paths crossed. I call him 'Anthony,' though," she said. "He's A-okay. I was cold and he gave me his gloves, and he didn't know me from Adam." Stan didn't speak so she continued. "You're a fine boy, Stanley. I just know it."

"How?" he challenged.

"Your eyes. They're honest eyes."

Stan refused to let himself be swayed by pretty words, even if the person who uttered them was very ill. "Why were you following me?"

The woman fingered her hair. It stood on end like Stan's did when it was dirty. "I needed to see…" she began, "…to see that you were all right. I was sick and…" Her voice failed her.

"What would you have done if I wasn't all right?" Stan prodded. For this, she had no answer. "They take good care of me," he told her.

"I know that."

"They love me," he added, hoping it would hurt her.

"I love you, too, son," she offered in a tiny voice.

"Then why did you give me away?"

The woman's hand trailed to her throat, which had a deep, hollow indentation at its base. Stan noticed that the skin around her nails was ragged. "That's a tough one," she admitted. "I couldn't give you much of a life, and I wanted you to have better."

"Better than what, lady?"

Her eyes met his, eyes which must have been nice once but now were red around the rims and painted with blood vessels. Her nose was rubicund also, and slightly bulbous. "Better than me, I suppose," she said.

Although Stan felt sorry for her, he wasn't certain he could be courteous. "And please," she added. "Please don't call me 'lady.' I ain't a lady. Never was."

"What should I call you, then?"

She thought for a moment. Thinking sapped her energy. "Well, not 'Ma.' I ain't that neither…I don't know."

"We had a name for you," Stan confessed. "Me and Wendy, when you were following us."

"What was it?"

Stan looked down. "You'll laugh."

"I won't. Promise," she swore, slashing an X over her chest. "Cross my heart. Honest."

He reddened. "We used to call you 'The Yellow Queen.'"

Stan noticed that the woman was missing a few teeth, and those left in her mouth were stained brownish and broken. "The Yellow Queen," she nodded. "I been called worse. Why the Yellow Queen?" she wondered.

Stan shrugged. "Wendy…that's my cousin. Wendy said you reminded her of the Red Queen. Except you had yellow hair."

"The Red Queen?"

"You know, from *Alice in Wonderland*. It's a book. Wendy likes to read. A lot."

"And you?"

"Not so much."

"But you will. I thought reading was the cat's pajamas once upon a time." Her last words came out as a rasp, and the rasp became a cough. The woman held a small, white hand towel to her mouth. It came away stained with a poppy flower pattern. She took a sip of water from a tin cup on the bed stand. "Reading takes you to these magical places you might never get to in real life."

"Okay," Stan relented, but only because she was ailing. He didn't really believe her.

The slender hand of a nurse named Marta rested on Stan's shoulder. Nurse Marta wore a stiff cap with a veil partially covering her hair, which made her resemble a pure-hearted nun—although in his short life, Stan had never met a kindly nun. All the nuns he knew were as mean as junkyard dogs. "It's time, child," she told him.

Before Stan left the sick woman's side, she grabbed him and pulled him closer. Rose saw Stan nod before he came back to her. "You all right?" Rose asked, squeezing his shoulders.

Stan nodded. "She wants to talk to you."

"Me?" Rose wondered incredulously.

"You," he said. "Go ahead. She doesn't bite."

Rose looked toward Bed Number Five. The shadow of a woman amid the sheets silently beckoning her, and Rose went. The nurse stopped her. "Miss Walters has had enough excitement for one day," the nurse cautioned.

"Jeeze Louise, Marta," Denise complained. "Can't a girl have a little visit?" Nurse Marta was unmoved. "I got to tell her something. Something important," Denise pleaded.

Nurse Marta's lips unpursed. "Two minutes, Denise. No more."

Rose stood at Denise Walters' bedside. This was someone Rose had despised for so long, someone she'd feared, but now Rose saw that Denise wasn't a monster or a harpy; she was just a woman, just like her, but a woman who was dying. Rose's chest was flooded with compassion and another emotion which puzzled her. Was it the forgiveness of one's enemies Father Dunn spoke so fervently of from the lectern at St. Catherine's? Was it the charity of Our Savior manifesting itself in her. No, Rose concluded, it was pity, plain and simple.

Rose looked at the dried-out husk of a woman before her. When Denise tried to take a breath it caught in her throat. "I wanted to say…that I'm sorry. I'm sorry for what I done to you," Denise sighed. She paused, hoping the woman would say it was all right, but Rose didn't utter a word, because it wasn't all right; it was just over. "And I also wanted to say…thank you. Thank you for looking after my son…my Stanley."

"He's my son," Rose said simply. "And you're welcome."

"You done a good job," Denise croaked.

"Thank you. Me and my Paddy, that's my husband, and my family…we love Stan like he's our own."

"He *is* yours," Denise admitted. "He's more yours than mine." Then the floodgates opened, as both women knew they would. "Everything I have is gone," Denise lamented. Her chest heaved with the weight of her words. "But it's my own fault. I only have myself to blame."

Even though it was true, Rose told her, "Don't be so hard on yourself."

"Why not?" Denise wondered. Rose couldn't figure out why not, so she was silent. "You must hate me," Denise added.

Rose considered this for a moment. "No," she said plainly. "I don't think I truly hate anybody. Not even you."

"Then you're a better man than I am, Gunga Din." It was a strange comment but Rose understood the reference.

Kipling's poem was one Poppa quoted often. Manny Ortez Vega at the Brooklyn Navy Yard even nicknamed Tiger "Gunga Din" when he was a water boy there one summer.

"I hated you," Denise hissed through her sniveling. "I hated you because he loved you, even though he had me."

"That was a long time ago," Rose said. "Water under the bridge. He's dead and buried almost ten years now."

Denise wiped her eyes and her dripping nose on the stained hand towel. "I'll be there soon enough. But not a nice place like Green-Wood. It will be Potter's Field for me, thrown into a mass grave like a mutt, with no one to mourn me. But I guess it's what I deserve." Denise started weeping, weeping as though her heart were torn in two.

Before she could stop herself, Rose heard herself saying, "I won't let that happen."

Gasping in mid-sob, Denise questioned, "You won't?"

"You gave birth to my son," Rose explained. Denise grabbed Rose's hand, kissed it. It smelled the type of clean Denise had never known, even as a child. For one so ill, she had a forceful grip. 'A death grip,' Rose conceded then pushed the thought from her mind.

Nurse Marta was upon them. She eased the women gently apart. "She needs to rest now, Miss."

This time, Denise didn't complain; she was too exhausted. She closed her eyes. "Thank you," Denise mouthed, tears leaking down her face. She immediately fell into a deep sleep.

The nurse walked Rose to the ward's door. "Thank you for visiting her," Nurse Marta said. "She's got no one. Except for the good-looking young man who comes." Rose knew at once that the man the nurse referenced was Tiger. It made her proud. "The poor dear," Nurse Marta continued. "She's as penniless as a church mouse."

Rose hadn't noticed the other women in the ward when she'd first come in, so focused was she upon the difficult task at hand. She hadn't noticed the disagreeable odor, though Stan had mentioned it. She hadn't even noticed the constant wall of sound, a buzz, a hum, the magpie chatter of voices, crying out to no one in particular. Rose had to get out of this stifling place, even if it was like an icebox on the street. She needed to breathe fresh air.

At the ward's doorway, Nurse Marta asked, "Are you and Miss Walters friends? Old friends?"

Rose was too weary to recount the whole story—of her husband's drinking, of his cruelty, of his philandering which led to Denise's bed. "Yes," Rose told the nurse. "Something like that."

Sully was waiting for Rose outside the door but Stan was nowhere in sight. For a moment, Rose panicked. Had Stan run away? Was he upset? Inconsolable? "Tiger went off with him," Sully explained. "He'll be okay." And Rose was sure he would be. When she fell into her husband's arms, exhausted and relieved, Sully held Rose fast and close to his heart.

Chapter Twenty

The Lucky Buck

Jack, the owner and main barkeep of The Lucky Buck, kept a tin of cocoa powder stowed in one of the cubbies beneath the polished wooden bar for this very purpose: for the rare times a man brought in a distressed child who needed pampering by way of something sweet. Jack prided himself upon making a mean hot chocolate, as memorable as his hot toddy. He also kept a hot plate behind the bar, plus a bowl of sugar and a canister of whipped cream, in case of emergencies.

Jack had always liked the Martino kid, although he couldn't say the same for his father, who'd been booted out of The Lucky Buck more times than Jack could count. He didn't run that type of establishment, a bucket of blood where fights broke out, illegal substances and women's charms were bought and sold. Jack did his best to keep the place on the up and up, to make The Lucky Buck a haven where a working stiff could toss back a few after a long shift spent walking the beat or riding the rails, a place where you could "get right" before you went home to the little woman and the little ones, not a place to get shit-faced. If you wanted that sort of joint, then you could just hightail it over to Mooney's on Flatbush or Lauderback's on Prospect. Jack would even spot you a token for the train fare.

Tiger introduced the child to Jack as his brother and the resemblance was uncanny. Tiger even introduced Stan to Jimmy Burns, his childhood friend who'd been bar-backing at the Lucky Buck for a few weeks. Jimmy would have been homeless if it hadn't been for Jack. He hired Jimmy to swab the floors and sterilize the glasses. In exchange, he let Jimmy sleep in the storeroom and threw him a few dollars to live on. Jack could never forget the dirty-faced, snot-nosed, raggedy child with two drunks for parents; he felt for Jimmy Burns, he really did. Heck, Jack remembered Tiger as a knock-kneed boy in knickers whose father, the stinking bum, had brought in once or twice when Tony was supposed to be minding the tyke. Tiger was a good kid who always remembered to thank Jack for the cup of ginger ale after he wolfed down the cherry. The boy also played nicely with his own son, Jack, Jr., who was about the same age.

Although Stan wasn't crying, the boy was clearly upset. Jack placed the mug of cocoa in front of him, no questions asked. The child's face lit up at the sight of it, like the Christmas lights on Fifth Avenue. Jack added an extra spritz of whipped cream on top, and a cherry, just to see that smile again. He had a soft spot for kids, had six himself, and soon, a grandchild on the way from Jack, Jr. and Meghan, God willing.

"Hold out your finger," Jack told Stan. The boy did. Jack covered it with a dab of whipped cream which Stan inhaled, thanking Jack with a full mouth. In front of Tiger, Jack slipped a mug of coffee. "It's fresh," Jack assured him, gesturing to a battered aluminum pot. "The wife brewed it not thirty minutes ago."

Then Jack left the two alone, for it seemed they needed to discuss grave things. Jack was that kind of barkeep; he surmised without being enlightened. A rare bird with a sharp sense of perception, Jack was part psychologist, part priest, part confidant. He knew when to speak and when to keep his big trap shut. He had a knack for remembering names as well as faces, a necessary skill for a barkeep. Jack was also the glue which held the fabric of his neighborhood together. Jobs were gotten at The Lucky Buck, solid fellows were set up with cousins once removed, apartments were found. Along with Houlie at Farrell's a few parishes away, fellows like Jack Link were pure gold.

For a time, Tiger and Stan said nothing, just sipped their mugs of steaming beige liquid from their bar stools, silently enjoying the other's presence. Stan couldn't believe his good fortune—two hot chocolates in two days. It was the boy who spoke first. "I didn't feel anything," Stan admitted to his brother. "I mean, I felt bad for her because she's so sick but I didn't feel like she was my ma."

"It takes a lot to be a mother," Tiger said. "A mother looks after you, no matter what. She's always there for you. When you're in trouble and when you win first prize for memorizing a poem. Get what I mean?"

"Yes," Stan answered. "I do."

Then they covered a number of topics, including the Yankees' spring training due to start in a few months. When Jack heard sports mentioned, he figured it was safe to return. "Do you think McCarthy can do it this season?" Jack ventured, drying whiskey glasses with a cloth.

"Why, sure," Tiger replied.

The door of The Lucky Buck opened and an icy whoosh of air swept in. From the corner of his eye, Tiger saw Poppa, Harry, and John enter the bar, removing their hats and opening their overcoats. "Mind if we join the party?" Poppa asked.

Stan leapt to his feet. Instead of a manly handshake, he hugged each of them. Having his family there filled Stan with joy—it meant he was still part of them. Stan was sorry Aunt Astrid had chased Sam away. Even though they weren't married anymore, Stan still liked him, probably even more than he did his aunt. "We were talking baseball," Stan told them.

"My favorite subject," Poppa conceded. Jack poured each of them their drink of choice—for Poppa, it was a shot glass brimming with *amaretto*, for Harry it was whiskey and for John, a ginger ale.

Sully came in a beat after they did, explaining that he'd just finished escorting Rose home safely from the hospital. "She's making chicken fricassee for supper," he said, chucking Stan on the chin.

"I love chicken fricassee!" the boy gasped.

"That's why she's making it," Sully told him, accepting the beer Jack slid in front of him. The barkeep knocked on the wood, signifying that the round was on the house. He preferred when men came into his establishment to celebrate instead of drowning their sorrows. The Lucky Buck was the type of place you were welcome to do both, but this was one of the happier times which Jack relished.

"How about number ten?" Harry posed.

"The Scooter?" Stan clarified.

Poppa nodded. "Old Phil Rizzuto. It'll be good to have him back from the War."

"He was born in Brooklyn," Tiger revealed. "And during the War, he played ball for the Navy team alongside Pee Wee Reese."

"Did you catch many games on the radio when you were overseas?" Stan wondered.

"Whenever I could but reception was sketchy," Tiger told him.

"Hell of a team, especially with Bill Dickey managing," Sully added. "Now with the War over, we'll see what happens."

Poppa took a deep sip from his aperitif. "What do you mean, we'll see what happens? Don't forget Jolting Joe."

Jack topped off Poppa's *amaretto*. "How could we forget him with you constantly reminding us?" he joked.

"Last season wasn't DiMaggio's best," Harry reminded the barkeep.

"You're lucky I let Dodgers fans into this joint," Jack said to Harry, who laughed. "No badmouthing Joe D in my place," Jack warned.

"Just you wait. Joe's got a lot of baseball left in him," Poppa said to his son-in-law.

Stan felt swell because he was part of something, something large and real and true which didn't have a name. Maybe there were no words for it, maybe it was just a feeling, a camaraderie, of being part of a whole which was bigger than you, bigger than the house you lived in, bigger than your neighborhood, bigger than all of Brooklyn, or the world, even. Stan knew that he was part of these people, of this place, no matter who had given birth to him, no matter who his Pop was, and he knew that nothing could ever change this.

"Never underestimate the power of the Scooter," Sully reminded everyone.

Poppa began, "Not only was he born in our fair borough. But he was the son of a streetcar motorman, not too different than you and Tiger," he told Stan. It occurred to the boy that he knew very little about his father. Stan would have to ask Tiger when the time was right and when he was ready to learn.

"Our Pop was a train conductor," Tiger qualified. "On the West End line. He opened and closed the doors."

Harry added, "Same union, though. The God-damned TWU, as Tony used to say."

Meanwhile, in the red brick house on Forty-Seventh Street, Rose was preparing the vegetables for the fricassee. The chicken, cut into pieces and seasoned liberally with salt and pepper, was already simmering on the stovetop. It browned in olive oil, roughly-chopped onions and minced garlic while Rose sliced celery and carrots into thick chunks. Sully preferred them cut into manly-sized mouthfuls as he phrased it, not chintzy K-ration portions. (Even though Sully was 4-F—his high blood pressure kept him out of the service—he knew about the horror that was K-rations. Everyone did.)

There was a peculiar happiness which accompanied making a dish someone loved, and Rose was experiencing this culinary euphoria as she cut and chopped. She winced when she added a dash of white wine to the chicken, recalling her New Year's Eve escapades. Rose gave the pot a stir, added the vegetables, then was satisfied.

Fitting the lid onto the pot, Rose set to making the biscuits, for what was chicken fricassee without crusty, crumbly biscuits on the side to sop up all that rich gravy?

Even inside the Lucky Buck Tavern, Stan heard the church bells ring in the dinner hour. It wasn't St. Catherine's but Holy Family, a few blocks away on Thirteenth Street. Or was it St. Thomas Aquinas down on Ninth? Stan would have to ask Sully. From years of walking the beat, he could tell the distinct timbres of the neighborhood's various church bells as easily as he could distinguish the voices of family members. "One more for the road," Harry announced. Jack filled their cups as well as his own. "But just one," Harry added. "I'm cutting back."

To reach The Lucky Buck, the four men had piled into Poppa's Buick, which he'd nicknamed Betsy, as he did all his cars, even the swanky Nash. John, who'd been dry since the Great War, would drive them home. They thanked Jack profusely for being such an agreeable host, tipped him well, and went on their way.

On the sidewalk outside, Sully posed that since it was such a fine winter evening his sons might fancy a walk home instead of squeezing into the Buick. It was several miles, most of it uphill, but both Tiger and Stan said "yes" at the same time. The brothers had taken the trolley there from United Israel and took pleasure in the chilly walk with their stepfather. There were parting handshakes as the men went their separate ways. The three walkers secured their gloves, hats, and earmuffs, and checked the fastenings of their galoshes, for it had started to flurry lightly. "Am I too old to hold your hand?" Stan asked his father.

"You'll never be too old," Sully certified, grasping the boy's leather-clad paw in his own gloved one. Stan reached for Tiger's hand as well. His brother accepted it readily and gave it a squeeze.

The three walked side by side, up Fourteenth Street, soon passing the Armory, with its statue of a bayoneted Doughboy out front. "The Armory is so huge, you can play a football game inside," Sully said to Stan. "They assembled tanks in here during the War."

"Which war?"

"Both," Sully admitted.

Tiger pointed out the Doughboy statue, eternally bent in a crouch, poised to charge. "Uncle John posed for that," Tiger told Stan.

"Really?" Stan responded, eyes wide with wonder.

His uncles had played the same joke on Tiger when he was Stan's age. It felt right to carry on the tradition. "Sure," Tiger lied, glancing at Sully, who went along with the gag with a glimmer in his eye.

As they walked, Sully remembered another meeting almost ten years earlier, before Stan came to be, at another drinking establishment. The Paradiso males had held court at Farrell's just up the road. The men who would come to be his brothers-in-law seriously discussed how they could get poor Rose of her predicament—being attached to a cheating, abusive husband. In the end, nothing they tried was successful, but problems have a way of resolving themselves sometimes. Back then, Sully never thought he'd have a family, and such a fine one at that. He rubbed Stan's thumb through his glove and smiled into the night.

Sully, Tiger and Stan turned down McDonald Avenue and surveyed the expanse of Green-Wood Cemetery to their right. "Can we walk on the other side of the street?" Stan requested with a quiver in his voice.

"Absolutely," Sully said, without asking why. Little did the boy know his father was buried there, but he soon would. Soon enough, he would.

The Lucky Buck Tavern was uncharacteristically empty. Jack had sent Jimmy on an errand and there were no customers. He took out his harmonica, a snappy little Hohner he'd had since he was twelve. The mouth harp was the sole item in his Christmas stocking that year but he didn't mind because it was all he'd wanted. The Hohner had accompanied him to the Big War in France. It had helped him woo a comely lass named Lily when he got home. It had helped him calm their babies on nights when they were fussy just as it had calmed the fears of the men in the trenches. Jack raised the harmonica to his lips. The song, which came out as familiar and easy as his breath, was a Rodgers and Hart tune called "Glad to be Unhappy."

Just then, Jack's wife Lily came down with two bowls of thick, golden chicken soup on a tray, softly singing the words to the song:

> *"Look at yourself, if you had a sense of humor*
> *You would laugh to beat the band.*
> *Look at yourself, do you still believe the rumor*
> *That romance was simply grand."*

Lily set down the bowls, napkins, silverware and pumpernickel bread, still warm from the oven, on the bar. Their eldest girl, Maureen, was supervising supper with her younger siblings upstairs. Occasionally, there was a crash or a raised voice, but Jack and Lily were confident Maureen could handle whatever arose. Lily set out the dish of butter, then sat on the barstool, and continued singing as her husband finished playing the song.

> *"Fools rush in but here am I*
> *More than glad to be unhappy.*
> *I can't win but here am I*
> *Oh so glad to be unhappy."*

When he was done, Lily smiled. Jack laid down the harmonica, sat beside her and picked up the spoon. They ate.

Chapter Twenty-One

Vigils

Wendy didn't probe about where her cousin Stan went every day after school but somehow she surmised he was going to visit the Yellow Queen. Wendy would stroll home with Janet or June, forlornly looking over her shoulder at Stan, walking with purpose down Fort Hamilton Parkway toward United Israel Zion, and away from her. Stan never brought it up the next day and Wendy knew not to bombard him with questions. There were things a person needed to keep to themselves. However, Wendy did write about her cousin and the Yellow Queen in her journal, but otherwise, she told no one about Stan's vigils.

Soon after Stan started going to sit with the Yellow Queen, the woman began falling in and out of consciousness, but even before then, they didn't talk much. What was there to say? What was there to ask? If she was sorry she given him up? If he was treated well by his adopted family? They already knew the answers. Although he couldn't explain why, Stan felt he ought to be in her presence. Mysteriously,

Denise began slipping away, letting go; it made no sense for her to stay. She had seen her son again, had gazed into his eyes, had held his hand. There was nothing else to do. The circle had been completed.

Day by day, Stan watched her fade. Little by little, the woman people said was his mother slowly became less human and more invisible, transparent, almost. It was interesting to watch, like a science experiment, observing a person become less alive, less present. Stan recalled the time in school when Mrs. McVay planted a lima bean in a Dixie cup filled with dirt, watered it and the class watched it grow, bit by bit. It was this way with the woman, but in reverse; instead of becoming more, she became less.

In her lucid moments, the Yellow Queen reminisced about the man she'd named Stan for, her father, Stanley Wallaski — although she knew she'd insulted him by shortening and Americanizing their proud Polish surname to "Walters." There was no question that the Yellow Queen loved him and that her father had loved her back. "The only man who ever treated me like gold, no matter what I did," she recalled. At times, she mistook Stan for different people: his brother, his father. Stan never corrected her. Instead, he let her yammer while he listened. It was like a serial or a picture show with twists and turns; Stan never could guess where it might go.

Occasionally, she addressed him in Polish, reverting to the language of her childhood. *"Kochanie,"* she would call him, which meant "Darling" or "Sweetheart." Or *"Mój syn,"* which was "My son." It made Stan especially uncomfortable when she uttered *"Drogi chłopcze."* The last one made his face redden when Nurse Marta translated it for him because it meant "Dear boy." The other nurses weren't as patient as Marta was with Denise or with her situation. A staunch Catholic whose family hailed from Krakow just as Denise's did, Nurse Marta would say, "But for the grace of God, go I." Stan tried to remember this adage. He hoped it would make him a more charitable person like Nurse Marta was.

Rose didn't question her son as to where he went after school because deep down she knew. He came home before sunset and managed to finish his homework, though he was quieter than usual. Sully and Tiger would occasionally go to United Israel to check on the boy, standing briefly in the charity ward's broad entrance, quietly observing. Sometimes Stan laughed when the woman chatted animatedly. Others, he merely watched the prone female form withering the bed or listened closely, trying to decipher Denise's addled words.

What a change had come over the woman who'd once resembled a bountiful version of Alice Faye, a gal with copious curves in all the right places, who favored hip-hugging frocks and sported perfectly curled and coiffed bleached-blonde tresses. Now, Denise's arms and legs were twig-like, and her once-magnificent breasts had all but disappeared into her armpits. "It won't be long now, Paddy," Marta whispered to Sully one day. They'd known each other since they were kids at PS 131. Both from broken homes, against all odds, Marta had become a nurse, and a damned good one, and Sully had become a cop, and a damned good one, too. Strange how life was a series of changes, ebbs, flows, and occasionally, instances of nature righting itself.

Angela also kept a vigil, but over the life which grew within. Her stomach was so gigantic that often she couldn't sleep, but this didn't bother her. She would give into her wakefulness and switch to a comfortable armchair, look out the window at the piles of snow, lit golden by the streetlamps. Or else, she'd sit up in bed, watching Augie sleep, breathing easily and deeply beneath his pile of blankets, topped with one of Bridget's afghans. Even if she sat in the chair, another afghan covering her belly and knees, Angela didn't feel alone. She felt almost as though the baby were on her dwindling lap. She took comfort in its movements, rubbing what could be a foot or an elbow with a flicker of a smile on her face. Angela had grown plumper and prettier during the latter part of her pregnancy, her gray-green eyes dancing with an inner light.

Sully's vigil was keeping watch over the streets. Sometimes he pictured himself a minor king surveying his kingdom, making certain everyone within it was safe. He didn't mind the winter. The air felt cleaner during that season, sharper, more refreshing. While his partner Izzy complained bitterly about the temperature, Sully, with extra meat on his bones, reveled in it. "The cold keeps the crazies off the streets," he'd note.

Izzy would reply, "And we're crazy to be out here."

Calmly, Sully would remind the cop about their decent pay scale, steady work and union benefits. Izzy would scowl in response. To appease the peevish Pole, they might pop into an all-night diner for a cup of Joe, and Izzy's mood would improve marginally—until his toes froze again. Then the two police officers would repeat their wintertime dance. In the summer, it was the same, except Izzy would *kvetch* about the infernally hellish heat instead of the subzero digits.

Sully had a particular talent for rescuing victims of the elements during his winter watches. He would be driven to turn down a specific street, to look into a certain areaway, and there, he would discover a vagrant who planned to sit down for just two short seconds and rest his dogs but ended up falling asleep. Or he would find a housewife who made a quick dart to the corner store and twisted her ankle on the ice. Patrolman Sullivan was Borough Park's own bearlike guardian angel.

Rose kept vigil in her snug, railroad-roomed apartment comfortably nestled atop her parents' place. The brick house on Forty-Seventh Street might look rickety at first glance but in reality, was as solid and stalwart as the people who lived inside it. The house had withstood torrential rainstorms, hurricanes, blizzards and nor'easters, and it would withstand additional harsh weather by the time the people who lived inside it no longer lived there.

Usually just after midnight, Rose would wake, stop in the bathroom, with its octagon pattern of black and white tiles, do her business, pull the toilet's chain in the wooden

box above, then check the boys' room. She would watch
Stan snore lightly with delight upon his face, then she would
leave when she was satisfied he was all right. Rose would
also look at Tiger's bed, often unslept in, say a short but
passionate prayer for his safety, wherever he was, then go
back to her own bed.

Finally, Rose would send up supplications for her
husband, who was out walking the beat, for Angela, for
Augie, for her unborn grandchild, and for her sisters (even
Astrid), her one living brother, her one deceased brother, and
her parents, who grew more delicate with each day. Rose
would pray for the people she liked, loved, and by the time
she got to those she didn't care for, she was already asleep.

In the bedroom directly below Rose's, Bridget fought
wakefulness which often became a vigil. Sometimes she
had an odd ache or pain she didn't have upon retiring. It was
strange, realizing that someday, maybe someday soon, she
and Poppa would be gone, and that none of this, nothing
that she knew would remain, at least not for her. Who would
occupy their apartment after they died? What would they
do with the old featherbed? What would become of the
collection of scallop-edged photographs she treasured, sent
to her from across the country and across the globe?

There were pictures Sophie Veronica dutifully sent of the
children who were growing like tumbleweeds, pictures of
everyday occurrences and milestones so her in-laws would
feel part of their lives, even though Kelly, God rest his soul,
was gone. There was a shot of Paul loading tubs of Brooklyn
Made potato salad (which used Bridget's recipe) onto the
delivery truck with Sophie Veronica. There was another
of Billie at her junior prom on the arm of a shy, toothsome
cowboy named Bob.

Would anyone think to flip over the yellowed, creased
picture from Father Carmine and read what he'd written
on the back? His inscription had both warmed and broken
Bridget's heart. He'd sent it out before Christmastime,
decades earlier, when he'd wished to be bathing in the

beneficence of his brother Michael Archangel, fattened by the cooking of his sister-in-law, and welcomed into the arms of his family. Instead, the Cardinal thought it prudent to send Father Carmine to Rome to study, and the young Jesuit suffered in silence, homesick for the holidays in Brooklyn.

Then there was the picture her son-in-law John had snapped of Bridget herself, at the front porch one long ago spring as she wrote to her friend Alice, who lived in the wilds of Van Nuys, near Los Angeles. Ankle wrapped in a bandage, reading glasses perched at the tip of her nose, sweater draped over her shoulders, deep in thought. It was the kind of picture of someone doing a seemingly insignificant act which spoke volumes—about their life, about how they were loved, cherished, even. Bridget always was partial to the photograph, and she was never pleased with the way she looked in pictures. Perhaps it was because of the way her blinded eye appeared unfocussed. Bridget reckoned that she liked John's snapshot of her on the porch because of its unspoken aspect, the emotions it implied. It was the type of picture taken of a someone who was adored, by a person who adored them.

Bridget wondered what would become of all these things, of everyone. This is one of the reasons she couldn't sleep and kept a quiet vigil many nights. Sometimes the only thing that helped her rest was reciting the Overlook Prayer. Before Bridget knew it, she was yawning, and soon enough, she was fast asleep.

Tiger's vigil was held at the shellacked wooden bars at a number of drinking establishments in the first-rate borough of Brooklyn. He was never actually drunk for he would think more than he would drink. Usually Houlie, Niall, Jack or Dermott would pour him a double shot of Dewar's and leave Tiger to his musings. Oh, they would chat him up if they sensed Tiger wanted to jaw about the virtues of the Yankees or Rita Hayworth (a product of Brooklyn like himself, *Cover Girl* being Tiger's favorite film of hers). But mostly, the barkeeps let him be.

The young man was relieved to be home, that was for sure, and he was lucky, he knew this for a fact. Tiger was lucky to be back and in one piece—a few of his friends, even his uncle, were not. But Tiger and his pal George, they were among the fortunate ones. Three weeks after his return, however, Tiger still didn't know where he fit in. Moe the Greengrocer had offered him his old job back but Tiger didn't take him up on it. To be polite, he'd thanked Moe profusely but told his former boss he was taking a little R&R. Packing and unpacking shelves, fetching fruits and vegetables from the Washington Market near Fulton and Vesey with Moe's rickety pickup truck, that was pleasant enough for a boy but Tiger was no longer a child. He wanted to do something else, something important, to be of value. Tiger wanted a career, a calling, not just a job. Especially after what he had been through in the War. Only, he didn't know what that "something" was yet. He would figure it out soon, though. He was sure he would.

Like Angela, Harry's vigil often took place at an apartment window. He pulled up the shade, careful not to rouse his wife, mindful the lamplight didn't fall across Jo's pretty face and wake her. When the glow did happen to caress Jo's visage, she looked especially lovely—skin pale and luminescent as the moon, hair a warm russet after all these years, her countenance peaceful and relaxed, his very own Kings County Sleeping Beauty. Harry would arrange the cherry wood rocker by the window, the same chair where Jo had serenely nursed Wendy when she was a baby. Harry would have a thick tumblerful of Irish whiskey at his elbow and methodically sip, only not the way he used to. Just one drink and that was it.

There, at his solitary windowsill, Harry sipped, keeping watch over the neighborhood, a sentinel, wondering what would become of him, of all of them: the Paradisos, the Sullivans, the Martinos, the Corsos and the O'Learys. Harry wanted to work, needed to work, but no one would hire him. Being on double disability (from the VA and the PD) was making him batty, he would be the first to admit it. Though Harry's body was broken, his mind was sharp and restless. Alcohol calmed it somewhat but this was a temporary fix, a Band-Aid on a severed artery. So, most nights, Harry sat watching, brooding, waiting.

He wouldn't keep the bottle by his side, but in the kitchen, forcing himself not to get up, even when his first glass went empty. And if he did rise, steadying himself on the furniture, the walls, Harry would hop and hobble, slowly picking his way through the rooms, using a cane if he felt especially wobbly. It wasn't to pour a drink, however. He would stop in Wendy's doorway, the paint glowing a cheerful pink, even in the dimness. Sully had recently repainted the room without complaint after Harry had come back from the War and the O'Learys moved downstairs. Life had been so different before. Harry never could have imagined this: being an amputee veteran. He never could have imagined a lot of things. Like his wife getting a job, for example. But life is always changing, evolving, and you've got to change along with it.

In his daughter's doorway, Harry would listen to Wendy breathe steadily, sometimes murmuring a random word like "doll" or "cake" or "Stan" in her slumber. If the girl had a fever, he would enter the room and place a concerned palm on her forehead, gently pushing aside the damp curls which were the same shade as her mother's. Convinced there was no danger, Harry would leave and head to the can or back to his chair. He could sleep after he saw Sully and Izzy pass beneath his window, usually between one and two in the morning. Then Harry's eyes would grow heavy, he would drain his glass and finally doze beside his bride.

The next morning, Jo would keep a brief vigil over her husband's sleeping form. She knew that the thick tumbler on the nightstand had held whiskey and not water but said nothing. She knew her Harry was lost and that only he could find his own way; there wasn't a thing she could do except love him. Harry had left parts of himself in Brittany, along with his leg, and she would be there, waiting for him until he found what he'd misplaced and returned to her.

Jo's other morning vigil occurred before she stepped out of bed. She would proffer little prayers in the dawn light: thanks for another day, entreaties for her family's safety, and for Harry to find the peace within himself he needed to move forward through life. Perhaps Jo would invite Bridget to do the Overlook Prayer on Harry's behalf. He might require a dash of divine intervention, though he was drinking a lot less these days.

Usually before her alarm clock rang at seven, Jo had already sat up, slipped her legs over the side of the bed, and greeted the ground with her bare feet. She wrapped the plaid flannel robe around her waist and began her day. After the coffee was done perking and she fixed cream of wheat for herself and Wendy, she would wake the girl for school or for church. If it was Saturday, she would let the child sleep in. Harry, she wouldn't wake, no matter the day.

So, this was Jo's silent vigil, at the solitary breakfast table before anyone else was awake.

Stanley Sullivan's vigil ended without incident one afternoon in mid-January, not a month before his ninth birthday. The Yellow Queen had been unconscious for several days, the life slowly sifting out of her in United Israel Zion's steel bed. Her breathing had been ragged, irregular. For some reason, Stan took her hand, which felt cool and dry, as if carved from wax. It was the first time he'd touched her of his own accord.

Nurse Marta kept her own vigil over Stan and Denise but from afar. She sensed the time was near and warned the boy when he first arrived that day, straight from the third grade at the same public school she'd attended. His cheeks were so red from the cold they looked as if they'd been slapped. Stan perched his book bag in the corner as was his custom and sat in the chair beside Denise's bed. "She's doing poorly," the nurse told him. "It won't be long now, I'm afraid." Stan sat and waited.

Death didn't happen as the boy had imagined. There was no dramatic finale like there had been in *And Then There Were None* or *Dillinger*, both of which he'd seen with Poppa and Wendy at the Loew's 46th the year earlier. (Bridget had been feeling too peaked to come to either movie with them.) No, in real life, death was quiet. It snuck up on you, a stealthy alley cat, and pounced on you mutely when you least expected it.

Still holding her hand, Stan watched the woman's washboard chest rise and fall. He studied her fingers, elegant and graceful, while his looked scruffy in comparison. Weeks earlier, she'd remarked that Stan was a nail-biter like her, but drifting in and out of consciousness, Denise no longer chewed her nails, whereas Stan chomped on his with zest. His nails were bitten to the quick and none too clean. Rose tried to get him to use a brush on them when he bathed, but Stan tended to forget. His fingers were also decorated with tiny cuts and scars. One was from sticking his pinkie into the triangular opening of an evaporated milk can he'd found near the curb. Another was where Butchie had nipped him when he tugged the skittish Pomeranian's intriguing, fanlike tail at age three. He was secretly pleased when the yapping dog died of old age. Stan thought of telling Denise the dog-bite story but doubted she could hear him.

Turning over his palm, Stan noticed how much darker his skin was than hers. It was beige, even in the dead of winter, while hers was a ghostly bluish-white, like the snow at night. He probably favored his father, Stan concluded, and tried to remind himself to study one of Bridget's family photographs when he got home later that afternoon. He was sure there'd be one of his father tucked away somewhere in a breakfront drawer.

The Yellow Queen's breaths came slower and slower, with more pronounced spaces between each one. Finally, she took in an impossibly long, deep breath and never exhaled. That was it, she was gone. Denise Walters, neé Wallaski, left the world with much less fanfare than she had entered it, and certainly, more sedately than she had lived. She died without ceremony, there one moment and gone the next.

Stan called Nurse Marta, who'd been watching from outside the supply closet. She came to him at a clipped pace, dropping the packet of bandages she'd been retrieving. "The Yellow Queen is dead," Stan told her.

The nurse pressed sure, gentle fingertips to Denise's neck, searching for her pulse, but found none. "Yes," Marta said to the boy. "She is." The nurse pulled the sheet up over Denise's face and tucked it around her. "Do you want to say good-bye?" she remembered, grasping the sheet top.

"I already did," Stan admitted.

"Should I call for your pa? Your brother?"

"Nah," the boy said. "I'm all right. I guess I'll be going now." Stan grabbed his book bag and ventured toward the door, then turned. "What will they do with her?" he wondered.

Nurse Marta smoothed down the sheet. "I'll fetch an orderly to take her down to the morgue."

"Like in the movie with Bela Lugosi?" he began. "*Murders in the Rue Morgue*?"

"The silly picture with the mad scientist, kidnapping women left and right?" she asked. Stan nodded, eyes wide. "It's not like that. It's just a quiet, peaceful place," Marta told Stan. He believed her. The boy was clear-eyed, not even close to crying. Marta was glad because too many tears had already been shed that day and she was only halfway through her shift.

"I'll be seeing you," he offered.

"Not if I see you first," the nurse smiled softly. She was a neighborhood girl and lived on Eleventh Avenue with her folks.

Stan smiled back. "Thanks for everything," he said to her. "You've been nice. You were her favorite one."

"I thought she was hunky-dory, too," the nurse admitted. Holding his book bag over his left shoulder, Stan shook the nurse's hand in his right, like a grown man, then took his leave of her. Marta watched Stan disappear down the hall, his galoshes making a faint squeak on the waxed linoleum.

Rather than send their son's mother off to a mass grave at Potter's Field on City Island, Sully and Rose decided to have her laid to rest in a single plot in Green-Wood Cemetery. It happened to be catty-cornered from Tony's, an undesirable piece of real estate not far from the train yard, on a bleak hillock where nothing grew, no matter how the groundskeepers tried. Old Man Lockman, who owned the funeral parlor on Twenty-First Street, sold the plot to the Sullivans for a song, having purchased it for a pittance himself. He had a tender spot for Polish girls, especially those gone astray through no fault of their own. Just like Nurse Marta, Gene, Sr. was known to say, "There but for the grace of God, go I."

Father Dunn agreed to say a few words at the church before laying Denise to rest, even though she wasn't a parishioner. (No one knew if she was even Catholic.) For this reason, it wasn't a proper mass, just a remembrance, a recognition of a girl who'd started out unblemished, as all girls do, but whose life had taken a wrong turn somewhere along the road, and she never could seem to find her way back onto the right path again.

The church was empty, save for the first two rows, which were filled with Stan's family. Gene Lockman, bless his heart, had secured a plain pine box for Miss Walters, as he respectfully referred to her. "It's on me," he'd told Sully. "I never forgot what you did for us," he added. Sully had done the family a favor during Gene, Jr.'s wilding days, burying an arrest for a "drunk and disorderly," in which a plate glass window came to be broken, but no other harm had been done. The window had been paid for and the young man's record expunged. Since then, Jr. was on the straight and narrow, the fear of God—and the law—instilled in him. One night in the holding tank of the Seventy-Second Precinct was all he needed.

Not only was Gene, Sr. thankful but he was also keenly moved by Sully's wife, Rose, who'd shown such a tender heart toward a woman who had been Rose's nemesis. When Gene said this to Rose in the basement of Lockman's Funeral Home, she actually blushed. Shrugging, Rose explained, "We're all God's children." Tiger had reminded her of this soon after his return—and she'd told him the same thing often as a youngster. Rose had scoffed at the statement in reference to Denise, but now realized its truth. How funny life was; it turned full circle and sons came to teach their parents sometimes.

Sully, John, Tiger and Gene Lockman served as Denise's pall bearers. The end stages of her disease had reduced her weight considerably, and they easily managed. Angela stayed home, complaining of swollen ankles. Augie had to work. Astrid did not attend either, not for that piece of trash, she'd snapped, in front of Stan, no less. "I can't see burying her like a dog, with no nothing," Rose explained to Sully in a whisper. Luckily, he agreed. Denise was the boy's mother, after all, and Rose could make good on the promise she'd made at the woman's sickbed.

The simple wooden box became beautiful when cloaked with the church's white satin, gold-edged funeral pall. Smoothing down the fabric, Father Dunn droned, "Not a sparrow falls to the ground without the Father's knowledge." Listening to these words, Tiger had to silently disagree; he believed the Father had indeed allowed Denise Walters to slip from between His heavenly fingertips, undetected. Not only did this sparrow fall, but she was crushed underfoot.

Stan marveled at the way the winter sun streamed in through St. Catherine's stained glass windows, making colors dance on the ground. The floor itself was marble, made of large, speckled squares and rectangles of pink with strips of brass inlaid between. The steps leading to the altar were also crafted of cream-shaded marble. There was no organ music to permeate the stillness, just Father Dunn's words.

As the priest stood beside the Yellow Queen's casket, Stan admired the vibrant daisy-shaped stained glass above the choir loft—the deep cobalt was his favorite. Wendy tapped him on the shoulder and made him face front. The church's golden dome depicted God on his throne, surrounded by a gaggle of saints. Sister Mary Hewer from Religious Instruction would have boxed his ears because Stan hadn't memorized the saints' monikers. But even nameless, the celestial get-together kept Stan's interest.

Father Dunn's words floated above his head, filtered through him:

> *"Do not let your hearts be troubled…"*
> *"For I am convinced that neither death nor life,*
> *neither angels nor demons…"*
> *"The Lord is my shepherd…"*
> *"…for His compassions never fail…"*
> *"The Lord is close to the brokenhearted and saves*
> *those who are crushed in spirit…"*

They were just empty words to the boy, rushes of air in the chill of the church, but they did sound pretty.

When the short service was over and the family was following Denise's coffin down St. Catherine's middle aisle, Stan noticed Nurse Marta standing at the back, wearing her starched uniform beneath her winter coat. She gave Stan a nod and he nodded back.

Before the funeral procession left the church, a frail, humped figure approached Rose and grabbed her with unexpected force. Through broken teeth and garbled speech, the woman introduced herself as Aunt Mimi. It seems she'd been Denise's landlady in a Sea Gate rooming house. "I knew that bum was *fershlugina*," Aunt Mimi sobbed. "I blame myself. If I hadn't put her out…but I didn't have a choice, did I? They made me, my family did. I got bills to pay. I'm a woman alone. I got to earn a living, don't I?" Rose didn't have to say a word because the woman had answered all her own questions.

The old crone eventually released Rose but before she turned to go, she noticed Stanley. "Is this the boy?" Aunt Mimi gasped. Before anyone could respond, the woman turned on her heels and rushed down the aisle, toward the church's exit, sobbing and muttering to herself.

It was a short ride to Green-Wood Cemetery from St. Catherine's. Its bells tolled sadly, marking the death of a lost lady whom few would remember a year from then. Gene Lockman also donated the use of his second-best hearse, only no one except he and Father Dunn rode in it. The other family members headed home on foot, leaving the Sullivans at the church steps. They slipped into Poppa's Buick, which he'd loaned Sully for the occasion. Tiger accompanied them—he felt he ought to.

The caravan of two cars drove deep into Green-Wood to reach the gravesite, almost as far as they'd driven along the icy streets. Stan watched with interest as Sully turned the steering wheel on the cemetery's winding roads. The boy had never been in Green-Wood before, even though he lived less than a mile from it. He thought the Gothic structure at the main gate resembled a spired Castle Frankenstein from *House of Frankenstein*, which he and Wendy had seen at the Minerva when Uncle John was running the projector. (The picture had scared them so intensely that for days, they thought they saw John Carradine, who'd played "Dracula," at every turn, on every street corner.)

In Green-Wood, there were tall trees, naked of leaves now, and fat shrubs as tall as Stan was. There were small headstones leaning to one side or another, like broken teeth. There were mausoleums decorated with Tiffany glass, pillars and urns. There were hoity-toity names like Chamberlin, Pardee and Durant. There was a dancing couple named Lawson and a podgy bear atop Mr. Beard's stone, dangling its leg over the side. Somewhere, Stan recalled, was the statuary of Rex, who stood guard over John E. Stowe's obelisk and behind it, a diminutive marble marker for "Our Little Adelaide," Stowe's daughter who predeceased him.

Only one dog was buried in Green-Wood, Elias Howe's, the inventor of the sewing machine. The dog's name was Fannie and though the beloved pup was put in the family plot, Fannie had a headstone of her own. Wendy had told

Stan about the cemetery's history. She knew more about Green-Wood than a young girl ought to, he decided. For a brief moment, Stan wished Wendy was beside him in the Buick's back seat instead of Tiger. Wendy would have taken his hand without saying why, just knowing it was right. Born a day apart, though worlds apart in opposite ends of Brooklyn, the two often shared the sensibilities of twins.

Sully followed the hearse down the curved roads dusted with snow. No one spoke. Sully even switched off the radio out of respect to the dead. Old Man Lockman had memorized the twists and turns of the almost five-hundred-acre cemetery by heart. They went by the frozen surface of the Sylvan Water, turned onto Spruce, then Maple, skimming close to where Green-Wood bordered Thirty-Sixth Street. The hearse stopped at a barren hillside which overlooked the train yard.

Despite the frozen ground, a hole had already been dug in the earth. Tiger and Sully effortlessly lifted the pine box which contained the remains of Denise Walters. Although they didn't need the help, two grounds men assisted them in placing the box on the woven fabric strips stretched across the yawn of the open grave. Stan grabbed his mother's arm, as he had when he was a toddler. Sully rested his fingers on the boy's shoulder while Tiger placed his palm on Stan's back.

Although the boy was supported from three sides, Stan still feared he might topple into the rectangular hole carved into the snowy dirt. Father Dunn said a few words, this time about a camel passing through the eye of a needle, which Stan didn't quite follow. Great puffs of smoke came out of the priest's mouth when he gave Denise's eulogy, out of all their mouths when they breathed, creating a flimsy partition of mist between the living and the dead. At the sound of the soil hitting the bare wood box, Rose led Stan away. Tiger followed.

Instead of immediately getting into the Buick, Rose and Tiger showed the boy his father's grave, which was steps away. It was the first time Tiger and Rose had visited since

Tony's funeral. "He worked on the El," Rose told him. Stan looked down at a flat stone barely visible above the snow line. All it bore were his name and the years he lived:

Anthony Joseph Martino
1896-1936

Nothing else. Stan felt strangely empty as he looked down upon the speckled headstone, then to the right at the gravediggers finishing up the Yellow Queen's final resting place. Sully had pulled the Buick up to the curb. They drove home in silence, Stan sitting on his mother's lap and Tiger sitting in the back seat, alone.

As Sully garaged Poppa's car, Rose and Stan went inside, greeted by the delicious aroma of polenta and pork. Bridget knew it was one of Stan's favorites in a sea of favorites. Comfort food, she called it. Coupled with crusty Italian bread from Piccolo's, it was a feast.

They took off their coats, hats, gloves, mufflers and galoshes, and tucked into Bridget's simple, satisfying meal. His grandmother smoothed down Stan's hair, which was standing on end from the static electricity of his watchman's cap, kissed him on his crown, and said, "Welcome home." Spoon in hand, warm, savory cornmeal mush slipping down his throat, Stan realized that his vigil was over, and that he truly was home.

Chapter Twenty-Two

By George

Although New York and New Jersey shared a border—and shared one word of their names—they couldn't have been further apart. To go from one to the other without an automobile in the 1940s required a number of modes of transportation: trolley, bus and ferry, and a considerable amount of travel on foot. Tiger didn't ask to borrow Poppa's Buick for this trip, even though the old gent would have surely said 'yes.' In fact, Tiger revealed to no one where he was going. He didn't know why, he just needed something which belonged to solely to him, something private.

When Tiger's friend George and his family had dropped by on New Year's Eve the month earlier, they fit right into the festivities. George's wife Elaine chatted with Bridget and the rest of the ladies as though they'd been acquainted forever. The Thomas's nicely-behaved children played with Stan and Wendy, letting out squeals of joy now and then, while the men discussed the War in hushed tones in a corner of the parlor. Before George left, Rose grasped his mahogany-shaded hand extra tightly. "Thanks for looking after my boy," she told him.

"Thanks for having such a fine boy," George responded, then kissed Rose softly on the cheek.

Early on a crisp, sunny February morning, soon after the bells at St. Catherine's had struck seven, Tiger slipped a meatball hero into his overcoat pocket and set out on a journey. Although there were probably swifter ways to travel, Tiger decided to take the trolley to Bay Ridge rather than the El to yet another train. His walk to the streetcar was brisk. The snow had all but melted except for grimy patches here and there. The groundhog had predicted an early spring. Always the first to blossom, the spear-shaped crocus leaves were peeking their heads out from the rigid earth. Soon, front yards would be decorated with their delicate white and purple flowers, signs of life, signs of hope, especially near the end of winter. The forsythia branches, though brown and woody, were preparing themselves to bloom. The nubs where their brilliant yellow flowers would pop were turning green, almost complete.

As he turned the corner, Tiger could see the trolley in the distance, hear the sobering clang of its bell. He rode it all the way to Sixty-Ninth Street. When it reached Shore Road, Tiger stepped down from the trolley car. A stiff wind battered the open-air ferry terminal. Tiger's coat flapped around his legs like dusky wings and he almost lost his hat. He flattened it down onto his head before it flew away and kept walking.

When Tiger was a boy, Poppa used to take him fishing on the Sixty-Ninth Street Pier, the very same pier where the ferry was moored. Sometimes it was so jam-packed with fishermen, they had to muscle their way in to find a spot. Tiger would sit with his legs dangling over the pier's side and Poppa would stand protectively behind him, showing his grandson how to bait a hook and cast out. If they caught blues or fluke, they'd take them home to Bridget, who'd turn their catch into a delicious supper after Poppa and Tiger gutted and scaled the fish. Bridget would soak the oily bluefish filets in a pan of milk, coat them with eggs and cracker meal, then fry them in olive oil until they crackled on your tongue.

A decade later, Tiger stood near the edge of the Sixty-Ninth Street Pier, gazing out toward Fort Wadsworth on Staten Island, admiring the view. Maybe this is why Tiger chose the mode of travel he did—trolley to pier—because it harbored memories. Good memories, not the sad, foggy remembrances of his father's blurred, drunken voice raised in anger when it was dark outside and everyone else in the house was asleep. Not the hunched shadow of his father's form near his sister's bed. Not the fumblings, shushes and terrified whimpers. When Tony stole into the room Tiger shared with Kewpie, the boy would sometimes feign a nightmare and start screaming. This would often drive their father from the bedroom, but not always. At times, the soused man would yell at Tiger to go back to sleep. Once in a while, there would even be a smack across the face.

But the Sixty-Ninth Street Pier held only pleasant recollections for Tiger. After a fruitful day of fishing, Poppa would buy him a Mello Roll, the short cake cone's rectangular opening waiting to be joined with the cylinder of ice cream, which you unwrapped yourself and fitted into the cone. It was challenging to accomplish with fishy, worm-soaked fingers but Tiger managed. In foresight, Bridget would always slip a moistened washrag into a waxed paper sack and tuck it into their lunch pail so the Mello Roll wouldn't taste like fluke.

Tiger walked beneath the metal canopy which announced, "Staten Island Ferry: Short Route to New Jersey." You could catch busses, trolleys, or drive to practically anywhere from St. George, where the boat docked in Staten Island. Tiger purchased his ticket for the ferry, which had just arrived. He waited first for the cars and then the passengers to disembark. There were a trickle of others making the trip with Tiger. With his round-trip ticket, he waited patiently with the men and women huddled against the relentless wind.

The "Brooklyn-Staten Island Ferry" itself was painted khaki green. The color was not unlike Tiger's service uniform, now in mothballs in the basement. The name painted on the ferry's side announced "Hamilton." Two or three cars waited to board the ferry when the crewmen opened the accordion gate. The drivers slowly eased their cars onboard. One by one, the pedestrians stepped onto the ferry's sheet metal flooring. Tiger wondered if Poppa and his men had ever worked on the *Hamilton* in the Brooklyn Navy Yard when it needed repairs. Though not as impressive as battleships like the *Arizona* or the *New Mexico*, which were built there, the *Hamilton* was important because it took ordinary people to the office, to visit family and friends, and in Tiger's case, to change their lives.

Tiger watched the proceedings and let the rest of the passengers board before him. "Welcome aboard, soldier," the ticket taker said, closing the gate behind him.

"Thanks," Tiger responded. "Does it show?"

"Lucky guess," the man admitted. "Plus you walk straight as an arrow, like you're still in uniform."

"Old habits are hard to break," Tiger smiled, shaking the man's hand. "You?"

"I was in the Pacific Theater mostly," the fellow, whose name tag stated "Frank," told him. Frank was short, built like a mule and had eyes the color of a cloudless summer sky.

"The European Theater," Tiger revealed. "A little in the Pacific."

"They moved us around like checkers, huh?"

"The game of war," Tiger said thoughtfully.

"I was a Seabee," Frank announced with pride. "Was in Bermuda for a time, fortifying the railroad. Then the party was over and we were shipped to the Marianas."

"Tough luck," Tiger admitted.

"Not as tough as some. I came back. You did, too." After a beat, Frank wondered, "Work?"

"Nothing yet."

"I was lucky they held my job for me," Frank said. "They're still hiring. It ain't easy work but the pay's all right."

"I'll keep it in mind," Tiger replied, tipping his hat. "Much obliged."

"Enjoy the ride."

Tiger climbed the ferry's covered stairway to the pedestrian area. His heavy footfall rang with each step. The narrow walkway was encased with chain link fencing and midship, there was an indoor waiting area, but Tiger didn't go inside. Instead, he stood beneath the wheelhouse, braving the determined wind with Staten Island over his left shoulder and New Jersey over his right. The coastline was rocky, mostly uninhabited. Behind Tiger, was the ribbon of Brooklyn's Belt Parkway, the section completed five years earlier with talk of linking it to a highway which would be known as the Brooklyn-Queens Expressway.

Near the Narrows was the taupe stone shadow of Fort Wadsworth. Built onto a bluff, it began as a blockhouse in the 1600s, and during the Revolution was named Flagstaff Fort. Captured by "the bloody British" (as Poppa called them) in 1776, it remained in British hands until the war's end in 1783. Poppa was fascinated with the history of his adopted land and passed along that very same fascination to his grandson. Tiger remembered how Poppa had explained that Fort Wadsworth's present name was chosen to honor Brigadier General James Wadsworth, who'd been killed in the Civil War's Battle of the Wilderness. In 1910, Fort Wadsworth fired a twenty-one-gun salute to former President Teddy Roosevelt as his ship chugged through the Narrows on his return from his adventures in Africa and Europe. "I heard it all the way at the Navy Yard," Poppa had told Tiger. "Hand to heart."

Tiger faced the Statue of Liberty, which turned her back on New Jersey, giving it the cold shoulder as she gazed stoically toward New York. It was just past eight, and Tiger was already famished. He took out the meatball sandwich he'd made hastily in the morning light. With a fork, he'd smashed down the remainder of last night's supper onto a piece of leftover Italian bread and folded it into a square of waxed paper. By now, the warmth of Tiger's body, had taken the chill off the sandwich. The savory mélange of ground pork, beef and veal, lightly seasoned with dried oregano, parsley, eggs, stale bread soaked in milk, and a dash of grated Parmesan cheese melted in his mouth.

The rooftops of the St. George section of Staten Island came into view. It was on the island's northeastern tip and loaded with posh homes, many built on Fort Hill where a British stronghold once stood. There was a slew of Victorian mansions, and way back when, St. George was a resort area, with elegant hotels festooning St. Mark's Place. The neighborhood was named not for the legendary dragon-slayer but after a prominent land baron named George Law who'd acquired the waterfront at bargain-basement prices. Old George was guaranteed immortality when a buddy pledged to canonize him in exchange for land rights for what would end up being the future ferry terminal.

Tiger disembarked the *Hamilton* and stepped onto St. George's Landing's wooden dock. Frank, the crewman, directed Tiger to the bus station, which he said was the quickest way to reach Jersey City, and the most picturesque. (George had written to Tiger that he could take either the bus or the trolley.) The bus traveled north, making its way across the graceful skeleton of the Bayonne Bridge. At the time of its completion in 1931, it was the world's longest steel-arch bridge. Soaring almost three-hundred feet above the tidal strait of the Kill Van Kull and a large stretch of swampland, the Bayonne Bridge resembled a parabola with its nearly symmetrical curve.

During the bus ride, Tiger realized how fitting it was to journey from a place named St. George to visit his friend George. Tiger figured it was a good omen. They'd stuck together like Elmer's Glue in wartime, George joking that he was literally the fly in the ointment because of his complexion. Could Tiger and George truly be friends in peacetime? Their lives were so unalike, having grown up in different States, in different cultures. George pointed out in his gentle manner that people were more the same than not. *"'We hold certain truths to be self-evident,'"* George would begin. *"'That all men are created equal...'"*

And like an Abbott and Costello routine, Tiger would chime in, "And how about women?"

George would shake his head, and continue, undaunted, *" '...that they are endowed by their Creator with certain unalienable Rights, that among these are Life, Liberty and the pursuit of Happiness...'"*

Tiger would pat George's shoulder. "Pal O'Mine," Tiger would sigh. "You realize the fella who wrote that owned slaves, don't you?"

George would usually throw his arms up, exasperated, and reluctantly agree. "But the idea sure is pretty, isn't it?"

Tiger couldn't believe how much Jersey City resembled Brooklyn, the brownstones with high stoops, the little shops, the neatly-painted wood-frame houses. Of course, Brooklyn didn't have the Colgate Clock, which decorated Jersey City's waterfront, but the timepiece embedded in the tower of Brooklyn's Williamsburgh Savings Bank was pretty impressive, too.

The bus went along Journal Square, by the Stanley Theatre, which was almost as fancy as the Brooklyn Paramount. Tiger thought he was seeing things when the stately Loew's Jersey Theatre came into view. He couldn't deny it was more glorious than the Loew's 46th. It was one of Marcus Loew's "wonder theatres," George would brag. "I don't sell tickets to the movies...I sell tickets to theaters," Loew was known to say. Tiger studied the Baroque façade and remembered to look up at the cupola and the life-size, mechanical statue of St. George on horseback, slaying the dragon. It was too early for the red lightbulb in the dragon's mouth to be blazing but Tiger was captivated nonetheless.

Soon, the bus turned off Jersey City's main drag. The houses became less opulent and more comfortable, more lived in. There was evidence that families made their homes here: melting snowmen and igloos in front yards, forgotten wagons, filled with slush. A few houses could have used a new coat of paint or needed a shutter repaired but most seemed well-tended.

As George had instructed, Tiger got off the bus at the Miss America Diner on West Side Avenue. He studied the letter which contained George's directions, beautifully written on linen writing paper in George's neat, former altar boy handwriting. The people around Tiger were more Colored than white but it didn't worry him. It was merely an observation, as Tiger might notice that the letters in the Miss America Diner's sign were red.

An older gent wearing a porkpie hat with skin the shade of orange blossom honey confirmed that Tiger was indeed walking in the right direction, and that Stegman Parkway was but a few blocks ahead. A woman with a pleasing toffee-colored complexion who was carrying a paper sack of groceries paused to add that Tiger must turn right once he got to Stegman. "If you come to Hudson Boulevard, you've gone too far, son," she added.

Tiger thanked them both and continued on his way, past Stegman Court, Stegman Place and Stegman Terrace, until he reached 315 Stegman Parkway. Tiger recognized it immediately from the creased photos George had carried with him throughout the War. It was a two-story brick building, unattached on either side, with a small stoop covered by a peaked roof which mirrored the main house's roof. A waist-high fence housed the tiny garden in which Tiger knew they grew both vegetables and flowers in the warm months. A rose bush, gray with winter, snaked its way up one of the porch's brick columns. An alley led to the garage out back. It wasn't so different than the home Tiger had grown up in. George was right, people were pretty much the same all over. They had similar wants and needs: a warm place to sleep, good food to eat, to feel safe and loved. During the War, he and George never had any of these things at the same time, but now they had all four simultaneously again.

"Anthony Martino, Junior, as I live and breathe," George's voice boomed. He must have been watching from one of the house's three front windows. "You finally made it."

George was down the steps in an instant, his ham-fisted mitt engulfing Tiger's long, slim fingers. "I wouldn't take you for a white picket fence kind of fellow," Tiger said with a cock of his head.

"That's Elaine's doing," George told him. "She painted it when I was away. How the hell are you?"

"Okay," Tiger admitted. "And you?"

"Okay, too."

George explained that Elaine was at the doctor with her mother—her folks lived in the upstairs apartment—but was expected be back in a few hours. In the meantime, George took Tiger on the grand tour of the neat, three-bedroom place. "It's almost twenty years old," George conceded. "But it has good bones." There was a formal dining room and parlor plus stained glass accents above many of the windows, parquet floors covered by rag rugs which were made by Elaine's people in the South, and a brick fireplace which actually worked. (In fact, George had a fire going in anticipation of his friend's arrival.) George and Elaine's bed was covered with an ivory-colored chenille spread, and the children's bedrooms housed two solid twin beds each. With his brother John, George had built and stained the maple furniture. He was proud of building the beds, proud of the house itself, and it showed.

The dining room table was already set with Elaine's best dishes—Blue Ridge Pottery, it read on the back of one of the luncheon plates, which were painted with bouquets of June flowers. Tiger followed George into the kitchen where a pot of beans and another of greens bubbled on the stove. It was a firetruck-red, industrial-sized O'Keeffe & Merritt with four burners, a griddle, two broilers and two ovens. "I treated myself when I got back," George almost apologized.

He poured Tiger a mug of coffee, mellowed with chicory. "You earned it," Tiger told George, gesturing at the gleaming stove.

"Did I?" George wondered after taking a sip. "Some gave more."

Tiger bowed his head. "Others gave less. Then there's the time, the time we'll never get back. The things you missed... like teaching Darryl how to ride a two-wheeler or seeing Liora Rose take her first steps."

George nodded. "How about you help me fry up a mess of chicken?"

"I thought you'd never ask," Tiger sighed.

George eased a tray of legs, wings and thighs out of the Frigidaire, the largest Tiger had ever seen outside of a restaurant. "I've been soaking them in buttermilk all night," George said. "Keeps them extra moist." He dumped the milk down the sink and gestured to a deep baking sheet already lined with pale, speckled powder. "Flour, salt, black pepper and a touch of cayenne."

"That's it?"

"That's all it takes," George conceded. "Some get real fancy with French mustard, spices and seasonings, but believe me, chicken don't need fancy. There's no reason to be highfalutin."

Tiger rolled up his sleeves, washed his hands and commenced to coat the chicken with the flavored flour as George heated the oil. "Now, you don't smother it. You just splash it, flip it, then splash some more. Ever watch a bird give itself a bath in the dirt?"

"Who hasn't?"

"That's the way you coat it. A number of folks double dip but not George. There's such a thing as too much of a good thing." He watched Tiger for a moment. "You got a nice feel for this," George admitted.

"I can hardly cook," Tiger told him. "But I'm an A-one prep man. Been helping Grandma Bridget since I could stand at the table."

"Before that, even, I bet. My Junior used to kneel on a chair to lend a hand when he was too short to reach the counter."

"Me, too," Tiger admitted. Both men smiled then laughed. "You can be my *sous chef* any day." George flicked a droplet of water into the oil-filled Dutch oven. It rippled and spat back at him.

"*Sous chef*? What's that?"

George took a coated chicken thigh and fed it into the oil. It shuddered, thanking him. He added two more pieces. "French for second in command in the kitchen. Sort of like a colonel. Learned it in Nice. Before I was stationed in Holland."

George added a couple more chicken parts. "Aren't you going to fill the pan?" Tiger asked.

George shook his head, moving the chicken slightly with the tongs. "Crowd the pot and you lower the temperature of the oil. Makes for a greasy bird." The men stood silent, watching the chicken fry. "What I got up here..." George said, gesturing to his close-cropped hair, "...could fill a book. Maybe two."

Tiger saw his opportunity and seized it. "See, that's what I wanted to talk to you about."

"I ain't writing no book," George stated, turning the chicken. "I barely finished eighth grade, Anthony."

"Not writing a book, opening a restaurant."

"Do you have any idea what it takes to open a restaurant? To run one, even?" George inquired.

"No," Tiger admitted. "But you do. You've worked in a kitchen your whole life."

As George fried the chicken, stirred the collards, salted the red beans and finished up the rice, Tiger explained his plan. By the time George unwrapped the gingham cloth from the cornbread he'd made earlier that morning and sat at the table, they'd looked at Tiger's plan from all angles, George playing Devil's advocate to Tiger's youthful zeal.

After saying Grace, they continued fleshing out Tiger's proposal. The chicken was exquisite. It melted in your mouth, "like a Communion wafer," Tiger admitted.

"That's probably sacrilegious but I thank you, sir," George said, chewing and inwardly agreeing.

"Most people live their whole lives without tasting chicken like this."

"Most white folks," added George.

"Or tasting *manicotti* like Grandma Bridget's."

George took a forkful of red beans, creamy with the perfect kick of spice. "So, you want it to be an Italian place?"

"Not exactly. Something different. A restaurant that's only open for lunch and an early supper. It would have a limited menu with a few items on it. But honest, first-rate dishes, the best. Comfort foods. Foods that make you feel good. Home cooking."

George eased collards onto his fork with some rice. "Whose home?"

"Any home." Tiger helped himself to another hunk of cornbread. He could taste the buttermilk in it, the texture of the cornmeal pleasing on his tongue. He spread it with butter. "Your home, mine, even Sadie Lieberwitz's."

"That woman bakes a mean *babka*," George admitted.

"And your Elaine's banana pudding…pure heaven on a plate."

George broke out laughing. "And you've never even tried her sweet potato pie. Tastes so good, make you wanna slap ya momma."

As George cut a slice, he explained what the colloquialism meant. "It's just a saying," George stressed. "Not that you'd ever hit Rose. It means the pie's so darned good you'd slap your ma because she don't bake pie like that. Comes from down Carolina, I suspect."

Tiger's first forkful of sweet potato pie was true bliss: the ideal blend of sugar, cinnamon, creaminess and flaky crust. He closed his eyes and slowly chewed, letting the heavenly mixture slip down his throat. "I can't describe this in words," Tiger admitted. He washed down the pie with George's chicory coffee. How the man managed to procure ground chicory root in Europe during wartime was anyone's guess, but he made converts of the men in his division. (Tiger suspected Elaine sent it to George, a New Orleans native, who couldn't live without his special coffee on any continent.) Tiger devoured the first slice of pie and even had a second wedge, as did George.

In between bites, George picked Tiger's brain. "How can you turn a profit on a place only open a few hours a day?"

"The food will speak for itself," Tiger said. "Great food that's cheap to make but big on taste. How can it not work?" George didn't know how to respond so he refreshed the coffee. Tiger continued, "There'll be a couple of choices on the menu and it will change every day." George still didn't seem to understand so Tiger plodded on. "For instance, Sunday could be my Aunt Jo's lasagna, with meatballs and sausages on the side. Monday could be meatloaf with mashed potatoes, and string beans. Tuesday, it'll be fried chicken. Wednesday, potato latkes, noodle kugel, and brisket—Sadie Lieberwitz will teach you how to cook them. Thursday, Thanksgiving dinner with turkey, dressing, yams, cranberry sauce, and all the fixings. Elaine can bake, so can Bridget and my Ma. We'll have the best of the best, everyone's specialty dish, at the place."

George nodded his head and smiled, showing off the gap between his front teeth which he usually tried to hide. "Feel good food," George agreed.

"That's what we'll call it! 'George & Tiger's Feel Good Food.'"

"Has a mighty nice ring to it," George admitted.

Stuffed almost to the bursting point, Tiger and George cleared the dining room table. It was a wreckage of chicken bones, cornbread crumbs and plates slick with grease. Tucked into one glass door of the china closet, Tiger noticed a sepia-toned photograph another GI had taken of the two friends in the mess tent. Tiger was honored to have such a prominent spot in the Thomas home.

In the kitchen, George washed and Tiger dried. "You won't have the long hours you do now," Tiger told him. "At least not after we get the place off the ground. No more six-day workweeks."

"How do you figure?"

Tiger had it all sorted out. He'd thought it through completely, during his contemplative sits at bars or as he walked in Borough Park late at night. "Some days, like when we serve Aunt Jo's lasagna, you can stay home, kick back, take the day off," he explained.

"It sounds good," George said in spite of himself. "Too good to be true. It would take a boatload of money."

Tiger nested one of Elaine's Blue Ridge cake plates onto a stack of others after he dried it. "I have a little put away," Tiger revealed. "I sent money home during the War. Instead of spending it, Rose put it aside for me. There's about a thousand bucks."

George's heart sunk as he poured the used vegetable oil into a tub. "That's a start, Anthony, but it's not nearly enough."

"I know it," Tiger conceded. "There's more, though. When my father died, there was an insurance policy through the TWU. All three of our names were on it. Rose didn't want any part of it. Neither did my sister. That was before my brother Stan turned up. So, they gave it to me."

"How much?"

"Ten grand," Tiger told him.

The Dutch oven slipped from George's fingers and jangled into the deep enamel sink. "You've been sitting on ten Gs for how long?"

"Almost ten years," Tiger admitted. "I couldn't touch it until I was eighteen. I've been saving it for something special. Something like this." Tiger threw the dishtowel across his shoulder. "Look, I never said much about my Pop but he was a real SOB. He wasn't much of a father but he was good at being a drunk. He ran out on us once or twice, but it was even worse when he came back. So, I figure, here's a chance to make it right. Here's my chance to make good from bad."

George nodded. "Like growing flowers in horse manure."

"Exactly!" Tiger exclaimed, grabbing his friend by the shoulders. "Hey, we can change our lives, change a slew of lives, and make a difference. So, what do you say, buddy?"

George picked up the bean pot and continued scrubbing. "It's a lot to think on, Anthony. I got a wife and four kids depending on me, and a mortgage. I'm just staying afloat as it is."

"You're busting your hump with little to show for it."

"I go to the diner when it's dark, come home when it's dark. I hardly see Elaine and the kids. I'm tired of slinging hash, of people sending back their eggs and complaining their toast is too dark."

Tiger took the heavy pot from George. "There'll be no toast. Maybe some cornbread, made one way: our way. Like it or lump it."

"Oh, I reckon they'll like it," George admitted. "And I like it, too."

Tiger proposed they would be equal partners in the venture, with him bringing in the capital and George contributing his expertise. The two men shook on it, an ebony, kitchen-scarred hand engulfing a smooth palm the color of buttermilk. The handshake became an embrace. "I'll have to discuss it with the Mrs., though" George said when they pulled out of the bear hug. "It's a big decision."

"It is," Tiger agreed. "Take all the time you need."

As Tiger was leaving, Elaine came in with her mother. The women bore a strong resemblance to each other, had the same easy chuckle, the same rich, nut-colored skin. Elaine kissed Tiger on the cheek, then introduced him to Miss Addie, fresh from her checkup with a clean bill of health. "Except for my danged rheumatism," Miss Addie sighed.

"Nothing a nice slice of pie won't fix," Elaine hummed. Tiger told Elaine how fantastic her dessert was. "Thanks, sweet pea," she gushed. "Momma taught me how."

"And now she makes it better than me," Miss Addie lamented, making her way to the dining room. "But I taught her all she knows," the old woman called out.

The children would be home from school soon, although it was a lengthy walk from PS 34 on Hudson Boulevard. It was almost ten blocks but George said there was talk of building another school on that very street. Elaine sucked her teeth. "I'll believe it when I see it," she snapped.

George offered to drive Tiger home but he refused the ride. "It's your day off," he said. "Spend time with your family."

Tiger enjoyed it all: the short walk to the bus, the brief wait at the ferry, the ferry ride itself, and the trolley ride home from the Sixty-Ninth Street Pier. It gave him extra time to contemplate, to map it out. During his pilgrimage home, Tiger took notes on the back of the directions George had written him. Tiger sat with a snub-nosed pencil, smiling with the bumps of the bus, the crumpled paper resting on his knee.

On the Staten Island Ferry, Tiger stood outside, grasping the railing in the steady wind, standing firm and sure in the iciness, facing his destiny, which lay waiting for him in Brooklyn.

Chapter Twenty-Three

Feel Good Food

When the telephone rang the very next day, it was George calling to tell Tiger that he had decided to become his partner in the Feel Good Food venture. Not only had his wife Elaine given her blessing but she'd shed a few tears of gladness when George told her about his friend's proposition.

Tiger revealed his plans to go into business with George Thomas at Sunday supper the weekend after he'd visited his friend in Jersey City. Everyone agreed that it was a wonderful idea. Why shouldn't Tiger start a restaurant? He'd grown up around simple, delicious, home-cooked meals and had been helping Bridget in the kitchen since he was a tyke. He always had a solid head on his shoulders and was practical with a dollar. True, there was some risk involved but it wasn't reckless. They couldn't fathom the place failing, and besides, there wasn't an eatery like Feel Good Food in Borough Park or anywhere else. If nothing else, it was unique.

The many-leafed dining room table at Bridget and Poppa's place was abuzz with talk of the eatery. Angela declared it a fine venture. Augie, too. When she spoke, Rose had a jittery vibrato to her voice, her excitement almost palatable as she passed Harry the gravy dish. "I'll be happy to whip up a pot of peas and macaroni now and again," Rose told Tiger.

"Thanks, Ma," he said. "That would be great."

"When I think of comfort food, that's what I picture," Sully admitted. "A big, steaming bowl of soup." He stabbed another meatball with his fork and plunked it onto his plate.

Astrid nibbled at her *ravioli*. She pierced the center and dug out the ricotta cheese. "Just eat it," Poppa admonished. "Don't kill it."

"I'm watching my figure," Astrid snuffed.

"Nobody else is, Maggie," Harry quipped. "Not since you gave Sam the old heave-ho."

Harry's sister-in-law glared at him and shoved the silk violets dusting her latest millinery masterpiece out of her eyes. "And the name's 'Astrid.' It has been for at least twenty years, but who's counting." Astrid prodded further, the jeweled veil on her hat obscuring her sour disposition. "Now let me get this straight," she clucked at Tiger. "People aren't going to be able to eat what they want, only what you have."

"Oh, they're going to want what we have," Tiger smiled.

"But they won't be able to choose."

"Sure, they will," Tiger said. "We'll have a few items on the menu. They can choose from those."

As was her nature, Astrid wouldn't let up. "What if I wanted an egg sandwich?"

"Then you'd have to go to Dora's Luncheonette," Tiger stated, his voice calm and even. "It's sort of like when you come here. You can't pick and choose. Grandma Bridget serves one main dish, and it's damn good."

"Well, I never…using profanity on the Lord's day!" Astrid gasped. "Mind your tongue, young man."

"Thank you, kindly, Tiger," Bridget blushed. "What a damned nice compliment." Astrid savagely carved off the corners of her *ravioli*.

"What did that *ravioli* ever do to you?" Poppa asked, moving Astrid's plate away from her. "*Basta*. Enough!"

Tiger tried again. "It'll be like home, only better. Reasonable, tasty, and you don't have to cook or clean up."

"I'll clean up!" Stan volunteered. "Can I be your busboy?"

"You can start by clearing the plates off this table," Rose suggested.

Stan rolled his eyes. "It's not the same," he whined. "I ain't getting paid to do that." Reluctantly he began piling up the dirty pasta bowls.

"Yes, you are," Sully told him. "Room and board."

"Three hots and a cot," John added. "Just like in the service."

"Aw, nuts!" Stan said, defeated, carried the soiled supper plates into the kitchen. "And it's my birthday, too. Or did you forget?"

"Your birthday's not till Thursday," Rose reminded him. "And nobody forgot!"

"And mine's Friday," Wendy added.

"I'll always be older," Stan informed his cousin. Wendy stuck out her tongue at him and Stan returned the favor. Then they giggled.

Bridget scratched her chin. "Did we say we were going to celebrate your birthdays today while we were together for Sunday supper?" she stammered. "I can't remember."

"You did! You did!" Stan and Wendy piped in unison.

"Oh," Bridget sighed, rising from the table. "I hope I can rustle up some dessert." Time had taken its toll on Bridget's bad ankle and the rest of her. She didn't believe her family noticed that she walked more slowly, more carefully these days, holding onto pieces of furniture as she picked her way through the parlor. Seeing Bridget hobble made Rose's heart ache so much that she had to turn away. To Rose, it was almost worse than watching Harry's pained, three-legged-dog gait.

Tiger had been astounded at how both of his grandparents had aged in the two years he'd been overseas. He tried to balance out their decline with how astounding it was to see how Stan and Wendy had grown and matured in the very same timeframe. It shattered Tiger how his grandparents were fading. It was strange how life could be both happy and sad for the same reasons: growing older. In the young, it was a wondrous thing; in the elderly, it was a curse. But Tiger figured getting older beat the alternative, just like Poppa always said.

Jo picked up the gravy boat and the bowl half-filled with meatballs, savory sausages, scraps of *braciole* and pieces of chicken stained a glossy amber from the tomato sauce. "I think Tiger's restaurant is a grand idea," Jo commented. "I'll bake a tray of lasagna whenever he says the word."

"I'd like that, Aunt Jo," Tiger told her. "It will be a big hit." Jo beamed as she took the leftovers into the kitchen.

"How about a pot of *pasta e fagioli*?" Camille offered, taking the ravioli platter. "Momma taught me how to cook it just like hers."

"Sounds good," Tiger admitted.

"I bet you could convince Ti-Tu to fry up some of his mom's potato *latkes*," Augie suggested. "Those are great." Everyone agreed they were scrumptious, and Ti-Tu said he'd be honored to make them for the eatery.

When Angela suggested cooking too, the aunties protested. With the baby coming soon, Angela's hands would be full, overflowing. As it was, her ankles were swollen and her back ached, so how could she stand at a stove? They wouldn't even let her clear the table. Angela pouted at being excluded but Tiger assured her, "I bet you can help in other ways."

Harry covered a hunk of Italian bread with butter before Rose carried the basket into the kitchen. "Could you stand corned beef and cabbage every once in a while," he wondered.

"Could I?" Tiger grinned. "Only if it's the O'Leary Special."

"With my secret ingredients," Harry smiled.

"It's no secret," Astrid snapped. "Garlic and pepperoni. Everyone knows!" She picked up the crystal bowl of grated cheese and stomped off.

"You'll be paid for the cost of the food plus a little extra," Tiger explained to everyone. "George will do a bang-up job with stuff like meatloaf, ribs and fried chicken, but with the Italian dishes…it'll be nice to have them coming from my family's kitchens." Tiger paused, "It'll be like you're all part of it. And George could use a break. I can't see him driving in from Jersey but four days a week. Though, once he spends time here, maybe he'll decide to move to Brooklyn. But until then…"

Although the chefs tutted and protested at the thought of being paid, Tiger insisted on compensating them. It was non-negotiable. Astrid, who was possibly the world's worst cook, or at least Brooklyn's, tromped back into the dining room. Tiger could tell she was feeling left out, forgotten. "Aunt A…" Tiger began.

She cut him off, "You know I don't cook, Anthony."

"No one ever called what you do cooking, Maggie," John joked, flashing her a wink. Astrid was visibly peeved and didn't see the humor.

Tiger continued, "But you have such a good eye for color, Aunt A. And you can sew like a son of a gun. I was wondering if you might pick out material for tablecloths and curtains."

"Gee, I could whip those up in a jiffy," Astrid trilled. "And it would cost a trifle."

Rose and Jo brought in cake plates and utensils. Wendy carried the heavy pastel porcelain *Capodimonte* bowl Bridget had already heaped with an assortment of nuts. It was so frilly, fancy and latticed that Poppa referred to it as "Capo Di Gaudy," but Wendy liked it. Filigreed and peaked with painted china blossoms, it reminded her of the top of Cinderella's coach. Stan reluctantly agreed that it did. What very few realized was that the nut bowl's lid of flowers had once been broken off by Tony when he set it down too roughly on a Sunday afternoon he should have been sleeping one off. Although Bridget had told Tony it was nothing, she had secretly gone off to cry in the kitchen—the bowl had been a wedding gift from her cousins back in the Old Country. The next day, when Bridget was grocery shopping on Thirteenth Avenue, Poppa laid down sheets of the *Brooklyn Daily Eagle* and glued the broken top with Duco Household Cement. Since its accident decades earlier, the *Capodimonte* was like new, except for an almost invisible scar. That's the way Poppa was—always fixing things, and setting them right.

Camille brought in a narrow cut-glass dish from the kitchen. At most family suppers, a plate like this held celery stalks, but in Italian households like the Paradisos', it held fennel. Peeled and sliced into elegant strips, fennel, or *finocchio*, as they called it, aided the digestion, especially after a heavy Sunday meal. Its clean taste and hint of licorice prepared their palates and their bellies for the next course: dessert.

The women did their best to keep Wendy and Stan out of the kitchen because Bridget was finishing up their birthday cake. She was frosting what was dubbed the "Happy Birthday, Anniversary and Wedding Cake" by Mrs. DePalma. (It was Mrs. DePalma's recipe, and that's what she called it. Her Dominic and Antoinette loved it, too. Everyone did.) The cake was Wendy and Stan's absolute favorite of many favorites. It included canned cling peaches, crushed pineapple and a luscious filling crafted with homemade whipped cream. As Bridget painted on the frosting, her wrist flicked from side to side like an artist decorating a canvas. This marvelous cake was Bridget's canvas. Next to last, sliced almonds were studded to the confection's sides. Then it was ready for a layer of peaches on top.

When Bridget was through, Jo put in nine candles and one for good luck. Rose lit the wicks with several wooden safety matches, tossing them into the sink to be disposed of properly later. Bridget warned Rose not to light "three on a match," which brought bad luck, but Rose was familiar with her mother's superstitions and already knew not to do this.

When the candles were ablaze, Bridget lifted the cake platter with both hands, careful to walk steadily. Camille shut the dining room lights so the table was plunged into momentary darkness before Bridget illuminated it with the cake. The men, charged with keeping the children distracted, had been watching John do card tricks. Stan and Wendy were mesmerized. The card deck fanned to the table when the cake arrived. They all sang "Happy Birthday," faces glowing in the candlelight.

"I thought you forgot," Stan chortled after he and Wendy had blown out the candles.

"How could I forget my babies?" Bridget asked, kissing each of them on the head, savoring the essence of the Johnson's Baby Shampoo their hair was washed with. Neither child protested at being called "babies," not when there was cake involved. Soon there would be a true baby to take the title from them.

Astrid, charged with perking the coffee, the one domestic chore she did well, poured steaming cups of the sable liquid. They permitted Angela to stand in place and pass people coffee, which she was delighted to be charged with. When Angela gave Tiger his cup, she said quietly, "It's a wonderful thing you're doing. The restaurant with George. I know it will be great." Tiger rested his head against his sister's stomach and felt a small tremor within. "And I can make a batch of lemon-ricotta cookies once in a while," she smiled. "Baby or no, I'd like to contribute somehow."

"Me, too," Bridget added. Even at her age, she could hear a pin drop. Stan swore his grandmother's hearing was her superhuman power, comparable to Superman's X-ray vision. "I could bake this cake in two shakes of a lamb's tail," she told Tiger.

Bridget cut thick wedges of the confection, giving Stan and Wendy the first, and biggest, pieces. It tasted as good as it looked: the layer of crushed pineapples mixed with the hand-whipped, sugared cream. The topping, the peaches, whose juice soaked into the light, white layer cake, mixed together to create exquisiteness. "I've been making this cake for fifty years," Bridget laughed. "And I never had any complaints—or leftovers."

Stan had to be reminded not to lick his plate clean. Harry warned Wendy that if she scraped hers much more, she might wear the painted roses from its surface. As Sunday supper wound down, dishes were collected, washed and put away. The silverware was closed into the breakfront until the following week. The remaining food was divided, packed up and carried away to everyone's respective homes to be enjoyed a few days later.

After hugs, kisses and good-byes, the family made their way to their own places. Last-minute homework was finished. Naps were taken on armchairs under the guise of reading the Sunday papers or "resting my eyes." Even the women sat and relaxed for a moment or two. It was almost six—they'd been eating since one—yet it felt late. In the thick of winter, the sun had already gone down. No one was hungry for a proper dinner that night, perhaps just a cup of tea and a slice of Italian bread with butter and jelly, but not a real meal.

Back at their limestone house, Harry's mind was too busy to doze on the sofa. With a notepad and pencil, he was adding up figures. Jo sat beside him, flipping through *Ladies' Home Journal* without much interest. Wendy occupied her favorite spot in the parlor carpet reading *Honey Bunch: Her First Trip on a Houseboat*. She'd already read it twice since Christmas, and was hoping for new Honey Bunch books for her birthday in a few days, and maybe even a couple of bottles of India ink for her fountain pen. She had been furiously writing in her journal, about her family mostly, and was running low on ink. The Ford Sunday Evening Hour played on the radio in the background. It was a program on the music of George Gershwin, which the O'Learys all enjoyed.

A few blocks away, Tiger sat at the kitchen table, trying to teach Stan how to play Blackjack. The boy insisted on getting a hit even when he had cards totaling fifteen or sixteen. It's not that he didn't understand the rules of the game; he did. But Stan was convinced the lower numbered cards would magically come when he needed them most. Instead, all Stan got were picture cards, jeering Jacks and sneering Queens, which put his score closer to thirty than twenty-one. Or when Stan had a hand totaling ten, he couldn't get a picture card to save his life. "Aw, nuts!" he would exclaim, exasperated. "For the love of Pete!" Tiger and Rose, who was at the stove, both smiled to themselves. Potatoes and eggs, and a nice cup of tea would tide them over until breakfast, Rose decided. It would also console Stan after he lost at every hand of Blackjack.

Sully was dressed in his work blues. He slipped on his heavy coat, ready to withstand another night shift. It was a warmish evening, at least, and spring was truly in the air, though it was technically a month away. Sully insisted he was stuffed, though he did take a forkful of potatoes and eggs. He stole a quick peck on the lips from Rose before he went on his way. She said a little prayer that he would safely return home to her when the night shift was over and dawn broke over Kings County.

Astrid was home in her compact Manhattan studio apartment, wrapped in her silk dressing gown from Lord & Taylor, pouring over fabric samples and patterns books, trying to discern what would be suitable for an eatery called "Feel Good Food." She guessed the men would veer toward the homey, comfortable materials of gingham and plaid, while she favored exotic splashes of color. Astrid ignored the note from Sam which had been slipped beneath her apartment door while she'd been gone. It was clear he felt snubbed but Astrid thought it was high time Sam sever himself from a family which was no longer his, starting with their Sunday suppers. Reluctantly, Sam did, but not without occasional love notes and gifts of magnolias. He was a Southern gentleman, after all, and would not go gently into that good night.

Meanwhile, John was in the projection booth of the Minerva Theatre, on the corner of Fourteenth Street and Seventh Avenue in South Brooklyn. Camille sat in the back row, the seat closest to the booth without actually being inside it with her husband. John took delight in looking down at Camille's strong Roman profile in the flickering light of *The Harvey Girls*. The picture starred Judy Garland, who was indeed a cutie, but John felt Judy couldn't hold a candle to his wife. He watched Camille tap her toes to the song "The Atchison, Topeka and the Santa Fe." The movie made Camille wistful for her brother Kelly and for the family he'd left behind in Tucson, not far from Monument Valley, where *The Harvey Girls* had been filmed. Perhaps she and John would go visit Sophie Veronica and the kids this summer if their finances allowed. A bus trip wouldn't be too dear.

Not an hour into their shift, Sully and Izzy popped into the Loew's 46th so Izzy could "use the can." Sully warned him sternly, "You gotta cut back on the Java."

"It's the only way I can manage a six-to-six without doing it sleepwalking," Izzy insisted, disappearing behind the door marked "Gents."

In the lobby, Sully was glad to run into his son-in-law. Augie was now manager and Mr. Acerno, the owner, was logging fewer and fewer hours, hoping to fully retire by year's end. Pete Acerno was grooming Augie to take over, and even had him placing the theatre's food orders and readying the film canisters for pickup. "How's your better half holding up?" Sully wondered, though he'd seen Augie and Angela a few hours earlier.

"Angie's a real trouper," Augie admitted. "But her ankles have been paining her real bad lately."

"I noticed," Sully said.

"Babies seem to be a lot more trouble on the inside than they are on the outside," the father-to-be sighed.

Sully laughed, remembering Stan as an infant and toddler. "Oh, they're heaps of trouble either way," Sully told him. When Augie's face dropped, Sully added, "But they're worth it."

Izzy came out of the Gents, adjusting his gun belt. Soon the two policemen were back on the beat, now passionately discussing where they would stop for supper. Late on a

Sunday evening, their choices were limited. Usually, they resorted to Miller's on the corner of Fifty-Sixth Street under the El, which had something for everyone, even heartburn. It was going to be a long night.

By eight, Bridget was already in her nightgown and in bed, snoring softly, while Poppa sat alone on the sofa, reading the news in the *Eagle*, then switching to *Il Progresso*, the Italian-language newspaper. It was as though he was compelled to compare and contrast the shenanigans from one press to another, like he didn't believe either source. For a brief moment, he wondered what it would be like to be alone, without Bridget beside him or in the next room, then flushed the thought from his mind. For Poppa, life without Margarita Virgilio Musto Paradiso, his Bridget, was unthinkable.

Next door, Angela sat alone in her parlor. Before Augie left to cover the last show at the Loew's 46th, he'd prepared a piping hot basin of water into which he'd dissolved a few tablespoons of Epsom Salt. Angela had soaked her aching ankles and feet until the water grew cool. She was now in her favorite overstuffed armchair with her feet up on an embroidered ottoman. Although a couple of Bridget's cardamom cookies sat in a little dish on the end table at Angela's elbow, she didn't feel like eating. The baby took up so much space that after just a few bites she was uncomfortably full. Angela still had almost two months to go. She figured she would be eating thimble-sized portions of food by then.

Astrid had given her niece a copy of *Cannery Row* that afternoon and she was already midway through it. Angela loved all things John Steinbeck. Her favorite book of his was a tossup between *Of Mice and Men* and *The Grapes of Wrath*. If a pistol were put to her head, she probably would have chosen the latter, and not because the actress who played "Ma" in the film could be her grandmother's *doppelganger*. (When she and Tiger saw the movie together when it first came out in 1940, they laughed that Bridget led a secret double life: as actress and homemaker.) In addition to Bridget's uncanny resemblance to Jane Darwell, the characters in *The Grapes of Wrath* reminded Angela of her own family. People crossing the Dust Bowl, settling in the Salinas Valley, or those living out their days in Borough Park weren't very different, Angela decided.

The baby stirred inside of her, earnestly kicking her bladder. She rested her palm on the child's foot to still it, and kept reading about *Cannery Row's* "Doc," who was a marine biologist, and the sea creatures, some phosphorescent, which Doc studied in the Great Tide Pool near where he lived. Angela liked Doc a lot, especially the part which went:

> *"Doc tips his hat to dogs as he drives by and the dogs look up and smile at him."*

To Angela, it sounded a lot like Poppa, and the good men in her life. But not men like her father, who tended to kick dogs and cats when nobody was looking, out of pure meanness. And then, there was this:

> *"Doc would listen to any kind of nonsense and change it for you to a kind of wisdom. His mind had no horizon. Everyone who knew him was indebted to him. And everyone who thought of him thought next, 'I really must do something nice for Doc.'"*

For Angela, the passage was so evocative of Doc's personality without going into the color of his hair or whether or not he had a beard (which Doc did), painting a picture by telling the reader what a person was and did rather than how they looked.

Cannery Row was a trim book, just over 200 pages. Its dust jacket had a watercolor painting depicting a couple of piers and rickety buildings. (It could have been Red Hook, Brooklyn. It could have been painted by Angela's Uncle Julius.) Underneath, the flesh of the cover was yellowish-beige, perhaps the shade of Mr. Chong, the grocer's, skin.

Angela read about the Palace Flophouse, the Bear Flag Restaurant, and Hazel, who was a man, and not a woman. Then there was Mr. and Mrs. Sam Molloy, the couple who lives in the boiler. Angela read slowly, savoring each word and phrase:

"Early morning is a time of magic in Cannery Row…"

and:

"I love you," he said one afternoon. "Oh, I love you…"

and especially, the beginning lines:

*"Cannery Row in Monterey in California is a poem,
a stink, a grating noise, a quality of light, a tone, a habit,
a nostalgia, a dream."*

Angela savored the words like most people savored a chocolate drop, slowly unwrapping the foil, placing it flat on the tongue then letting it gradually melt and fill your mouth with its beneficence. This was the sort of book Angela didn't want to end, like a pleasant dream or a lingering Sunday dinner down at Grandma Bridget's. Or a baby she wanted to keep safe inside, forever. But Angela realized none of this was possible, and continued reading as slowly and completely as she could, reaching for a cookie, taking a bite and momentarily becoming lost in a land of exotic spice and warm sugar where all is sunny and good.

She turned the page.

Chapter Twenty-Four

Room to Grow

George made the drive from Jersey City to Brooklyn the
following Wednesday, his next day off. Tiger wanted him
to look at a few prospective locations for Feel Good Food.
George's brother-in-law Tyrone offered him the use of
his Chevy sedan for the trip. It burned a little oil but
made the trip without a hitch. As George turned down
Forty-Seventh Street, he noticed an empty storefront beneath
the El, between a bakery and a pizzeria. Besides the fact that
it wouldn't be wise to open so close to other eateries, George
didn't like the idea of having the clatter of the El overhead.
It wasn't a peaceful cooking or eating environment, even
though people in this neck of the woods were probably
used to the sound the elevated train permeating everything
they did.

George eased the cake platter out of the Chevy's
passenger's seat with the same delicacy he would have
lifted one of his children. Beneath the aluminum cover was
one of Elaine's superb red velvet cakes. She remembered

that Anthony's little brother had a birthday the following day and that Anthony's cousin's birthday was the day after. (Elaine, like George, was one of the few people who used Tiger's Christian name.) "There's not much sweeter than a Valentine's Day Baby," Elaine had grinned as she added a shot of Coca-Cola to the cake's batter. "And no husband of mine ever goes calling empty-handed," Elaine said as she mixed a splash of leftover coffee into the batter then folded it into the rust-red concoction.

While the cake baked and saturated the rooms of their apartment with layers of sugariness, Elaine made the cream cheese frosting. She was always remembering little things about people—birthdays and anniversaries, favorite dishes, even with all she had to do. This was one of the reasons George loved Elaine so hard for so long, through wartime, bliss, grief, striving, struggle, and everything else in between.

As he rapped on the Paradisos' front door, George wondered if he was the first Colored fellow to turn up at their threshold. Then he remembered the many shades of brown at their New Year's Eve open house: coal-black Panamanians, *café con leche*-tinted Cubans like Sandra Santiago and her husband Enrique, folks with brick-toned skin (and hair to match) from Georgia to "light Egyptian"-shaded folks. (When they were in the Service, watching *Stormy Weather* together, Tiger told George "light Egyptian" was the name of the cosmetics shade created by Max Factor to duplicate Lena Horne's smooth-as-caramel skin tone, and George never forgot it.) Even Sicilians visited the Paradisos, which George also learned from Tiger, were considered by some Italians to be the Negroes of Italy—both because of their complexions and their earthy demeanors. Tiger's people didn't prescribe to this sort of racial nonsense. They judged the worth of a man by content of his character, not the color of his skin.

Tiger's grandfather answered the front door. He could hear the man taking each step slowly with his loping, slightly bowlegged gait. Just as Poppa and George were shaking hands, Tiger bounded down the stairs as he had as a child.

In ways, Tiger still was—a child who had gone to war, come back, and was now stuck in between. There wasn't simply a handshake between the two men but an all-engulfing hug, initiated by Tiger. 'I'll never get used to these Eye-talians,' thought George, smiling to himself. 'They're such emotional folk.'

Bridget wouldn't hear of sending Tiger and George out into the winter streets without a cup of coffee to brace them but Tiger insisted they had to go. "We've got an appointment with Mr. Ingar at eleven," he explained, "and we don't want to be late." Mr. Ingar owned the building with the empty storefront between Moe's greengrocery and Gus's dry goods store. A former truck driver for Eagle Warehouse near the Red Hook docks, Roberto Ingar invested wisely, purchasing dilapidated buildings and fixing them up on weekends and nights, putting out-of-a-job carpenters, plumbers and electricians back to work. Before long, Mr. Ingar had a sprinkling of buildings throughout Borough Park. He became known as a standup guy as well as a decent landlord.

George didn't even remove his overcoat. He gave Bridget the cake platter, put his hat and gloves back on and ducked out the door with Tiger. They promised to be back in time for lunch and a proper visit. "You'd better," Bridget chided.

On the short walk to Thirteenth Avenue, George learned more about the borough, which, at first, seemed as foreign to him as the wilds of Borneo. Tiger went on about Coney Island then discussed Brooklyn's now-defunct horseracing tracks. "There was the Gravesend Race Track, the Sheepshead Bay Race Track, the Brighton Beach Race Course..." Tiger began. "Thoroughbred racing, harness racing...Most tracks opened in the 1880s but they closed by the 1920s." George was surprised to hear that a considerable population of Coloreds had settled in town. Tiger said, "A lot came up from the South as grooms and there were even Negro jockeys."

"You sure they weren't Sicilian?" George pondered, well-schooled with how Italians felt about their darker-complected cousins. As they strolled, George took note of the front yards, and imagined that the backyards were just as well-tended. He thought he spotted the purple bud of an early crocus coming up through the melting snow.

"Absolutely sure," Tiger told him.

"Name one," George challenged.

Without skipping a beat, Tiger said, "Isaac Murphy, for instance."

"Sounds like a nice Jewish or Irish boy to me," George laughed.

"Except he wasn't," Tiger pointed out. "Isaac Burns Murphy was the toast of the town. He was considered one of the best jockeys of all time. Won almost half of his races."

"Do tell," George prodded.

"Murph was the jockey when 'Kingman' won the Kentucky Derby—the first horse co-owned by a Negro to win it."

Now George was really getting interested. "You don't say."

"Murphy was also the first jockey to win three Kentucky Derbies," Tiger added. "Started out as a jockey when he was only fourteen."

Tiger and George paused at the DeMeos' house. Nunzi was outside, brushing the snow away from his prized rosebushes. Tiger introduced George to Nunzi. "Whatever happened to Old Isaac?" George wondered when they started walking again.

"He died young," Tiger said gravely. "Murphy was only thirty-six but he was a drinker. That plus gaining a ton of weight forced him into retirement. Got pneumonia, then *kaput*, he was gone."

George didn't know what to say. He knew Tiger's father had been a drunk and died young, too, but George was unclear on the circumstances. He also knew a lady friend of Tiger's had also passed recently. By the little he knew of Denise, George suspected she'd been a drinker as well. "Happens to the best of them," George admitted.

"I suppose it does," Tiger conceded. He steered the conversation back onto the safer ground of racetracks.

"Poppa tells me the First Baptist Church out in Sheepshead Bay welcomed lots of the tracks' Negro workers and a many of them moved around there. Why, I've met Colored folks who were fifth generation Brooklynites."

"What's this I hear about a place called Weeksville? A big Negro community, I believe," George said.

Tiger nodded. "It wasn't just a community," he qualified. "Weeksville was the first place in Brooklyn where Coloreds were landowners."

"Landowners," George repeated in marvel.

"It was in the 1830s, after slavery ended in New York State. A stevedore and ex-slave by the name of James Weeks bought a piece of property along with a bunch of others to form an independent, free Negro community," Tiger said, proud of his borough. "Some of the houses are still standing a century later."

George broke out into a large grin. "Is that so? I'll tell you, Anthony, I'm liking Brooklyn more and more."

"Enough to move here?" Tiger wondered.

"We'll see," George told him.

The two men didn't find it necessary to discuss their upcoming business venture for they had talked and written and figured and planned it to the hilt. It was good to converse about a host of other things, to revisit how Tiger and George had gotten acquainted overseas: through quiet reminiscences, thoughtful observances, and laughter.

After a block, Thirteenth Avenue came into view. The knife sharpener's wagon chugged down the street, chiming a bell in its wake. Although it was raw outside, the street was bustling and busy. After all, people have to eat and clothe themselves, no matter what the temperature. "Reminds me a lot of Jersey City," Tiger admitted.

"Only lighter," George smiled. Yes, Borough Park was similar to his hometown, but vaguely more affluent, the streets a bit tidier, the shops better tended. The paint on the storefronts was fresh, not so sun-bleached. The sidewalks were newly swept and cleared of snow. There was also more variety in the shops. One place sold Talmuds and another sold Catholic articles—crosses, rosary beads, pyxes to carry Communion hosts, and religious books. There was even a *botanica* which sold herbs and elixirs as well as statues of saints endeared by the Hispanic people—like Santa Barbara, Saint Martin and Lazarus. There was also a *smorgasbord* of eateries—German delis, Italian butchers, Norwegian specialty shops, knish shops, and French bakeries—but nothing like what they planned to open. "A true mish-mash," George commented as they walked.

"Like Brooklyn itself," Tiger agreed. "A little of this, a little of that."

"It works for me," George admitted, taking in Lane's pharmacy and the children's clothing store. He caught a noseful of vinegar, garlic and pungent spices, then noticed a row of wooden pickle barrels outside a store off the corner of Forty-Fifth Street.

"Herb's place," Tiger announced. They approached the barrels so George could have a closer look. Herb, who'd known Tiger since he was a scrappy kid, recognized him immediately and came outside wearing his apron. When George shook his hand, he noticed that even Herb's skin was perfumed with pickle juice.

"Your Ma's kept me up to date about you," Herb said to Tiger. "Welcome back."

Tiger thanked Herb, then asked George, "Half or full sour?" (Herb already knew Tiger's preference.)

"I'm a half sour man myself," George conceded.

Herb dipped his arm elbow-deep into the barrel. The vinegar prevented the liquid from freezing in the wooden casks on the pavement. Herb fished out two perfect half-sour pickles, which looked like slick, shiny cucumbers. When George and Tiger took a bite, the pickles snapped back with a crispness. "Now that's a pickle!" George exclaimed.

Tiger pulled two bits from his pocket and tried to give it to Herb, who refused it. Then Herb added quite seriously, "I appreciate your service, fellas. It's the least I can do." They thanked him then continued on their way.

When they were a safe distance, Tiger confided, "Herb's son Larry...he didn't make it." George bowed his head and mouthed a silent prayer for boys like Larry who didn't come home as he and Tiger had.

"There but for the grace of God..." George said simply. "...go we."

Tiger and George walked further down Thirteenth Avenue. It was slow going because every few steps they ran into someone who was acquainted with Tiger, his mother, his stepfather, his sister or any number of his relatives. There were kind words looking after Angela's pregnancy, his grandmother's leg, his brother's performance in school. It was either, "Tell Mike that Big Andy says 'Howdy'" or "How's your Grandma been keeping?" or "Come spring, I'll need a boy like Stan to help weed my yard." Tiger introduced George whenever they stopped. There were warm back-pats and chucks on the shoulder. With each step, George's heart grew lighter for he surmised that Feel Good Food would do well in this neighborhood, especially with its close-knit fabric. George could envision events like Soup Night, Blue Plate Specials, sing-alongs, and then...

"I hope you don't mind..." George heard Tiger saying. When he glanced up, George saw one of Tiger's uncles standing in front of an abandoned storefront, awkwardly shifting from foot to foot, waiting for them. George thought his name was Harold or Herb. That's right, it was Harry. Harry O'Leary. Harry was a vet, like them. Only he hadn't been as fortunate as they'd been. "It's just that Harry's got a keen eye," Tiger continued, "and he's handy with a hammer. Plus, Harry knows everybody in the neighborhood—he used to be a cop."

"The more the merrier," George told him. "We could use an extra set of eyes since we have no idea what we're doing."

"But when did that ever stop us?" Tiger reminded him.

"My granny down in Jefferson Parish likes to say all it takes is heart. When you got heart, the rest of it falls into place."

Tiger smiled. "I like your granny down in Jefferson Parish."

"And she would like you," George conceded. "She'd try like hell to fatten up your scrawny ass, boy. Taught me everything I know in the kitchen by watching, smelling, and eating."

"What's her secret, then?"

"Aw, Miss Helen would say, 'I just quit stirring when the tasting's good.'" Both men laughed. "It's true," George added.

"You'll have to bring her up when we get on our feet. So she can see what you've done."

"What *we've* done," George corrected.

They reached Harry at the empty storefront. With a quick glance through the dirty windows, George saw that the place was a wreck but also, that it had great promise. It seemed to have been a food shop, for the wooden bins which might have held vegetables or meats were still there, half torn down, half standing. The floors were bare pine boards, filthy with scraps of paper, clumps of dust and unnamable refuse. The space was deep, poorly lit and cellar-like. Yet...yet... George could envision the walls painted a bright color, the raw wood floors covered with linoleum squares. He could picture checkered curtains on the front window which would be so clean it would shine like the sun.

Harry's bear paw swallowed George's in greeting, milky white against burnt umber skin nicked with years of chopping, mincing and scarred from lifting hot pots off the range. Harry grabbed his nephew in a clinch. "You sure you don't mind me being here?" Harry wondered. "Because I could..."

George told him, "Naw, you stay. We can use a third opinion. And a lot of luck."

Mr. Ingar showed up a beat later. He was a squat man, perhaps five foot five, and solidly built. Well-dressed in a matching charcoal topcoat and fedora with a blue band and feather, he cut an impressive figure. When he unfastened his coat, you could see the suit he wore was skillfully-made, probably sewn by Calabrian immigrants. (The Calabrese were acknowledged for their exemplary tailoring skills.) His shoes were newly polished. Anyone who knew him knew Mr. Ingar grew up poor and earned whatever he had through hard work, frugal living, wise investments and elbow grease. He had a loving wife named Fortunata and two beautiful daughters. Mr. Ingar was nothing if not trustworthy and deeply enjoyed giving a good guy (or two) a break. He'd already made up his mind that he would offer the vacant store to the pair of vets for a decent rent, if they wanted it. The rest was a formality, a necessary dance that had to be done.

The four men shook hands before Mr. Ingar produced a key and unlocked the door, which stuck somewhat. The second it swung open they were nearly bowled over by an intense oceanic odor. "Did I mention this place had been a fish store?" Mr. Ingar wondered.

"I never would have known," Tiger remarked.

When they stepped inside, Mr. Ingar wisely left the door ajar behind them. "It's been sealed up for a few months," he apologized. "Needs a little airing out."

"Needs a lot more than that!" Harry said. He had been acquainted with Ingar, as he called him, when he was little more than a street urchin. Harry had given him a pass for mischief-making, letting him go when Harry should have hauled him in for a misdemeanor. But as Harry had surmised, Ingar turned out all right, which is why he'd set him free.

George and Tiger were the only ones brave enough to venture into the depths of the store at first. The debris looked worse when they were wading through it. The tin lining the boxes which had once held fragrant cod and mackerel was encrusted with the type of green slime you'd find at the bottom of a boat docked in Sheepshead Bay. A rat the size of a housecat scuttled across the floor and under a pile of discarded *Herald-Tribunes*. "It has potential," George nodded.

"That, and rodents," Tiger admitted.

"My Granny Louise has a remedy for the stank," George said.

"A clothespin on your nose?"

George ignored Tiger's feeble attempt at a joke. "You familiar with the God-awful smell when a critter dies in the walls?"

"Yes," Tiger told him warily. "It smells like death."

"You just boil a mess of cider vinegar in a tin pot, and like magic, the stank is gone."

"But then the place reeks of vinegar," Tiger pointed out.

"Naw, that fades. Believe me, it fades. That, plus a few coats of paint, and it'll smell like a brand-new dollar bill." Tiger wasn't entirely convinced.

George walked toward the back of the store. "We could put in a kitchen, right here. Can't you see it? A big, old stove with six burners, an oven and even a broiler. Then, right next to it, a griddle for flapjacks and eggs. I was thinking of having 'Breakfast for Supper' nights. I mean, who doesn't crave a mess of corned beef hash, johnnycakes and eggs for dinner every once in a while? Not to mention cathead biscuits."

"Cathead biscuits?" Tiger asked.

"Biscuits big as a cat's head," George explained. He trudged through the room's wreckage, gesturing. "A sink over here, open shelves for dishes, pots, pans, and the like..." In spite of himself, Tiger could envision it the way George described it. "We can make it work, I tell you."

"Okay," Tiger said.

"Okay," George replied, grabbing hold of his friend's hand as though it were a lifeline. "I'm so darned tired of busting my back for other people. It's time we had a piece of the pie."

"Sweet potato?" Tiger grinned.

"Any pie you say, brother," George told him.

Mr. Ingar was surprised when Tiger and George agreed to take the store. They, in turn, were pleasantly floored when Mr. Ingar told them the rent. They'd expected a haggling match but the cost was half of what they'd anticipated.

What's more, the first two months would be rent free. "I figure that's how long it will take to do the renovations," Mr. Ingar explained. "How does it sound?"

Tiger and George were speechless, so Harry piped up. "Sounds fair, doesn't it, boys?"

"Extremely fair, sir," Tiger admitted.

Looking at Harry, Mr. Ingar conceded, "Somebody gave me a good break once, and I never forgot it. Sometimes, a good break is all you need."

After they shook hands, Mr. Ingar gave George the key. "Start fixing it up as soon as you'd like," he added. "Your place will be a welcome addition to the neighborhood," Mr. Ingar nodded. "With room to grow."

There was no talk of money up front, no mention of money under the table, only a vague, "You can start paying rent on April 15th, okay?"

"That's better than okay!" George burst out, then added, "Sir, you've got free grub for the rest of your life." The man smiled, softening his usually grave, guarded face. His brown eyes shone like those of a faithful German Shepherd as he walked away. And just like that, the short, barrel-chested man was gone, his nicely-tailored overcoat swishing in the breeze, his shiny Florsheims clicking on the pavement.

Finally alone in the broken-down palace, Harry looked around and scratched his chin. He pushed his pork pie hat further back on his head. "This place is a holy mess," he sighed.

"True," Tiger relented. "But with a little elbow-grease..."

George sighed, "And a lot of dough..."

"We got that, too," Tiger said.

Harry watched in blissful awe as his nephew and his business partner dove into their plans for the future: what had to be done and how to do it. Nothing ate away at their optimism. Harry longed to feel passion like this. Oh, he loved Jo and Wendy, and the rest of his family deep and true enough, but he didn't have this kind of blind faith in anything. Whereas Tiger and George's belief in humanity and in all that was right had become more indomitable during the War, Harry's had flagged. "I've seen this man take chipped beef on toast and turn it into a true thing of beauty," Tiger explained. "So, I believe Old Georgie can do anything."

George's coppery skin actually blushed a deeper shade. "Thank you. I won't let you down."

Next, Harry watched as the men politely argued about George leaving his job early so he could help with the renovations. "I have some rainy day money put aside," George admitted. "Plus Elaine brings in wages from her job at the school cafeteria."

"But that's only part-time," Tiger reminded him. "I won't hear of it. You've got four kids at home and her folks upstairs." The willowy man was resolute, standing up firmly to the broad, gentle man almost a decade his senior. Tiger explained how his own days were free and how his childhood friend Jimmy Burns could be hired on. "I ran into Jimmy at the Lucky Buck last week," Tiger said. "He just got back in town."

"You mean from Rikers," Harry added.

"For panhandling and loitering this time," Tiger explained to George. "Jimmy's a good egg. He just didn't have the same breaks as you and me. Didn't come from a great family. Both folks were drinkers. Never had much of an upbringing. He could use a fair shake."

George nodded. "Any friend of yours…"

They decided to move the large, deep wooden bin to unearth what lay behind it. Wedged between it and the wall were rotting paper sacks and what looked to have been fish parts: heads, bones and scales. "That explains the stink," noted Harry. They cleared up as best they could, moving the trash to a pile in the middle of the floor with an old broom that was lying there. Since all three were wearing their best dress suits, they were careful not to ruin them. Tiger and Harry would return the next day in their work duds and really dig in. They'd have nearly eight weeks to whip the place into shape. "It'll be a long road," Tiger admitted, "but it'll be worth it."

Harry and Tiger managed to convince George not to feel guilty about being unable to pitch in with the cleanup when George apologized about it again. "We each have our parts in this," Tiger told him. "Taking care of your family until this place is up and running is yours." At last, not only did George accept it, but he quit bringing it up.

With a lightness in their step, the three men headed back to the little brick house on Forty-Seventh Street. Harry thought this was the perfect time to bring up his proposition. Although he had been a soldier and before that, a beat cop and had dealt with all sorts of people, Harry felt nervous addressing Tiger and George. His heart beat fast in his chest and when he spoke, his voice was tight, higher than usual and unfamiliar even to himself. Harry talked fast, breathlessly, so they couldn't cut him off. "Boys," he began. "I'd like to get in on it. This restaurant of yours is really going to take off and I want to be an investor. I've been looking for something to sink my teeth into, something I could believe in. I think this is it."

They proceeded several steps until they were beneath the Callery pear tree near the corner which had recently begun to bud. Tiger and George exchanged silent glances before either of them said a word. They'd already discussed people asking to invest so Tiger knew exactly how to respond. Although he'd practiced his speech over and over in his head, he assumed it would be Poppa or his Uncle John who would approach him with a proposition. The men stopped walking. Tiger looked directly into his uncle's eyes. "Harry, we appreciate your faith in us…" Tiger began.

"And your generous offer," George added.

"Right," Tiger nodded. "But me and George need to do this on our own." The bulky man looked visibly deflated. "I know it's not the answer you were hoping for but we would still like you to be involved, though."

"If you'll have us," George tagged on.

Tiger continued, "We're looking for a reliable man for the front of the house. A trustworthy sort to oversee the cash register. Someone who will make sure the place runs smoothly. I'll be helping out Georgie in the kitchen and waiting tables. I couldn't keep an eye on register as well."

George continued, "I can see you're respected in the neighborhood. You'll keep out the riff-raff and bring the good folks in. Not only do you know everyone around here but they like you. That's saying heaps."

Tiger could see that Harry was puffed up with the infusion of sincere and flattering words. "We won't be able to pay you much at first," Tiger told him. "But we want you here from Day One. Neither of us knows squat about contracting and fixing up a place but you're a pro. We hope you'll decide to be part of this."

Harry answered immediately. "How could I not?" he said. Together, they made their way toward 1128 Forty-Seventh Street where Bridget and Rose had prepared splendid meal. They served the luncheon downstairs where there was a proper dining room instead of just an expansive eat-in kitchen. Within minutes of the trio's arrival, the table was covered with a number of dishes, despite Bridget's insistence that the meal was "nothing special."

First there was PR Soup, a family favorite. Short for potato-rice soup, it was another of Mrs. DePalma's own creations: a diced-up potato, leftover rice, chicken broth, onion, garlic, a sprinkle of dried spices, and *voila*. Topped with a scattering of Pecorino Romano cheese, it was perfect to chase away the winter blues. George made a mental note to add it to Feel Good Food's menu.

After the empty soup bowls were cleared away, then came the potted meat, which was what Sadie Lieberwitz called pot roast. So, since it was Mrs. Lieberwitz's recipe, it was referred to as "potted meat" in the Paradiso home. Melt-in-your-mouth beef (like Elaine's red velvet cake, Coca Cola was the secret ingredient), and on the side, whipped potatoes and carrots…it was heavenly. George noted potted meat would make a great sandwich, slapped between two slices of hearty bread the following day… if there were any leftovers. Then there was a simple green salad of lettuce, thinly-sliced red onions, cucumbers, tomatoes and green pimento olives, tossed lightly with oil and red wine vinegar. When George asked Bridget how much she added of which ingredients, she responded, "I just eyeball it." This reminded him of Miss Helen's stirring sentiment, and he smiled.

In addition to these dishes, there were two types of bread: Italian and pepperoni, the latter Bridget insisted was left over from the night before. There were also small bowls of olives, roasted peppers (to go with the bread), marinated celery and the sharp perfume of Provolone cheese, "to whet the appetite," Rose told him.

And finally, when George sighed that he could eat no more, even after loosening the top button of his slacks, there was Elaine's Red Velvet Cake. They would save Stanley and Wendy each a pre-birthday slice to enjoy when they came home from school. The entire table oohed and aahed over it—the subtle sugariness, the magic of its texture on the tongue, the whipped cream cheese icing. "I've never tasted anything like it," Poppa admitted, patting his belly. Coffee was served, Cuban-style, like Consuelo Ortez Vega had taught Bridget to prepare it: thick, sweet, with a sliver of lemon rind. "So strong the teaspoon stands up in it," Harry joked.

When George let himself back into his brother-in-law's Chevy, eased himself behind the Bakelite steering wheel, and left Brooklyn for Jersey City, he was satiated, blithe, and full of hope.

Chapter Twenty-Five

Hide and Seek

Tiger looked high and low for Jimmy Burns but couldn't find him. It reminded him of when they'd played Hide and Seek as boys; Tiger's friend had been impossible to locate, even then. Perhaps this was because Jimmy was so used to making himself disappear. When you're invisible, you don't get hit. When you're invisible, you can't be the victim of a drunk's wrath. When you're invisible, you don't get hurt but you also don't get love. You don't get fed. You don't get a lot.

None of the neighborhood kids could find Jimmy during Hide and Seek. The boy had an easy time crouching, still as a stone, beneath front porches or behind gingko trees until someone cried, "Olly olly oxen free," signifying that Jimmy had won the game. Whereas Tiger would become fidgety whenever he hid, Jimmy found strength in the very act of hiding. It was one of the few things he did well.

Even though Jimmy was invited to the Paradisos' backyard cookouts, they would often find him secreted away beneath the table built from a four-by-eight and a pair of sawhorses, his grubby paw reaching up to snatch a chicken wing or a biscuit, then stealing off like a rodent to gnaw away at his loot in private. It was as though Jimmy were afraid the food would be snatched from him. Perhaps this had happened in the past, and he was scared it might happen again.

Tiger's family's attitude about "that Burns boy" was extremely charitable. Rose thought all Jimmy needed was a bit of tenderness and understanding to set him right, having been raised by wolves (drunken parents) with a cast of unsavory characters waltzing in and out of his life. Whenever Rose tried to give the unkempt boy a hug, he stiffened like a bag of sticks and slithered out of her embrace. Bridget contended all that Jimmy needed was to be fattened up, and tried to accomplish this whenever she had the chance, sending him home with containers of thick soups for the family or pushing him out to play with an apple in each fist. However, Jimmy needed a lot more than being hugged or a few meals to fix him.

Finding Jimmy Burns as a grown up entailed methodically visiting the local watering holes one by one and seeking him out. The first place Tiger tried was the Lucky Buck, but Jack Link informed him that he was forced to let Jimmy go when a customer's lost wallet was found on the floor beneath Jimmy's cot with no explanation from Burns. Jack seemed crestfallen Jimmy had let him down. "I thought I could trust him," Jack sighed. "But he started drinking hard again and…"

The Pink Pussycat, Tiger's father's favorite drinking establishment, perhaps because it was within spitting distance of the train yard, proved fruitless. The owner, Bledso, had a slew of rude words about boys like Burns who stayed put at home, wreaking havoc wherever they went, while others, like Tiger, had served overseas. (In actuality, Jimmy was 4-F on account of "mental deficiency.")

A trip to The Stumble Inn elicited a litany of tuts from Teddy Long, the saintly barkeep, who confessed that Jimmy had left him with a five-dollar bar tab for weeks. "If I ever catch up with him…" Teddy warned as Tiger headed for the door. But Tiger knew Teddy was far too compassionate to do more than scold Jimmy when he did turn up. Besides Teddy believed so fervently in the basic goodness of humanity that he'd probably end up trusting Jimmy again.

Tiger ventured as far as Tilly's Tavern in Bay Ridge and received the report of no Burns sightings for a month, but finally struck gold at Farrell's. Tiger entered the stained-wood door of the pub, a stone's throw from Holy Name of Jesus Church, only to find Jimmy carrying a tub of used beer glasses to the back to be washed.

His childhood friend looked vaguely sober but hung over, bloodshot and battle-worn, and thinner than Tiger had ever seen him. As Jimmy disappeared into Farrell's back room without spotting him, Tiger ordered a glass of beer from Houlie, the no-nonsense barkeep. He quickly learned that Houlie had taken pity on Burns, who was homeless after he'd been cast out of the Lucky Buck for stealing. Houlie hired Jimmy on as a bar-back—with Old Man Farrell's permission, of course. "James knows this is his last chance," Houlie explained to Tiger. "Or else he'll be out on the street."

Jimmy had a cot in Farrell's storage room and heated water in a kettle to take farmer's baths there. Houlie was doing his best to steer the misguided boy on the straight and narrow. So was Father Shine at Holy Name, Houlie said. At the mention of the church, its bells chimed eight in the distance, followed by a tinny version of "A Mighty Fortress is Our God." For a moment, Tiger envisioned stern-faced Bishop Boardman or even Father Shine pulling the bells in the brick tower bordering Prospect Avenue, but he knew bell-ringing was an altar boy's duty since there was no Quasimodo in the parish. (*The Hunchback of Notre Dame* has been one of Jimmy and Tiger's favorite movies as teenagers, but perhaps this had to do more with the sultry Maureen O'Hara's heaving bosoms rather than the acting prowess of Charles Laughton. He and Jimmy were randy teen-age boys, after all.)

When Jimmy came out of Farrell's back room, his face first brightened upon seeing his childhood friend, then reddened. This time, Jimmy seemed shameful, like perhaps he knew Tiger was aware of his recent situation at the Lucky Buck. But Tiger greeted him with the same enthusiasm he did when Jimmy called for him to play stickball when they were ten. "How have you been?" Tiger gushed.

"Oh, I been better and I been worse," Jimmy admitted.

With a nod from Houlie, Jimmy took a break. He showed Tiger his neat bed in a corner of the storage room, surrounded by piles of crates, shrugging, "Nothing fancy, but it beats Rikers or Sing Sing."

"Or a pup tent," Tiger conceded. Jimmy admitted he'd fallen upon bad times while Tiger had been overseas and had taken to petty thievery in order to put food in his gut. Jimmy seemed to regret it but said he had little choice. He acknowledged flashing a switchblade if money didn't easily exchange hands. (But Jimmy would never use it; he was so benign he wouldn't hurt a mosquito.) One unfortunate evening, the drunken gent in question stumbled and fell onto Jimmy's knife, which pierced the man's ample abdomen. If not for the quick action of Tiger's stepdad, who responded to the scene, the old cocker would have bled out, turning armed robbery into murder. Not only did Sully staunch the bleeding but he spoke on Jimmy's behalf in court. Sully's testimony lessened Jimmy's sentence considerable, which was mercifully light since it had been Jimmy's first offense. Sully had taken to looking after the Burns Boy since he breathed life back into him after "the garage incident."

They shifted their conversation back to the bar, where Houlie poured them each a glass of ginger ale. "I could use a dependable guy," Tiger began. He told Jimmy about Feel Good Food and all the work which had to be done. Jimmy listened closely, sometimes mouthing a word here and there. When Tiger was done explaining, Jimmy said it was a wonderful opportunity and he was grateful Tiger had thought of him, but he couldn't leave Houlie, who depended on him.

"That much is true," replied Houlie, who heard everything which passed above his shellacked bar, "but I can spare you a few hours a day." Jimmy looked doubtful and opened his mouth to protest. "Besides, Tiger needs you as much as I do," Houlie pressed. "And I bet you could use extra dough." Still, Jimmy was silent. "Don't worry, you'll always have a place to stay as long as you want it," Houlie pledged. This apparently did the trick.

Tiger gave Jimmy the particulars and wrote down the address on a cocktail napkin. He was to report at the storefront the next morning at nine when they'd begin demolition. Jimmy shoved the napkin into his pocket, excused himself and went into the back to wash the tub of glasses, for Houlie was running low. Tiger drained his soda and went for his wallet. Houlie protested until Tiger explained that the money was for Burns—a little incentive for his friend. Houlie said he'd give the tenner to Jimmy. "What are the chances he'll show up?" Tiger wondered.

"If I were a betting man, I'd say about 50/50," Houlie wagered.

"Better odds than I thought," Tiger smiled.

But the following morning, a crystalline blue February day, Tiger was surprised to find Jimmy Burns waiting for him at the storefront. After bagels from Heshe's and coffee in paper cups, they dove into their project, swinging hammers, pulling down walls, wading through the mess, all the while, reminiscing about their childhood. They shared tales of pinching grapes from Rizzi's cart, running wild in those very streets. Jimmy recalled the afternoon when Tiger was sick in the curb, spewing great rivers of orange vomit before his Uncle Harry rescued him and ferried him home. "He never liked me much, your uncle," Jimmy concluded.

"Harry likes you okay," Tiger told Jimmy, gathering up an armload of ruined plywood. "It's just that he's a hard nut. On the outside, that is. On the inside, he's a big mush."

Jimmy's expression darkened when Tiger said his uncle was helping to oversee the project. The thought crossed Tiger's mind that his friend might not have even showed if he knew of Harry's involvement from the get-go, and that he might not turn up tomorrow because of it.

Burns was tireless. Already, his gently-used collared shirt was drenched with sweat. He was dwarfed inside the voluminous fabric and Tiger thought it might have been one of Houlie's cast-offs, which the barkeep had passed along to the young man so down on his luck. "I know what people say about me, about my family," Jimmy muttered quietly.

"People say lots of things," Tiger told him. "I never pay them any mind."

His face smeared with dirt and soot from the demolition, Jimmy gathered a pile of debris which seemed impossible for a man of his build to lift, yet he did. "Ant strength," Tiger's neighbor Eileen Daly dubbed it—when a flimsy human could tote several times their own body weight, like an ant could. Yes, Jimmy Burns was the epitome of ant strength. "Sure, I've made some dumb mistakes…" he acknowledged.

"Who hasn't?" Tiger pointed out.

"But not like me," Jimmy said. "Only I paid for them. I paid for them fair and square. I never had it easy. Neither did my folks but then they were degenerate drunks." Jimmy turned to Tiger and said, without remorse, "You're lucky."

"I am," Tiger conceded, taking a sledgehammer to a stubborn board. "But what my family got, they busted their humps to earn."

Jimmy took the hammer from Tiger and knocked down twice of what Tiger could in ten hesitant taps with one well-placed swing. "I ain't talking about dough," Jimmy explained. "I mean that you always knew you were loved. You knew you were wanted." Tiger opened his mouth to speak but couldn't conjure up any falsehoods to make Jimmy feel better about the fact that he wasn't either. "That's okay, though," Jimmy added. "I ain't sore about it. Your people went out of their way to be nice to me, no matter what everyone else thought. Your Ma gave my Ma Kewpie's old duds for my sister Mary. Your grandma was always trying to feed me. Still is." Jimmy gestured at the lunch pail in the corner, stuffed with fat sandwiches of leftover gravy meat, a thermos of soup, and hunks of cake wrapped in waxed paper. "All I'm saying is that I appreciate it. I appreciate everything," Jimmy added.

"It's okay," Tiger managed to choke out. "We're friends."

Jimmy's dusty, sweaty face beamed. "Yeah, we're in it for the long haul." He wiped his eyes with a corner of shirtsleeve. "I won't let you down, Tiger, I swear."

A loud din outside drew them both to the gritty front window. Harry had arrived with a battered green pickup truck. Tiger had no idea where he might have procured it and didn't ask. He noticed his uncle's brief frown when he caught sight of Jimmy Burns, mucky from the intense work, and wondered if Jimmy saw it, too. Harry did his best to mask his disappointment, slapping his great meat hook into Jimmy's calloused, less substantial hand and shaking it vigorously. "Glad to have you aboard," Harry grinned, perhaps too widely.

They toted the refuse out to the truck, first bagging the smaller chunks into burlap trash sacks then taking the slats of wood which smelled of damp and fish and rodent. When they were done, Harry drove off. To where was another mystery. Harry simply said he would make the stuff disappear, and did. By the end of the day, the place looked more like a shop and less like a junkyard. Although there was still much to do, Tiger and Jimmy left satisfied with a job well done.

Since his friend had to toil at Farrell's through most of the night, Tiger wasn't hopeful about Jimmy showing up the next morning, but he appeared soon after Tiger did, looking slightly worse than he had the day before. He wore the same dingy clothes but smelled and looked clean. "My uniform," Jimmy joked. Tiger gave him a buttered roll and a carton of coffee. "I ain't had a drink in three days," Jimmy told Tiger.

"That's good," Tiger nodded, mouth filled with fluffy Kaiser roll.

"That's great," Jimmy responded. "It's the most I gone without it since I was fourteen."

"How do you feel?" Tiger wondered.

"Not so bad as I figured I would," Jimmy concluded.

"Will it be tough, you moonlighting at a bar and all?"

"Nah," Jimmy said. "Houlie ain't a drinker. If he can do it, I figure I can, too." Jimmy wiped the crumbs from his slacks and stood. "One's too much and ten's not enough," he added. "Get what I mean?"

Tiger crumpled up the waxed paper from his roll. "I think I do."

The sweeping was endless. The floorboards were brushed with one of Bridget's old corn husk brooms. While Jimmy was still sweeping, Augie arrived with a friend who worked at Dykes Lumber. The flatbed contained enough drywall to cover the place. DeGaetano, who sometimes stuttered, had convinced his boss to give it to Tiger wholesale. In no time, DeGaetano and Augie had the new walls up. DeGaetano was a master at the craft, patiently taping and plastering the nail holes and the creases where the sheetrock joined, then sanding them smooth after the plaster dried. DG, as Augie called him, moved slowly and surely, creating a thick coating of dust on the floor planks, but the shop still seemed cleaner. Jimmy swept up as methodically as DG sanded, reflective as he did so. Tiger wondered what Jimmy was pondering, hopefully not a pint of Ruppert's or Rheingold.

Poppa stopped by with pepper and egg sandwiches for the crew. They were still warm. The men ate them rapidly in great hunks, washing them down with Dr. Brown's Cel-Ray soda. Poppa, who'd eaten earlier with Bridget, surveyed their progress and approved. After touching up a few spots, DG took the truck back to Dykes and said the walls would be ready to paint the following day.

With a large bucket each, Tiger and Jimmy tackled washing the floor with Spic and Span, water and sweat. They started at opposite ends of the room and made their way to the center, crawling about like scullery maids. They had to laugh at themselves, especially when Jimmy commented that they looked like Sara Crewe and Becky from *The Little Princess*, who worked their fingers to the bone before Captain Crewe came back from the Boer War and rescued them from their fates. The fellows had seen the picture with Poppa and Bridget at the Fortway when they were twelve. Neither boy would admit their secret crush on Shirley Temple back then, but somehow, each of them suspected it.

The grueling labor at the shop paid off and eventually, Tiger and Jimmy could discern the natural color of the pine planks beneath. The floor had to be absolutely spotless so the linoleum glue would stick. There could be no scraps of dirt remaining or else it would show through the floor covering. Tiger and George had already selected black and lemony linoleum squares because the sunshiny shade was so cheery (and white was too plain—plus, it would scuff too easily). They'd also found a wall paint to match the yellow of the floor tiles.

Tiger's Aunt Astrid had already bought the material for the curtains from her favorite shop on Bridge Street downtown near Abraham & Strauss. It sported a cream and yellow gingham pattern with darling little flowers sprinkled throughout. Astrid had also found a durable cotton which came in a wide array of colors. She said it would be perfect for the tablecloths and that she'd drop off some swatches so they could take a look. A rarity for Astrid, she refused to take money from the budding restauranteurs, explaining that both the curtains and the tablecloths were her "break a leg" gift to wish them well in their new venture. Poppa accused Maggie of getting soft. To which she responded with her usual, "Pish posh...and the name's Astrid."

What to hang on the walls was a matter for gentle debate. The women were leaning toward tasteful paintings of flowers, from van Gogh's sunflowers to Monet's water lilies to the peonies of a local artist named Christine Lafuente. Astrid suggested a series of still life paintings of food which were classy and guaranteed to whet the appetite. Stan had an affinity for movie posters of Betty Grable, which had nothing to do with the notion of food that made a body feel good. "But Betty Grable sure makes *me* feel good," Stan had explained.

They hadn't decided on wall decorations, even on the Saturday they were painting the sheetrock a pale yellow. Jimmy casually remarked how George and Tiger should cover the walls with pictures of their families if they really wanted to make it homey. George, his deep brown skin spattered with Benjamin Moore's "Lightning Bug," looked at Tiger. They both smiled at Jimmy's idea. "That's perfect!" Tiger exclaimed, clapping Jimmy on the back, staining his hand-me-down shirt with the shade. "It would give the place a personal flair, like they were eating in someone's kitchen."

"They are," George laughed. "Ours."

It so happened that Tiger's friend Dan Fiorino, who'd recently returned from the War (where Dan had been a field photographer), had opened a portrait studio nearby on Fort Hamilton Parkway. Dan agreed to blow up any family pictures they desired, at cost. He also offered to frame them, at cost, too. Dan told them the time he spent reproducing the photographs would be his pleasure, and his gift to his fellow servicemen. George said there would be free eats whenever Dan liked. Dan thanked George but said he wouldn't hear of it. "At cost, then," George winked. The deal was sealed, and soon Feel Good Food's walls would be adorned with framed portraits of Granny Louise hung up beside Grandma Bridget, Miss Helen beside Poppa, Uncle Kelly, Sophie Veronica and the kids. Why not include photographs of the people whose recipes they used? For instance, Mrs. DePalma and Sadie Lieberwitz? Dan volunteered to take these portraits with his military issue Contax camera. "It will be a welcome change to use it for something like this, something positive," Dan admitted. He had documented far too many war dead and bombed-out villages in Europe with the Contax. He hoped taking pictures of friends and neighbors might cancel out all the bad.

The days melted into weeks as the snow gave way to spring blossoms budding in front yards. The tulips and daffodils came up after the crocus. The cherry blossoms began to bloom soon after, the tree branches bare one day and bursting with brilliant pink the next, like magic. The Paradiso women toiled diligently under Astrid's supervision, sewing the hems for the curtains by hand. Angela struggled to see the needle and thread past her bulbous belly. Everyone joked that she was so huge she might be carrying twins but Angela would be content with just one healthy baby in her arms come the end of April.

When he heard about their ambitious sewing project from Bridget, the Paradisos' neighbor Antonio DeMuccio, a retired tailor from Calabria, offered to hem the tablecloths on the old Singer sewing machine he had in his basement. It was the kind operated with a knee pedal instead of electricity but it spun like a top. In his prime, Antonio used to sew costumes for Broadway showgirls, and later, dress suits for men. His wife Evalena, who also worked on the tablecloths, had made ladies housecoats and pajamas in a factory, so table linens were a snap for her.

In this manner, Feel Good Food became a true neighborhood effort. It was beautiful to behold, how it evolved each day, more resembling an eatery than an abandoned dream as the weeks went by. People couldn't resist peeking into the soaped window as they walked by, trying to gauge the progress. Even Bridget's heart was light and cheerful as she listened to Poppa detailing the day's achievements. She'd been a bit melancholy and poor of health lately but didn't tell anyone except for Poppa. "I've got no oomph or get-up-and-go," Bridget sighed to her husband. The prospect of Tiger's business, and of her timeworn recipes taking on a new life in the restaurant, filled Bridget with a brightness of spirit.

The pieces were falling into place. The appliances would soon be delivered from Bowery Kitchen Goods near Houston Street. Tiger and George had met there one day and picked out everything for Feel Good Food, from tables and chairs to the refrigerator and stove to tableware. George was like Tiger used to be in Dora's Luncheonette as a kid: wide-eyed, fingering all the penny candy and coveting each one. The difference was that Tiger told George he could choose whatever he wanted for the restaurant, that money was no object. Even with setting aside a bit of cash for Stan when he grew older, Tiger still had a sizeable nest egg from his father's TWU death benefit, and he intended to spend it.

George's dark eyes widened as he fondled the gleaming stainless steel surface of the sleek Vulcan stove. He fingered his cap nervously as they placed the order for the most enormous Frigidaire they made. They picked utensils which were sturdy and had heft to them, and drinking glasses which were thick and solid. The dishes were simple—white rimmed with a yellow stripe. They purchased sugar bowls and creamers to match. Tiger insisted they buy the best pots and pans, and new bakeware for the ladies who would be creating their signature desserts in their home kitchens to be sold at the diner. The bill made George's head spin and he had to loosen his shirt collar as Tiger signed his life away. His friend laughed at George's expression. "If you weren't so colorful, I'd swear you'd gone pale on me," Tiger joked.

"I do believe I have," George admitted.

To help him recover from spending so much money, Tiger took George to the Nom Wah Tea Parlor for lunch. They walked through a labyrinth of fragrantly-pungent blocks to reach it, on the part of Doyers Street which curved, the same place it had stood since 1920. Poppa's crony, Mr. Wong, had enlightened him about the Nom Wah, the Chinaman's favorite haunt in Chinatown, and it had become a Paradiso haunt, too.

The Nom Wah's red banquettes were always full and their Formica tables were always overflowing with delicacies. Tiger had the waiter bring them a selection of *dim sum*, two of at least a dozen dishes, even chicken feet in black bean sauce. The pork dumplings, hand-wrapped and infused with a savory broth which flooded your mouth when you bit into them, were George's favorite, although he liked the turnip cakes a lot as well. "Not your Momma's turnips," he concluded, smacking his lips. They washed the meal down with two pots of jasmine tea, which George had never tasted before. He thought they might serve it iced at Feel Good Food during the summer months, and Tiger agreed that it would be a nice touch.

George and Tiger were pleasantly stuffed when they left the tea parlor. From one of the fish stalls lining Canal Street, George couldn't resist buying a sack of shrimp with the heads on, to boil in a pot when he got home to Jersey City. He would season the water with his own concoction of herbs and spices, like a New Orleans crawfish boil. In broken English, the fish shop's owner told George to come back, that crawfish would be in season soon. He also managed to convey that he had a truck and would deliver to Brooklyn if the order was large enough. They shook on it, and George left beaming, talking of the wonderful dishes he would create: huge, steaming pots of jambalaya and a crawdad étouffée that would curl your hair *and* your toes.

Tiger led George further down Canal Street. He made his friend laugh with tales of how the scent of the neighborhood made his cousin Marissa gag and retch, though she did like the Nom Wah. They made a right onto Mulberry Street from Canal. Another right onto Grand led them to Ferrara's, which had been there since 1892. It was another place to which George had never been. Tiger ordered them each a vanilla *cannoli* and George watched in wonder as the counterman cradled a crispy tubular shell in one hand and wielded a pastry bag in the other. He stuffed the shell with a heavenly mixture of fresh cream made with ricotta and confectioner's sugar, studded with chocolate chips and citron. The man filled one shell, took up the next, then passed them to Tiger and George when he'd finished. They accepted them readily, like boys receiving an ice cream cone. When George tasted it, he groaned audibly. "Now, I've had *cannoli* before," he explained. "But never like this." While Piccolo's under the El was exceptional, and Jersey City's new place Monteleone's was even better, there was nothing quite like a just-made Ferrara's *cannoli*.

A box of pastries each, tied up with candy-striped cord, Tiger and George made their way to the Grand Street station.

There, the West End train would deliver them safely to Borough Park, where George's brother-in-law Tyrone's car was parked. As they descended into the train station, off in the distance, the bells of St. Patrick's Old Cathedral tolled three.

Chapter Twenty-Six

Crackerjack

Among other things, Angela was a crackerjack typist. She had an affinity for it from the first time her fingertips lightly hovered above the keys at New Utrecht High School's typing class ten years before. She easily memorized the positions of the letters, numbers and symbols. While her classmates were struggling or hunting and pecking their way through "Learn to Type!" Angela was building speed and accuracy. It even astounded her teacher, Mrs. Yamin, who said that if she kept it up, Angela, who was dubbed "Angie" at New Utrecht, would be a more skilled typist than even she. (Angela did keep it up, and she was.) She even received a merit award for "outstanding achievement" in recognition of her keyboard prowess.

Mrs. Lieberwitz let Angela borrow her old Royal so she could type menus for George & Tiger's Feel Good Food. The machine was black, sleek and portable, and came in a nifty carrying case. Although it wasn't heavy, neither Mrs. Lieberwitz nor Augie would let Angela carry it up the flight of steps. (She wasn't strong enough to carry it up the long flight of stairs herself.) Ti-Tu, who had just come home from his job at as a rate analyst for Yale Transport Corporation in the City, gallantly ferried it upstairs to the Corso residence because Augie was still at the Loew's 46th when Mrs. Lieberwitz dropped it off. "Keep it for as long as you like," Mrs. Lieberwitz told Angela. "It's been collecting dust in the basement but it works like a dream." There were even a couple of replacement ribbons to go with it.

Angela set up her home office on the dining room table, first putting down a cotton cloth to protect the finish. It was a beautiful piece of furniture and had been Augie's grandmother's. Angela took pride in polishing it with lemon oil once a week, even though she, Augie, and sometimes Ti-Tu, generally ate their meals in the kitchen.

Beside the Royal, Angela had a stack of flaxen paper George and Tiger had chosen with much consideration. It perfectly mirrored the shade of the restaurant's walls and the curtains. They also had a rubber stamp custom-made which proclaimed the name of the eatery in bold Times New Roman lettering, surrounded by an oval and two buttercups. Though it was costly, they managed to find ink pads in a mustard yellow, which matched the containers of French's they would keep on each table.

Angela's routine was to type the menu first, then carefully stamp the logo on top when she was through. In case she made a rare typo, Angela didn't want to ruin a stamped page, but she never did. She hummed as she typed, even enjoying the clang of the bell which sounded when she came to the end of a line.

For the time being, Feel Good Food planned to have the same menu the same day of each week. Monday would feature a handful of items, including meat loaf and a hearty *pasta e lenticchie* (a thick lentil soup topped with plenty of Parmesan cheese) plus there would be cream-cheese iced carrot cake for dessert. Tuesday would be shrimp and rice, mac and cheese and escarole soup, and so on. Angela didn't mind typing the same lines over and over. It became a meditation, an incantation, listening to the rhythmic tap of the metal keys against the thick paper. She liked the surety and the repetition. It lulled her into a quiet place. Her belly was so large that she had to sit far back from the table. Her arms barely reached the keyboard, that's how far away she had to sit. After an hour or so, her lower back would begin to ache. Whether the pain was from the typing or from the baby, she didn't know. She got up to stretch anyhow.

Typing Feel Good Food's menus was an easy chore for Angela. First, because she did it with a spirit of confidence that everything would work out for her brother and his business partner George. Second, because she was thankful to have something to do during the lonely days of late pregnancy besides listen to the radio, read and worry. She missed her office friends at *Ladies' Home Journal*, where she'd gotten a job after high school. Angela knew she could continue typing for Feel Good Food even after the baby came, while her child napped or lay gurgling nearby in the white wicker bassinet. But the baby wouldn't come for another month. At least that's what Dr. Schantz said. Angela relished doing a task which mattered, while she waited for her baby to be ready to be born.

That was the worst part, the waiting, the fretting. What would labor be like? Was the baby stirring too much in her womb? Or too little? Would the baby be healthy? Would Angela be a good mother? Although no one in the family brought it up, every so often Angela couldn't help but recall the time her Aunt Jo gave birth to a stillborn child when Angela had been a teenager. When she thought about her aunt's tragedy, a chill ran up her spine and she would suddenly feel squeamish. Angela couldn't imagine the anguish of coming home from the hospital without a child in her arms. She remembered how Aunt Jo had nudged Angela out of her depression when she'd been terrified she'd miscarry again, and the young woman never forgot her aunt's compassion.

Because of what had happened to Aunt Jo, Angela was extra cautious. Most Italian families were superstitious where expected babies were concerned, but Angela elevated it to a new dimension. The future Corso child's room was completely empty and scrubbed clean as a whistle but Angela wouldn't permit Augie and Ti-Tu to repaint it and she wouldn't let them move in the nursery furniture. The basinet which had been used for Angela, Tiger and Wendy had already been scoured with disinfectant and a damp washrag. It stood at the ready in the basement next door, covered with new plastic sheeting, along with an arsenal of neatly-boxed undershirts, cotton diapers, burp cloths, hooded towels, booties, bonnets, gowns and sleepers. A separate crate held items like diaper pins, thermometers, eye droppers and aspirators. Angela wouldn't allow these things into the apartment before their time. While her family thought it was odd, they sympathized with her trepidation.

There it was again, the pain at the base of Angela's spine, bone deep and a sick green in color, if pain could have a shade. It took her breath away. Angela had to concentrate hard to breathe deeply, which seemed to dissipate the discomfort. Perhaps it was the uncomfortable dining room chair she'd been sitting in or perhaps she'd been sitting for too long. Angela placed her palms firmly on the tabletop to stand. 'Soon, I'm going to need a fork lift like Stan says,' she thought, smiling to herself.

When Angela found her footing and reached her full height, she felt a sharp stabbing sensation in the pit of her abdomen, on the right side. Then there was a sudden whoosh of fluid between her legs. At first, she thought it was a gush of urine, only the color was wrong. It was clear, smelled slightly sweet and was flecked with blood and mucus. There was a great deal of it, soaking through the seat of her grandmother-in-law's pretty chair cushion of needlepoint daisies. Besides spoiling the chair, it also seeped into the rug. Angela hoped the maple floor beneath the carpet wouldn't be ruined.

When Rose heard her daughter's cry, she was at the side window in a flash. "Momma!" Angela called again, moments after the first time. It reminded Rose of the girl's plaintive wails when she fell off her red tricycle in the alley and skinned both knees. This sounded more frightened, more dire, though. Rose flung up the window sash to see Angela in her own window across the alleyway. Her face was a ghostly white. "It started," Angela cried. "The baby. It's coming. Now."

"But it's too early," Rose told her. "A month too early."

"There's blood," Angela said. "Lots of it."

In a moment, Rose was down the house steps, down the front steps and at her daughter's side with no recollection of how she got there. Stan was still in school, Sully was doing an overtime day shift and her parents were probably taking their customary afternoon nap, so she didn't breathe a word about Angela to anyone. She didn't even stop to put on her coat. Rose ran outside wearing her cobbler's apron over her everyday dress.

The Corso apartment, usually as neat as a pin, was a wreckage of murky fluids, fallen papers, a ruined pot of African violets and a broken china teacup overturned in the excitement. Usually a worrywart, Rose was oddly calm, as though she knew in her heart it would turn out all right, and that by the end of the day, she would be cradling her grandchild, hale and healthy, if not diminutive.

Rose took her sobbing daughter into her arms and eased Angela back into a dry chair. Then she ran the tap and brought her daughter a cup of cool water to calm her. Rose went to the parlor telephone and dialed Dr. Lewis's number, which she had memorized. Rose could have dashed across the street to fetch him but she didn't want to waste time, and she couldn't leave Angela, who begged her not to go. Moments after she hung up the phone, from the window Rose saw Dr. Lewis on his front porch, Mrs. Lewis behind him, guiding him into his jacket, then handing him his aged leather medical bag. The portly, light bulb-shaped man rushed across the street. On the way, he passed Nunzi DeMeo, who was watering his sidewalk. Nunzi alerted his wife Violetta, who was cutting down a cluster of early lilacs to grace their dining room table. "Everything okay?" Violetta asked the family doctor.

"It's Angela," Dr. Lewis told her, breathlessly. "The baby's coming."

"But it's not time!" she cried. Dr. Lewis hustled across the street without responding.

When Violetta DeMeo knew something, soon all of Borough Park knew it, too. She was on the telephone immediately, not spreading gossip but alerting her fellow St. Catherine of Alexandria Sisters of the Rosary so they could gather for an emergency novena prayer vigil as soon as possible. Meanwhile, Eva Lewis was already on the horn, summoning an ambulance to whisk Angela to United Israel Zion under her husband's care. Eva's next call was to Dr. Schantz, who'd been seeing Angela through her pregnancy. Dr. Lewis was mainly there for moral support.

Meanwhile, upstairs in the Corso apartment, Dr. Lewis stabilized his patient, reminding her in an unwavering voice, "I brought you into this world. I'll help bring your baby into this world, too."

At first, no one could imagine how word got to Tiger so quickly because Feel Good Food did not yet have a telephone installed. It was actually thanks to Billy-the-Bike-Boy, who was far from being a boy but was still delivering meats for Moskowitz on the rusty Schwinn. Billy must have heard it from Mrs. DeMeo. He spread the word up and down Thirteenth Avenue as he made his deliveries. A furious ringing of Billy's bicycle bell drew Tiger out of the shop. He managed to decrypt Billy's news of Angela's early labor through the maze of misinformation. "Your ssssister's water balloon broke!" Billy spat out, then rode on.

Spattered with Benjamin Moore's Navajo White (Tiger and Jimmy were in the middle of painting the shop's moldings), Tiger ran the two blocks to the Loew's 46th. He left Jimmy alone to accept the tables and chairs from Bowery Kitchen Goods, confident his friend would double-check that the order was correct and undamaged.

Jimmy Burns' very bearing had changed greatly in the weeks he'd be working for Tiger and George. He stood taller, bathed more frequently, washed and Pomaded his hair, even when it would be covered with a painter's cap. "Don't worry, I'll hold down the fort," Jimmy told Tiger, and Tiger was sure that he would.

None of Augie's employees at the movie house were able to locate him. Augie wasn't in the projection booth or supervising a delivery of York Peppermint Patties and other confections from the Hershey Company, but Tiger knew precisely where he would find his brother-in-law: in the can.

By the time Tiger and Augie were zipping along New Utrecht Avenue, Harry and Jo were hustling down Forty-Seventh Street from the opposite direction. As the runners turned onto the block, an ambulance came careening down the road, going the wrong way on the one-way street. Mr. Lieberwitz noted this while taking out a paper sack of trash. "Is the baby on the way?" he asked of the sprinters.

"Seems so," Augie gasped, running his hardest.

"But it's way too early," Mrs. Lieberwitz yelled from the second-story window, from which she'd been beating a throw carpet with a stick.

"Tell that to the baby," Tiger said, struggling to keep up, moving apace with Augie.

Mrs. Lieberwitz spat over her left shoulder to bring Angela luck, and hit her husband on his silvery pate. Yiddish epithets were exchanged but soon forgotten for there were more important things to worry about. Sadie Lieberwitz hastily stripped out of her housedress and put on street clothes to join her friend Rose, who surely could use her support.

Out of breath, the running duo reached 1128 Forty-Seventh Street as Poppa and Bridget were helping each other down the front steps, avoiding the loose brick in the right-hand corner which Sully promised to cement but never got around to doing. Wendy and Stan were walking home from school, pausing to sniff the lilacs and taking a few nibbles of red bud, which had recently bloomed. Their skipping turned to a full-blown jog when they spotted the ambulance's swirling lights near the family compound. As she dashed, Wendy's chestnut braids took flight behind her just as her Aunt Rose's used to do decades earlier when she ran relay races in grade school. Wendy made it to the house before Stan, as usual.

By then, a small crowd had gathered in front of 1130 Forty-Seventh Street as Angela was being carried down the steps on a stretcher, her stomach a mountain beneath the sheet which covered it, Augie bent close to her ear, whispering fervently into it. The intimacy between the two young marrieds was so palatable, so real, it could be spread onto thick slabs of bread or stirred into a batter to create something delicious and unforgettable.

Augie climbed into the back of the ambulance with Angela and the attendant while the driver leapt into the front and sounded the siren. It was so loud the children clapped their palms over their ears. Tiger came out of the house carrying his mother's coat. He guided Rose's arms into the sleeves in a deft motion and even helped her button it. Wendy and Stan were brought up to date, instructed to keep their grandparents company and to do their homework. Tiger, Rose, Harry and Jo speedily made their way to United Israel, only a few blocks away, on foot. They arrived seconds after the ambulance.

The operating theater was so bright it hurt Angela's eyes: white tiled walls, white ceiling, glaring white light bulbs. It wasn't nearly as big as she thought an operating room ought to be. She was grateful they let Augie in with her, though he had to scrub up and don a cap, gown and put funny booties over his shoes. A nurse with thoughtful, worried eyes above her mask told Angela they didn't normally allow husbands in the operating room but the young couple was so dear—and so frightened—they made a concession, at least until the pushing started in earnest.

Angela could see that Augie was smiling even though the lower half of his face was covered in mint green cotton. His eyes crinkled up in the corners, a giveaway that he was grinning, though it was out of nerves, not humor. "Tell me something wonderful," Angela begged him.

"We're going to have a baby," Augie said. The contractions were coming quicker and more intensely now. Angela couldn't imagine how she could endure childbirth. In the ambulance, it felt as if the baby were going to slip out, but now it felt like it was stuck, as though there were a great stone within her which wouldn't budge.

"I know that," she responded. "Tell me something else."

"I love you," Augie stammered. Angela knew he would say this next.

"I love you, too," she encouraged. "But I need you to take my mind off the pain. Tell me a story…" Augie was stumped. "I don't care if you make it up," she pressed. "But make me believe it. Or else tell me something true. A memory, a good one."

"How about driving down to Florida on our honeymoon?" he offered.

"That was a nice trip," Angela sighed. The nurse slipped a blood pressure cuff onto her arm. "I'd never been so far away from home before."

"Me neither," Augie admitted.

"It's getting lower," the nurse whispered to Doctor Schantz, who'd just scrubbed in. "She's lost quite a bit of blood."

Angela was staring deep into Augie's eyes as though there were no one else in the operating theatre. Her face wrinkled into sadness. "I liked Florida but in another way, I hated it. I hated the South," she recalled. "I couldn't believe there were separate bathrooms and separate water fountains marked 'Colored.' I felt so embarrassed. It's not that way up here."

Augie shook his head. "In Brooklyn, we're all the same," he told her.

"Not the same," Angela corrected him. "We're different but it's all right, isn't it?" She winced with the next contraction but didn't cry out.

Dr. Lewis entered the operating room but not so much to assist Dr. Schantz as to comfort Angela when Augie had to leave. "Dr. Lewis brought you into the world," Mrs. Lewis liked to remind children when her husband had to perform a particularly unpleasant duty like giving a vaccination or cauterizing a nose. Hearing this always calmed them down, imagining Dr. Lewis, his stubby fingers at the ready, his rotund body in a crouch, a baseball catcher ready to grab their teeny bodies the second they shot out.

Dr. Lewis's eyes were sharp and concerned above the cotton mask. Augie recognized him by the protrusion of his pulpy nose beneath it and also by the way he nervously droned in a monotone hum. Dr. Lewis had brought Augie into the world as well, and practically everyone else in Borough Park, it seemed. The good doctor stepped beside Dr. Shantz and whispered, "Is it still alive?"

"As far as I can figure," the senior doctor responded. "But we've got to get this baby out now. She's losing a lot of blood."

"Caesarian," Dr. Lewis said.

"Hopefully not. She's fully dilated."

Angela sobbed silently as the nurse tapped Augie's shoulder. "I'm sorry, Mr. Corso, but it's time for you to leave."

The tall, young man hesitated, his sable eyes growing moist with emotion. "Augusto, I'll take care of her," Dr. Lewis told him. "I promise." Augie left without a word for if he spoke, he would have cried, too.

On one side, Dr. Lewis stood, holding tight to Angela's hand. On the other, the nurse changed the bag of saline solution which emptied into Angela's arm. The nurse smiled at her terrified patient then continued humming "I'll Get By" as she checked Angela's pulse. Through wet eyes, Angela smiled back weakly. "My grandpa used to sing that song to us when we went on a long drive," she said. The nurse nodded, then began to sing in a voice that was girlish and soft:

"There may be rain
and darkness, too,

but I'll get by
as long as I have you."

The song sounded even sweeter than Aileen Stanley's or Billie Holiday's version because it was sung just for Angela. "What's your name?" Angela asked the nurse.

"Sally," she said, as she slipped a rubber mask over Angela's nose and mouth. The gas smelled vaguely of lemons, half-rotted lemons. "This will put you to sleep, Angela," Nurse Sally continued. "And when you wake…" Those were the last words Angela heard before slipping off.

The maternity ward's waiting area had been commandeered by the Paradiso Family. Augie's parents had arrived. So had Astrid, straight from her job at B. Altman's. She was still wearing her work smock. Mrs. Lieberwitz, who was there, too, had run into Sully and Izzy as they walked the beat, so the patrol cops were in the waiting room as well. Although they tried their best to stay at home with the kids, Poppa and Bridget were too antsy to wait in their parlor for word from the hospital. Ti-Tu offered to sit with Wendy and Stan, who were not old enough to enter the maternity ward. When their grandparents left for United Israel, Stan bellyached and Wendy pouted but their countenance changed when Ti-Tu offered to teach them how to fry up his famous grilled cheese and tomato sandwiches, slathered with mayonnaise on the outside to toast them perfectly, just like they did in diners. He also brought with him two boxes of Crackerjacks to seal the deal.

Camille and John were the last to arrive, out of breath, practically running from the El, which stopped three blocks away from the hospital. Including two additional expectant fathers, there were over a dozen stuffed into the alcove. This was above the hospital's limit but because of the presence of two cops, certain exceptions were made, however, only if the group remained quiet. "If anyone else comes, it'll be like that scene in *The Big Store*," Poppa concluded. Everyone looked at him curiously. "You know, where Chico's looking for hardboiled eggs. Groucho comes in, too, then the maids, the engineer, the manicurist..." Poppa explained.

In addition to mixing up the names of actors, Poppa was forever confusing the names of pictures. Izzy scratched his head. "Do you mean *A Night at the Opera*, Mr. P?"

"Is that the one where the girl's looking for her Aunt Minnie?"

"I think so," said Izzy.

"Then yes. If Margaret Hamilton shows up..."

"You mean Margaret Dumont," Sully corrected his father-in-law. "Margaret Hamilton was in *The Wizard of Oz*."

"Whoever. If either of them shows up, we'll be in trouble."

Despite the tension and the frazzled nerves, everyone couldn't help but burst out laughing. The welcome sound subsided like rain soaking into a thirsty sidewalk—first undeniable and present, then it was gone. Space was made for Poppa and Bridget to sit on the waiting room chairs. Though her right ankle was tightly wrapped, it was clearly swollen. Bridget's daughters gently chastised her for walking to the hospital, but these days, Poppa felt too unsure and unsteady to drive, even though the Buick was a fine example of American engineering. Sully even managed to convince his wife to sit, though Rose admitted, "I'm as jittery as a jitterbug."

In the delivery room, Angela was deep asleep, the rubber mask obscuring half of her face. As Nurse Sally rechecked her blood pressure, she noted that the young woman resembled a fairy princess under a magic spell. Her skin was deathly pale like Snow White's, perhaps too pale. Dr. Lewis noticed too, his eyes meeting the nurse's above their masks. "More blood," he told her. She fetched another pint as Dr. Schantz wrestled the forceps into the recesses of the mother-to-be. The baby was limp when he drew it out of her, lifeless and small. Perhaps four pounds, the nurse estimated, but it didn't cry or stir. "It's a boy," Dr. Schantz announced calmly, suctioning the child's nose and mouth. Miraculously, the rag doll came to life, pinked up, and began wailing. Nurse

Sally's eyes crinkled with relief as she took the baby from the doctor.

The girl on the operating table grew blanched. "She's losing blood as quick as we give it to her," Dr. Lewis commented. As Dr. Schantz considered his options a second nurse cleaned up the pools of red. "I'll do my best to stop it," Dr. Schantz sighed. "Her uterus might be torn. If I can't repair it…"

"Do whatever you have to, just save her," Dr. Lewis snapped. He began muttering in Hebrew, prayers he hoped would save the girl he'd brought into the world not twenty-five years earlier with his own hands.

But when Dr. Schantz tried to feel inside the new mother, something blocked his entrance. His face registered shock. "It's a head! There's another one."

"Twins?" Nurse Sally exclaimed. "No wonder she's early."

With adeptness and care, Dr. Schantz eased out the second baby. This one was a girl, smaller than her brother, but feisty, indignant, and crying at the top of her lungs, as though she were annoyed she'd been overlooked. Nurse Sally took the second baby and cooed her into silence as she weighed her and cleaned her.

Even after the placentas were removed, Angela's heavy bleeding persisted. They gave her two additional pints of blood. "You tried everything," Dr. Lewis said to Dr. Schantz. "You have no choice." He nodded and told his staff to begin prepping for an emergency hysterectomy. They did so swiftly and seriously. The babies slept curled into each other's bodies in a single incubator, breathing on their own and resting comfortably.

When Dr. Schantz was done, although he was exhausted, he changed his soiled operating gown, scrubbed his fingers, arms and face thoroughly, and went out into the waiting room to tell Angela's family the news.

Chapter Twenty-Seven

Two Peas in a Pod

Although the nurses tried putting the Corso twins into separate incubators, they cried and cried unless they were nestled together in one. "Like two peas in a pod," Angela remarked as she studied them from her wheelchair. She dipped her hand into one of the holes in the incubator's side. Augie fit his fingers into the other. Their babies were petite, yet perfect little creatures.

Baby X, the girl, favored her father with her thick shock of black waves, serious ebony eyes and olive skin while Baby Y favored his mother with light hair, peach-toned skin and green-gray eyes. Angela had never felt anything as silky as their skin. Softer than velvet, perhaps their hair was even downier than their flesh—a wisp of a breeze, the kiss of a ghost.

Looking at her babies, Angela's heart was filled with joy and sorrow all at once. The word "bittersweet" didn't quite describe it. Mr. Wong said there was a phrase for this emotion in Chinese which loosely translated to "happy-sad" or "joy and sorrow mixed together." The Cantonese *bei hei gaao jaap* was very difficult for Western tongues to pronounce—Angela had tried several times, to Mr. and Mrs. Wong's peals of covered-mouth laughter—so she just called it "happy-sad."

The Wongs visited Angela and the twins at United Israel, and with them, brought a womb-strengthening concoction made especially for women who had just given birth. "Ginger vinegar soup with pig trotter," Mrs. Wong announced proudly. Angela's stomach withered after just one spoonful. There was another fortifying dish made with beef, carrots and Chinese yam, which Mrs. Wong swore smelled less noxious. She would bring Angela a pot of it when she was home from the hospital. Mrs. Wong also told of a Chinese tradition, *zuo yuezi*, which literally meant "sitting the month." It was the thirty-day period where new mothers rested, ate foods which restored their bodies, and were waited on hand and foot. "All you do is take care of you and take care of baby," Mrs. Wong explained. "Babies," she corrected.

During the two weeks Angela was in United Israel, her neighbors visited her one by one or in pairs. Mrs. Lieberwitz brought her cinnamon *babka*, which Angela loved. "Cinnamon's good for the blood," Mrs. L said. Augie's boss Mr. Acerno and his wife Marianna brought a thick pastina-chicken soup broth made with hearts, kidneys and assorted blood-bolstering innards. Like Mrs. Wong, Marianna explained, with a blush, "It helps your female parts recover."

Meanwhile, George's wife Elaine was more concerned with Angela's spirit, which she claimed chocolate worked wonders reviving. This is why Elaine and George brought a chocolate pecan pie, her first ever. Angela didn't mind being Elaine's guinea pig to try out a delicacy for the Feel Good Food menu. After the first bite, Angela sighed pleasurably, "I'll have to retype the menus and add this in…but it'll be worth it." Elaine and George had driven in without the kids, who her parents were minding. As they crossed the George

Washington Bridge, Elaine declared their Brooklyn jaunt a mini vacation.

Of course, Angela's in-laws were at United Israel at least once a day, often twice, with items like *biscotti* and *spaghetti carbonara*, and other dishes Mrs. Corso knew her son enjoyed. It was a mere coincidence that Angela favored them, too. Even Olie Olsen from Kreske's stopped by with a tray of his wife Tomina's *fiskeboller*, a wonderful Norwegian codfish cake which was healthful as well as delicious.

Rules were bent because of Sully's connections at the hospital—United Israel was on his beat and he protected it capably. Because of this, the staff even permitted Stan and Wendy to visit Angela and the twins briefly. They brought handmade cards crafted with crayons and pipe cleaners on construction paper. Tiger led them to the nursery's showcase glass window where the children examined the newborns with a sense of wonder and horror, especially Baby Orenstein, who had a full head of hair which looked like a toupee. "They're so squirmy and ugly," Stan remarked. "Like baby rats without their fur."

"Except ours," Wendy pointed out. "Ours are cute."

Stan wrinkled his nose. "Were we that ugly when we were babies?" he wondered.

"Probably," Wendy conceded. "But our parents didn't think we were. I bet they thought we were adorable." Wendy noticed Stan stiffen, perhaps recalling his mother, the Yellow Queen. "I know your Ma loved you a lot," Wendy added. "No matter how ugly you were." Stan smiled.

Ti-Tu even showed up, toting his violin case. He shyly began to play "Embraceable You." The tune had warmed Angela's heart since she originally heard it in *Girl Crazy*, the first Broadway show she'd ever seen. (Uncle John had taken her when she was ten.) It's the song she and Augie chose for their first dance at their wedding a decade after she'd attended the show. Ti-Tu remembered this and reverently played the song. Since the nurses kept encouraging Angela to get out of bed and walk, Augie managed to convince her that dancing was probably even better than walking. They stood

close on the speckled linoleum and swayed in place, barely
moving. Hearing the achingly beautiful notes of Ti-Tu's
violin, a security guard came running. "That's not allowed
here," the uniformed man told Ti-Tu. The nurses and patients
implored the guard to let the music continue; he did.

When Ti-Tu was done playing "Embraceable You," he
took requests of jigs and popular tunes, stopping once to
visit the room of a dying man who implored him to play
Kol Nidrei. Although usually a solemn chant (a prayer for
the dead) the song is generally sung on *Yom Kippur* or at
funerals. However, when the man heard the strains of Ti-Tu's
heartbreaking violin, with fading breath, he asked his wife
to fetch the musician and have him play *Kol Nidrei* at his
bedside. Ti-Tu quietly complied but he left the hospital
soon after.

And Rose, Rose practically lived at United Israel Zion.
The outpouring of food and music reminded her of the way
the entire neighborhood had banded together to shower her
with sustenance and wishes for a speedy recovery when
she'd had emergency surgery a decade ago. Although Rose
wanted to pamper her daughter, she held back, allowing
others to take the lead, deriving pleasure in seeing how much
her child and how much the newborn babes were loved.
Besides, there would be plenty of time for Rose to spoil her
daughter once she was home.

The doctors suggested that Angela stay in United Israel
for three weeks but she was itching to go home sooner. She
felt more able-bodied with each day and had very little pain,
even with the hysterectomy. Angela hated spending all that
time in bed. The women tried to convince her to stay in the
hospital for as long as she could because soon enough, she'd
be kept hopping as she tended to the twins. It was tough
enough getting sleep with one newborn in the house and
Angela would have a pair to care for. But the babies weren't
ready to come home yet, and as much as Angela hated the
thought of arriving at the apartment childless, she was more
than ready to leave United Israel Zion.

Although the babies were holding their own, Angela worried as she watched them from outside the incubator walls. To her every sneeze, every hiccough meant the twins had taken a bad turn. "They're so wee," Angela would sob, though she fought to hold the waterworks in check.

"They're doing fine," Augie would tell his wife, kissing her hair, which always smelled of roses. "Remember Baby McHaffay," he'd whisper. A few days before the Corso babies were born, the *Brooklyn Daily Eagle* ran a story about Baby McHaffay from the *Chicago Tribune*. Augie reminded his wife of it often, so often he could recite it word for word:

A two-pound baby girl born St. Patrick's Day was reported doing nicely in an incubator in St. Francis Hospital, Blue Island, yesterday. She is the first child of Mr. and Mrs. Ray McHaffay, 13416 California Street, Blue Island.

"We should send them a card," Angela said, wiping her eyes with the sleeve of her flannel nightgown.

"We will," Augie promised her. "We will." The next day, he brought Angela a notecard from Lane's Drugs and a three-cent stamp. She puzzled over the note, getting sparkles on the side of her hand from the card's cover as she wrote. Augie watched Angela with a whisper of a smile on his face. Her hope and determination was palpable, growing with each word, with each delicate cursive letter, carefully formed with the fountain pen. He could read his wife's silent thoughts forming: 'If Baby McHaffay could live, then so can my babies.' Augie shared same hopes.

At first, Angela refused to name her children. Somehow, she thought that if she put names to her love, she might lose them. At the hospital, the miniscule tags around the children's wrists read Baby X and Baby Y Corso. Soon, Angela felt she would be ready to give them names, but not just now. "I haven't even held them yet," Angela cried. "Once I can feel them, smell their skin, their hair..." her voice wavered. Augie understood.

Choosing a name was more complex than either Angela or Augie would have thought. They both shared the belief that to name a child after another person, either living or dead, was too weighty an onus for someone so new to the planet. A name had everything to do with the person you grew to be, they thought, not what someone else was. For example, Grandma Bridget's sister Henrietta was named for their grandmother, carrying on the Italian tradition of naming the first girl after the child's father's mother. Bridget swore that if her sister had been named "Jenny," for Jenny Lind, the Swedish Nightingale, who'd been their father's favorite singer, Henrietta/Jenny would have been a completely different person. Instead of being burdened with the name of a dusty harridan, Henrietta would have been named for a woman with the voice of an angel, and it would have made all the difference.

Augie himself was the third in a long line of men named Augusto Corso, and he wanted it to end with him. Angela's father had insisted that Tiger be named for him, and Anthony, Jr. regretted it deeply. To name the babies after one side of the family and not the other would have caused ill feelings. To name one child for one side and the other for the other side…was it more respectful to name the boy after someone or the girl? It should be an equal honor, shouldn't it? To recognize either Poppa or Grandma Bridget (or both!) with a child named after them would have been lovely, but neither expected it. "Our great-grandchildren should be individuals," Poppa explained. "Not saddled with old people's names."

"Plus they're a mouthful!" Bridget agreed.

Although they weren't Jewish, the young couple even considered the Hebraic tradition of remembering a departed relative by giving a newborn their name. Immediately, Angela thought of her Uncle Kelly. But his real name, Nicholas, was too cumbersome for such a teensy one. Not only that but Augie's parents had lost a daughter at age three to polio soon after Augie was born. Angela and Augie were afraid his folks might take offense if they named their son after an uncle on Angela's side and didn't name their daughter for Little Wilhelmina (which, to be honest, was a hideous name). So, the fact that there were two babies made the name dilemma twice as complicated.

The day before Angela was to leave United Israel, Nurse Sally took her and Augie into the room attached to the nursery. They layered pressed johnny gowns over their clothing and covered their feet with booties. "I feel like Mickey Mouse," Augie quipped. "How about you, Minnie?" Nurse Sally explained that the strange outfits were to keep the babies as germ-free as possible. Though Augie and Angela had physical contact with their children through the incubator's portholes, today they would actually get to hold them *and* feed them. The twins were finally strong enough. Nurse Sally put the couple into comfortable chairs and went to fetch the incubator. Moments later, she rolled it in on wobbly wheels. The babies slept soundly inside of the Plexiglas rectangle.

The twins seemed to have grown overnight but Nurse Sally said they were still too small to take home, but soon, very soon, she vowed. Baby Y's reddish hair was sparse while Baby X's dark patch stood up like an Indian brave's. "No wonder you had heartburn," Augie remarked. "Look at that moptop."

As Nurse Sally opened the incubator, she told Augie and Angela it was a very state of the art piece of equipment. "United Israel Zion is a teaching hospital," she revealed proudly. "We're often the first with a lot of things. Incubators have been around for decades but they were perfected in the early thirties. By Henry Ford, believe it or not." Augie said he didn't believe it, until Nurse Sally explained further. "A doctor named Robert Bauer at Henry Ford Hospital in Detroit combined oxygen, heat, humidity, and easy access in 1931. This is what he came up with."

"How about that doctor who put incubator babies in a Coney Island sideshow?" Augie asked.

"Oh, you mean Dr. Martin Couney?" Sally stated. Augie nodded. "They called him 'The Incubator Doctor.' He started exhibiting babies in Luna Park near the turn of the century. Couney's facility was top-notch. He employed six nurses and two wet nurses. Plus he didn't take a penny from the parents; the twenty-five cents people paid to see the babies more than covered the expenses for their care. Couney saved thousands of little lives with his incubators."

"What did they do before then?" Angela wondered.

"Since incubators were expensive, sometimes they kept the whole room hot. But infections spread easily this way and parents could only look at their babies through the nursery windows."

"I wouldn't like that very much," Angela said.

"I believe the human touch is important," Nurse Sally told her. "Skin to skin contact. It's comforting and healing."

With its top lid open, the incubator reminded Angela of the glass coffin where the Seven Dwarfs had laid Snow White to rest after she fell into a deep sleep from eating the poison apple. Of course, Angela never uttered this out loud.

Nurse Sally placed Baby X into her mother's waiting arms. The little girl cooed in her sleep and cuddled against Angela's chest. "She feels lighter than air," Angela sighed. "You're pure heaven," she whispered into the child's hair, which was black as coal and plentiful. Nurse Sally showed Angela the proper way to hold her daughter. "Keep her head up," she instructed. "Yes, like that." The child's entire head fit perfectly into Angela's palm. She loved her daughter's softer than spun silk hair, the warmth of her body, the scent of her baby skin.

Meanwhile, Augie was becoming acquainted with his son, who was several ounces heavier than his sister. Baby Y's lips were two curved rose petals and his eyebrows were so wispy they were almost invisible. The boy sighed and opened his eyes, pondering his father. Augie's heart sunk and he was instantly smitten. For a breath, it was only the two of them in the universe. "Do you like him?" Angela asked.

Augie nodded; he couldn't speak. He traced the miniscule face with his pointer finger. "I think I'll keep him," Augie said. "He has your chin."

"And if he didn't?"

"I'd still keep him. Her, too."

"Want to switch?" Angela wondered. Augie did.

Nurse Sally rested Baby Y in the crook of her arm. Hesitantly, Angela gave Baby X to Augie. "Mind her neck," she said warmly to her husband.

"I will," he assured her.

"She won't break," Nurse Sally admitted, giving Angela her son. This was her favorite part of the job: introducing new parents to their babies. The worst part was telling them that their child didn't survive. Nurse Sally brushed away the thought, focusing instead on the hardy little fighters under her care right then and there. "And neither will he."

The boy held his mother's finger firmly, especially tenacious for a creature so small. It did not go unnoticed by his father. "He's got some grip," Augie pointed out. "A future Yankee, maybe?"

"Poppa would like that," Angela admitted. "Stan and Tiger, too."

Nurse Sally interjected, "I'm a Dodger's girl myself, but a future Yank would be just peachy with me."

Angela's milk hadn't come in yet and she doubted it ever would. Nurse Sally told her that worry didn't help; in fact, it might even keep the milk away. For the twins' feeding, there were two little bottles of formula warmed up and waiting. "In the hospital, we feed preemies every two hours, even at night," Nurse Sally explained. As small as they were, the babies ate well, greedily even, making almost imperceptible grunting noises. Angela thought it the most beautiful sound. "Little piggie," she cooed to the boy in her arms.

Burping was tricky for the new parents. "Harder," Nurse Sally coaxed. "They're more resilient than they look." With each firm pat, Angela felt Baby Y's ribs, thin as fresh, new pencils, felt his chest rising and falling, a miniature bellows beside her shoulder. Finally, he let out a voluminous burp. Angela noted that Augie handled Baby X with a nervous surety as he cajoled a belch out of his daughter and laughed at its voracity.

When the twins were back in the incubator, Angela felt deflated, as though she'd lost them. She and Augie endured the slow walk back to her room, feeling strangely empty and full at the same time. "I've baked chickens heavier than those two," Angela pointed out. "I'm afraid they'll never come home. And when they do, will I be able to…"

"They will, and you will," Augie said firmly. "Just not today." They were quiet for a few steps. "Imagine, calling your babies chickens," he laughed, shaking his head. "Still, you'll do okay. You and me both." Augie looked at Angela with a love so fierce it made her turn away. Right then, Angela felt a heaviness in her chest, a tightening and a squeezing, then a release. She knew at once that her milk had come in.

For their next feeding, Nurse Sally showed Angela how to suckle the twins. Tiny as they were, they each latched on easily. It seemed the most natural act in the world. Rose had breast-fed both Angela and Tiger, and often bragged that she'd had enough milk to be a wet nurse. Bridget had nursed all six of her children. Angela hoped the two women would have plenty of advice for her once she and the babies were home together. Angela also hoped her milk was as plentiful as theirs. "Eat right, get plenty of rest, and it will be," Nurse Sally assured her. "The Irish believe a glass of Guinness every day fortifies a woman's milk supply," she added. "But you didn't hear it from me."

Despite Angela's protests, Nurse Sally convinced her to try suckling both children at once. They fit easily into the curve of each arm, and even with their eyes closed, were able to find her nipples. "See?" Nurse Sally said. "There's nothing to it." She watched the young mother's face melt from contentedness to worry. "What's wrong, child?" the nurse asked.

"They're so little…" Angela faltered. "Do you think they'll make it?"

Nurse Sally squeezed Angela's shoulder. "Why, of course I do."

"If you didn't, would you tell me?"

"No," Nurse Sally admitted. "But these two…I'm sure they'll make it. And I'm never wrong."

Angela nodded, convinced of it now herself. "David," she proclaimed, "and Beth."

"I don't follow you," Nurse Sally admitted.

"Those are their names: David and Beth. I've been afraid to say them out loud until now."

Nurse Sally took David from Angela to burp while Angela put Beth over her own shoulder. "Those are beautiful names," Nurse Sally said.

Angela smiled dreamily. "David means 'beloved' and Beth means either 'God is my oath' or 'house of figs,' depending on which book you read. But me and Augie just like how they sound: strong and soft at the same time."

That night, Angela slept soundly in the hospital bed, unaffected by the stir of activity around her, the around-the-clock temperature-taking, the bells and buzzes. And in the morning, when he visited her on his way to work, Angela told Augie the names of their children out loud, putting Baby X and Baby Y to rest, and all of her worries along with it.

Chapter Twenty-Eight

A Shower of Roses

The following day, Angela came home from United Israel Zion Hospital without her twins. It was a lovely, early spring afternoon and she asked to walk home, even though Sully, Augie and Rose had come to fetch her with Poppa's Buick. It was only a few blocks and Angela reasoned that she should get accustomed to the walk since she'd be doing it at least three times a day to feed David and Beth. Nurse Sally explained that they would be supplementing those feedings with formula so Angela could conserve her strength and increase her milk supply, both of which she would need when the babies were living under their parents' roof.

Angela was surprised she fit into the checkered suit from Abraham & Strauss downtown which had been a favorite of hers before she'd gotten pregnant. Rose brought it to the hospital along with a few other choices. They decided on the checkered suit, sensible pumps with Cuban heels, and a tasteful hat Astrid had designed. It was difficult leaving the babies behind, but Angela did so without a tear, following a lengthy nursing and cuddling session. She would be back at suppertime for another feeding. "They'll be home in two weeks, tops," Nurse Sally confided. "They're growing in leaps and bounds, no fevers."

When Augie came to the hospital to get Angela, she felt as though she were being picked up for a date. He was dashing, handsome and happy to see her, as she was him. Sully put Angela's overnight satchel into Poppa's car and took it home. Rose let the two lovebirds stroll alone, excusing herself to pick up a few groceries she didn't really need on the Avenue.

The young couple didn't speak. Hand in hand, they passed beneath the El's elevated tracks and made a detour to St. Catherine of Alexandria Church. There, Angela wanted to pray her thanks for their two healthy, if not miniature babies. Although Augie feared his wife was taxing herself with too much exercise her first day out of the hospital, he didn't say a word. He knew visiting the church was important to her.

In the dim coolness of St. Catherine's, Angela made her way to the side altar beneath the statue of St. Therese, the Little Flower, with her beneficent face, meek eyes, rustic wooden crucifix and armful of multicolored roses. A Carmelite nun at the age of fifteen, Therese offered up to God what she referred to as "flowers"—little kindnesses to others, tiny sacrifices, all done to demonstrate her ardent devotion to God. She called her faith her "little way." Therese was canonized in 1925, only twenty-eight years after her death. It's said that throughout the world, miracles have been granted through her intercession. Before she died, Therese supposedly declared, "I have never given to the good God anything but love; He will return that love. After my death, I will let fall a shower of roses."

The church's hard wooden kneeler felt familiar beneath Angela's knees. She had come to St. Catherine's throughout her pregnancy, praying for strength, praying for a healthy baby. Angela folded her hands, closed her eyes and thanked the Little Flower. She began:

"O Little Therese of the Child Jesus
Please pick for me a rose
from the heavenly garden
and send it to me
as a message of love..."

Angela paused and smiled, for she now had not one
"rose" but two. Augie knelt beside her, watching his wife
pray, wishing he shared her faith, regretting the fact that
this place was merely a building to him, nothing more. To
Augie, churches were structures filled with pretty stained
glass, empty-faced statues and mumbo-jumbo in a long-dead
language he didn't understand, nor did he care to. (Augie
had purposely forgotten the Latin he'd learned as a child.)
It surprised him that Angela could believe so vehemently
in a God she couldn't see, especially after what she'd been
through with her father. But if this place gave his wife solace
and a sense of comfort, it was all right with him. Augie
closed his eyes and pretended to pray, too. He might have
even dozed a little.

Since Angela's prayers had already been granted, she left
out the part of St. Therese's invocation about granting favors,
but she did ask for decency and strength.

"St. Therese, help me to always believe
as you did, in God's great love for me,
so that I may imitate your "Little Way" each day."

When she was done, Angela realized that her face
was covered with tears, which she wiped away before
Augie noticed. She knew he didn't believe the way she
did—maybe it had to do with being an altar boy and being
smacked by mean priests like Father Dougherty for ringing
the bells too late during mass or spilling a tiny smidge of
wine as he assisted the priest in preparing the Communion
offering—but Augie didn't begrudge Angela her faith and
wouldn't balk at having the twins christened when the time
came. Even though the baptism ceremony's words about

renouncing Satan (several times), its superstitious practices and preoccupation with sin were harsh and frightening when you thought about them. Angela still believed in the sanctity of baptism, so that's all that mattered. Augie thought baptism was just a way for the church to milk money out of poor people who were led through the sacraments like frightened lambs. But to Angela, the thought of baptism was a comfort, so he relented on her behalf.

Finally, Angela lit a candle at St. Therese's altar, taking a stick from the sand, touching it to a quivering flame until it too caught fire, then bringing it to a fresh candlewick before doffing out the glowing tip into the sand. When she was done praying, Angela slipped a whole dollar bill into the brass box's slot. "Okay," she told Augie. "I'm ready. We can go now."

Augie held open St. Catherine's wide, wooden door with the bulk of his weight so his wife could pass through. The bells tolled overhead, deep and loud and grim. They played the hymn "Star Upon the Ocean," one of Angela's favorites.

Borough Park beyond the church seemed suddenly bright, alive and enchanted. There was the scent of sweetness in the air, something Angela couldn't quite put her finger on. Perhaps she'd been in the hospital too long and had gotten used to breathing its antiseptic air. This aroma of the streets was so very different. Early April, the forsythia was almost gone—and they didn't have much of a scent anyhow. It wasn't the cementlike fragrance of the Callery pear trees or the sugariness of hyacinth, and it wasn't lilacs. Roses, Angela decided. She smelled roses, although they were out of season, too. Roses usually bloomed in late May or early June, depending on the variety.

With their arms intertwined, Angela and Augie walked down Fort Hamilton Parkway, toward Forty-Seventh Street. The scent became more intense. Even Augie, who had a dulled sense of smell, noticed. "What's that?" he wondered. "Smells like flowers."

"Roses," Angela said knowingly, her heels tapping on the concrete.

"Already?" Augie wondered.

When they turned down their block, the aroma was overwhelming, heady and seductive. It was then when they noticed that every rose bush in front of every house on Forty-Seventh Street between New Utrecht Avenue and Twelfth Avenue was in full bloom. Back then, most Brooklyn homes had at least one rose bush in their gardens. The rose was a hardy, forgiving plant with woody branches. Roses thrived even when they were left untended and uncared for. Few living things flourished under neglect like rose bushes did. This was indeed a good example for humans as well as flowers, because it gave even abandoned souls a sense of optimism.

Nunzi DeMeo was in his yard, staring at it in wonder. His garden was brimming with early roses. The largest specimen held a place of honor beside "Mary on the Half Shell," as he affectionately referred to his statue of the Madonna ensconced in a scalloped grotto. "*Sacrilig*," his wife Violetta often rebuked him but Nunzi meant it with the utmost admiration for the Mother of Our Lord. For the safekeeping of his soul, Vi was known to slip off to St. Catherine's after Nunzi uttered what she considered a religious epitaph. Nunzi clipped the most perfect pink rose from the biggest bush. It trailed up one of the columns which supported his wooden porch and continued up to the second porch on the house's next floor. "It's the funniest thing," he began. "The roses weren't blooming last night. Then, suddenly, this morning...pop! All of them at once." Nunzi presented Angela with the rose. She thanked him. "A rose among women," he said, "Just like your momma."

Angela and Augie walked on, bathed in the flowers' heady scent, dizzy with it. Every yard on Forty-Seventh Street was bursting with a kaleidoscope of roses, in every shade imaginable. American Beauties as red as blood. Pashminas the color of a blush. The yellow variety the song was written about. Roses as brilliant orange as a November sunset over Staten Island. White Polar Stars the color of fog. Tea roses, primroses, desert roses, Rose of Sharons. Purple, even blue roses. Roses the color of a bruise, lemon with crimson-edged petals, and vibrant fuchsia, too, or as hushed as a whisper. Saint Anthony statues were embraced by Mrs. Franklin D. Roosevelt's golden blossoms. Front gates were intertwined with apricot-tinted Benitas. Trellises were exploding with Toscanini, cream dusted with light cerise.

"I've never seen anything like it," whispered Angela.

"Me neither," Augie admitted.

The couple slowly made their way up the block, pausing often to close their eyes and just breathe. They stopped at Poppa and Grandma Bridget's place before going home, the 1-1-2-8 on the wood porch post obscured by frilly, salmony Empress Josephine roses, whose shrub seemed to have doubled in height in the weeks after Angela had given birth. Since she'd been a little girl, Angela knew that Napoleon's wife was crazy for roses—Empress Jo's garden was legendary, not sheerly for its size but also for the fact that its inhabitants were imported from across the globe, including China. The rose named for her was cultivated the year after her death and christened in her honor. Angela also knew her Aunt Jo was named not for an obscure "guinea from the Old Country," but for Napoleon's wife.

Bridget's roses almost blocked the footpath, joining together in an arch overhead. They seemed to move away almost imperceptibly as Angela and Augie approached to retrieve her overnight bag. Angela's grandparents and mother were waiting for them on the porch on this unseasonably temperate spring day. Only the couple couldn't see them until they had actually climbed the steps because the rose branches thickly covered the front porch, obscuring the view of the street. "Can you believe it?" Rose asked. "These roses?" They couldn't believe it; no one could.

It's all Wendy and Stan could talk about when they came home from PS 131 for lunch. Tiger was in shock when he headed over to the house from Feel Good Food to unearth a hacksaw in the basement. That morning, Tiger had left before daylight, and hadn't noticed anything awry. But now, now the entire block was blooming. "It's a miracle," Stan gasped, as he blew on his fried macaroni. Reheated from last night's supper, Stan loved the crunchiness on the ends of the *rigatoni* where the heated sauce crusted. Wendy did not, so she was satisfied with peanut butter and jelly.

"Miracles are all around us, every day," Rose told the two children at her kitchen table. "You just have to know where to look."

From all the walking, Angela felt tired and had to go lie down for a spell. She turned down Rose's offer to fix her lunch and headed directly to the apartment she and Augie shared in the house next door. Angela took the front steps cautiously then wearily considered the steep flight which led up to their place. Without saying a word, Augie put down the suitcase and scooped his wife into his arms. "I'm a fat cow," Angela protested.

"You're light as a feather," he said.

When Augie opened the apartment door, Angela was surrounded by the scent of roses. A dozen long-stemmed reds stood in the cut-glass vase on the dining room table, awaiting her return. She smiled. "I got them last night," Augie explained, setting her down on the Oriental rug. "Before this happened out on the street. I wanted the place to smell of roses when you got home. I know how you love them."

The apartment was exactly as Angela had left it, except someone had straightened up the mess she'd made. The puddle where her water had broken was gone, the African violets righted, the papers straightened and the shattered tea cup tossed into the trash. The Royal remained on the dining room table and there also were the small pile of menus, but they'd been rearranged into a neat pile. Angela would pick up where she'd left off, only not just yet. She needed a nap.

Before she laid down, Augie convinced Angela to have something to eat to keep up her strength for nursing the twins. "Anything you eat, they eat," he reminded her. He had taken to heart Nurse Sally's breastfeeding lecture. The icebox was stuffed with casseroles and soups. Piled on top of it were the desserts, including an iced bundt cake, a mint green and brown striped box from Ebinger's and an apple

pie from Elaine Thomas. Angela saw that Mrs. DePalma
had sent over a loaf of her homemade date-nut bread, which
she knew Angela liked to eat slathered with plenty of cream
cheese. She sat at the table as Augie heated up the pot of
soup Mrs. Wong had dropped off. It was fragrant, flecked
with chicken, dried dates and ginger. Although it was a
special concoction to help new mothers' bodies recover from
childbirth, Augie had a bowl, too. It was delicious. After
treating herself to a slab of date-nut bread, Angela lay down
for a nap and Augie went back to the Loew's 46th.

The bed was comfier than Angela remembered. Cradling
her body like a familiar hand, it felt heavenly, especially
after the narrow hospital bed. Although she was tired, Angela
couldn't sleep. Her mind dashed from one thought to the
next: from the babies to the roses to the wonderful food
in her stomach, flooding her with a sense of comfort, of
being cherished. Angela closed her eyes and covered herself
with her favorite quilt. She truly felt as though Grandma
Bridget, who'd made it years earlier (before she'd turned her
attentions to afghan-making), was hugging her close, just
as she had when Angela was a girl and was lulled to sleep
on Bridget's wide, welcoming lap, her head nestled on her
grandmother's pillowy chest.

Half asleep, Angela mused about the language of roses.
Each color had its own meaning: red for love, pink for
appreciation and admiration, white for marriage, spirituality
and new beginnings... An orange rose signified enthusiasm
and passion. Yellow bid friendship, joy and fair health. Deep
burgundy meant unconscious beauty. Yellow with red edges
was for companionship and falling in love. Peach meant
sincerity but light peach was for modesty and coral was for
desire. Lavender was for enchantment...love at first sight.
Angela didn't know how she remembered all of this but she
did. It made her delightfully sleepy as her wavering eyelids
took in the single pink rose from Mr. DeMeo which Augie
had put into a bud vase on her nightstand.

Even the number of roses were significant. A single
rose embodied the utmost devotion. Two intertwined said

"Marry me," while six signified a need to be loved, to be appreciated. Eleven roses ensured the recipient that they were truly, deeply idolized while thirteen indicated a secret admirer. A dozen roses, especially red roses like Augie had given her, represented complete dedication and gratitude, the definitive symbol of true love.

While she adored roses, Angela knew that real love wasn't represented by flowers but by what people did for you: cooking your favorite foods, carefully trimming your toenails when your pregnant belly was too massive to do it yourself, putting a cool rag on your forehead when fever raged through your body, sitting awake to watch you sleep. Angela was very fortunate, she realized, because not only were these things done for her, but she would do these things for David and Beth, and for the people she loved. It felt good to be treasured, she thought. It felt like a fleecy afghan you wore on the inside instead of on the outside.

The twins! Angela leapt out of sleep. Where were they? She rushed into the nursery to find it empty, no little bodies curled against each other in the wicker basinet. It was then when Angela remembered that the twins were in the hospital, safe and sound under the watchful eye of Nurse Sally and the rest of the staff. Angela also realized that her chest was soaked and that she needed to feed her children. She was glad she'd had the foresight to put a towel beneath her body while she napped because it was damp when she woke.

Angela changed her clothes then called Rose from the side window. Her mother met her in front of the house so they could walk together to United Israel. They linked arms, both gratified to be strolling silently among the profusion of aromatic blossoms. "It's lovely, isn't it?" Rose asked.

"Lovely while it lasts." Angela nodded.

At the crowded desk in the closet beyond the projection booth which served as his office, Augie was busy at work, sketching plans for an incubator of sorts. When he was a lad, he remembered his neighbor Marie Dolan saying how she was born at home two months early and how her dad had put her in a peach crate down by the boiler in the basement to keep her warm. At first, Augie thought Mrs. Dolan was pulling his leg but she swore it was so. Old Mrs. Dolan not only thrived but lived to be ninety-three.

Little as they were, Augie was determined to get his children home as soon as possible. He knew they'd grow hardier faster among their family rather than in the sterile austerity of the maternity ward. Besides, it would be less strain on his wife, not having to walk back and forth to United Israel three or four times a day. He was confident that Poppa, who was quite handy, could guide him in constructing a home incubator for the babies. Augie couldn't wait to tell Angela his idea when he got home later.

After the hospital, Angela was ready to rest again, though it restored her soul, holding and smelling her babies. To her, the scent of their hair, their skin, was even more delicate than roses, which were still blooming when she and Rose walked home in the dusk light. Augie arrived soon after— Mr. Acerno insisted on coming in to close the theatre so Augie could have dinner with his wife. "I've had plenty of suppers with mine," he sighed. On the way back, Augie stopped at his parents' place to pick up the supper his mother had set aside for the new parents. When he got home, Augie began heating the tray of pasta with broccoli in the oven as he excitedly told Angela about his plans to build an incubator. She ate hungrily, listening to him. Ti-Tu, who had to work late, came afterwards, and agreed that the home incubator sounded like a outstanding plan.

After the men did the dinner dishes and Angela dozed in front of the radio with Ti-Tu to keep her company, Augie went next door to share his plan with Poppa. As soon as he stepped outside into the night, he sensed that the fragrance of the roses was fading, although it was too dark to see them clearly. Poppa was excited about the plan to build a home incubator and had a few suggestions which Augie readily incorporated. He would share it with the hospital the next day and hopefully, the doctors would agree to let them take David and Beth home sooner rather than later.

By the time Augie went back next door, he could barely detect the scent of the roses. They were a distant memory, reminiscent of the swirl of fragrance left behind when a well-coiffed lady exited the room. The next morning, Nunzi DeMeo's rose in the bud vase on Angela's nightstand had withered. When Augie and Angela left for the hospital, the roses of Forty-Seventh Street were gone. The woody branches had receded and were now brown with nary a green bud visible. "Did we dream them?" Angela asked.

"Then we were all dreaming the same dream," Augie said as they approached Nunzi DeMeo, who was shaking his head in disbelief. At Mr. DeMeo's feet lay a single, fallen red rose petal, nothing more.

Chapter Twenty-Nine

New Beginnings

Poppa and Augie worked fast and fastidiously because the twins could be sent home any day now and they wanted to be ready. Stan was particularly proud of the makeshift incubator because the men had let him help build it. "It's a cradle fit for Baby Jesus himself," he said.

"But Baby Jesus's was stuffed with hay," Wendy reminded him. "Weren't you paying attention during Religious Instruction?"

"I was," Stan insisted, but in truth, he wasn't. Wednesday afternoon Religious Instruction class at St. Catherine's was Stan's best opportunity to daydream. None of what he learned in religion class made sense to him. For instance, the Holy Ghost, Lazarus rising from the dead, Jesus walking on water...and that was just for starters. Although Stan was happily terrified by the notion of lepers, which Sister Mary Hewer said, with a sordid glee, were indeed real. At first, Stan didn't believe her, as he didn't believe most things nuns told him. Especially when they addressed the class as, "You public school children…" with contempt, like they were criminals, even lepers themselves.

The only nun worthwhile in Stan's book was Sister Lucide, with her olive skin and compassionate, brown deer eyes like Bambi's mother in the movie. That was the last time Stan had cried during a picture. He was five at the time and it was during the part where Bambi's mom was killed by that rotten hunter. But Sister Lucide…she wore sandals in the summertime (he'd been surprised that nuns even had toes and previously, had pictured some manner of winged feet). Sister Lucide referred to her sandals as her "Jesus shoes," which Stan appreciated. He liked to think the Son of God had a sense of humor.

"Were not," Wendy snapped, shaking her cousin out of his reverie. "Were not." She folded her arms across her chest, upset she wasn't allowed to hammer nails yet. Wendy lent a hand in other ways though, learning how to change diapers by using her baby doll as a model, getting pointers about how to hold a baby and how to lift an infant the correct way. Stan was learning these things, too. Poppa and Augie promised they'd let Wendy help with some of the finishing touches on the incubator, perhaps even hammering, and she knew that they would.

You'd never believe they'd started with a deep drawer from an unwanted dresser. It was beautiful, lined with cedar, its edges dovetailed, not a nail in it. The children were currently working on creating the incubator's comfy lining, and in doing so, their Great Aunt Astrid was teaching Wendy and Stan how to sew. When the boy balked, she explained, "It's a good skill for a young man to have: how to darn his own socks. This way, you won't need a woman to take care of you when you're older." Knowing how to wield a screwdriver was a necessary skill for a young lady, too, she added—"So you can hang pictures yourself, and such," Aunt Astrid explained. Wendy couldn't wait for her grandfather and cousin to teach her.

As the children sewed the cotton padding for the bottom and sides of the incubator, Aunt Astrid tutted whenever they made a mistake and had them start over. The project was coming along, little by little.

Poppa showed Augie how to bend the wood to create the incubator's rockers as well as the legs which would attach the rockers to the incubator itself. They'd cut a U-shape from a wood scrap with Poppa's jigsaw, clamped the wood between the U-shaped jig and the cutout, and let it sit overnight. When they checked on it the next morning, Stan and Wendy were flabbergasted at how the wood had miraculously curved. When satisfied with it, the men set to making another rocker.

A few blocks away, at George & Tiger's Feel Good Food, the awning and signs were going up above the storefront. Tiger watched, *kvelling*; it was a Yiddish word with no precise English counterpart, which meant "swelling with pride." He wished George could be there to see the signs put into place. As with all else, the duo spared no expense. In addition to the awning, there was also a neon sign which stood out from the building on a post, and a painted sign on the brick building's front wall. (The latter was done by Weiss, an out-of-work artist who'd studied at Pratt Institute.) Ralph Signs had sent a truck with a crane and three employees to mount the awning, one of whom was redirecting Thirteenth Avenue shoppers from walking into their work zone.

The activity had attracted a handful of onlookers. Sully and Izzy, who were on the clock, even paused to watch. Tiger was pleased to run into Rose's friend Anna Pateau on her lunch hour with her brand-new employee, a slender, sepia-eyed beauty named Teresa. When Anna introduced them, Tiger stood taller and ran his fingers through his thick tuft of hair which he was certain was dappled with paint and sawdust from the finishing touches he and Jimmy were putting on the shop. Teresa didn't seem to mind, and smiled widely, revealing her dimple (just on one side, the left) and her strong, straight teeth. She offered Tiger her hand and he took it. "What does Tiger stand for?" Teresa wondered.

"Anthony," he said shyly. "But no one calls me that."

Anna oversaw the Prudential Insurance office a few blocks away. Aunt Jo was helping out there a few hours a week or when one of Anna's employees fell ill. (Jo lived close by and could be there at a moment's notice, and what's more, Harry thought this a good thing since he was so busy helping to get the eatery off the ground.) Anna promised she'd take "the Girls" there once Feel Good Food was up and running. "We're having our grand opening on the fifteenth," Tiger told her.

"I usually bring my lunch from home," Teresa announced.

Anna flashed Teresa a quick glance. "Well, that day you won't," Anna said to her. "We'll be there," she assured Tiger. "Terry, too." The young woman's blush didn't go unnoticed by Tiger or by Sully, who was watching the interaction intently. Tiger kissed Anna on the cheek and took Teresa's gloved hand again, perhaps lingering longer than was typical. Teresa and Anna chatted enthusiastically as they walked away.

Tiger shook his head. "There goes trouble," he said to Jimmy Burns.

"She seems like a nice girl," Jimmy told him.

"That's the trouble," Tiger concluded. "She's the kind of girl you marry." The sort of girl who wore a dainty gold safety pin clipped to her brassiere from which dangled a religious medal depicting the Blessed Mother. Tiger was sure Teresa wore this amulet, which was meant to deter bad boys from exploring the warm, moist skin beneath the pin.

"And?" Jimmy asked.

"And nothing," Tiger responded. "Don't you have floors to sweep?"

Jimmy went back into the shop, laughing to himself. There was very little left to be done. Maybe he could go over the floor again but the checkerboard linoleum was spotless. The brand-new kitchen sparkled behind the half wall they'd built. There were swell-looking framed family photographs of all sizes adorning the walls, which Jimmy and the guys had painted a creamy yellow. The gingham curtains Tiger's aunt had made were already up on the picture window and looked rather smart, even though the woman herself was a bit of a pain. The tables and chairs, chrome-legged with black tops and seats, were already set up. Before the shop opened, they would put out the tablecloths, already pressed and waiting, and top each table with a bud vase and a single daisy. Tiger had arranged to have the flowers delivered from Bill's Buds, a wholesaler in the Flower District near Twenty-Eighth Street in Manhattan, every couple of days. Not only was Bill a vet, but he delivered to Shannon's nearby, so he didn't charge Tiger extra for dropping them off.

Speaking so quickly he became breathless, Augie had told the doctors about Mrs. Dolan and her peach-box incubator. Instead of pooh-poohing the idea, Dr. Schantz closely examined the blueprint Augie had made with Poppa's assistance, nodding and hmmming as he shared it with Dr. Lewis, who gently fingered his large nose as he read and thought. The Corsos were surprised Dr. Schantz had agreed to their proposal and almost cried when he said he'd let them take the twins home earlier than planned and care for them in the handcrafted incubator.

Before they gave their final assent, the medical team went to look at the area around the boiler in the basement of Ti-Tu's house. Unlike the Paradisos' place next door, the cellar floor was cemented. A narrow cot was set beside the incubator/cradle. There was a changing table, too, and cloth diapers neatly stacked there. Next to the boiler, the cement ground was covered with a new area rug. Ti-Tu's cellar was more immaculate than most people's homes. Boxes were piled on shelves in an orderly fashion. The stored furniture was draped with dust covers. Before Mrs. Rosenkrantz passed, she'd had the house converted to gas heat. It wasn't just more efficient but it sure beat shoveling coal. Dr. Schantz nodded, examining the cellar's shiny furnace, which Ti-Tu wiped down regularly. "Gas burns cleaner than coal," the doctor noted.

Nurse Sally, who also lived on Forty-Seventh Street, but in Sunset Park down near Sixth Avenue, offered to stop by once a day and check in on the babies. "It's on my way," she said to the doctors. This wasn't really true, but she'd become very attached to David and Beth, something she tried not to do with the newborns in her charge. However, these two were different—they were much cherished and terribly adorable, each in their own particular ways. David was sedate, Beth demanding. She was dusky haired and eyed while David was pink-skinned and pale-haired, with inquisitive sea-gray eyes like his mother.

While Sally Hinton didn't have children of her own, she had hundreds of her heart, hundreds she'd tended to over the years who thrived and went on to do things great and small. Thankfully, very few had died, but she remembered those, too, recalled holding their tiny bodies long after they'd gone lifeless and cold. She had prayed for them, named them, and immortalized them in a leather journal of forest green with a floral design etched onto its front cover. Sally recorded their names, the date they were born and whatever else seemed significant. It gave her closure, helped her grieve and move onto the next baby.

Sally never told anyone about her journal, not even her husband, though he stumbled upon it once in her unmentionables drawer—Mark had been looking for a misplaced sock. Was it a diary of illicit acts, of men's names and addresses? Mark was sure it wasn't—his Sally was as true as steel—but he opened the journal anyway. With one glance, he closed it sadly, rueful that he'd ever looked. Mark placed the diary back where he'd found it. Only Sally knew he had discovered her secret baby book, for the journal had been replaced in the drawer upside-down. She never said a word about it, and neither did he, but Mark held Sally extra tightly in bed the night he found it.

But the Corso babies, Sally reminded herself, these babies didn't require her care anymore and it was time to let go.

Nurse Sally slipped out of her memories as deftly as she'd slipped in. She cleared her throat and told the doctors,

"I think it's an excellent idea. As well-watched as the twins are at United Israel, there's no place like home."

Angela smiled upon hearing Nurse Sally quote the line from *The Wizard of Oz*. During the many hours they'd spent together, the nurse had learned this was Angela's favorite movie. Though it might be dismissed as a children's film, there were so many layers to it, so many messages. Yes, Angela was familiar with the saying about movies and their meanings—"If you want to send a message, try Western Union"—but *The Wizard of Oz* was an exception. It wasn't just about Cowardly Lions and witches and flying monkeys; it was about family, dedication, and sincere friendship. So, when Nurse Sally referred to the movie, Angela knew what she meant without her actually saying it.

Although the first day of spring had already come and gone, the Friday the Corso twins came home felt like the season of hope and renewal had truly arrived. Gone was the wintery chill lurking in the corners. Gone was the evening frost. Gone was the morning mist. Augie and Angela hugged Nurse Sally and said good-bye to the other nursery attendants, then placed David and Beth into the carriage. It was a big, navy blue pram with a bonnet and white piping. They looked so diminutive inside the cavernous carriage, pressing into each other for comfort and warmth. Angela tucked in the buggy blanket Bridget had hurriedly crocheted for them. She began it the day they were born and finished it up the evening before they came home. It was made with a special blue, pink and ivory yarn. David wore a blue beanie and Beth a pink one, both of which had been tenderly knitted by Aunt Jo. They were bundled up in matching cream-colored sweaters, safely tucked into the cozy pram and ready to go.

If you would have told Angela months earlier that she would be proudly strolling along Fort Hamilton Parkway with her twin infants in a sturdy carriage with Augie at her side, she wouldn't have believed you. With all of her worry, she never imagined having one baby in her arms, let alone two. A torrent of love awaited the Corso Family at home.

Everyone was gathered at Ti-Tu's apartment—Rose, Sully (who'd stopped there with Izzy on their patrol), Poppa, Bridget, Harry, Jo, Tiger and Jimmy Burns, too. Stan and Wendy bellyached that they had to go to school but they went to PS 131 anyway, although grudgingly. Camille and John were there also, as was Astrid and her new beau Al. A warmhearted man with a genial laugh and a balding pumpkin head, he was far too pleasant for the likes of Astrid. Sadie Lieberwitz also stopped by to wish the new family all the best.

Everyone stayed briefly. After Rosanna served chicken soup for lunch, Angela and the twins retreated to their basement refuge. Instead of imagining of it as a concrete prison, Angela considered it a haven, a place where they would grow strong together. It was comfortable and snug in the cellar. Ti-Tu had even propped a painting against the wall, a pastoral scene of the Polish countryside where his people were from, making the basement even homier.

Angela and the babies had many visitors but for short periods of time. This filled her with a sense of being cherished but never to the point of exhaustion. She never had to entertain or lift a finger. Mrs. Wong reminded her of *zuo yuezi*, which some called "30 days in your pajamas." Angela did nothing but rest. Her food was taken down to the basement by a revolving door of family and neighbors. Meals were eaten while the babies slept, which they did a great deal. Ti-Tu found a cherry wood side table the perfect size to host meals for two. A pair of card-table chairs were set up at either end, where Angela and a companion would sit and sup. When she had no visitors, Angela rested, reading while she reclined, or she slept.

In halting English, Mrs. Wong made it clear to Angela that she was not to eat or drink anything icy (for it chilled the womb), nor have raw fruits or vegetables. Foods or fluids taken into the body had to be hot or tepid. "You must balance the yin and the yang," Mrs. Wong explained. It made perfect sense to the women in the family: the resting, the warmth, the nurturing essence of hot foods. The soup Mrs. Wong brought of pigs feet and peanuts was actually quite tasty, and it was supposed to stimulate the milk supply. "It can't hurt," Rose shrugged. But Angela drew the line at the notion of not bathing for a month; she refused to be wiped down by washcloths and relished her lingering sits in the claw-footed bathtub upstairs while Rose sat with the twins, although no one told Mrs. Wong about Angela's transgression.

She slept well in her basement retreat, though not deeply. Whenever the babies stirred or cooed, she awoke, slipping back into slumber when they did, waking fully when they did not. She soon became used to this dreamless sleep, her body adapting to the new normal in her life. A week or two of living like this would do the trick, Dr. Schantz said. Once the babies reached the five-and-a-half pound mark, they would be able to move upstairs to their own room or to their parents' bedroom, if it made Augie and Angela more comfortable. Or when the furnace no longer fired, whichever came first.

Tiger and George were at Feel Good Food bright and early the morning they were to open, but not earlier than Jimmy Burns, who stood outside waiting for them, rubbing his palms onto the cardboard coffee cup he cradled. It had been several weeks since Jimmy'd had a drink and he no longer had the shakes. He felt clearheaded and happy, two things he hadn't remembered feeling since he was a boy. Jimmy no longer bunked in Farrell's but had a room at the YMCA on Ninth Street. He was relieved to be away from the stench of smoke and beer, though he did miss seeing Houlie every day. Jimmy had been going to Alcoholics Anonymous meetings in the back room of All Saints Episcopal Church, and he tried like hell to follow the steps. His sister Mary said that if Jimmy stayed dry, she'd let him visit her kids again, maybe even let him take them to Luna Park in the summer.

Although Jimmy had the key to Feel Good Food, he waited near the curb, intent on giving his bosses the pleasure of unlocking the front door on the first day. They were planning to open at half-past eleven for the lunchtime crowd.

Tiger and George arrived before nine, walking close together and chatting up a storm, as was their custom. As unalike as they looked on the outside, their commonalities ran deep and they never seemed to run out of conversation. Bridget noted that George and Tiger "came from the same place," and it was true. They came from the same kind of people, had the same values. Tiger had the notion that the doe-eyed beauty from Anna Pateau's office came from the same place, too. The very thought both excited and frightened him. In one way, Tiger hoped Teresa was there at the grand opening, and in another, he hoped she wasn't.

Everything was ready. The stove was fired up. The refrigerator was stocked. The tables were set. The cash register was in working order. George began prepping the yams then the okra, and Tiger helped. Next, George made three meat loaves and put them on a slow cook in the oven. Then he and Tiger readied a mess of cocktail franks wrapped in dough for "pass arounds." They'd made the potato and macaroni salads the night before. The desserts sat beneath glass domes—Elaine's sweet potato pie, Grandma Bridget's butter sunshine cake and Aunt Jo's ice box cake plus bite-sized versions of two types of cookies to offer to customers *gratis*. George would start frying up the chicken at about eleven and keep it hot under the heat lamp. Yes, they were more than ready.

Before he left for the Loew's 46th that morning, Augie set the carriage in the areaway in case Angela decided to take the babies to Feel Good Food's opening. Angela so wanted to be there but was on the fence about exposing the twins to so many people and so many germs. She admitted to her mother as they changed diapers, "I'm feeling a little stir-crazy, though."

"Then let's go out on the town," Rose told her.

Once dressed, the children were carried outside and nestled into their pram. Only Beth woke, momentarily piqued about being disturbed, but she soon fell back asleep. David and Beth lay ready for their first foray into Borough

Park. Bridget's blanket was tucked around them and a mesh netting was fastened to the carriage hood to protect them from the sun and from microbes. Although some mothers didn't take their babies outside for weeks or a month, Dr. Schantz was a firm believer of boosting the immune system by getting babies out and about. "The fresh air will do them a world of good," he'd said to Angela.

Although it was a Monday morning, Rose and Angela were turned out in their best Sunday suits and snazzy shoes. It was a fair April day, and had warmed up nicely. The sun shone and there were a few high, wispy clouds decorating the sky. Angela gave her mother the honor of wheeling the carriage, which Rose did with a straight back and a regal step, bursting with pride. They were stopped often by curious neighbors itching for a look at the twins. "At this rate, we'll never get there," Rose gleefully admitted as they turned onto Thirteenth Avenue.

There was already a congregation beneath the banners which ran from the storefront to the telephone pole at the curb in front of George & Tiger's Feel Good Food. As Rose and Angela drew closer, they could hear the excited chatter of voices and catch a whiff of a symphony of delicious scents: garlic mixed with fried scrumptiousness combined with after-supper treats baking in the oven. With pure delight, Rose took in the whole scene: the signage bearing her son's nickname, the curtains and tablecloths lovingly made by family and friends, the comforting aroma of dishes she and her children were raised on, the unguarded smile and unabashed elation on Tiger's face, and Jimmy Burns looking healthier than she'd ever seen him. The entire neighborhood had turned out to congratulate her son and support Tiger and his friend's new endeavor.

Although it was a blissful occasion, in a way, it reminded Rose of a wake: where all the important people in your life come together. When Rose told this to Angela, she gently chided her mother. "Really, Ma? A wake? How about a wedding without a bride?"

"I like that a lot better," Rose said to Angela, straightening the netting over the carriage, smiling.

The moment he saw them, Tiger came over and folded his mother and sister into an embrace. "What do you think, Rosie?" he asked.

"Oh, I think it's grand, just grand," Rose swelled.

The tables inside were full. On the sidewalk, Tiger heard the ding of the bell which signified that orders were ready to be delivered. He excused himself and ducked inside. Jimmy made his way through the swarm with a tray of pigs in the blanket which were soon gone but he made certain Rose and Angela each got two before tucking back inside to help George and Tiger. Jimmy felt good about feeding Tiger's folk for a change.

At one table, Rose noticed Tiger lingering over the three pretty girls who accompanied Anna Pateau. One in particular, slim with short, dark, wavy hair, seemed to catch Tiger's eye. It was enjoyable for Rose to watch how their bodies leaned toward each other, observing their wordless, pantomime from afar. It was like watching a silent picture show unfold in real life. Anna caught Rose's eye and winked, mouthing, "That's her." Rose nodded in silent response.

Harry manned the cash register, which rang out an order every couple of minutes. They'd bought a high stool just for him so Harry wouldn't have to stand and could rest his leg. The next time Tiger came by with a plate of steaming meat loaf, mashed potatoes and okra, Harry quipped, "We're busier than a one-legged man at a butt-kicking contest." Tiger was taken aback by his uncle's new-found humor and by his poking fun at himself. "It's okay to laugh," Harry assured Tiger. They did, heartily, with George joining in behind the stove.

Jo arrived with Poppa and Bridget in the back seat of the Pontiac. Sully and Izzy came soon after, under the pretenses of keeping the horde under control, but they managed to eat a couple of chicken wings in the process. Augie took a break from the Loew's 46th with Mr. Acerno in tow. His boss cooed like a nursemaid over the twins. Sally Hinton came, too, in her gum-sole shoes and spotless white uniform. Sully introduced his family to a blue-eyed gent with a devilish grin named Houlie, who tended bar at Farrell's. Everybody was delighted to be there, and hungry. Space was made for Tiger's family at a large table but Rose, Augie and Angela remained outside. They didn't want to jam up the eatery with the huge pram or expose the twins to so many people in so close a space.

George's clan would soon arrive from Jersey City, to be chauffeured by Tyrone after school let out and before the dinner rush. John, Camille, Astrid and her new beau would come after work. Hopefully, there'd be food left when the others arrived. But there would be, of course there would be. The two partners had prepared their whole lives for this moment, and they were more than ready.

As Anna Pateau and her gals were leaving, she introduced them to Rose. There was Francine, Grace and Teresa, the one who'd been giving Tiger the eye. Rose immediately liked her, the unapologetic Roman nose (similar to her own), bright smile and intelligent gaze. Anna said they'd lingered too long at lunch already and still had the monthly invoicing to do at Old Pru, as Anna affectionately called the parent company. (It was as if Pru were a woman rather than a business.) Rose asked after Karl, Anna's husband, who had been a supervisor with Poppa at the Brooklyn Navy Yard, and promised to come visit them both soon.

Tired from her adventurous day, Angela thought it best to go home with the twins and settle down for a family nap after a hardy feeding. But not before George sent out a covered tastings plate for her to enjoy back at the house. Angela waved a thank-you to George, who was off in the kitchen, happily busy at the stove, beaming from ear-to-ear. The babies were beginning to stir and it would only be a matter of time before they woke up starving, inconsolable until they were satiated. Augie saw his family home before he headed back to the movie theatre, but Pete Acerno lingered—Augie hadn't seen the man smile like that since they'd made buckets of money when *Gone with the Wind* had played at the Lowe's 46th. A picture called *The Best Years of Our Lives* was due out in the fall and was expected to shatter previous box office records. Augie thought of this as he tucked in Angela, David and Beth, and watched them drift off to a peaceful sleep. Then he strolled back to the theater.

When school let out, Wendy and Stan were instructed to go straight to George and Tiger's. They did, and were thrilled with what they saw—lots of family, friends, and neighbors, and even more exciting, strangers. Wendy would have to write about the day in her journal, she decided.

The two children endured multiple repetitions of "You've gotten so big," "If I tripped over you in the street, I still wouldn't have known you" and "What grade are you in?" They tolerated several cheek-pinches as greetings. ("Why do Italians always pinch your cheek when they say hello?" Stan groaned to Wendy after the fifth pinch.) But these indignities were well worth the excitement of a restaurant opening, and well worth the food. Neither had ever tasted hush puppies before and instantly fell in love with the fried corn lusciousness, especially when dipped into the maple butter George made to go with them. Neither was a fan of greens but fried okra was a whole different ballgame.

Tyrone had borrowed his foreman's huge Ford truck because George had taken his Chevy to work that morning. The Ford, packed with Thomases, arrived, dispensing George's wife Elaine and their four children while her brother found a parking space. (Elaine's folks would come at a later date.) The two eldest kids burst out onto the sidewalk, elated to see their father's name painted in fancy script above the storefront and also, immortalized in neon. Elaine got out of the car slowly, George, Jr. pausing to hold the door open for her. She wore a lovely dress of lavender which brought out the honey tones of her skin and a hat with little blossoms which suited her outfit perfectly. Elaine stood on the curb with their youngest, Liora Rose, on her hip. Gazing up at the sign, at all of the people, Elaine beamed, tears rimming her eyes. One slid down her cheek. "What's wrong, Momma?" her daughter Pamela asked in alarm.

Elaine was too overcome to answer. George appeared at her side, rubbing her back. She noted that he smelled pleasantly of Aqua Velva and corn fritters. "Nothing's wrong, child," George told his daughter. "Your momma's just crying because she's glad. Now run and play. Wendy's waiting."

Sure enough, there was Wendy O'Leary not far off on the sidewalk, anticipating Pamela's arrival like an expectant puppy. She'd saved her friend a piece of cantaloupe wrapped with salty, savory *prosciutto*, a cured ham she knew Pamela would savor, because Wendy herself did. Not far from the girls Stan played tag with George, Jr. and Darryl, who were careful not to fall and ruin their dress clothes. When they were hungry and tired, they found the kitchen, where Jimmy Burns had put aside a plate of finger foods for them. "Uh-uh," Bridget rebuked from her perch nearby. "Wash your hands first. And use soap!" she called.

All three groaned but said, "Yes, Ma'am," as they ran off toward the restroom.

Day turned into night and Feel Good Food was still packed. Customers ebbed and flowed like the tide. Tables filled and emptied, then filled again. Rose was thrilled when her sister-in-law and girlhood friend Irene arrived with her husband Raymond and two of their three sons, extremely moved that they'd made the long trip from Queens to attend the restaurant opening. Ti-Tu came straight from his desk at Yale Transport, stopping briefly at home to fetch his violin. As always, Tyrone had his harmonica stuffed into his jacket pocket, just in case. The unlikely duo played together as if they'd done so for ages—the introverted Jewish boy who'd dreamed of becoming a classical orchestra musician and gave music lessons in his spare time and the rough Negro dockworker who taught himself to master the Chromatic in between unloading ships.

Surprising everyone, even her, Astrid's beau Al grabbed a cast-off orange crate Moe the Greengrocer had put out near the curb. Al set it on its highest side, sat on top of it, and beat out a rhythm on the wooden box. There wasn't a tune called out that this ragtag band didn't know, and if they didn't know it, they faked it. The music reminded Rose of the times the whole of Forty-Seventh Street would gather for sing-alongs when she was a girl. They would congregate on a front porch, usually Poppa and Bridget's, and warble old-timey songs together, slightly out of tune. Years later, outside of Feel Good Food, Rose called out "Smile A While," which had been one of her favorites as a child. Though some called it "Till We Meet Again," the trio was familiar with it and played it without skipping a beat. Even Sully, who wasn't from the singers, joined in.

The sun had long gone down. Tiger had gotten so carried away he'd almost forgotten a very important part of the celebration. He went into the shop and flicked on a light switch. The neon sign outside blazed red, white and blue, announcing "George & Tiger's Feel Good Food, Est. 1946." Everyone cheered. Tiger's aunts, grandmother and mother cried, as did Elaine. Poppa was overcome with emotion as well. It was a splendid night.

When the roar died down into silence, with little Liora dozing on her lap, Elaine suddenly began singing "Hard Times Come Again No More." As her chest rose and fell, the sound was reminiscent of a church's pipe organ. Her song was just as holy. Her daughter's drowsy head lolled to the side as Elaine sang. With a contralto so deep and warm and beautiful that it moved some to weep, Elaine sounded like a misplaced angel.

> *"Let us pause in life's pleasures and count its many tears,*
> *While we all sup sorrow with the poor;*
> *There's a song that will linger forever in our ears;*
> *Oh! Hard times come again no more."*

Everyone joined in for the chorus, whether they could sing or not.

" 'Tis the song, the sigh of the weary,
Hard Times, hard times, come again no more
Many days you have lingered around my cabin door;
Oh! Hard times come again no more."

George joined his wife on the next verse, his voice as dark and sweet as molasses. It spoke of bayous, Spanish moss, wrought-iron balconies, beatings, white hoods, fires, lynchings, and shame, but also of things of great promise which Colored folk had sought for ages but rarely attained. Until tonight. As for George, he'd seen it, tasted it, witnessed it, lived it, that very evening.

"While we seek mirth and beauty and music light and gay,
There are frail forms fainting at the door;
Though their voices are silent, their pleading looks will say
Oh! Hard times come again no more."

George and Elaine's intertwined voices lit up the night, tangling together like the strings of joyous kites which had somehow gotten loose and were soaring up to the heavens, ecstatic and eternally free.

Chapter Thirty

Coda

The days were growing longer and warmer. Already the lilacs had given way to rhododendron and daylilies. The rose bushes were starting to bud, this time for real. Bridget couldn't decide which season she liked best: the autumn with its cooling days, brilliant palate of leaves and chilly evenings, or the spring, with its sense of freshness and rebirth. Yes, it was probably the spring, with its promise of a new day. Only that morning, as Bridget lay in bed, too stiff in her muscles and joints to rise, she wondered if she would live to see another of either season dawn. And it was all right with her if she didn't.

A few weeks shy of her seventy-fifth birthday, Bridget was tired, deep down in the bones tired. A few days earlier, she had overheard Rose telling Dr. Lewis her concern about her parents' recent decline. "They're up there in years," Dr. Lewis reluctantly admitted. "They're both in reasonably good health, but they're wearing down, aging." In her heart,

Rose knew this was true. She knew growing old was part of life's natural cycle but she had a difficult time accepting it.

Bridget had been feeling poorly since the opening of Feel Good Food a few weeks earlier. Perhaps it had been the bite of the night air or staying out so late. She and Poppa wouldn't have missed it for the world, though. It was so nice to have people besides Bridget's family appreciating her recipes, and to see folks of all shades of beige and brown getting on so well together. Everything was as it should be.

Her great-grandchildren David and Beth were thriving, growing more solid each day. Why, last week, Dr. Schantz had even given permission for the twins to move upstairs and out of their dresser drawer incubator/cradle in the cellar. They adjusted nicely to the wicker basinet which had sheltered most of Bridget and Poppa's grandchildren. In fact, the twins were doing so well that they were growing chubby.

Though it was no longer necessary for Nurse Sally to check in on them daily, she came a few times a week because she'd grown close to the twins and to Angela as well. She called Angie the sister she never had, and vice versa. Of course, Sally had been there the Sunday earlier for the babies' baptism at St. Catherine's. She'd gasped and cried quietly into a Kleenex when Father Dunn asked, "What name do you give this child?" and Jo, the godmother, responded, "Elizabeth Sally." Nurse Sally was still crying when Tiger told Father Dunn that the boy would be called "David Rosario." Then Rose started crying for the way Angela and Augie had chosen to honor her.

The christening party, held later at Feel Good Food, certainly rivaled the eatery's opening-day festivities, although nothing could top the excitement of that day. The food, the fellowship, the singing…George and Elaine Thomas sure could carry a tune.

Reflecting on the eatery's opening made Bridget remember the music at the twins' christening, which was just as moving. A delicate, little child with a big voice named Diana Marie had sung. Her mother, Anna Marie, was a gifted vocalist, too. From St. Catherine's choir loft, Diana

Marie sang Kewpie's favorite hymn, "Ave Maria" as though she'd been touched with the Blessed Mother's grace, like her mom Anna Marie before her. Kewpie…nobody called her granddaughter Kewpie anymore, but for the life of her, Bridget couldn't remember her granddaughter's real name. She pondered for a long moment. Angela…her name was Angela.

The space beside Bridget in the bed she'd shared with Poppa for going on forty-eight years was empty, but the starched sheets embroidered with pastel-colored flowers were still toasty from his body. Bridget caressed the scooped-in spot where he'd recently lain, cradled by the feather mattress. Poppa's heavy bones and tired joints were just as weary as Bridget's were. "I'm older, after all," he liked to remind her.

To which Bridget would respond, "Only by six months." The bedclothes smelled of him, of Michael Archangel's familiar skin, of Kirkman's soap and bay rum. Bridget smiled in the daylight.

As though her thoughts had summoned him, Poppa stood in the doorway of their bedroom, in his neatly-pressed white shirt and baggy pants. He had lost weight recently, though his appetite was as hearty as ever. They should really go see Dr. Lewis about it but neither of them had the energy or the desire. It was as though Poppa's body were fading, as if his very physical being were shrinking, but his spirit was still larger than life.

Poppa held an earthenware mug of coffee, black and thickened with sugar. He placed it on Bridget's bedside table. Slowly, she sat up, not without great effort, hoisting the frame which had grown more generous with each passing year while Poppa's grew smaller. Bridget winced from her arthritis, which seemed to invade her every joint. "Arthur's visiting this morning," she sighed to Poppa.

"Arthur It-is?" he asked. It was a joke they shared almost every day.

Bridget nodded slowly. "Thank you," she said. "For the coffee."

Poppa sat on the edge of the bed while Bridget took a deep sip from the mug. The bed's weary slats groaned. "And thank you," he replied.

"For what? I haven't done anything."

"For everything," he told her.

To Bridget, that first sip of coffee, dark, complex and syrupy, was a piece of paradise. "I couldn't have done it without you," she admitted.

"We've done all right for ourselves, haven't we?" he noted. "Came over from Italy as kids. Worked hard, have a house, a car, six children, ten grandchildren, two great-grandchildren…Even got to hold them at the christening last week."

"Was it just last week?" Bridget wondered.

"Yes," Poppa said. "Time flies…"

"…when you're getting old," she concluded, taking another swallow of coffee.

"*Getting*? Margarita, we're already old. Very old."

Bridget ignored him. "The christening was grand, wasn't it?" Poppa nodded. "George cooked up a feast. And Tiger, he went and got himself a fine gal, didn't he? I like her…What was her name again?"

Poppa thought for a moment. "Teresa. Think of The Little Flower."

"That's right," Bridget said. "She's got a pure heart. Comes from good people. You can just tell."

"She's got some gams on her," Poppa joked.

Bridget gave Poppa a playful poke. "And kind eyes." She looked worried for a moment. "Now, what were we saying?"

"We were saying how lucky we were, what we've got," her husband reminded her.

"Yes, we were. We've got a nice house," Bridget repeated. Poppa eased his body back into the bed beside her. He kicked off his slippers. "A nice car…"

"I miss the Nash, though," he lamented.

"The Buick's a good, solid automobile," she pointed out.

Poppa patted Bridget's thigh through the sheets. "I like them solid." Bridget smiled; she was well aware he wasn't talking about the car.

"What's new in the world?" she wondered. "Did you read *The Eagle* this morning?"

"Too tired," he told her. "I feel a little out of sorts today."

"Me, too," she admitted. "Maybe we slept funny."

"Could be," he conceded. "Besides, I doubt much has changed since yesterday."

Bridget drank the coffee. It was stronger than she usually made it but it was still good. "None for you?" she wondered, gesturing with the cup as she put it on the nightstand.

"My stomach's on the fritz again," he said.

"Maybe you'll stop in at Dr. Lewis's across the street?"

"Maybe," he said. But she knew he wouldn't.

Poppa lay on top of the covers. He eased his head onto the pillow next to his wife's. "It all pans out in the end, doesn't it, Bridget O'Flynn?"

"Yes, I suppose it does," she told him.

When Poppa kissed Bridget on the lips, her heart stirred with barely imperceptible dragonfly wings, still, after all these year. It had been ages since Poppa had used his old nickname for her, an Irish moniker because his Italian girl looked Gaelic rather than from an insignificant town east of Naples in the south of Italy. Avellino, it was called. Poppa himself was from a village called Laurenzana, little more than one hundred miles away. "I'm ready," she said.

"Ready? For what?" Poppa wondered.

"To hear it," she explained. "It's been a while."

Poppa scooched up higher on the bed so his lips tickled Bridget's ear. He began reciting her favorite poem, whispering it to her:

"When you are old and gray and full of sleep
And nodding by the fire, take down this book
and slowly read, and dream of the soft look
Your eyes had once; and of their shadows deep;

How many loved your moments of glad grace,
And loved your beauty with love false or true;
But one man loved the pilgrim soul in you,
And loved the sorrows of your changing face.

And bending down beside the glowing bars,
Murmur, a little sadly, how love fled
And paced upon the mountains overhead,
And hit his face amid a crowd of stars."

Bridget smiled in the weak morning light. "I would have taken you for a Walt Whitman gal," Poppa commented.

"Not me," she said. "It's Yeats all the way."

Glancing at the beautiful face beside his in bed, Poppa gazed into Bridget's luminous green eyes, ivory skin creased with tiny lines, like the finest crepe paper. He traced one of the deepest grooves, at the right side of her mouth, with his pointer finger, which was also wrinkled. She smiled once more. Then Poppa stroked Bridget's flowing hair which was once golden brown but was now was flecked with the threads of a dozen different metals. By day, Bridget generally wore it pinned up but she took it down at night. It was a sight which never ceased to thrill Poppa—his wife's lush hair spilling over her shoulders and down her back. This morning, Bridget's hair was unfastened for she hadn't yet pinned it up for the day. Poppa stroked her silken tresses then clutched a gentle handful in his fingers. "You're going to put me back to sleep, Mike," she said.

"Just another forty winks," he told her.

When Rose came into her parents' apartment after calling their names several times to announce her arrival, she was surprised to find them still in bed. They were early risers, even on the weekend. The *Brooklyn Daily Eagle* sat on the kitchen table, undisturbed. There were no breakfast dishes either in the sink or on the drain board. There was only a mug of coffee gone cold on the nightstand beside where her mother lay beneath the covers. Her father was curled up next to his wife atop the bedspread, her brilliant hair clasped lightly in his fist. Neither Poppa nor Bridget stirred when Rose entered their room, still calling their names.

At first glance, Rose's parents resembled the couple in the painting which had hung above their parlor sofa for decades. It was named "The Innocents," and showed a young boy and a young girl, tangled together in the ecstasy of sleep. Except the pair in the bed before Rose was not young, and they were not sleeping. Rose touched each of their cheeks, already gone cool like candlewax.

Far off, Rose heard the bells in St. Catherine of Alexandria's stone tower toll ten times. Although it was many blocks away, the sound startled her, even from a distance. At that moment, Rose knew that her parents were gone. But before she called for Sully, she watched Poppa and Bridget lying there peacefully. Rose smiled vaguely to herself, crying softly at the same time. Then she remembered something Sadie Lieberwitz had told her when they were girls. Decades later, Rose had never forgotten her friend's words. "Angels die in their sleep," Sadie had said. It was a Jewish belief that truly blessed people passed away in slumber. Rose herself had come to believe this, too, even before she found her parents lying still and motionless in their bed.

'Sleep well, dear ones,' Rose said aloud as she smoothed down the covers. Only after the sound of the bells faded on the quiet morning air did Rose turn to fetch her husband.

Publisher's Note

While this book is inspired by real people, places and some actual events, *The Bells of Brooklyn* is a work of fiction and in no way meant to be a historical accounting. Any resemblance to persons, either living or dead, is purely coincidental. This book is intended solely for entertainment purposes.

About the Author

Catherine Gigante-Brown is writer of fiction, nonfiction and poetry. She was born in Brooklyn, where she still lives with her husband and son. Her first novel, *The El*, was published by Volossal in 2012, and her second, *Different Drummer*, was released in 2015.

Acknowledgements

As always, I would like to thank my family for their patience with me while I birthed another book. Especially my husband Peter. I'd also like to thank my friends for encouraging me to write a sequel to *The El*, mainly because they wanted to know if Sully and Rosanna got together. (My Aunt Lucy warned me not to let anything bad happen to Poppa and Bridget because she loved them so.)

A big, juicy thank you to Vinnie at Volossal for his friendship, wisdom and for publishing my books, and to his wife, my dear friend Jackie, for being its first reader. And gratitude to my cousin Bobbi Wicks (who inspired the character "Billie") for giving it an early read—and for spotting those errors everyone else missed with her eagle eye and attention to detail.

I'm indebted to my parents, who are long gone, for teaching me first-hand what true, unconditional love was. Now you each have a book dedicated to you.

Thanks also to my cousin Jediah Cirigliano for giving me permission to use the name "Feel Good Food," which is also the name of his food business. Additional thanks go to my cousin Maria Calabrese Saffi for her love and support, for teaching me the Overlook Prayer, and for her advice on that chapter. And to Ruth and Mary Lok Neighbors for puzzling over Chinese phrases which would describe "happy-sad," and figuring out whether the Wongs would speak Cantonese or Mandarin.

It took me many months to "say goodbye" to this book, slowly, painstakingly editing it, savoring certain phrases, getting misty over particular passages. It was almost as though I didn't want to let go of the Paradiso clan. But now I'm ready, and I entrust them to you.

CPSIA information can be obtained
at www.ICGtesting.com
Printed in the USA
BVOW03s0512310817
493578BV00006B/2/P